The Language of Suspense in Crime Fiction

Reshmi Dutta-Flanders

The Language of Suspense in Crime Fiction

A Linguistic Stylistic Approach

Reshmi Dutta-Flanders
English Language and Linguistics
School of European Culture and Languages
University of Kent
Canterbury, UK

ISBN 978-1-137-47027-0   ISBN 978-1-137-47028-7   (eBook)
DOI 10.1057/978-1-137-47028-7

Library of Congress Control Number: 2016962740

© The Editor(s) (if applicable) and The Author(s) 2017
The author(s) has/have asserted their right(s) to be identified as the author(s) of this work in accordance with the Copyright, Designs and Patents Act 1988.
This work is subject to copyright. All rights are solely and exclusively licensed by the Publisher, whether the whole or part of the material is concerned, specifically the rights of translation, reprinting, reuse of illustrations, recitation, broadcasting, reproduction on microfilms or in any other physical way, and transmission or information storage and retrieval, electronic adaptation, computer software, or by similar or dissimilar methodology now known or hereafter developed.
The use of general descriptive names, registered names, trademarks, service marks, etc. in this publication does not imply, even in the absence of a specific statement, that such names are exempt from the relevant protective laws and regulations and therefore free for general use.
The publisher, the authors and the editors are safe to assume that the advice and information in this book are believed to be true and accurate at the date of publication. Neither the publisher nor the authors or the editors give a warranty, express or implied, with respect to the material contained herein or for any errors or omissions that may have been made. The publisher remains neutral with regard to jurisdictional claims in published maps and institutional affiliations.

Cover image © Caspar Benson / Getty Images

Printed on acid-free paper

This Palgrave Macmillan imprint is published by Springer Nature
The registered company is Macmillan Publishers Ltd.
The registered company address is: The Campus, 4 Crinan Street, London, N1 9XW, United Kingdom

To the late Professor Lawrence Goldstein who gave me the opportunity to resume my career in Linguistic Stylistics.

Acknowledgements

I would like to thank the following Lecturers and Senior Lecturers at University of Kent for providing me with their own insights and astute observations on crime studies: Dr Marian Duggan in Criminology and Dr Will Norman in American Studies. Dr Tony Bex, both from English Language and Linguistics, for helping me with his helpful suggestions at the early stages of my writing and to Dr Vikki Janke with taking interest in my progress. Without the support of my department and Head of School Professor Shane Weller for providing me with my honorary fellowship, I would not have been able to continue with my book and complete it. My thanks also go to all Associate Lecturers from different disciplines at the postgraduate offices for their lively debate and challenging discussions at various stages of my writing.

Contents

1	**Introduction**	1
	Bibliography	4
2	**Manipulated Context**	5
	2.1 Introduction	5
	2.2 Context Function	8
	2.3 Frame Analysis (FA)	15
	2.4 Distortion in Plot Sequence	20
	2.4.1 Manipulated Context: The Classification	24
	2.4.2 Discourse Referent: The Classification	27
	2.5 The Processing of Manipulated Context (MC)	28
	2.5.1 Manipulated Context: Case Study—*The Murder of Roger Ackroyd*	30
	2.5.2 The Principle of Relevance: Case Study—*The Murder of Roger Ackroyd*	36
	2.5.3 Manipulated Context: Case Study—*Cover Her Face*	43
	2.5.4 Manipulated Context: Case Study—*The Good Soldier*	48
	2.5.5 The Principle of Relevance: Case Study—*The Good Soldier*	58

	2.6 Microcontexts: Scenarios (Case Study: *The Good Soldier*)	68
	2.7 Conclusion	70
	Appendix 2a	72
	Frame Analysis: *The Murder of Roger Ackroyd* (*Ackroyd*), 1993	72
	Frame analysis (FA)	73
	Appendix 2b	84
	The first story of crime	85
	Appendix 2c	90
	Frame Analysis (FA): *Cover Her Face* (CHF), 1974	90
	Frame analysis (FA)	91
	Appendix 2d	98
	Frame Analysis (FA): Moser (2008)	98
	Frame Analysis (FA)	99
	Maisie Maidan's death scenario (pp. 85–88)	107
	Appendix 2e	126
	Manipulated Contexts (murder mystery)	126
	Bibliography	133
3	**Double Function**	**137**
	3.1 Introduction	137
	3.2 The Double Function (DF) Principle	144
	3.3 Storyworlds: Inter diegesis Space in the Narrated World	147
	3.4 Narrative Act: Narrating Discourse and Narrated Discourse	150
	3.5 Storyworld Analysis	157
	3.5.1 Case Study: Storyworld for Offender Dr. Sheppard	157
	3.5.2 Case Study: Storyworld for Offender Mrs. Maxie	171
	3.5.3 Case Study: Storyworld for Abettor Dowell	175
	3.6 Conclusion	183
	Bibliography	185

Contents   xi

4 Disposition   187
    4.1   Introduction   187
    4.2   Story Resolved, a Criminal Revealed   190
    4.3   Villains: Their Contextual Background   193
    4.4   Framework: The Grammar of Experience   200
        4.4.1   Experiential Function: Transformational Outcome   200
        4.4.2   Interpersonal Function: Passivity and Modality   209
        4.4.3   Referential and Evaluative Function: Truth-Value   217
    4.5   Findings: Linguistic Dysfunctions   224
        4.5.1   Perpetrator: Bud Corliss   227
        4.5.2   Villain: Raven   237
        4.5.3   Perpetrator: Ripley   247
        4.5.4   Offender: Mrs. Maxie   261
        4.5.5   Offender: Dr. Sheppard   265
        4.5.6   Abettor: Dowell   269
    4.6   Conclusion   275
    Appendix 4a   278
        Perpetrator Bud Corliss: *A Kiss before Dying*   278
    Appendix 4b   305
        Perpetrator Raven: *A Gun for Sale*   305
        Perpetrator Raven   328
    Appendix 4d   344
        Offender Mrs. Eleanor Maxie: *Cover Her Face*   344
        Perpetrator Mrs. Eleanor Maxie: *Cover Her Face*   353
    Appendix 4e   360
        Perpetrator Dr. Sheppard: *The Murder of Roger Ackroyd*   360
        Perpetrator Dr. Sheppard: *The Murder of Roger Ackroyd*   364
    Appendix 4f   367
        Abettor John Dowell: *The Good Soldier*   367
        Abettor John Dowell: *The Good Soldier*   379
    Appendix 4g   391
        Offender, Perpetrator Engagement Discourses   391
    Bibliography   405

5 Orientation — 409
- 5.1 Introduction — 409
- 5.2 Hypothesis: Narrating-I, Narrating-He and Experiencing Self — 416
- 5.3 Offender Texts: The Characteristics — 418
- 5.4 The Framework: Orientation Techniques — 419
  - 5.4.1 Orientation in Behavioral Science — 420
  - 5.4.2 Orientation in Modal Senses — 420
  - 5.4.3 Counterfactual Implicature — 424
  - 5.4.4 Hypothetical Implicature — 427
  - 5.4.5 Binary Pair of Events: Hypotheticality in Counterfactual Inferences — 428
- 5.5 Findings: Counterfactual Recount and Hypothetical Utterance — 428
  - 5.5.1 A Counterfactual Context — 429
  - 5.5.2 A Hypothetical Context — 439
- 5.6 Conclusion — 446
- Appendix 5 — 448
  - *Ted Bundy: Conversations with a Killer: The Death Row Interviews* (2005) — 448
  - *The Diary of Jack the Ripper: The chilling confessions of James Maybrick* (2010) — 450
- Bibliography — 454

6 Contrasting Mind-styles — 457
- 6.1 Introduction — 457
- 6.2 Framework: Image-Structure-Mapping — 460
- 6.3 Text and Hypothesis: Fictional World — 462
- 6.4 Analysis: Contrasting Mind-styles — 466
- 6.5 Conclusion — 472
- Bibliography — 473

Conclusion — 475

Bibliography — 479

Index — 493

List of Abbreviations

DF	Double function
DR	Discourse referent
DS	Direct speech
DT	Direct thought
FA	Frame analysis
FIT or FIS	Free indirect thought or Free indirect speech
IS	Indirect speech
MC	Manipulated context
NO	Narrative object
PoR	Principle of relevance
SW	Storyworld

List of Figures

Fig. 2.1	Discourse referent: *Ackroyd*	32
Fig. 2.2	The concealer's PoR (Dr. S)	40
Fig. 2.3	The revelator's PoR (RP)	40
Fig. 2.4	Discourse referent: *The Good Soldier* (TGS)	55
Fig. 2.5	The abettor perspective: Dowell	62
Fig. 2.6	The victim perspective: Dowell	63
Fig. 3.1	Tense forms in HP	147
Fig. 3.2	Narrator intervention	153
Fig. 4.1	Linear and non-linear model	202
Fig. 4.2	Ergative transitive constellation	205
Fig. 4.3	Modal system	210
Fig. 4.4	Narrative categories	210
Fig. 4.5	The modal schema	215

List of Tables

Table 3.1	Storyworld reference points	154
Table 3.2	The character in speech (S) and thought (T)	155
Table 3.3	Storyworlds in *Ackroyd*	159
Table 3.4	Storyworlds in CHF	161
Table 3.5	Storyworlds in TGS	162
Table 4.1	Double analysis	203
Table 4.2	Modal tendencies in narrative categories: A (homodiegetic) B (heterodiegetic); **N**—narrator, **R**—reflector	211
Table 4.3	Syntactic devices to undercut agency	212

1

Introduction

This book is not about the 'who' committed the crime, but about 'how' criminality is presented in a criminal narrative. It analyzes the offender intention, the 'goings on' that happened prior to, during and following the act.

Crime narratives can be classified as murder mystery (whodunit) stories, or thrillers or a combination of both, as hybrid stories. 'Hybrid' crime narratives, such as *A Kiss Before Dying*, and 'thriller' narratives such as *A Gun for Sale* and *The Talented Mr Ripley*, analyzed in this book, have a more chronological order of events than a causative plot structure. All crime narratives use *curiosity* factor based on the presented facts on crime. However, in a whodunit narrative, one is unaware of the 'who' behind the crime, whereas, in thriller narratives, the readers are aware of the 'who' but are blinded by the violence that is going on without knowing the 'why' behind the crime. *Suspense* in both whodunit and thriller narratives is also about the unfolding of protagonists' stories in the first story of crime. The story related to an antihero precedes its story of murder or the violence committed in crime stories. This embedded offender story narrated in anticipation initiates a tripartite narration in its story of crime, alongside its acts of prospection and retrospection in a criminal context.

Conventionally, there is a *first story of crime* in prospection and a *second story of investigation* in retrospection. In Todorov (1987: p. 44), *the first story of crime* and *the second story of investigation* is a 'duality' (a dual state) found typically in whodunit mystery stories.

The term *story* is distinct from a *narrative*. In narratology, there is a well-known distinction between the *fable* (the story, **what** has happened in life) and the *subject* (the plot, **the way** the author presents it to us). The *story* is the **content plane** of the narrative, 'the what' of a narrative, the narrated, as in Prince (1987). The *discourse* is the **expression plane** of the narrative, 'the how' of a narrative, the narrating. Additionally, the concept of ***storyworld*** in Prince (c2003) is added to the distinction between story and discourse, creating a three-part model. Storyworlds are **alternative worlds** constructed in the language through a performative force, which carried out by a criminal is akin to a cultural convention.

For the reevaluation of the criminal act, the narrative universal *suspense* is of more significance than *surprise* and *curiosity* factors in a crime story. Suspense is not related to a situation, as in Hitchcock's definition of suspense where the theatre audience knows that there is a bomb under the table and it is about to explode, but the characters in the play are unaware of the bomb. *Suspense* is more about unfolding the offender traits in a storyworld backgrounded in the dominant narrative, and is essentially an emotional process unlike *mystery* (the gradual revelation of criminous information), which is an intellectual process, as in a whodunit. The emotional process rationalized in the linguistic stylistics of the offender discourse enables the analyst to look behind the crime in the first story and link to the third story of mystery revealed or violence resolved in the crime.

As suspense emerges in the unfolding of the criminality, it has the ability to provoke an intellectual as well as an affective response, shaping our overall outlook of the crime. For instance, reevaluation of the plot or narrative form in a story reveals that the criminal setting is anchored on an unfounded motive that drives the life of crime. The criminal orientation, when linked with the motive, functions as a *stimulus* (something that incites an action), formulating a *trigger* (to initiate, to activate) for the criminal act in order to fulfil a self-gratifying criminal intention stemming from personal desire in the criminal profiling process, as in social sciences studies. Thus, from a two-dimensional circumstantial detection in mystery stories to a three dimensional re-evaluation of the offence in criminal orientation, the criminal motive is obtained in the experiential and interpersonal functions in clauses, using approaches such as transitivity framework from systemic functional linguistics, and modality framework from critical stylistics. Additionally, a 'discourse-based' frame analysis for realizing the causative plot structure, and an Agent-affected schema for the construction of an alternative offending 'self', contextualizes further the offender into the theme of crime. Finally, a counterfactual recount of a perpetrator versus a hypothetical utterance of an offender and their grammaticization in linguistic aspects, all provide a rationale for offender-based themes analyzed in each chapter:

2 the plot structure for an offender based 'manipulated context' in the narrative form;
3 the 'double function' as the functional environment for the narrative gaps in offender narrative;
4 the post-murder-participant disposition in linguistic dysfunctions;
5 an 'intermediary' orientation of an offender;
6 the mind style for the worldview in the fictional world in which the offender lived.

A sentence-level microstructural analysis is implemented for each offender engagement discourse analyzed, to gain a microscopic view of the message backgrounded in the offender narrative that shapes the suspense respective to each offender. By keeping to a case-by-case investigation method, as in the criminal detection process, each offender is individually studied. All are adopted from fictional as well as true-crime narratives. The crime themes with reference to each criminal are objectively introduced through linguistic stylistics framework analyses.

Linguistic stylistics analyses of crime stories started with my doctoral research. However, with recent advances and interest in crime studies in literature, forensic linguistics and social sciences, the ground I cover has been expanded to take an interdisciplinary approach to an offender engagement discourse in criminal narrative analysis.

Bibliography

Sources cited: Chapter 1

Prince, G. c2003. *A Dictionary of Narratology*. Rev. ed. London: University of Nebraska Press.

———. 2003[1987]. *A Dictionary of Narratology*. Lincoln: University of Nebraska Press.

Todorov, T. 1987. *The Poetics of Prose*. Trans. Richard Howard and Jonathan Culler, 43–52. Ithaca, NY: Cornell University Press. Reprint, 1977.

2

Manipulated Context

2.1 Introduction

Crime stories are studied extensively in literary texts (Boltanski 2014) and the criminal process is researched in forensic linguistics (Coulthard and Johnson 2007) and in forensic semiotics (Danesi 2014). In criminological research recommended in Glenn and Raine (2014), the space–time budget method is nominated as a data analysis method for retrospectively recording the whereabouts and activities of respondents involved in crime and victimization on an hour-by-hour basis. By adopting this notion in a **discourse-based frame analysis** in literary texts on crime, it is possible to monitor a cluster of events based on a topic and singularized as frames based on specific themes (**thematic frames**) in the narrative. In crime fiction, an event (microcontext) may stand out against the background of other thematic frames in the **narrative frame** (the skeleton of the story) when creating a risky point (**cardinal point**) in the narrative. This formulates narrative options (**alternative narrative paths**) to provide a secondary narrative positioned on the concealer (**perpetrator**[1]) and the revelator's (the participant framed) **Principle of Relevance** (PoR) in the context of murder, and the relevance is based on the **logical fallacy** of **consecution** and the **consequence of events** centering a participant's motive, belief or desire in the narrative. The belief or desire as an utterance or statement in the **first story of crime**[2] has the backward- and forward-oriented referential function of a **discourse referent** (DR), which is different from an anaphoric or cataphoric referent. By centering this DR, a referential layer is formed in the referential process of *priming* and *focusing* (Emmott 1999: pp. 123, 221). Such referential layer as a **manipulated context** (MC) is devised in the **bidirectional functionality** of DR, formulating at the vertical axis of different narratives an offender narrative which is distinct from the revelator narrative in the story.

Following this notion, this chapter focuses on the process of isolating MC from a range of novels in order to understand the manipulation process of a linguistically created **double function** (DF), a narrative act as functional environment effective to resurface the process of manipulation in the deep-structure analysis of clauses in offender discourse.

The monitoring of events in a narrative with information stored in one's memory for **episodic links** (*contextual monitoring* in Emmott 1999: p. 115) is not enough to understand a **narrative gap** in the **prospective reading** of the story. Using discourse-based frame analysis (FA) of a story, which is different from Emmott's (1999: p. 121) *contextual frames* (a mental store of information) enables one to follow the way a complex plot form is constructed as the narrative's discourse.

---

[1] Perpetrator and Offender: The word perpetrator refers to someone who has committed an act of sexual coercion but has not been convicted. The term offender is used to refer to a man who has been convicted of a sexual offence. (Cowburn 2005: p. 2)

[2] From Todorov, the first story of the crime tells "what really happened", whereas the second – the story of investigation – explains how the reader (or the narrator) has come to know about it." (1987: p. 45) The first story ends before the second starts. The first corresponds to the notion of **reality** evoked, events similar to those which take place in our lives; the second corresponds to the narrative (plot). The first is absent but **real**, cannot transmit the conversations of characters implicated; the second present but insignificant, a mediator between the reader and the story of the crime. The first involves literary devices: temporal inversions and individual point of view. Therefore, in whodunit there is retrospection followed by prospection in the first story.

In FA, storylines for ***curiosity gaps*** (note 6) or ***surprise gaps*** are also tracked in the plot form of a story, as monitoring of frames enables the reader to focus on the

> 'Suspense arises from rival scenarios about the future: from the discrepancy between what the telling in the narrative lets us know about the happening. [As the] *tale communicates in a sequence discontinuous with the happening*. [This is because of the] *gaps and twists* [introduced] *in the chronology of narrative events* [for mystery], *disclosed to* [the readers to cause their] *misreading and enforce a corrective rereading in late re-cognition*.' (Sternberg 2003: p. 327)

The secret or mystery constituted as *suspense* in prospection or *curiosity* in retrospection in detective narratives such as Christie's *The Murder of Roger Ackroyd* (*Ackroyd*), James' *Cover Her Face* (CHF) and an **experientialist**[3] **novel**, Ford's *The Good Soldier* (TGS). The unravelling of this secret is usually in the final disclosure of the sequence of events, as in a detective narrative, or in a corrective rereading, or re-cognition of microcontexts (scenarios) (Sect. 2.6) respective of vantage points of participants' (offender or victim) Principle of Relevance (PoR) in the narrated story. The PoR is related to participant desire or motive in the story, and centers on this bidirectional discourse referent (DR). New narrative relations are instantiated as a **manipulated context** (MC) where gaps or disconnection between events are interjected to process the mystery for a corrective re-reading or re-cognition of the actual happenings in criminal context. A MC foregrounds specific themeframes in microcontexts corresponding to the offender motive in the story.

MC analysis (Sect. 2.4.1) is about processing a criminal context, and fulfils various functions in the narrative discourse. Understanding of context is carried out from a linguistics perspective, as comprehension of context in linguistics occurs at multiple levels. The more the analyst knows about the features of context, the more likely the analyst will be able to predict what is likely to be said.

---

[3] *Experientialist novel*—Normally the narrator is the functional agent who verbalizes the story's nonverbal matter. However, the Modernists focus on a reflector's mind, the experiences, a figural style, which tends to avoid background information to familiarize with characters and their actions. The narration may restrict to reflector's stream of associative consciousness and move towards interior moment of revelation or recognition (epiphany) rather than reaching a suspense-filled climax. (Jahn in Herman 2007: p. 96)

2.2 Context Function

Context is dynamic in character where there is change of state in the course of events in an episode. In Chatman (1978: p. 21), **events** in the narrative context tend to be related or mutually entailing, while an **episode** is a sequence of events that form part of the narrative, but may be a digression from the main story. Context can be also about 'pragmatic success' or appropriateness of an **utterance-act**, denoting which utterance is successful in which situation (Van Dijk 1977: pp. 191–192). For example, if the structure of an utterance as in clauses 1 and 2 below, is placed in a communicative situation of at least two persons such as the speaker and hearer,

1. May I borrow your bike tomorrow?
2. Tomorrow I borrow may bike your.

the **concrete situation** for utterance-act 2 needs to be defined; is it an act of language, or is it at the level of linguistic description of a sentence, or an act of communication spoken by a foreigner? For this, coordinates of context can specify what aspects of situation are relevant for supporting an intended meaning in a made utterance.
Coordinates of context are,

Possible-world coordinate: to account for states of affairs, which *might be*, or *could be* or *are*
Time (Hymes' setting) **coordinate**: to account for tensed sentences and adverbials like *today* or *next week*
Place (Hymes' setting) **coordinate**: to account for sentences like *here it is*
Speaker coordinate: to account for sentences which include first-person reference (I, me, we, our etc.)
Audience coordinate: to account for sentences including you, yours, yourself etc.
Indicated object coordinate: to account for sentences containing demonstrative phrases like *this, those* etc.
Previous discourse coordinate: to account for sentences including phrases like the latter, the aforementioned etc.

Assignment coordinate: an infinite series of things (sets and sequence of things) that enables the hearer to interpret what is said in the light of what has already been said.

(Brown and Yule 1983: p. 40)

Readers can characterize in coordinates the context against which the truth of a sentence is judged, which provide characteristics of the context in which the text has occurred, for instance microcontexts in **repeated** or **recalled** contexts in frame analysis (Appendix 2a, 2c, 2d). This context condition is *post hoc*, which is an issue of calculability, and relates to the manner of **intentionality** of participants involved in a given communicative situation.

Intentionality in Text Linguistics is about the text-producer's intention, such as to deceive or to conceal some knowledge; intentionality therefore creates a text condition like the appropriateness of an utterance-act above. An example is participant disposition (Chap. 4), where there is impaired textual coherence or disturbances of coherence for a desired contextual effect (Beaugrande and Dressler 1972: pp. 115, 153). **Disturbances of coherence** could get in the way of narrative comprehension, such as in a **withheld frame**, illustrated in example 3 below (Frame 14, Appendix 2a). The intentionality in example 3 below is to withhold the cause for the decision made in the utterance, making it unavailable in the immediate context, but recoverable from episodic links formulated in the FA of the narrative discourse in *Ackroyd*.

3. '*Could I do anything with the boy? I thought I could.*' (*Ackroyd*)

As a **discourse cue**[4] (as opposed to **clue**), the utterance in 3 is a **mismatch** in the immediate context. With reference to the murder in *Ackroyd*, readers need to look for the narrated elements to provide value to this utterance. The value being that Dr. Sheppard, the murderer, implicated

---

[4] Discourse cue—in Weizman and Dascal, 'The cue question is: are there any missing elements, any variables whose values should be determined? Are there any gaps to be filled? An affirmative answer entails the clue question: what values should be assigned to the missing elements. In other words, the contextual meaning relative to speaker utterance is labelled clue, whereas when contextual information is used for the detection of an interpretation problem (i.e. mismatch) it is labelled cue.' (1991: p. 21)

Ralph as the suspect relative to Frames 11 and 21 (*Ackroyd*, Appendix 2a). This frame as a **risky point** in the *Ackroyd* narrative formulates paths or narrative options in the first story of crime. These options are **alternative worlds**[5] relative to a revelator and a concealer in the story. For instance, information (**cue**, note 4) in the **repeated frames** (4, 6, 8) and **frame recalls** (3, 11, 21, D1) provide the **clue** (contextual meaning) for processing of the referential layer and consequently the substituted narrative (Figs. 2.1 and 2.2) related to the offender motive in example 3, which was to frame Ralph to avoid detection. The cluster of repeated and recall frames as a **microcontext** for perpetrator motive functions as the cardinal point to create a *curiosity gap*[6] in retrospect to the third story of investigation in *Ackroyd*.

Paraphrases[7] in frame theory, like **repetition** in stylistics, are repeated frames, not present in films, which emphasize and evoke an **indirect item (narrative object)** in the cognitive world. For example, on taking a **multimodal** approach from the storyboard (SB) in the film version in *Ackroyd* (Appendix 2b), SB frame III is a **diegetic** means to make prominent Ursula, the parlor maid secretly married to Ralph, reacting to the news of Flora being engaged to her husband Ralph in story reality. This clip functions as the information for the contextual meaning that is embedded in the chain of retrospective SB frames V, VI, then VIII, and IX, and the frames are a clue to the secret marriage between Ralph Paton and Ursula, the Ralph episode (Appendix 2a). In the story, Ralph's stepfather wants him to marry his cousin Flora, but Ralph has married Ursula, the house parlor maid at Ferny Park. SB frame III becomes the **cardinal point** in the film version of the story, with its contextual meaning gathered from the chain of SB frames mentioned above to provide the **valued context** for this risky moment in the film. In this way, in

---

[5] Alternative world that has its own temporal and spatial parameters, where hierarchical relations between world levels are formed based on narratives temporal and spatial zones (Bridgeman in Herman 2007: p. 52). In addition, possible worlds (storyworlds) are also formed based on the chronology of events as the real vs. the reality of fictional universe.

[6] Curiosity gap—'… gapped antecedents, trying to infer (bridge, compose) them in retrospect. … For *surprise* … the narrative first unobtrusively gaps or twists its chronology, then unexpectedly discloses to us our misreading and enforces a corrective reading in late re-cognition. (Sternberg 2003: p. 327)'

[7] Paraphrase, unlike anaphoric reference, allows the referenced object to be directly evoked by using a label (a concept represented as frame) (Rosenberg 1980: p. 98).

utterance 3 from the novel, **participant intentionality** needs working out, as the intended meaning in an utterance is *post hoc* in the alternative narrative world.

The **appropriateness** and **intentionality** of SB frame XI, when Parker was run over by a taxi, is interpreted as a **narrative surprise** in the film narrative, which is not available in the written narrative. The relevance of this frame is related to the time of **murder** that was manipulated by Dr. Sheppard, which Parker figured out due to the armchair found out of place when Roger Ackroyd was found dead. Parker's death in the film is then the **content factor** that foregrounds the importance of the Dictaphone episode. Being the butler, Parker noticed the armchair in the office where Roger Ackroyd was murdered was out of place. Dr. Sheppard (unknown to Parker and the other staff) obscured the Dictaphone, set up to manipulate the time of death, with the displaced armchair. The SB frame XI thus constitutes the **real intention** for an **intended outcome**; that is the distortion of the time of murder. As **text-presented knowledge** in the film, SB frame XI also interacts with the **world-knowledge** that readers need to gather about the time of murder to connect the **content value** of the Dictaphone episode with Parker's death to overrule Ralph as the suspect. **Content factors** thus cannot be ignored as they are important for the **text informativity** for reader focus and narrative interest.

Furthermore, the **restricted context**[8] in SB frames VIII and IX in fictional reality functions as an alibi for Ralph, and contradicts the incident in SB frame VII, when Major Blunt saw someone (Ursula) going up to the summerhouse to meet Ralph. Therefore Ralph could not have been with Ackroyd (set up by the Dictaphone) as is implied in SB frame VII. Ralph could not be in the office with his stepfather and be at the summerhouse secretly meeting his wife at the same time. This **communicative situation** for an **episodic link** in the overall Ralph episode (Appendix 2a) set up between SB frames VII and IX is restricted in the story for the intended proposition of Ralph positioned as a suspect. Following which, the reality

---

[8] In restricted contexts, participants in two boats, distant from each other, are aware of each other's presence, but cannot hear each other or see anything else in the boat because of the distance between them. In the two contexts created, individuals in each have the same temporal and spatial orientation, but are not aware of the information flow in the other. Such is a *restricted context* in Emmott's term (1997: p. 130).

embedded in SB frame VII, synonymously in the written narrative in **recall frames** (3, 11 and 21) provides an episodic link between events for an (external) **alternative construct**, which occurs over large stretches of text. In the **nonlinear** orientation in **content factor**, there is a successful concealment of the intended purposes in the first story of crime in film story. A victim (synonymous to an **object**[9] as in Rosenberg in Metzing 1980: p. 102, see also notes 4 and 5 in Chap. 3), is instantiated in the narrative **circularity** which is created in retrospection of the first crime following which Roger Ackroyd was murdered. In other words, the first crime (Frame 1, Dr. Sheppard blackmailed Mrs. Ferrars for poisoning her alcoholic husband and she consequently committed suicide) is not linked to the logical consecution of events relative to a second crime (in Frame 22, Ackroyd's death due to the revelation of the blackmailer). The readers are restricted to this **concrete external setting** (time and place). However, readers are provided with a text condition for **desired contextual effects** such as the **microcontext** (an internal context) as **repeated or recalled frames** in written narratives, or the **surprise frame** in film discourse for conjoining what is actually said about existing assumptions in the context; therefore drawing a **contextual effect** for an intended outcome.

Context thus functions as a **cognitive construct** (Widdowson 2004: chapter 3) and conjoins what is actually said as a **cue** for the existing assumptions in the context as the **clue** to the intended purpose, and draws a **contextual effect** (meaning) as explained above. This could not be inferred from either the text or the context alone. By taking into account the intra- and extra-linguistic **contextual factors**, one can infer the relevance and the required contextual effect in a communicative situation, where **context** is an abstract and internal location for communication, as well as a **concrete external setting** for the intended function in a specific context.

Besides the microcontexts formulated with reference to the Repeated or Recalled Frames in FA, there is no pragmatic coordinate to infer the manner in a propositional content. In understanding the text by linguistic analysis, and then its evaluation in relation to contextual factors, one

---

[9] Object refers to a person or other entity involved in the situation. In criminal context, the person is an object (a narrative object) of the cime narrative. The object is the narrative focus that coincides with a character who then becomes a fictive subject of all perceptions.

can further index the **propositional content** linked to the concealed or backgrounded manner, as in example 4 below.

4. *He has much in common with John McEnroe* (JM). (Widdowson 2004: p. 50)

The linguistic formality, *has much in common with*, **directs** the reader towards the inference of *He* as bad-tempered rather than a good server like JM. How do readers arrive at the intended **contextual effect** of *he* being referred to as bad-tempered like JM in example 4?

Contextual assumptions are born from personal experiences or they are **culturally shared** as **schematic knowledge** and define a state of an individual. The **schema** constructed about JM as an ill-tempered tennis player is **a social construct.** The readers have to access this **shared contextual assumption** related to John McEnroe in the proposition and relate it to the second-person pronoun *he*. So in the **scenario** of example 4 (as part of the bad-tempered JM Theme Frame), the schematic knowledge specific to McEnroe must be presupposed to start the **inferential (interpretation) process.** Widdowson expresses these constructs as the *frames of reference* (microcontext), and this is necessary for recovering or decoding the underlying propositional content of utterances, as they provide bearings on the propositional content of a **context of situation.** Frames of reference, as explained in Sect. 2.4, constitute **cardinal points** for alternative narrative options respective to an offender motive or desire.

In this way context enables one to take into account both the direct and indirect proposition to constitute the **intended context. Content factors** in a context constitute the intended narrative interest as the reader focus, whilst **coordinates** as **context of situation** help to **characterize the context** in which the text occurred. '**Microcontexts**' (Sect. 2.3), as *frames of reference* in a narrative frame, draw upon the context functions for the intended **contextual effect**, which would be otherwise overlooked in a nonlinear story plot. Microcontexts as *contextual clues* (Emmott 1992: p. 227) can enable readers to realize the intentionality construct (motive) embedded as a referent (discourse referent) in criminal narrative.

According to Schank and Abelson (1977), a **restaurant frame schema** would contain information about the entities present in a restaurant. The temporally ordered information in the form of a *script* focuses on goal-oriented sequences that define a well-known situation, in other words, **schema** is based on the principles of organization which govern events. One may argue that such a **schema-consistent context** may be drawn up for solving the mystery in Christie's *Death in the clouds* (Emmott 2014: pp. 274–276). Synonymous to parallelism, this schematic construct is **two-dimensional** and works best as an ingredient for pattern recognition. However, for a **pronoun-less discourse referent** (DR) (synonymous to antecedentless pronouns), the value of this DR can best be understood in the *instantiated expectation* for a **narrative object**, as in Rosenberg in Metzing (1980: p. 102),

> '*Intersentence anaphoric references were more susceptible to processing difficulties.*'

That is, a **referent in discourse** is synonymous to an intersentence anaphoric reference, and, as an **object** for the **offender intention**, is difficult to process in a **circular** crime narrative. However, the *discourse cue* associated the DR without its referent in the immediate context is possible in the **forward-oriented** as well as **backward-oriented** (bidirectional) contextual function of the DR in the story. The inexplicit **discourse object** (e.g. Ralph's secret marriage), for instance, is instantiated as a DR and links **forward** with Dr. Sheppard's **motive** instantiated in Frame 14 with the respective context in Repeated Frames (4, 6, 8). The **backward orientation** is when Dr. Sheppard took advantage of Ralph's secret marriage to the parlor maid, Ursula, in Repeated Frames 6, 7 and 8; the equivalent is in SB frames V and VI, in the film version, to formulate a narrative option, constituting in prospection, Ralph as the suspect in utterance 3, Frame 14.

A discourse-based frame analysis of selected stories is therefore carried out to work out the microcontext for manipulated contexts (MC) in the first story of a detective discourse. MC constructed (Appendix 2e) in the **narrative frame** is based on the bidirectional function of the DR as the risky point in the plot form.

2.3 Frame Analysis (FA)

Frame analysis is beneficial for the processing of MCs in a mixed up plot structure, characteristics of an **offender narrative** to conceal their backgrounded motive for the crime.

Frames are **episodic** (nonlinear) in nature. Monitoring of frames helps with the plot form (the order of the appearance of events), e.g. '[whether] *normal (abc), flash-backed or begun in medias res*' in the work itself (Chatman 1978: p. 20). The sequence of events when broken down into individual frames in FA helps to work out events functioning as ***kernels/ nuclei***[10] (also note viii) or as ***catalysts/satellites***,[11] or microcontexts in the narrative. Microcontexts for scenarios[12] are created in ***microsequences***,[13] and one becomes aware of these scenarios in the narrative's discourse via theme frames in the plot form, like the **victim scenario**, the offender disposition, a **deception scenario**, the **desire scenario** (Sect. 2.6). Following the FA of 3 stories in Appendix 2a, 2c and 2d, the **scenarios** presented are found to be a *circular affair* (nonlinear) over a linear configuration of episodes (e.g. thrillers) in the plot form of the story.

To work with an unchronological plot structure, it was necessary to work out the **discourse processing** carried out in the story narratives. In addition, retrospective characterization of the same events, in which types of frames are **withheld**, **recalled** or **repeated**, differ widely based on the individual who is undertaking the role of narrating the events. For the purpose of the concealed motive, in the aforementioned frame types, there is **evaluative assessment** of **events** leading up to and following the crime. For instance, in nonlinear frames in *Ackroyd*, Dr. Sheppard's **greed,** which leads to blackmail and murder, was concealed by the narrator,

---

[10] Nuclei or cardinal points are risky moments in the narrative and gives rise to options which will carry the narrative along different path, and are both consecution (logic, the relation of consequent to antecedent; deduction) and consecutive (following one after the other without interruption).

[11] Catalyzers as fillers are only consecutive (following one after the other without interruption) and as trivial incidents have discursive function: to accelerate, delay, summarize, anticipate, revive semantic function, give fresh impetus to the discourse.

[12] Scenarios - In Minsky (1980: 16), key words and ideas of a discourse evoke substantial thematic or scenario structures, drawn from memory with rich default assumptions. Thematic Frmes in Minsky are scenarios concerned with topics, activities, portraits, setting, such as the party scenario.

[13] Microsequences, 'Events combine to create micro-sequences which in turn combine to form macro-sequences which jointly complete the story.' (Rimmon-Kenan 2002: p. 16)

Sheppard, until the second murder (of his patient's fiancé, Roger Ackroyd). Similarly, in *Cover Her Face*, the housemaid Sally's **secret** motive was to manipulate and victimize Mrs. Maxie's reservations about her son Stephen wanting to marry her, when in story reality (unknown to her murderer) Sally was married. Finally, in *The Good Soldier*, Dowell's love for Nancy Rufford is concealed and his **desire** to marry her is only voiced following his wife's suicide.

Without the support of FA, the contextual configuration of Dr. Sheppard, Sally and Dowell's **motives** remain backgrounded, while in the mixed up narrative discourse, the **victim story** is foregrounded. For example, the victim Florence's manipulative character in TGS and her flirtatious nature is foregrounded in the readers' mind (TGS Frames 50). Similarly, Dr. Sheppard's motive is backgrounded when the doctor framed Ralph Paton as the prospective blackmailer and the murderer of his stepfather (*Ackroyd* Frame 14).

Besides **motive identification** as **protagonist intentionality**, FA was also necessary for **microcontext** (*micro themes*) formation in complex discourse, as stated by Van Dijk.

> 'Large amounts of detailed information [were] … reduced and then organized according to the micro themes in the macro narrative, also available for retrieval in recall, in integration of incoming information, and in problem-solving.'
> (Van Dijk 1977: p. 158)

For **discourse comprehension**, our interpretation of the **discourse world** requires formation of episodic links or contextual configuration of events for **contextual monitoring** of microcontext for microthemes, otherwise backgrounded in the narrative. Events in the microcontext are not in the sequence they occurred in the content plane. They are situated at considerable distance from each other in the plot form of the story. Hence, facts in a ***contextual frame*** (Emmott 1999: p. 121), the loosely connected parts of a story are true on a particular occasion within a story, and are relevant from a particular vantage point. If this point in the narrative changes with the **intentionality** of the narrator as a character, significance of a frame *slot* (e.g. the DR as the cardinal point) constitutes an alternative narrative, based on the vantage point from where the story was narrated. For example, the concealed desire (motives) of principal characters Dr. Sheppard and Dowell formulate sequence of events (Figs. 2.1, 2.2, 2.4, 2.5 and 2.6) which is different from the sequence constituted with reference to the revelator.

Any event can be described in terms of focus that is **close-up** from a revelator perspective, or made **distant** from a concealer perspective. The work of those who study **fraud, deceit, misidentification** and other effects include the way in which concealing and revealing bear upon a situation based on one's experience, such as *what is play for a golfer is work for the caddy*. Following such an experience-based organization of events, frame analysis is *an examination of the organization of experience* (Goffman in Lemert and Branaman 1997: p. 155), where presentation of events is not linear. Linear presentation **constrains** the writer to give an alternative experience of the same event for a different focus, constituting a nonlinear circular presentation. This constitutes microcontexts for different **discoursal focus**, and for alternative scenarios like the concealer tale of Dr. Sheppard (Fig. 2.2) as opposed to the revelator tale of Ralph Paton (Fig. 2.3), simultaneously in TGS the abettor tale (Fig. 2.4) foregrounds a fourth triangle, Edward, Nancy and Dowell as opposed to the tale of a deceived husband (Dowell) (Fig. 2.5).

As a concept, the term *frame* belongs to cognitive theory. It denotes a **conceptual structure** in **semantic memory** and represents a part of our knowledge of the world. In this respect, a frame is an **organization principle**, relating a number of concepts as in Van Dijk's *Text and Context* (p. 159),

'... *which by convention and experience ... form a unit ... actualized by cognitive tasks, such as language production and comprehension, perception, action and problem-solving. Thus, ... a restaurant-frame ... would be general but culture-dependent, ... That is a frame organizes knowledge about certain properties of objects, course of event and action which typically belong together. ... The explicit propositional knowledge from the frames establish the explicit coherence between sentences of a discourse ... This explains ... in the noun phrase the waitress is definite though no waitress need have been referred to by previous expressions in the discourse.*'

A frame is seen as equivalent to schemata, plan or a script and, according to Minsky (1980: p. 3), serves as a two-dimensional ingredient of the perceptual processing of schemata (patterns) but fails to cope with complicated three-dimensional scenery for concealment and restricted revelation in a scenario such as in an **offender scenario**. Supplementing the above with Minsky's FA for discourse, one can work with larger structures than sentential grammars. For example, for the **frame system** (defined below) in the discourse in the fable below, how do we know the wolf is lying?

> *'There was once a wolf who saw a lamb drinking at a river and wanted an excuse to eat it. For that purpose, even though he himself was upstream, he accused the lamb of stirring up the water and keeping him from drinking …'*
> (Minsky in Metzing 1980: p. 12)

We realize this because a contamination cannot flow upstream, and through the use of the conjunction *even though* which form a causal link to Wolf's **desire frame** to eat the lamb, which is **withheld**, but *inferred* in the narrative.

The **frame-system** (event or action in a two-frame generalized event to build an appropriate instantiated frame-pair) then has *slots* for action or events; one can build a *frame-pair scenario* to understand if one has understood an event or action. In any event, any individual statements of a discourse lead to further representations, like the **withheld desire frame** of the offender wolf in the fable narrative. This corresponds to the **deep structure of the narrative** (Chap. 4), where frames are rearranged or consumed for a growing **scenario representation**, and analyzed in the **frame levels** such as:

Surface syntactic frames: Prepositional and word order indicator conventions.
Surface semantic frames: Qualifiers and relations concerning participants, instruments, goals, consequences and side effects.

However, in representing changes by simple **before–after frame pairs**, as in the **contamination frame** in the fable example (*he accused lamb of stirring up the water and keeping him from drinking*) complex situations and sequences are condensed representing strategies such as:

Thematic frames: **Scenarios** concerned with topics and setting. Thematic frames are also **culture-dependent**. For example, in a party scenario, the dominant frame is about celebrating and the default frame may be cutting a cake, or going to a pub.

Narrative frames: Skeleton forms for typical stories. Conventions about foci, protagonists, plot forms, development designed to help a listener (reader) to construct a new instantiated thematic frame in the mind. (Minsky in Metzing 1980: pp. 14–16)

In TGS, for instance, the **deception frame** of prussic acid for amyl nitrate and the development of this deception in the alternative frame scenario (Figs. 2.5 and 2.6) constructed in TGS, is possible when Florence's deception frames (TGS Frame 96) are aligned with Dowell's concealed desire (TGS Frames 80, 85) of narrator Dowell as an abettor. An alternative narrative is formulated which centers Dowell's desire as the median point in the abettor perspective in Fig. 2.5, and a deceived husband as the median point in the victim perspective in Fig. 2.6. The **median point** is the cardinal point (hinge point, risky point) for consecution of an alternative narrative plot summary.

Events, utterances, activities, whereabouts, crime and victimization are identified as specific frames, functioning as information by which the mind forms connections to build their own respective specific **theme frames** in the plot form of a crime narrative. The connections are, as mentioned earlier, are **episodic** (*a* [nonlinear] *contextual configuration*) and can be accessed via microcontexts from FA to create an inherent link between instantiated **entities** (events that imply or index **existents**/a character/an element of setting), creating a context from fragments of information which are at a distance from each other in the narrative. The principle of **microcontext** is formed from fragmented information and disjointed events, which are at a distance from each other, just like the **restricted situation** in Emmott (1999: p. 121) (note viii) is therefore necessary to form an episodic link for narrative comprehension. For instance, participants L & Y are in one location in one occasion, but somewhere else on another occasion. At the point of narration, no inherent link is formed between these occasions and this configuration somehow needs to be retained and then linked to create a (micro)context from these disjointed incidents. Similar to this act of inference, unlike parallel processing in the restaurant frame, a microcontext is formulated in the FA of the story, providing a three-dimensional link for inference making during reading by:

- Providing links between unconnected events in large stretches of narrative; and
- prompting an event evaluation due to nonstandard actions like repeated or recall frames within a narrative discourse.

For suspense in narratives, understanding of the reality following event organization, that is, the sequence of events that line up to the abettor protagonist (Dowell in TGS) or to the anti-hero motive (Dr. Sheppard in *Ackroyd*) are different constructs constructed according to the concealer and revelator perspective in the story of crime. Unlike the restaurant frame, the constructed story lines do not have a set of related mental data that relate to a **murder schema**, apart from the fact that there is a victim and a perpetrator in the criminal (offender) narrative. The narrative reader is not aware of which of the participants is the victim or the perpetrator.

The **victim–offender narrative analysis** is carried out in the plot summary of the first story of crime using the FA of 3 stories. The second story of investigation in *Ackroyd* and CHF is not analyzed for FA, as it starts when the first story of crime stops. The FA of the first story is synonymous to a retrospective recording of the narrated story on an **event-by-event basis.** While aiming to focus on a specific frame as the risky moment (the cardinal point) for narrative option, the analysis also concentrates on the narrative's plot form in the first story. Through FA, the plot summary in three stories is presented in Appendix 2a, 2c, 2d, in which each distinct action of the story has a corresponding proposition as pointed out by Todorov in Howard and Culler (1977: p. 110). From the plot summary of each story, the MCs (Appendix 2e) are formulated at the cardinal point in the story, and follow the **episodic links** formulated with reference to the framed DR as the cardinal point in the discourse (Sect. 2.4.2).

2.4 Distortion in Plot Sequence

An utterance in the discourse narrative can prompt narrative forking or option in the primary story, causing delay, generating mystery or reader suspense or surprise, or mere reader curiosity. If the story of crime is the primary narrative, then the assumption is that there is another secondary narrative caused in the manipulation of the event sequence in the primary story for perpetrator motive or desire. As a narrative episode, this **secondary narrative** is **dynamic** by causing movement in the way of distortion, but is **iterative** where the same event but with slight variation is repeated in a frame. This narrative entails concurrence of two temporal sequences (**duality**) in which events that happened are **dynamic**, but are **manipulated** in the way events unfold in narration, i.e. the unchronological manner of frame sequence in narrative.

In such **narrative duality**, the move away is from narratives as reference to a single time axis (**mimesis**), to a **narrative layering** constructed in the intersequencing of the dynamics **of prospection, of retrospection and of recognition**, for constituting narrative universals like *suspense, curiosity and surprise* (Sternberg 2003: p. 326). Furthermore, there may be single or multiple narrative forking for a **circular narration** constructed due to *logical fallacy* (Barthes 1977: p. 119) for different narrative purposes, for instance to conceal in the consecution of the sequence events that reveal the perpetrator motive. As Barthes comments,

> [To understand a narrative, it is not merely] '*to follow the unfolding of the story, it is also to recognize its constructions in 'storeys' to project the horizontal concatenations of the narrative 'thread' on to an implicitly vertical axis; to read (to listen to) a narrative is not merely to move from one word to the next, it is also to move from one level to the next.* [Barthes continues] ... *meaning is not "at the end" of the narrative, it runs across it .... meaning eludes all unilateral investigation.*' (1977: p. 87)

There is thus distortion of the original sequence of events following a murder, not just for concealment, but also for reader suspense. To follow the processing of this manipulation in MCs (Sect. 2.4.1), the reader needs to locate the narrative options centering on a **cardinal (hinge) point** in the narrative. The reader then needs to track the narrative relations for options and follow the systematic application of *logical fallacy* centering this hinge point (the motive Frame) when mapping relations from the setting (horizontal) on to the telling (vertical) axis of a **content plane**. The *logical fallacy* in Barthes' *Image Music Text* is in the way of confusion of the logic for the chronology of event relations instantiated; that is, what comes *after* being read in the narrative as what is *caused by* (1977: p. 94) for delay and attempted concealment of the offender. This fallacy is constituted following the referential layering of an **indirect discourse referent** (DR) functioning as the bidirectional cardinal point in secondary (alternative) tales due to the perpetrator's motive or desire backgrounded in the first story of crime (Figs. 2.1 and 2.4). In such application, there is a form of ***distortion*** (Barthes 1977: p. 119) at structural level of the story, where specific microcontexts from the plot form, creating a referential layer for the construction of a MC, in which offender **intentionality** is embedded in the discourse, forming a narrative more **circular** than **linear**.

It is '*Often the complaint of the writer that linear presentation constrains what is actually a circular affair.*' (Goffman in Lemert and Branaman 1997: p. 155). A **circular narrative** achieved due to *narrative forking* presents alternative continuations as suspense-causing **discontinuity** in the sequence of events. This discontinuity in Sternberg (2003: p. 327) is two clashing components of *suspense* causing **two possible expectations** about the future resolution of a conflict in the narrative, and is:

- Between narrative *curiosity* and narrative *suspense* **in *prospection*** relating to the process of gapping (**curiosity gaps**) in the chronological direction of the missing and the desired information (the narrative past vs. the future); or
- Between narrative *curiosity* and narrative *surprise* **in *retrospection***, relating to the perceptibility of the process of gap filling (**surprise-gaps**), to the awareness of the existence of the gap not foregrounded at the point of the opening and delayed in the narrative. [My emphasis as bullet points]

The processing of discontinuity thus constitutes **gaps** in the way of suspense, surprise or curiosity, and is of the view that it centers an indirect DR which is the motive or the desire in the first story of crime. For example, if utterances 8–10 below (p. 26) by Dr. Sheppard are hinge/cardinal points in the narrative discourse, a **conflict** in prospection is constituted in these utterances, which functions as the raison-d'-être in the alternative discourse. These utterances occur after the first crime and second murder in the story in *Ackroyd*. Also, as narrative options, these utterances in perpetrator context become the cause for the narrative effect of **misdirection** by directing our **gaze** towards a **framed suspect** Ralph Paton (Frame 14) and Parker (Frames 33, 27) as possible *blackmailers*, away from Dr. Sheppard, the real blackmailer and murderer, in Frames 23 and 29.

At the cardinal point, the narrative option in the discourse carries the narrative along different paths, for instance Ralph or Parker as suspects in *Ackroyd* versus the actual offender in alternative storyworlds (Sect. 2.5). This option is found in the logical linearity of events disturbed in the first story of crime formulating a layered discourse based on the **Principle of Relevance** (PoR) of the concealer and the revelator in the narrative discourse. PoR is in turn related to the referential layer of the indirect DR, which has the **bidirectional functionality** (both backward and forward orientation) and double functionality of a **cardinal function** different from a backward-oriented anaphoric and forward-oriented cataphoric referential function. For instance, the **referent function** in 7 is different from utterances 5 and 6,

5. Antecedent anaphora (backward pointing): e.g. *Look at the moon, I can't see it.*
6. Antecedent cataphora (forward looking): e.g. *Look at that.*
7. **Discourse referent** (forward and backward pointing): e.g. *Kill an active plump chicken, prepare it for the oven.*

The pro-form *it*, in example 7, has the **double functionality** of *nuclei* (note 8) in the referential layer and in the criminal context appears a) at once chronological (consequential) and logical (consecutive) in sequence, but b) distorted (dystaxia) at horizontal level of the narrative thread, to form c) an illusion of chronological sequence (layering) created for delay as well as for movement (acceleration) in the story.

This is termed *logical fallacy* (Barthes 1977: p. 94). A **discourse layering** thus formulated is at the level of the **concealer**, according to the principle of concealed motive, and deception in Figs. 2.2 and 2.5, and at the level of the revelator according to the principle of actual truth in Figs. 2.3 and 2.6 below. The **concealer's PoR** is relative to the concealed desire, while **revelator's PoR** is relative to the actual happening of events. The referential layer (Figs. 2.1 and 2.4) arises in the bidirectional functionality of an indirect DR functioning as the cardinal point, and is a **direct referent** to the mystery, motive or desire, which is linked to the murderer.

2.4.1 Manipulated Context: The Classification

Manipulated context (MC) is one such referential layer (Sect. 2.5) formulated in the bidirectional functionality of a discourse referent relative to an offender motive or offender desire. In MC (Appendix 2e) there is not necessarily any lack of continuity of space, time or participants, but rather a lack of a consequential link between frames to establish real **causality** following a chronological order. This lack of contextual configuration in immediate contexts does not necessarily cause disorientation in the reader. It is not the case that readers fail to respond to the text signals and move to the next context. For reasons of inexplicit information flow in the way of mixed-up sequence, text signals are manipulated and understood when taking into account:

- the inference processing of the cardinal point in the discourse referent, distinct from a cataphoric or anaphoric referent;
- subsequently the microcontexts formed in the frame analysis;
- the logical fallacy in the dual function of showing and telling when following chronological sequence of thematic frames (the microthemes) within the macro narrative in the story.

There is then **frame modification**[14] (Emmott 2004: p. 142) in MC that is **withheld** in prospection, but **realized** in retrospection. In MCs there is not necessarily any lack of continuity of space, time or participants, but there is **lack of episodic link** between frames to establish **causality** in the chronological order provided.

---

[14] Frame modification: the most obvious one is if the text explicitly states that a character has left or entered the location and there is no change in the contextual configuration of a frame. In the reader's assumption however, the frame remains intact. (Emmott 2004: p. 142)

The processing and structure of MC in the discourse is understood with reference to:

- The referential layer of a **framed discourse referent** (a backward- and forward-oriented DR);
- The confusion of the consecution and consequence of events in the plot line (the **logical fallacy**); and in
- The **Principle of Relevance** (PoR) based on the concealer and the revelator.

The processing of MC centers on the indirect DR as the perpetrator motive in the narrative. As stated above, the cardinal point in the story has double functionality of a forward- and backward-oriented function in the narrative discourse, and is different from an anaphoric and cataphoric referent in the narrative. Halliday (in Bloor and Bloor 2013: p. 96) establishes the referent function on the **principle of reference**, referring to entities **outside** the discourse.

The **referent function** is also relative to **Relevance Theory** in Sperber and Wilson (1986) and to **Reference Theory** in Emmott (1997: chapter 7). For example in 7, the indirect referent *it* is referring to an entity which is identifiable as the bird in the **situation of utterance**. The demonstrative *that* is an **exophoric reference** (reference **outside** the text as in Bloor and Bloor 2013, p. 96). In 5, the referent *it* is **coreferential**, an **endophoric reference**. In reference theory, forward-pointing is cataphoric, and backward-looking is anaphoric, and involves a direct referent. However, in 7 the reader must **amalgamate** the antecedent NP, *active plump chicken*, with the verb *kill* to form a **new** mental **entity** referred as the pro-form *it*. This new entity formed is by an amalgamation of information from immediate/given context (*focusing*) and from the background /surrounding /old context (*priming*), which is also a **common-sense assumption**, termed as *conceptual accessibility* as in Bock and Warren (1985: p. 50). This **situation of utterance** becomes complex if the **new entity** (offender-in-prospection) is not given and **outside** the immediate clausal discourse and is to be inferred by taking into account the backgrounded information relevant to this entity in the story context. The reference to the sense of **new entity** inferred in immediate context materializes in story prospection.

To work this out, an *optimal relevance* (the ***stimulus*** as in Sperber and Wilson 1986) is necessary for a made assumption, and the assumption is in **anticipation**[15] (different from anticipation of events in Prince 1982) of what the narrator anticipates while situated in the **discourse-now** of the **narrating-I**, than in retrospective **story-now** of the **experiencing-I**. Anticipation is based on *focusing*, synonymous to a forward-looking cataphora, where information is carried forward about an inexplicit referent, such as with the pronoun *anything* in example 8, which then links with the common-sense assumption from the context **primed**[16] as seen in Figs. 2.1 and 2.4 below. These assumptions together **trigger** the appropriate entity representation for the DR *anything* in example 8, a pro-form for the new entity of Ralph Paton in prospection, a 'framed' suspect. The key point here is that Dr. Sheppard, in utterances 8–10 from *Ackroyd*, formulated a **new entity** disposition as the **narrative object (NO)**, which is inexplicit in the immediate discourse,

8. '*Could I do <u>anything</u> with the boy* [Ralph Paton, Ackroyd's nephew]? *I thought I could.*' (p. 27, Frame 14),
9. '*I hesitated with my hand on the door handle, looking back and wondering if there was <u>anything</u> I had left undone.*' (p. 41, Frame 23 (B4)),
10. '*I did <u>what little</u> had to be done.*' (p. 45, Frame 29), (my emphasis)

The pro-form, *anything*, and *what little* are an **indirect discourse referent** to a perpetrator manipulation and therefore concealment in post-murder context. Reference to the **new entity** of Ralph as suspect is outside the immediate discourse and is thus in anticipation.

---

[15] Anticipation—In Prince (1982: p. 49), when the narrator presents an event or a series of events before its time, we have an example of anticipation.

[16] Primed event—One particular contextual frame, or frame which is a mental store of information about the current context built from the text itself and from inference made from the text, becomes the focus of attention for the reader. (Emmott 1999: p. 123)

2.4.2 Discourse Referent: The Classification

Discourse referent (DR), following from the section above, is an entity articulated in the course of narration, where a reference in a specific frame is indexed to an object in the immediate context, which functions differently to an anaphoric and cataphoric referential pronoun. The reference is to a framed but indirect discourse referent, which has the double functionality of a cardinal function (the *nuclei* in Barthes 1977: p. 94).

Function 1. At once providing, by priming and focusing, a chronological (**consequential**) and logical (**consecutive**) sequence of events relative to an entity inexplicit in the discourse.
Function 2. When mapped as the mediation point for an alternative discourse with additional reference to why this event is important and no other in the discourse, the sequence found is altered (**distorted**, *dystaxia*) in vertical reading. The altered sequence reveals an **illusion** of narrative relations when it is mapped on to the vertical axis from the narrative horizontal setting relative to the median (cardinal) point.

This is in line with the characteristics of crime (*Crime Science: A Springer Open Journal* 2014: p. 1), the offending process is **covert and indirect**, associated with offender motive or desire, and constitutes **alternative narrative relations**. These **scenarios** are alternative (chrono)logical sequence (Figs. 2.2 below and 2.5), and are **MCs** (Appendix 2e) formulated in the priming and focusing of the motive as the cardinal point in the perpetrator discourse, which is set in opposition to the revelator's narrative discourse.

MCs are analyzed in Christie's *The Murder of Roger Ackroyd* (*Ackroyd*), James' *Cover Her Face* (CHF) and Ford Madox Ford's *The Good Soldier* (TGS). Narration in these stories is in retrospect by a first-person, third-person and a first-person narrator respectively, with **hybrid voice**[17] which is defined by **multivoicedness** of simultaneous **mimetic** and **diegetic** lin-

---

[17] Hybrid voice is an existence of 'dialogic relations and hybrid combinations … occurring … at the intersection … between the depicting authorial language and the depicted language of the hero.' (Scott 2009: p. 123)

guistic aspects. In *Ackroyd*, the principal narrator is also the murderer. In CHF, the **focalization** in the story is mainly through the principal character, Mrs. Eleanor Maxie, who is also the murderer. In TGS, two suicides and one accidental death take place, and again narration is in retrospect by the principal character Dowell, who is the **affected** tragic hero in the narrative.

2.5 The Processing of Manipulated Context (MC)

I now set out how MCs are understood in *Ackroyd*, CHF, and finally in TGS. Firstly, the hinge point in the plot form with its bidirectional function and its respective referential layer (Figs. 2.1 and 2.4) is established for realizing narrative options as MC formulated in each story. The hinge point is commonly the referent for the desire or the motive of the concealed perpetrator in the story. Corresponding to the hinge point, frames are selected from the plot form and are mapped on to the horizontal and vertical axis of the alternative narrative thread (following the median point for alternative story lines), to compare the relevance of the concealer from that of the revelator in the story.

Before the analysis, the terms used in the figures are defined again:

Concealer—relevance agrees with the principle of concealment, or distortion.
Revelator—relevance agrees with the principle of revelation, i.e. the actual sequence of actions that reveals the set of actions leading to the murder.

Several instances of a **cardinal event** at the median point are linked together to realize the narrative thread with reference to the desire or motive as the indirect **discourse referent** (DR) providing a narrative option in a story. Within a hierarchical perspective of a murder story, the **indirect DR** is also the **mainspring** (the impelling cause, the principal spring) of the narrative.

Median point, also referred as the hinge point or the risky point in the story is typically an utterance in the discourse positioned in the moment of narration (Storyworld c, Chapter 2.6), which is given in anticipation.

The median point is the **discourse referent** with reference to the concealer motive or its desire in the story. This relevance as the discourse point is presented with an * on the horizontal axis. Following the point where the * appears on the horizontal setting, the sequence of events are pre- or post-hinge points based on the context centering of the median point.

Horizontal axis (setting): —the distributional relation of events in linear fashion, with reference to the median point, describing the 'before-and-after' setting for the risky moment, which formulate the narrative option.

Vertical axis (showing): —is an integrational narrative relation of events showing the events sequenced in a hierarchical order with reference to the median point. This is where the grasped relations show event (frame) sequence inversion which causes the creation of the hinge point as the climactic point in the alternative narrative.

Bidirectional axis: the narration in prospection (future) and in retrospection (past), of narrative events with reference to the median point on the horizontal axis in a narrative discourse.

A *cardinal function* in a murder context is a dual function of **consecution** (the logical relation of a consequent to an antecedent as the deduction) and **consequence** (the linear sequence of events corresponding to the **nuclei** (risky moment) in the discourse). The search for the *nuclei* with cardinal function operates over a horizontal and vertical set of narrative relations based on the PoR at the level of the concealer and revelator.

The **episodic links** between events formed at the horizontal level are then logically mapped on to the vertical axis of the narrative, where it is necessary to work out how the events are sequenced and then layered in the alternative concealer or revelator's narrative.

There is *logical fallacy* in the logical sequencing of events, where causal relations are altered. The altered relevance is based on *what* [event] *comes after* [which is] *being read in the narrative as what it is caused by*. This relevance is *post hoc* and is in opposition to the actual happenings in the story. That is, the concealer **calculates** how the interpretation is reached; '*why this interpretation and not that*.' as stated by Sperber and Wilson (1986: p. 37).

Before the processing of MCs in each story, it is helpful to skim through the plot forms of each story (*Ackroyd* in Appendix 2a, CHF in Appendix 2c and TGS in appendix 2d) and to become familiar with the frame sequence for the different episodes (**theme frames**) in each story. This is also to track the complex episodic links plotted for theme frames significant for the story suspense. For reasons of space constraint, initials of each character from the story are used in the analysis.

2.5.1 Manipulated Context: Case Study—*The Murder of Roger Ackroyd*

Dr. S (Dr. Sheppard), RP (Ralph Paton), Mrs. F (Mrs. Ferrars), C (Caroline), RA (Roger Ackroyd), FA (Flora Ackroyd)

The context in each frame from *Ackroyd* is,

Frame 14—*Could I do <u>anything</u> with the boy* [RP, RA's nephew]? *I thought I could.*' (p. 27)

Cardinal point

Frame 1—Mrs. F found dead by Dr. S. (p. 7)

Frame 3—Dr. S remembered Mrs. F talking to RP the day before she was found dead. (p. 15)

Recall Frame 21   **RP Episode**

Frame 4—RA unaware that his stepson was at King's Abbott and not in London. Dr. S remembered seeing RP at King's Abbot talking to Mrs. F. (p. 16)

Episodic link to Frame 3   **Repeated Frame 11**   **RP Episode**

Frame 6—C informed her brother Dr. S of RP staying at Three Boars instead of Fernly Park, and he had met up with *a girl* (Ursula, RP's wife). (p. 19)

Repeated Frame 7   **RP Episode**

Frame 7—Dr. S came to know from RA that RP was engaged to Flora. (p. 25)

RP Episode

Frame 8—RP is in the woods expressing his concern to a girl (Ursula) about his stepfather, RA will cut him off his inheritance, as he was secretly married to Ursula, and not his cousin FA against his stepfather's wish (p. 203), ... and also he was in need of money (Frame 37) and he would become a very rich man when RA was dead. (p. 26)

Repeated Frame 6   RP Episode

Frame 10—C's assertion: Mrs. F's husband died over a year ago (Frame 1). He was an alcoholic and was poisoned by Mrs. F. Overcome by guilt, Mrs. F committed suicide. (p. 9)

(implied) Blackmailing Episode

Frame 11—Dr. S recalling RP and Mrs. F together the *day before* (the day is left unclear in prospective narration) walking along, side by side, and Mrs. F had been talking very earnestly. This tête-a-tête between RP and Mrs. F the day before Mrs. F died struck the doctor as being odd,

'*I think I can safely say that it was at this moment that <u>a foreboding of the future</u> first swept over me.* (p. 15) ... *That earnest tête-a-tête between Ralph and Mrs Ferrars the day before struck me disagreeably.*' **(Episode D (Event 1))** (p. 15)

Repeated Frame 3, 21   RP Episode

Frame 15—Dr. S meets RP at the Three Boars and offers to help, but RP refuses help and acknowledges that he has to deal with his personal matters directly with his stepfather and reveal his secret marriage to Ursula the parlor maid. (p. 28)

Episodic link to Frames 6 and 7   **RP Episode**

Frame 20—Dr. S and RA leave for the study where RA shares his knowledge of Mrs. F having poisoned her husband, about how she was blackmailed for huge sums of money (p. 38). Dr. S narrates that the blackmailer was referred to in the letter as a person, and he took this to be a man.

Letter Episode

Frame 21—recalled by Dr. S,

'*Suddenly before my [Dr. S] eyes there rose the picture of Ralph Paton and Mrs Ferrars side by side. .... I felt a momentary throb of anxiety. Supposing—oh! but surely that was impossible.*' (p. 37)

Repeated Frame 3, 11   RP Episode

Recall frames 3, 11 contextually forming an episodic link with Frame 21, manipulate the **agent parameters** relating to the possible blackmailer by directing the reader's gaze to Frame 7, where C overhears RP with a girl, Ursula, and foregrounds the story about RP. In retrospect, in Frame 21, Dr. S was aware of RP being married without the knowledge of his stepfather. Dr. S exploited this withheld knowledge in Frame 21, when he advised RP in Frame 15 to stay away until the investigation of his stepfather's death was over. Because of his secret marriage to Ursula (also Repeated Frames 6, 8) and to avoid suspicion that he killed his stepfather for his inheritance, RP agrees to Dr. S's arrangement to conceal him in a mental hospital.

Frame 27—Parker is astounded to hear from Dr. S that he received a call from someone who introduced himself as Parker requesting him to come to Fernly Park where his master has been found murdered. (p. 43)

Murder Episode

In Fig. 2.1 below, the cardinal point is the utterance in Frame 14. The utterance is **covertly** related to the perpetrator's desire/motive as an intended outcome; that is, to frame RP as the suspect. The referential layer of Frame 14 as the cardinal point is,

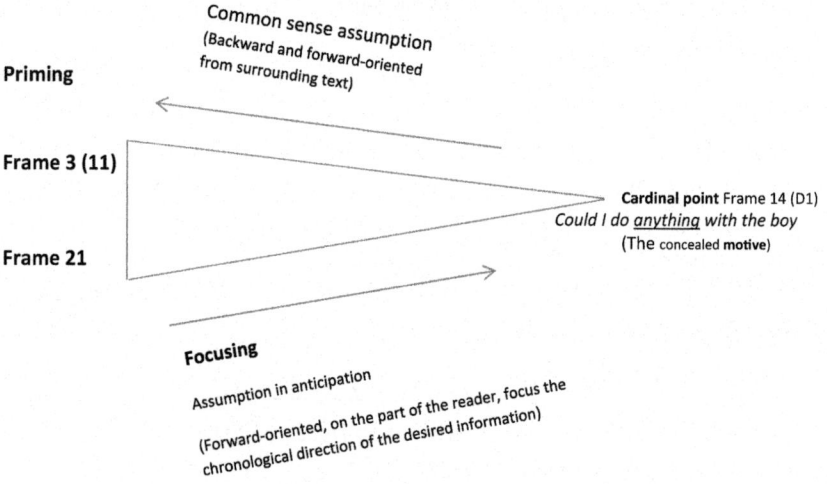

Fig. 2.1 Discourse referent: *Ackroyd*

Explanation
Frame recalls 3 and 21 (doctor saw Mrs. F and RP talking the night before Mrs. F committed suicide) are **salient assumptions** for the pro-form *anything* in Frame 14. That is, as primed frames (a background context) in prospection, form the context for RP to become the most likely blackmailer in the story. This is **covertly** indexed as the pro-form *anything*. With reference to the primed frames as the background, the inference for the pro-form in anticipation formulates a forward- and backward-oriented common-sense link with other frames related to the cardinal point.

For instance, in the primed frames, the narrator (Dr. S) in prospection creates inferences for the indirect referent *anything*, in the story. That is, as a **content factor**, the repeated frames (4, 6, 7, and 8) about RP at the Three Boars and not at his family home in Fernly Park in the discourse, provide further **text informativity** for the pro-form *anything*. In the properties of the **here and now** of the repeated frames (RP meeting *the girl*) are logically, physically and cognitively (Van Dijk 1977: p. 192) established the cause for the ***storyworld*** (Palmer 2004: p. 194) centering on Frame 14. The repeated frames are a referential context in the primed events, and function as underlying discourse content for the pro-form, *anything*. Consequently, directing the reader's gaze towards RP's secret meeting with his undeclared wife Ursula, when his wife came to know that RP was compelled to fulfil his stepfather's wish and be engaged to his cousin Flora (SB frame ff III, Appendix 2b). A **microcontext** is formed in the repeated and recall frames, which formulates a referential layer for the DR at the median point.

This analysis does not undertake a comparative study of the way the story is narrated in the film compared to the novel. However, SB frame ff III, at the outset is the cardinal point in the film; unlike Dr. S's utterance in prospection in Frame 14 in the novel. In the film, SB frame ff III foregrounds RP's secret marriage to Ursula, while Frame 14 in the novel, as an event in prospection, gives rise to the narrative option when Ursula revealed to RA her secret marriage to RP (this fact is withheld in the 1st story of crime and comes to light when Poirot interviews Ursula the maid in the 2nd story of investigation). Consequently, in the novel, unlike the film, Dr. S took advantage of RP and Ursula's secret marriage and compelled RP to hide in a hospital to avoid being suspected of killing his stepfather, as he had defied his stepfather's wish to marry his cousin FA and keep the inheritance in the family. Dr. S also knew that Ralph was in need of money, which additionally made him a suspect as a murderer.

In the novel, the secret marriage in SB frame ff III is foregrounded as repeated frames in the novel. The repeated frames (6, 8, 13, and 15) are ***discourse cues*** to the ***clue*** (note 3) in the RP episode. That is, RP's secret marriage in the repeated frames is the contextual information (cue) to the contextual meaning (clue) embedded in Frame 15. The clue in Frame 15 relates to Dr. S compelling RP to remain in a mental hospital until RA's murder investigation was over. RP agreed to this as his suspicion could not fail to attach to the facts that he was married and could not marry FA. Unknown to RP, this framed him as a suspect, providing Dr. S the scenario to frame RP. This scenario is withheld in prospective narration, revealed in the third story of the investigation (in Todorov the 2nd story) by the inspector.

The overall context constructed in Fig. 2.1 is not a physical episode like Frames 1 and 8, where Mrs. F died and C saw RP talking to a girl, but is a **narrative gap** (Prince's *disnarration*) contextualized in the utterance in anticipation about an event (RP to hide in a mental hospital in Frame 15) to follow in the prospective narrative. Additionally, the **conceptual accessibility** (the common-sense assumption) for indirect antecedents of *anything* as the mainspring of the referential layer in Fig. 2.1 (also for *what little* in Frame 29) is ***post hoc*** in the narrative (Sperber and Wilson 1986: p. 37). The notion of *post hoc* is an **issue of calculability** and functions like the relational hierarchy of a grammatical subject, where the subject is before the direct object (DO), and the DO is before the indirect object (IO) and IO before all lower-level relations. In keeping with this logic, the primed (background) events, relative to the median point becomes the highest point in the hierarchy of events in the discourse, to which other events stem from it. Like the repeated frames, the recall frames for episodic links are related to provide the microcontext for the referential layer instantiated in Fig. 2.1. In other words, in the **referential layer**, the teller of the utterance in Frame 14 creates a conceptual accessibility for the pro-form *anything* where Ralph is a **narrative object** (NO), and the NO becomes a **covert textual antecedent** with the referential function of a **framed discourse referent** (DR).

Thus pro-form *anything* as a referent does not refer to a direct discourse antecedent *blackmail*, but to a **mental representation** (a sense of entity) of a blackmailer indexed in the microcontext in repeated frames (4, 6, 8) and recalled frames (3, 11, 21) in the discourse; a new **entity** of Ralph as the *blackmailer* in prospect. The primed events then link as a forward-orientation with Ralph as **new entity**; that is, a framed suspect for two crimes in the story,

(a) blackmailing Mrs. F for poisoning her alcoholic husband (Frame 20); and
(b) the murder of his stepfather, RA (Frame 23 (B4)) for inheritance (Frame 8).

As a secondary context, this overall **microcontext** comes into existence in **anticipation**. With a forward and backward common-sense assumption, this anticipated referential layer is connected further in the discourse to other events in the Ralph episode, such as his secret marriage in Frame 7 and 15, his inheritance in Frame 8 and 32. This scenario is summarized as Event C1-6 in Appendix 2a, formulating a nonlinear narrative centering on Frame 15, but realized, following the desire Frame 14, as offender motive at the median point.

All this is also possible by working out the **stimulus** (*optimal relevance*) for the indirect DR *anything* in Frame 14 relative to the assumptions in Frame 8 (RP needs money) and in Frame 10, C's assertion that Mrs. F killed her alcoholic husband and, overcome by guilt, committed suicide. These assumptions, when linked with the primed events in Frame 3 and Frame 21, along with the **discourse content** in the repeated and recalled frames as **common-sense assumption** from the **surrounding context**, these assumptions **trigger** appropriate context for the indirect DR. An **episodic link** is thus formed for the pro-form *anything* in anticipation, and constitutes a MC in the referential layer associated with the new entity of RP as a **fictive subject**, the *blackmailer* and consequently the murderer of RA.

Todorov, in Howard and Culler (1977: p. 45) stipulates,

'*In the story, there is no inversion in time, actions follow their natural order.*'
[That is], '*the kind of relation established between propositions in the narrative plot is of the temporal kind, where events follow one another in the text.*'

However, in the inference processing for Frame 14 in anticipation, there is **simultaneity of prospection and retrospection**. Unlike thrillers, the events in prospect do not take the place of events in retrospect or the reverse in the plot summary of a whodunit narrative as in *Ackroyd*. Dr. S constructs the embedded RP episode (Frames 11, 21) as *suspense* in prospection for Frame 14, and *curiosity gaps* in retrospection relative to the letter episode in Frame 23—*if there was anything I had left undone*—when Mrs. F's suicide note is removed from the crime scene in the narrative discourse. The conflict between narrative *curiosity* (in prospect) and *suspense* (in retrospect) in the story of crime in *Ackroyd* generates *curiosity-gaps* (conflict between narrative universals, curiosity and suspense) not foregrounded at the point of the narration in Frame 14, but contextually delayed as **withheld Frame** 23 for the letter episode. Such a **process of gapping** fulfilled in the chronological direction of narration, is in the anticipation of RP framed as the blackmailer, and in the prospection to achieve the desired outcome of RP framed as a **narrative object**. Such intentionality then influences the episodic links in the plot form for alternative formulations in consecution, as we shall see in Figs. 2.2 and 2.3.

Frame 14 established as the **mainspring** (the impelling cause, the principal spring in the narrative) in the hierarchical perspective of the murder story in *Ackroyd*, this event at median point operates over both the horizontal and vertical set of narrative relations in a Dr. S discourse. In mapping this cardinal point as in the figures below, changes are shown in the narrative relations of events based on the PoR of the offender and the victim.

2.5.2 The Principle of Relevance: Case Study—*The Murder of Roger Ackroyd*

The alternative world in distortion is analyzed at the structural level. That is, the way narrative relations are consequential to the desire frame along the horizontal narrative thread, which then formulate consecutive hierarchical relation of events when mapped on to the vertical axis from the horizontal axis. The event line in consecution then lines up with the **desire frame** at the median point in the narrative. The theory of levels adopted is initially based on Benveniste in Barthes (1977), where the distributional relation along the horizontal axis is the described setting, and the integrational relation along the vertical axis is where events are grasped from the setting to integrate the **climactic point** in the narrative to realize the instantiated alternative discourse layer. Based on the ***nuclei*** (DR) as the common point of relevance for each discourse, this grasping of narrative relations and then the mapping on to the vertical axis of the concealer discourse is distinct from the revelator's discourse. The mapping of the nuclei in *Ackroyd* appears thus:

The context in each frame on the narrative thread is quoted in the sequence in which they took place in the context of crime. The frame numbers are not sequential as they correspond to the way they appear in the actual plot form of the story. The underlined text is the mainspring, the hinge point of the narrative in the murder context.

The context in each frame is,

Dr. S (Dr. Sheppard), RP (Ralph Paton), Mrs. F (Mrs. Ferrars), C (Caroline), RA (Roger Ackroyd), FA (Flora Ackroyd)

Frame 1: Mrs. F found dead by Dr. S (p. 7)
Frame 3: Dr. S remembered Mrs. F talking to RP the day before she was found dead (p. 15)
                    Recall and Repeated in Frame 21   **RP Episode**

Frame 4: RA unaware that his stepson was at King's Abbott and not in London. Dr. S remembered seeing RP at King's Abbot talking to Mrs. F
                    Repeated Frame 11   **RP Episode**

Frame 6: C informs her brother, Dr. S, that RP was staying at Three Boars instead of Fernly Park, and met up with *a girl* (p. 19)
                    Repeated Frame 4   **RP Episode**

Frame 8: C overhears RP in the woods urging a *girl*, assumed to be Flora (p. 26), but actually Paton's wife Ursula the parlor maid at Fernly Park (pp. 203, 219). C overhears RP's concerns about his stepfather RA, how RA would cut off his inheritance if it was known that RP was secretly married to Ursula, when his stepfather wanted him to marry his cousin FA, and keep the inheritance within the family (p. 203).

Repeated Frame 6   **RP Episode**

Frame 13: RP at Three Boars and not at Fernly Park, but Dr. S insists that RA told him he was in London,' (p. 19)

Repeated Frame 4 and 6   **RP Episode**

Frame 14 (Frames 23: B4, 29): '*Could I do <u>anything</u> with the boy* [Ralph Paton]*? I thought I could.*' (p. 27)

Desire Frame   **Cardinal Point**   **RP Episode**

Frame 15: Dr. S met RP at the Three Boars and offers to help, but RP refuses help and acknowledges that he has to deal with his personal matters directly with his stepfather and reveal his secret marriage to Ursula the parlor maid. (p. 28)

Episodic link to Frame 8, 32   **Withheld Frame**   **RP Episode**

(In this frame, when Dr. S met RP at the Three Boars (p. 27) he came to know that RP was married to Ursula, the parlor maid (p. 219). In prospective narration, this information is **withheld** by narrator/doctor)

Frame 7: Dr. S came to know from RA that RP was engaged to Flora (p. 25)

Withheld Frame   **RP Episode**

Frame 20: Dr. S and RA leave the dining room after dinner for RA's study where RA shares his knowledge of Mrs. F having poisoned her husband (p. 38) and tells him how someone was blackmailing her for huge sums of money. He requests RA to punish the person who made her life hell for the last year. Dr. S narrates that the blackmailer was referred to in the letter as a person, and he took this to be a man. (pp. 37, 40, 108)

RP Episode

2 Manipulated Context   39

Frame 21: Dr. S **recalls,**

> '*Suddenly before my* [Dr. S] *eyes there rose the picture of Ralph Paton and Mrs Ferrars side by side. ..... I felt a momentary throb of anxiety. Supposing—oh! but surely that was impossible.*' (p. 37)
>
> **Recall Frame (3)   RP Episode**

Frame 23 (B4): Dr. S murdered RA and then removed the letter that revealed him as the blackmailer before he left the study. However, this is hidden in the prospective narration.
Dr. S narrates that the letter was brought in by Parker at 8.40 pm when RA read the letter to Dr. S. Ten minutes later the doctor leaves RA in his study to get back home. Before he leaves the study the doctor narrates,

> '*I hesitated with my hand on the door handle, looking back and wondering if <u>there was anything I had left undone</u>, I could think of nothing.*' (p. 41)

The underlined narrator utterance conceals the committed murder and the removed letter that disclosed the blackmailer.
B(4) Event 4: Dr. S checks the study for <u>*anything* left undone</u> and leaves the study by the open window, under which footprints of RP's shoes were discovered. (p. 228)

Withheld Frame   Cardinal Point   RP Episode

Frame 27: Dr. S finds RA murdered, and Parker is astounded to hear from Dr. S that he received a call from someone, who introduced himself as Parker, and requested him to come to Fernly Park where his master has been found murdered. (p. 43)

Parker framed

Frame 37: Lawyer tells Poirot that RP inherits RA's large fortune—Fernly Park and all the shares on his company, Ackroyd and Son, making RP a wealthy man. However, RP has a chronic condition, he spent money like water. (p. 97)

RP Episode

40 The Language of Suspense in Crime Fiction

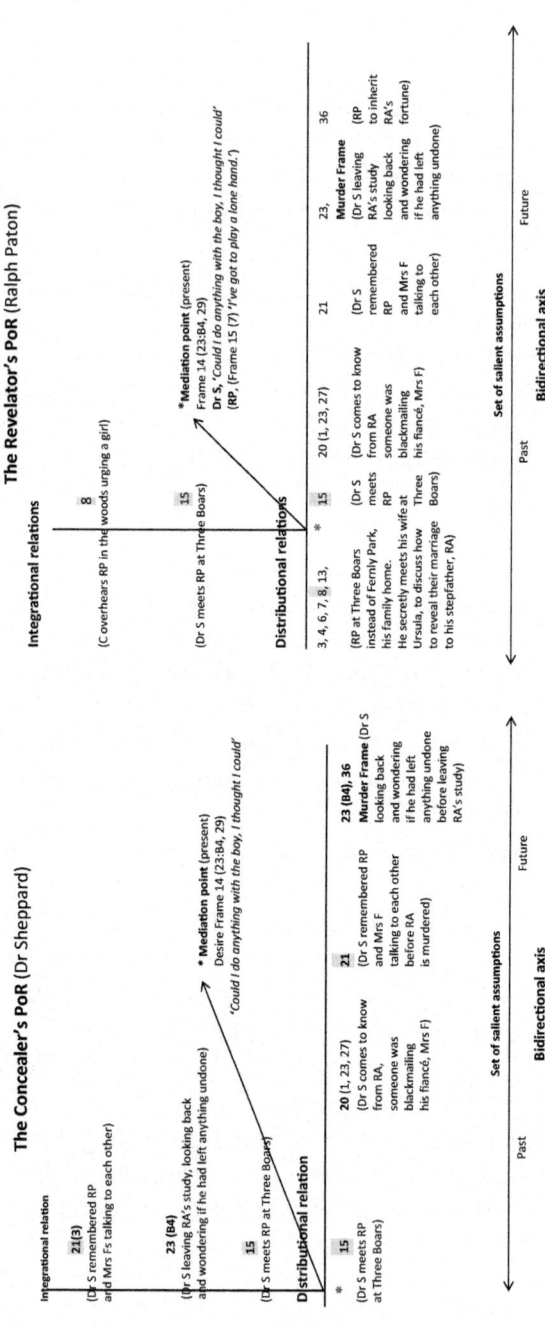

Fig. 2.2. The concealer's PoR (Dr. S)

Fig. 2.3. The revelator's PoR (RP)

Explanation

The motive in the **Desire Frame** 14 is the median point in the 2 alternative narratives (Figs. 2.2 and 2.3).

As established above, in the hierarchical perspective, the issue of *blackmail* is of hierarchical importance in the story of the concealer. Dr. S, the real blackmailer, and also the murderer, tried to establish RP as the perpetrator; contextually backed by Frames 3 and 21, when Dr. S *remembered* the sight of RP and Mrs. F together. Unlike the material process, *inform* in Frame 6, the mental process *remembered* in the repeated frames (3 and 21) make the hinge point a **cognitive process** in the doctor's mind, rather than a factual account. In addition, the use of the common noun *girl* is also significant with reference to information being **withheld** for anonymity and therefore a **suspense** in prospection.

In the concealer narrative, **relevance** formulated in the **repeated context** in Frames 3 and 21, with episodic link to the context in Frames 7, 15 and 32, foreground a **scenario** where Frames 15 and 21 are **overlapping** at both the integrational (showing), and distributional (describing/setting) levels of the concealer's narrative thread. We already know that this cognitive layer is a *post hoc* (calculability) anticipation by the concealer in Fig. 2.2. Such as, in fictional reality, Frame 15 takes place after Murder Frame 29. That is, Dr S visits RP at Three Boars; and unknown to RP, this visit was following the murder of his uncle in Frame 29. Moreover, Motive Frame 14 in the setting is before Frame 15, sequencing the perpetrator (Narrator) utterance in Frame 14 before the act of framing RP by Dr S the character. There is thus, distinction between the Narrator utterance and a character performing in Frames 14 and 15 respectively, and is of significance with reference to post hoc anticipation in the plotting of Roger Ackroyd's murder story.

In the revelator narrative (Fig. 2.3), the relevance is in the **overlapping** of Frames 8 and 15. Both appear at the integrational and distributional levels of the narrative thread. In the revelator's discourse, Frame 8 is of hierarchical importance. That is, when RP surmised that his wife Ursula had revealed their marriage to his stepfather (p. 204), he realized that the suspicion for the death of RA would fall on him and his wife that he loved.

Dr. S visited RP (Frame 15) and suggested for him to stay away for a while at a home for the mentally unfit (**withheld event** in Frame 15) until the investigation of his stepfather's murder was over (p. 220). This withheld event in the first story of crime is revealed in the third story of investigation. This argument is reinforced in the *logical fallacy* following the cause–effect consecution when following the DR in both the concealer and revelator discourse.

In the **concealer's** discourse, there is causal reversal in the vertical axis; Frame 21 is followed by 15 and 23. That is, Dr. S hypothesizes about framing RP as the blackmailer in Frame 21 and presents a mental cognitive picture of RP and Mrs. F being together in Frame 11 and 21. This cognitive process in the actual story happened soon after Dr. S murdered RA in Frame 15, when Dr. S met RP at Three Boars, as was backed by Poirot, '… *he had come straight* [to see RP at Three Boars] *from the scene of crime*' (p. 219). Here is a **narrative conflict** between curiosity and suspense; Frame 21, relative to the blackmailer, as a *curiosity gap* in retrospection, conflict between universals, *suspense* and curiosity, planted in Frame 20 (1, 23 and 27).

Conversely, the consecutive relation in the vertical axis in the **revelator's** discourse follows the narrative sequence of Frame 8 (Ralph at Three Boars) followed by 15 (doctor meets Ralph following RA's murder). Unlike Fig. 2.2, the revelator sequence is not an evaluative sequence of events in the vertical axis. The concealer narrative is in prospection, although the first-person narration in the story by offender/narrator Dr. S is in retrospection. The cause and effect chain is linear in Fig. 2.3: the cause in Frame 8 (his secret marriage) is followed by the effect in Frame 15 (Dr. S exploited the knowledge of RP's secret marriage, when RP was also engaged to Flora against his stepfather's wish, a fact unknown to his wife Ursula. Poirot supports this sequence later in the story of investigation; [Dr. S] *must know that things looked very bleak against him* [RP] (p. 219) in the narrative sequence.

In Fig. 2.2, the causal relation in the concealer's discourse is distorted in the vertical axis, and a logical fallacy is formulated in the causal relations. In the actual story the consecution of 'what' (Frame 15) must come after the 'caused by' (Frame 21), but in the hierarchical relation in Fig. 2.2, there is **causal reversal**, 'what' in Frame 21 is caused by Frame 15. In other words, the **cognitive process** in Frame 21 (3), Dr. S remembered RP and Mrs. F together talking earnestly occur before Dr. S met RP at Three Boars (Frame 15). Poirot (p. 219) supported this sequence in the third story, when he revealed, Frames 21 (3) followed by Frame 15 was to make RP appear as someone in hiding after having murdered his stepfather. Such hierarchical relations of events revealed in evaluation, constitutes the doctor as an **offender** long before the detection, who framed RP as a suspect on exploiting his secret marriage and his problems with money. Unlike other family members and staff at Fernly Park, the doctor was aware that RP was at Three Boars and had a secret to hide (Frames 15, 32). Also being the blackmailer, the doctor suspected that Mrs. F might have left a suicide note for her fiancé (Frame 20) which later compelled him to murder RA. All this, as an **external construct** in the concealer narrative, made RP the **mainspring** of his murder story and prompted Dr. S to frame RP over Parker, as being the best option to manipulate RP's situation and conceal his own offence, and also save his trust as a community doctor.

2.5.3 Manipulated Context: Case Study—*Cover Her Face*

The above **causal fallacy** is also considered in the plot summary of James' *Cover Her Face* (CHF). The story in CHF is different from *Ackroyd*. The story narrator is omniscient. Unlike the first-person narrator/criminal and two deaths in *Ackroyd*, there is one murder in CHF, committed by Eleanor Maxie, which is accidental and **not consequential**. Also unlike *Ackroyd*, the narrative does not open with a crime which then then leads to another.

In the retrospective narration, events in CHF lead up to the first crime narrated at the outset in the **recalled Frame** 1. Unlike the whodunit plot form in *Ackroyd*, the event sequence leading to the murder in the plot summary (Appendix 2c) is linear and not circular. To conceal the first crime in *Ackroyd*, and then to shift the identity of the perpetrator on to other, the events in the story lead to the second crime. Conversely, in

CHF there is no consequential crime. Hence, the plot summary in CHF does not give rise to narrative options where the criminal, as a victim of circumstances constitutes a logical fallacy in the layered discourse, as found in *Ackroyd* with reference to the Desire Frame 14.

As a retrospective narration, the development of events leading up to the first crime in CHF is mainly recalled frames. There is an underlying propositional content present as indirect context in the cognitive context 'C' adopted from the story of investigation. The indirect contextual reference to *death* by Dalgleish, by Deborah Maxie and Martha is to decode the veiled propositional content relating to the forthcoming *death* of Sally Jupp in the story. While the indirect propositional content related to the *motive* in the cognitive context 'B' is to recover the contextual assumption about the murderer being within the family. On the other hand, the ***surprise* context** in cognitive construct A is a schematic construct with reference to Sally Jupp *as a model of all virtues* (p. 17) despite her 'breach of the moral code' for being an unmarried mother with child.

The intended reader focus and the narrative interest is in the **cognitive constructs** rather than in the content factors in frame recalls (1–18), and is unlike the formulated microcontexts like the RP episode in the repeated frames, recall frames and in the withheld frame in *Ackroyd*. Similar to Frame 14 in *Ackroyd*, there is an abstract internal situational setting functioning as the nuclei in CHF in clauses 12 and 13 below. As **restricted context** these frames below are not specific to the characters of Mrs. Maxie in CHF or Dr. Sheppard in *Ackroyd* in the story, but are relative to a participant utterance, such as the one underlined below,

Frame 1: 12a. '...*But the air of constraint which burdened the meal could hardly have been caused by the occasional presence of Sally Jupp who placed the dishes in front of Mrs Maxie and removed the plates with a dextrous efficiency which Miss Liddell noted with complacent approval.*' (5)

Frame 4: 12b. '...*She could not be expected to foresee the magnitude of those complications... violent death.* (10) 12c. ...*But things were happening at Martingale which were difficult to overlook.* 12d. *What she had not*

expected was that it should become progressively more difficult as the weeks wore on.' (23)

(**Cover Her Face** 1974)

Frame 2: 13a. '... *When had I last seen her* [Mrs. Ferrars]? *Not for over a week. Her manner then had been normal enough considering—well— considering everything.*' (15) **Frame 14**: 13b. '... *Could I do anything with the boy? I thought I could.*' (27) ... **Frame 21**: 13c. '*Suddenly before my* [Dr. Sheppard] *eyes there rose the picture of Ralph Paton and Mrs Ferrars side by side. .... I felt a momentary throb of anxiety. Supposing— oh! but surely that was impossible.*' (37). **Frame 29**: 13d. '... *I did what little had to be done.*' (45)

(**Christie** 1993)

In these utterances, the context is constructed over large stretches of text, and refers to **withheld events** like 'foresee *the magnitude of those complications*' (12b), which are left incomplete and unconnected at the point of narration in Frame 1. To accommodate and orientate contextual changes that take place in prospection in Frame 1, there is tense shift and modal shift in the utterances. This is in line with a **dual-functional environment** in tense aspects in MCs, taken up in Chap. 3.

In the tense aspects and stylistic features like the speech and thought presentation, the utterances in 12a-d and 13a-d have the appearance of **FIT** (free indirect thought). However, 12a seems like a reported thought (for example, the verb *noted*). 12b is a report of a negative (she did NOT foresee), so it seems that the thought did not occur. The author, then, appears to be prefiguring a series of events which are part of the narrative flow (and therefore in the mind of the narrator), but not part of the character's thoughts. 12c is characterized as reentering the mind of Miss Liddell and characterized as FIT, 12d, on the other hand, reverts to an absence of thought.Following the thought convention in Short (1996: p. 317), the utterances in clause 12 are akin to conscious reasoning, a **cognitive meandering** in the version of DT (direct thought) to evoke a mind working associatively. However, despite the subordination in 12d, the language breaks the convention of the **maxim of quantity** (Grice's (1975) four conversational maxims), because of the **restricted content** in 12a, for example, [what caused] *the air of constraint* is withheld. The language also breaks the narrative convention when following maxim of manner when the modal shift to future tense in the past, *could hardly have been caused*, is from default narrative past tense in the passage. This writing behavior is more akin to a relevant participant with an **authorial purpose** than a third-person omniscient narrator.

In addition, utterances 12a–d (by a floating omniscient narrator in prospect, or is it the post-murder character Mrs. Maxie in retrospect?), narrative paths, commonly constructed in anticipation, are not constructed in narrative futurity, unlike *Ackroyd* in Frame 14. The narration in anticipation is supported by participant Stephen Maxie, when he exclaims in hindsight to Cathy how his mother would have never been found out if she hadn't confessed to committing the murder (p. 204).

On comparing 12a–d (CHF) with 13a–d (*Ackroyd*), utterance 13b is the cardinal point in *Ackroyd*. A secondary narrative option is constituted at this point in the story where Ralph is framed as the *blackmailer* (13a and c) in the forward and backward-orientation of frame relevance as the cause for subsequent suicide that takes place at the outset in Frame 1 in *Ackroyd*. Similarly:

While **utterance** 12 (a, b) in CHF functions as the DR, it only has **forward-oriented reference** to frames (8, 9, 10 and 13 below), unlike the bidirectional discourse referent *anything* in 13b in *Ackroyd*. The events referred in 12 are to appear in the narrative, but in fictional reality are events in retrospect in the spatiotemporal parameters of the narrated story in CHF. As suspense (in *prospection*) with **restricted context**, the **narrating reflector** constructs a **possible world-state in futurity**, which pushes forward the narrative for the reader in a linear fashion.

Following the context in each frame,

Mrs. M (Mrs. Eleanor Maxie), DM (Deborah Maxie), SJ (Sally Jupp)

Frame 1: Mrs. M remembered the ritual gathering of her guests for the summer church fete that took place three months before the killing of SJ

'*But the air of constraint which burdened the meal could hardly have been caused by the occasional presence of Sally Jupp who placed the dishes in front of*

Mrs Maxie and removed the plates with a dextrous efficiency which Miss Liddell noted with complacent approval.' (p. 5)
Restricted Frame   Cardinal point

Frame 8: Mrs. M's reaction follows when SJ made the discovery about the tablets under her husband's (Simon Maxie's) bed. The tablets were unauthorized pain killers, that could kill the patient. A heated conversation followed between Mrs. M and SJ, when Mrs. M threatens to sack SJ for accusing her of wanting her husband to commit suicide. (p. 33)
Frame 9: SJ in return threatens to reveal Mrs. M's intention of keeping quiet about the tablets to her son Stephen.

'… I'd like to see Stephen's face if I told him that you knew all the time.' (p. 33)
Provocation Frame Tablet Episode (SJ Episode)

Frame 10: Martha overheard this conversation (Frames 8 and 9) and her cognitive world of disgust for SJ is revealed when she wished SJ banished from Martingale House.

'… And, … all things possible, Sally dead.' (p. 34)
Tablet Episode (SJ Episode)

Frame 13: SJ appears at the fete wearing the same dress as DM (p. 39/40)
Provocation Frame (SJ Episode)

Examples 12 and 13 are contextually dynamic, and as a possible worldstate, there is change of state in these contexts embedded in retrospection, but restricted in prospection. In CHF, a **final state** is predicted in the context, Sally dead (p. 34), while an **intermediary state** is presented in *Ackroyd*. On the surface, these contexts appear **concrete** in maintaining the narrative tense, a default past and present for a third-person (CHF) and first-person (*Ackroyd*) narration respectively. On a closer analysis of speech and thought presentation, the clauses are not presented as DT of the character, or as FIT of the narrator, the texts appear as **an internal construct** for communication by a 'post-murder' participant. The thought presentation is not distancing, or creating closeness, rather it is the creating of **reader confidence** constructed with the adverbial, *hardly have been caused*, in circumstantial adverbials *considering, supposing*, to foreground the significance of the events referred in the utterance. While spatial deictics *then* place the narrating omniscient participant as **focalizer** in the context, who is reflecting in prospection the past from the moment of narration in the progressive aspect '*considering—well—considering, Supposing—oh!*' in *Ackroyd*, and also in future tense in the past (a literary tense in Quirk et al. 1985), '*could hardly have been caused, could not be expected to foresee*' in CHF. The futurity in tense aspect is relative to the story in prospection, when story reality narrated is retrospective.

For the analyst, it is evident that a **secondary narrative in prospection** is constituted in **licensing** a restricted **omniscience** (Chap. 4), and is functioning as a prerequisite to orientate the readers to a **death by provocation** to take place in the first story of crime (provocation in Frame 9 and 13 in CHF and the death for concealment in Frame 14 in *Ackroyd*). Without the second crime, and only recalled frames as the plot structure, the MC is visible more in the stylistic and linguistic reading of the clauses in CHF and not in the forward and backward resequencing of retrospective events.

In the analysis so far, whilst MC is in the first story of crime with narrative interest of curiosity and suspense, as in *Ackroyd*, a **possible world-state** as MC is constructed for reader focus in CHF.

2.5.4 Manipulated Context: Case Study—*The Good Soldier*

The final story considered for MC is *The Good Soldier* (TGS) by Ford Madox Ford. It is not a typical murder mystery story, but a story with complex *narrative frame* for the misreading of the protagonist motive in prospection. Three deaths take place in the narrative; the first is an accidental death (Frames 34, 45), the second and third are suicides (Frames 79 and 171). The narration of the deaths is unusual and draws reader attention. The questions raised are, 'Is Dowell looking for an alibi [for the deaths that took place]?' Also, 'Did Dowell fix his wife Florence and his best friend Edward to get rid of them, so that Dowell could marry Nancy Rufford (the concealed fourth tale in the story), whom Edward Ashburnham and his wife Leonora took into care?' Dowell is one of the principal participants in the story, who narrates the incidents he heard from the sub narrators Edward and Leonora. Incidentally, Nancy and participant Maisie Maidan were from the same convent as Leonora, and taken into care by the Ashburnhams with whom Edward subsequently went on to have affairs. This was encouraged by Edward's wife Leonora on the rationale that

'... *when Edward had exhausted a number of other types of women he must turn to her* [Leonora his wife]' (p. 210).

The complex narrative technique in TGS is a method of '*impressionism*' and

'*the quest of impressionism, in keeping with the word's history, is the quest for knowledge*' (Moser 2008). [According to the impressionistic technique, in fiction], '*it was truer to experience, more real, to focus upon a single observer-narrator, but then it is truer not to tell the stories chronologically.* [It is not realistic to] *get a man* [here mainly about Dowell the narrator and people around him] *in the fiction, to begin at his beginning and work his life chronologically to the end. You must first get him in with a strong impression, and then work backwards and forwards over his past.*'

A fictional **layering** is thus constructed in the communicative act (Clark 2014: p. 161) with the embedding of representations within other representations (**metarepresentations**) in the process of anticipation and retrospection. As Dowell himself states in the story,

'... *when one discusses an affair—a long, sad affair—one goes back, one goes forward. ... I have explained everything that went before it* [Maisie Maidan's affair] *from several points of view that were necessary, from Leonora's, from Edward and to some extent my own* [Dowell].' (p. 213)

To follow this embedding of representations, it is necessary to recognize its construction, the way the horizontal concatenations of the narrative thread are mapped implicitly onto the vertical axis of the narrative with reference to Dowell's **PoR** as a first-person narrator in the story. In addition, if there is systematic application of the logical fallacy by this observing narrator, also a principal participant in the story, the **restricted point of view** constructed in the story is restricted to the consciousness of a single observer Dowell in TGS.

With the help of FA in Appendix 2d, the **complicating action** in the story in TGS is based on two couples in the story: **couple 1**, Florence and Dowell, and **couple 2**, Leonora and Edward. They met annually at Nauheim, a health spa for heart patients. Florence and Edward both suffered from heart condition and visited **Nauheim** annually with their spouses. The couples were childless. Dowell as a narrator moves through three story triangles:

- Florence, Edward and himself;
- Florence, Edward and Leonora;
- Leonora, Nancy and Edward,

The last portions of each of the tales were written long after the earlier portions of other triangles were narrated. This forms a mixed up, unchronological narration of events, where Dowell sometimes tells the same story twice to render his superimposed emotions relating to other triangles in the narrative. The way the story is narrated foregrounds Dowell as a deceived husband, and consequently as a victim of circumstances, a victim of affairs. However, Dowell's desire to marry Nancy, the **withheld fourth triangle**, and his violent self are backgrounded in the story by Dowell's narration in the discourse. Without FA, it is not possible to have a full grasp of the manner of complexity and backgrounded causes in the narrative frame in TGS.

In first reading, the foregrounded image that remains is Dowell as a deceived husband. This appears to be too good to be true, especially when Dowell, as a principal carer, was not aware of his wife Florence's intention to commit suicide (Frame 96). This is because Dowell was unaware of his wife's affair with Jimmy in the past (Frames 64, 65) when in *story logic* Florence was openly having an affair with Leonora's husband Edward. In Frame 13 Leonora also made Dowell aware of this affair. Hence, to one's amazement, it is hard to believe that Dowell was ignorant of Florence's secret in Frame 96, where prussic acid was disguised as amyl nitrate, a fact that again Leonora knew and not Dowell in Frame 84.

In addition, it is also puzzling that throughout the narrative Dowell established his admiration for his friend Edward as a war hero with a generous personality, and sympathized with him for being financially controlled by his wife, Leonora. However, Dowell was unhappy with Nancy being sent away to her family in India in Frame 166. Dowell did not intervene when his friend set out to commit suicide in Frame 171.

It is also puzzling that without introducing Nancy as the character in the story, in ambiguity Dowell creates a **suspense** in prospection at the outset, as there is **repeated**, but **restricted narration** of Nancy Rufford as '*the girl*'. For instance, without any prior context provided, in Frame 7 *the girl* was to return to her father in India, repeated again in Frame 166, in Frame 8, *the girl was out with the hounds*, in Frame 23, the girl *was on her way to Brindisi*, in Frame 139, the girl *was on her way to India*, and then in Frame 116, the girl was described *like the sail of a ship*, [who] *will never do anything again*. The full episode relating Nancy Rufford comes to light only at the end, in Part 3 of the novel. A **microcontext** in repeated frames is thus constituted at the outset which, when linked with Dowell's **desire frames** 80 and 85, indexes to the Dowell **motive frame** 103 as the real hinge point around which the main narrative takes shape.

The **iterative** (repeated) frames about '*the girl*' Nancy Rufford (Frames 7, 23, 80, 85, 145), about the Protest scene and about Florence's conspiracy relating to her heart condition emphasize the importance of these episodes in the story; foregrounding a **semantic field** of storyworlds as the **turning points** in the narrative. The repeated frames as a ***discourse cue*** also evoke a **discoursal focus**, such as the microcontext in repeated frames about the girl evoke the discoursal focus to a **fourth triangle**, Dowell, Edward and Nancy. This fourth tale truly came to light only after Florence committed suicide and Dowell remarked *Now I can marry the girl* (p. 123) (Frames 80, 85). At this point in the narrative, as narrative ***surprise*** (different from Sternberg's *surprise gap*) the Frames 80, 85 provide **discoursal focus** for Dowell's desire for Nancy, and this tale is set out at the story outset as NR episode marked out in the FA. The NR episode set out at the outset in the narrative frame foreground Dowell's withheld desire for Nancy, which makes the TGS narrative begin *in medias res* and constitute a **causative** and consequently, a **circular** narrative. The construction of the past and the future in the story narrative is made dependent on this initially withheld fourth triangle. The fourth tale is a tale of desire and motive; a preoccupation of narrator Dowell from the outset in the story.

Contextually the motive in question is, with the view to fulfil his self-gratification to marry Nancy, why Dowell was ignorant of the fact that Florence had prussic acid in the phial that should have contained amyl nitrate for her heart, (p. 119)? Moreover, why did Dowell not interfere with Edward and his intention to cut his throat (p. 270) with a penknife (p. 294), when he loved Edward so dearly (p. 290)? By his own admission, Dowell was just like Edward, '*in my fainter way, come into the category of the passionate, of the headstrong, and the too-truthful*' (p. 291), and was it therefore Dowell who wanted Edward out of the way so that he could marry Nancy Rufford (Frames 80 and 85)? This **intentionality content** is emphasized further when Dowell admits that he wanted to make Nancy happy and make a positive impression on her (Frames 105, 106, 116, 148, and 167). Additionally, Dowell's reaction to Nancy's departure from Branshaw Manor (Frame 166, pp. 149 and 166) and finally his reaction to Florence and Edward's death (Frames 79 and 158) together enforce Dowell's intended desire, which was in place long before Dowell set out to write his personal account of a deceived husband. Arguably, Dowell's desire frame (Frames 80, 85) becomes the **mainspring** of the story in TGS and thus the cardinal point in the discourse.

The Dowell desire frame as the hinge point in TGS also indexes to an **offender notion**, when Dowell appears self-contradictory and dishonest as a narrator. Dowell presented Edward's love affairs (the Kilsyte case, Maisie Maidan and Nancy Rufford) as acts of a helpless sentimentalist (Frame 130) who was on the rebound to ease the tension between him and his wife Leonora (p. 182). To protect his friend, Dowell comments that he was '*forced to attempt to excuse him* [for his affair with Maisie Maidan]' (134) and] *in this* [that Edward loved Nancy and had no idea of corrupting NR in Frame 111]. In Frames 107–109, however, Dowell self-contradicts when he narrates that Edward regarded Nancy as his daughter. Dowell also narrated that Nancy received news of her mother's death (Frame 114), but later in the narrative (Frame 154) Nancy received a letter from her mother where she '*upbraided the girl with living in luxury* *whilst her mother starved*' (p. 243). Dowell's **backgrounded abettor self** believed that '*proud, resolute and unusual individuals* [like Florence and Edward] *are splendid and tumultuous creatures, who are best off being gone from this earth. Society needs only normal types* [like Leonora and Rodney Bayham]'. (Moser 2008: p. 274) All this foregrounds Dowell's accountability as an **unreliable narrator**. The critics in the anti-Dowell camp also saw,

> '... *Dowell as not merely misled and self-deluded but consciously dishonest.*' (Moser 2008: p. xxii)

The **desire frame** 80 and also repeated in Frame 85 as the hinge point, functions as the **discourse referent** to the withheld fourth tale, and formulates an alternative discourse which indexes Dowell as an **abettor** alongside the popular disposition of being a deceived husband, a victim of affairs and deception.

At this point, it is best to skim through the plot form of TGS in Appendix 2d, and familiarize oneself with the frame sequence for different episodes (theme frames), and track the microcontexts in the complex episodic links plotted in the plot form of the story.

The **desire frame** 80 (85) as the hinge point in the main narrative form formulates alternative narrative paths related to,

- Dowell's secret wish to marry Nancy (Frames 80, 85)
- Florence's desire to divorce Dowell (Frame 70) to live with Edward at Fordingbridge (Frame 75) and also to conceal her affairs with Jimmy (Frames 54, 55).

Dowell's desire to deceive is also surfaced in the story when Dowell's states with reference to his marriage,

> '... *as a constant factor in any matrimonial association—a desire* [is] *to <u>deceive</u> the person with whom one lives as to some weak spot in one's character or in one's career.*' (138).'   [my emphasis]   **Desire Frame**

The **desire for deception** as a weak spot in both Florence and Dowell tale are,

Frame 96
Florence could not bear to have Dowell *discover her early escapade with fellow Jimmy* [two years at Havre] (139), which was the determining influence in her suicide (140). Also revealed by Leonora,

> '*how she knew* [Florence] *had that flask, apparently not of nitrate of amyl, but actually of prussic acid, for many years and that she was determined to use it if ever I* [Dowell] *discovered the nature of her relationship with that fellow* [Jimmy]' (138).

Florence's Deception Frame

Frame 99 (103)
Dowell had *taste for good cookery and a watering tooth* (139), and *was in love with Nancy Rufford* ... [and following Florence's death, had to] '*get certain matters out of the way, ... certain negligible complications* [i.e. the inheritance] *before* [he could] *go to the place that has, during all your life* [when married to Florence] *been a sort of dream city?*' (143)

Dowell's Deception Frame

Contextually thus, Frames 96, 99 (103) provide referential environment for the risky point in Frames 80, 85 and 90 in the narrative frame and consequently formulating the sub-narrative (a MC) relative to the secret desires of the couple Dowell and Florence.

The **catalytic events**[18] as the contextual environment in the referential layer of a MC centering the discourse referent in the desire frame in Fig. 2.4 below are,

Repeated Frames concerning

- *the girl* (Nancy). Dowell *called to talk with him* [Edward about Nancy] in Frame 7 (145) and this happened in story-Now before Nancy was on her way to India (Frames 23, 139) to join her father (Frame 166) and
- Dowell's love for Nancy (Frame 116, 148)

Recall Frames (Frames 4 (51, 53) relating to

---

[18] Catalytic event as units (distributional or integrational) constitute real hinge-points of the narrative ... others merely 'fill in' the narrative space separating the hinge functions. ... the former [is the] cardinal functions and the latter ... catalysers.' (Barthes 1977: p. 93)

- Jimmy affair (Frames 49, 54–58) indexing to fake a heart condition (Frames 4, 51, 53), and
- Julius episode as the discoursal focus to Florence's fear of her husband Dowell's violent temper (Frames 56, 65) if he were to find out about her Jimmy affair. This was confirmed, when Leonora uncovered Florence's deception (amyl nitrate replaced by prussic acid) in Frame 96, following Florence's suicide on Bagshawe's revelation of Florence and Jimmy affair (Frame 77).

Withheld Frames (Frames 11, 12, 13) in the Protest scene foreground indirectly the Florence Edward affair (Frame 135).

These **primed catalytic events** (note 9) in Fig. 2.4 provide a referential environment and form a referential layer for Dowell's desire and Florence's secret in Frames 80 (85) and 96, functioning as the nuclei for Dowell Florence tale. In the processing of Dowell desire (Frames 80, 85) in the narrative, which is also relative to Florence secret/deception (Frame 96), the referential layer for the DR as cardinal point in the MCs (Figs. 2.5 and 2.6) is,

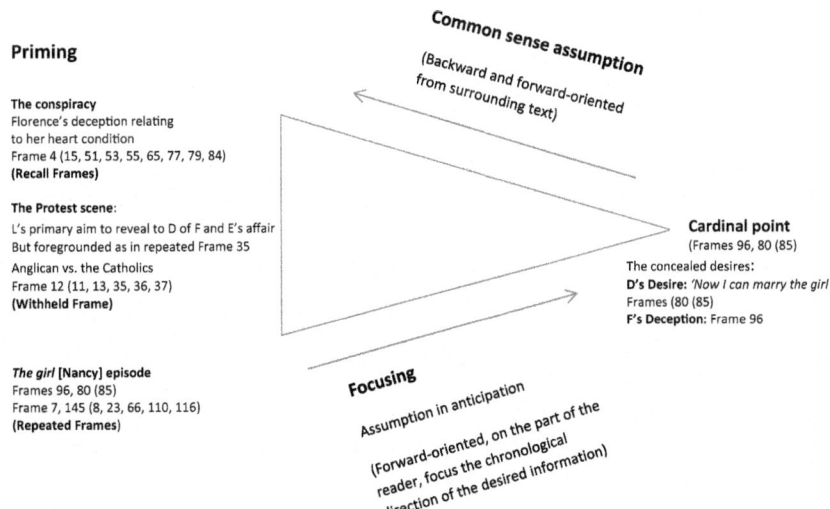

Fig. 2.4. Discourse referent: *The Good Soldier* (TGS)

Explanation

The primed frames constitute the storyworld discourse for the referent in the cardinal point. Figure 2.4 as a three-dimensional inferencing process in frame resolution **triggers** an appropriate entity representation for the DR as the cardinal point. As already explained, this processing is different from a signaling pronoun. The Dowell **desire frames** and Florence **deception frames** indirectly evoke as referents, Dowell's object of desire Nancy and Florence's secret and are formulated in the microcontexts as the referential layer: the conspiracy context, the Protest scene context and in the Nancy episode, instantiating the fourth tale concealed as the narrative purpose that is backgrounded in the story.

Priming inferences are generally **direct**. However, the sequence of events (the microcontexts mentioned above) relative to the cardinal point is indirect and more causally related. As in Fig. 2.1, the episodic link between the microcontexts is established using the **reference resolution processes** of both *priming* and *focusing* (Emmott 1997), where readers amalgamate information from:

- the immediate accompanying text;
- the surrounding text;
- inferences made from the intervening text;

to resolve the reference to inexplicit discourse referent in Frames 80 (85) (the fourth tale in the story). For instance, like forward-oriented anaphora, the mental inferences drawn from the **recall frames** provide **optimal relevance (cost)** to **bring forward** Florence's Deception Frame, as an entity representation for the concealed Jimmy affair (Frames 54–58). Then **brings forward** the Julius episode (Frames 59–64) to foreground the violent anger as the **trigger factor** and link this with Florence's deception in Frame 96 (98, 138). Dowell's violent orientation revealed in the Julius episode (p. 107) (Frames 59–64) was the **stimulus** for Florence (Frame 59), to conceal amyl nitrate for prussic acid (Frame 64), as she feared Dowell would murder her (Frame 65) if he found out about her affair with Jimmy (Frames 64, 96) soon after she married Dowell and sailed off to Paris. To continue her secret affair with Jimmy, Florence made up her heart condition

(F conspiracy frame) to keep Dowell from her bedroom (Deception Frame 55).

Similarly, entity representation in the recalled Protest scene forms an episodic link with the Bagshawe incident (Frame 77), where the Florence–Jimmy affair brought to light the fact that Dowell was deceived, consequently with Florence committing suicide in Frame 79. The Protest scene also anaphorically links with the Edward–Florence affair, revealed by Leonora to Dowell (pp. 22, 168) and consequently linking to Florence's desire to divorce Dowell in Frame 70 and return to her ancestral home England with Edward; this linear sequence is jumbled in the narrative discourse. Like a backward-oriented referent, the deception frame 96 links to the repeated frames relating to *the girl*, which emphasizes Dowell's desire for Nancy Rufford in the circular narrative. Subsequently the deception frame works as an indirect catalytic event for the hinge point, Dowell's secret desire to marry Nancy in Frame 80 (85).

In the **resolution process**, the reversal of the linear cause and effect chain is evident. The unchronological structuring involves the readers in the novel's psychological, moral and philosophical questions, as well as the **suspense** in prospection, when the narrating observer is moving through the three triangles while backgrounding the fourth tale of his desire. The **causal reversal**, where the effect precedes the cause, is also effective for the purpose of confusion and delay in the revelation of the fourth tale in the story.

The act of contextualizing entities, as seen above and with reference to *Ackroyd* MC, the 'reference resolution' inference process is bidirectional (backward- and forward-pointing in the discourse). Desires and deception of both Florence and Dowell as withheld intentionality is thus **orienting backward** to the direct discourse referent in the primed events: the conspiracy surrounding Florence's heart condition, the Florence–Edward affair in the Protest scene, and the Nancy episode in the repeated Frames about *the girl* in the discourse. These **microcontexts** then are **forward pointing** to Dowell's secret wish to marry Nancy (Frame 80, 85) and Florence's desire to divorce Dowell (Frame 90). The relevant discourse for the indirect discoursal referent in the cardinal point is assimilated thus from the immediate context within the cardinal point and from the microcontext as the primed backgrounding discourse, centering also the cardinal point in Fig. 2.4. The referent is not an immediate context in the clause or sentence functioning as the cardinal event. The reader needs to build an appropriate microcontext of what is being referred to in Frames 80 (85) and 96 (the embedded discoursal focus in the story), and then an antecedent referent is made in the immediate context (Dowell's true intent) to resolve the indirect context centering the DR at cardinal point. As was the case for Frame 14 in *Ackroyd*, DR is associated with a motive or desire backgrounded in the main narrative, making TGS a mystery story with whodunit characteristics.

2.5.5 The Principle of Relevance: Case Study—*The Good Soldier*

In following the linearity of microcontexts for the DR in Fig. 2.4, the causal reversal in Fig. 2.5, raises the question of whether to analyze Dowell's **PoR** as an abettor or a deceived husband. If Dowell knew all along, that Florence had a strong heart like Edward (Frames 16, 17); he then trapped Florence deliberately on the continent (Frame 56) for his inheritance. Dowell then must have also known of Florence's deception about the prussic acid for amyl nitrate in her brown flask prescribed for her heart condition. In the actual chronology of events, the Julius episode (p. 107) (Frames 59–64) takes place before the Jimmy affair (p. 102) (Frames 54–58). However, contrary to the story in real time, the Julius episode is made consecutive to the episode relating to Florence's (faked) heart condition; also, the Protest scene takes place after, and not before Dowell meets Nancy at Nauheim. Together this causally reverse microcontext forms a referential layer for the Dowell desire that he must be free to marry Nancy (Frames 80 and 85), and for this Dowell had to get rid of his wife, not by divorce (Frame 70), as this would not allow him to inherit the money left to Florence (Frame 146). Hence, Dowell's conspiracy was the indication of his ignorance of the replacement of amyl nitrate with prussic acid by Florence (Frame 96). It is therefore justified to say, Dowell thus remains consciously ignorant of prussic acid replaced for amyl nitrate, an event triggered by Florence's fear relating to Dowell's violent orientation revealed in the Julius incident.

The erratic chronological structure overall helped the narrator to form such **narrative gaps** in the story to portray Dowell as the deceived husband rather than abettor in the story. Moreover, by giving portions of tales long after the earlier portions are narrated, enabled the **unreliable narrator** to background his offender **stimulus**, Dowell's violent orientation as evidenced in the Julius episode (p. 107) (Frames 59–64). This **backgrounded orientation** occurs before Florence's deception to conceal amyl nitrate for prussic acid. Dowell's backgrounded orientation then logically indexes to an abettor disposition (Fig. 2.5) otherwise presented as a deceived husband (Fig. 2.6)

The context in each frame for Fig. 2.5 is,

D (Dowell), F (Florence), L (Leonora) E (Edward), NR (Nancy)

Frame 80 (85), 96—**The cardinal point**

Frame 80 (85)—D's remark, '*Now I can marry the girl*' (p. 129)
Frame 96: L knew for many years that the flask contained prussic acid and not amyl nitrate, to use it if her true relationship with J was ever discovered (p. 138)

Frame 77—**The Bagshawe incident** (p. 119)

Bagshawe surprised to see F at the lounge of Hotel Excelsior. When Bagshawe revealed to D of seeing F coming out of Jimmy's bedroom when they were at his house in Ludbury with her uncle during his world trip, '"*Do you know who that is?*" he [Bagshawe] *asked.* "*The last I saw that girl* [Florence] *she was coming out of the bedroom of a young man called Jimmy at five o'clock in the morning. In my house at Ledbury.*"' (p. 119)

Frame 92—**The Casino Park scene** (p. 137)

F overheard E from behind the trees saying that N was the person he cared most. On hearing this, F ran back to the hotel with pallid face, when her eyes fell upon Bagshawe beside D at the hotel lounge, which according to D was the determining influence in F committing suicide (p. 137). This was because, F's main idea was to return to Fordingbridge and be a county lady in the home of her ancestors; she had taken on E at this time as she was sick of Jimmy. (p. 105) (Frame 76, 78)

Frame 4 (55, 56)—The Jimmy affair

F and Jimmy accompanied uncle Hurlbird on his world trip. Hurlbird had a heart condition, and Jimmy was to keep F's uncle from discussions that were not good for his heart (p. 24). Jimmy then met F and D when they had to discontinue their trip on *Pocahontas* at Le Havre (Frame 54) due to F's heart condition, where Jimmy met the couple and lived with them for next two years in their Paris flat (p. 102). D continues to narrate (Frame 55) how he was not to enter her room due to her heart problem, the rules were made between the two, and '... *her* [Florence] *heart demanded the sacrilege. So at ten o'clock at night the door closed upon Florence,... she would wish me good night ... Her room door was locked because she was nervous of thieves. ... It was pretty well thought out, you see.*' (p. 104)

Frame 61 (64, 65)—The Julius incident

Is significant as it narrates Florence that was frightened for her life. '*Yes, she was afraid of me* [Dowell]. *I will tell you how that happened.*' ... *Julius, a darky servant, valeted Dowell at Waterbury.*' Julius looked after both D and F, and was like a father-figure to F. But F was not keen to take him to Paris. '*He would have inconvenienced her. ... to conceal from me* [Dowell] *the fact that she* [Florence] *was not ... "a pure woman". ... She was afraid I should murder her. So she got up the heart attack at the earliest possible opportunity.*' (p. 107)

Frame 12 (11, 13, 35, 36, 138)—The Luther-Protest scene (p. 53)

At the museum (p. 49), F explains the letter about the Protest and compliments E as an '*honest, sober, industrious, provident and clean-lived*' individual because of this letter, who would otherwise be like the Irish (53). E's wife L was an Irish Catholic. Following this incident, L tried to warn D that F was trying to seduce E (Frame 138, p. 222 and Frame 135, p. 221). Maisie had real passion for E, but F played a nasty trick (Frame 44) and as a result, Maisie Maidan died (Frame 34) when F became E's mistress a week after (Frame 135, p. 221). D, contrary to L's revelation, requests L to accept the situation as F's '*mere silly jibes at the Irish and at the Catholics could be apologized out of existence.*' (Frame 35, p. 78)

Frames 69 (135, 37)—Florence's (F) affair with Edward (E)

F *'called for more and more attention from him* [Edward] *as the time went on. She would make him kiss any moment of the day.'* (p. 116) F became E's mistress a week after Maisie's death, when L saw E coming out of F's room (p. 224). F tries to convince L *'that her love for E was quite spiritual—on account of her heart. If you can believe that of Maisie Maidan, as you say you do, why cannot you believe it of me?'* (p. 84)

Frame 70—**Florence wanted to secure divorce**

F wanted to *'secure a divorce from Dowell. And go with Edward and settle in California, as her situation was too unbearable with regard to me* [D].' (p. 116)

The context in each frame in Fig. 2.6 is,

Frame 92—**The Casino Park scene** (p. 137)
Frame 77 (95)—**The Bagshawe incident** (p. 137)
Frame 12 (11, 13, 35, 36, 138)—**The Protest scene**
Frame 44 (19)—**The trick**

Played by Florence on Maisie Maidan. F warned E of how he might *be making in the girl's* [Maisie Maidan's] *heart* (p. 87). Dowell here is an unreliable narrator; like Leonora, D is implicating F to be responsible for Maisie Maiden's death, '"*You* [Florence] *murdered her. You and I* [Leonora] *murdered her* [Maisie Maidan]. *I don't like to be reminded of it.*"' (p. 84). When in fictional reality, Maisie Maidan overheard F and E discussing how L paid Maisie Maidan's husband for her to be an adulteress, '"*How could you* [Leonora] *buy me* [Maisie Maidan] *from my husband … I did not know you wanted me for an adulteress"* (p. 86). This upset Maisie, as revealed in her letter addressed to L (p. 85), but concealed from E. Following this, Maisie Maidan is found dead in her hotel room, in her effort to strap up a great portmanteau, her body fell into a trunk and it closed upon her. The key was in her hand. (p. 88)

Frames 69 (135, 37)—**F's affair with E**
Frame 70—**F wanted to secure divorce**

There are 176 Frames in total in the four-part narration of three triangles in the story in TGS.

The Language of Suspense in Crime Fiction

The frames cited in the figures below, and their numbers, correspond to the order in which they appear in the plot form of the novel in Appendix 2d. In TGS, the motive behind the suicides was not typically related to a participant who was a **conventional criminal**, as in a murder mystery or thriller narrative. Dowell's ignorance as the motive frame is the cardinal point in the narrative form. This motive has the dual function of

- illusion and
- distortion in causal reversal (*logical fallacy*).

The encoded referential layer in the two figures below is according to the abettor Dowell (2.5) and Dowell the victim of circumstances (2.6). The narrative layers are affected by what has gone before (Barthes' *logical fallacy*), that is, Dowell is aware of Florence's manipulative nature in Frames 11 and 23 and creates *expectations of relevance* (Wilson 2011: 77) for what comes after in Frame 6, 146 (D's Inheritance Frame) in the figures below:

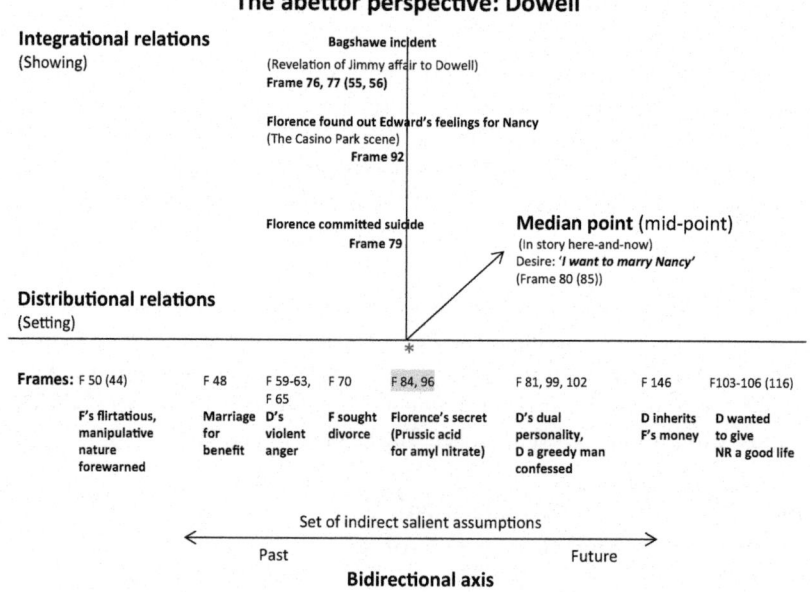

Fig. 2.5. The abettor perspective: Dowell

2 Manipulated Context 63

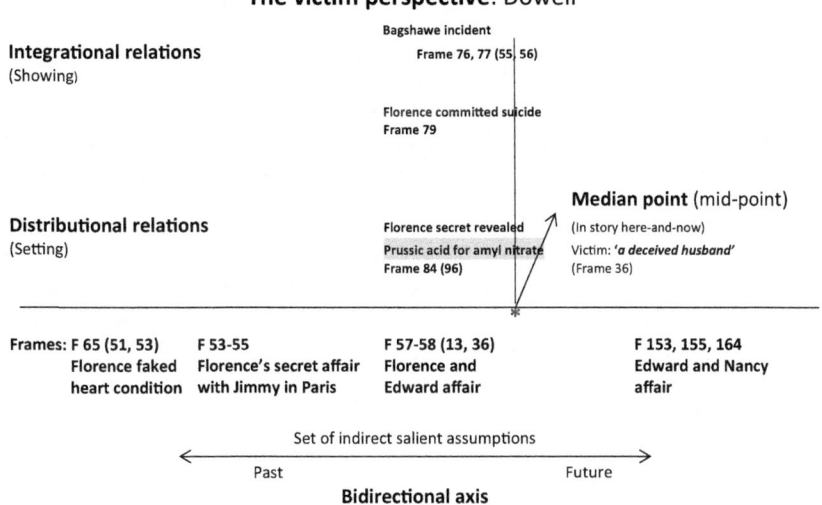

Fig. 2.6. The victim perspective: Dowell

Explanation

In the two narratives above, sequential position of the median point is different. In Fig. 2.5, the median position on the horizontal axis is about events that reinforce Dowell's underlying motive, while in victim perspective the median position is about events that reinforce Dowell as a deceived husband due to Florence's deception with amyl nitrate due to her secret affair with Jimmy, which was revealed only because she committed suicide.

In the abettor perspective, the narrative relations on the horizontal axis shows that Dowell was fore warned of Florence's flirtatious nature. Earlier in the story, following their marriage (Frame 48), Dowell narrated how Florence *faintly hinted* that she did not want much physical passion in the affair when she planned the Europe trip. In addition, two aunts and uncle Hurlbird (Frame 50 (44)) forewarned Dowell of Florence's life characterized by flirtations, and of her manipulative nature (Frame 44).

According to the **story logic** in Fig. 2.5, if Dowell was forewarned of his wife's flirtatious nature, and also knew of her true intentions on marriage, one may then ask, why did Dowell go on to marry Florence? Dowell was rich enough and did not need to marry for inheritance. This

intentionality is supported further in Frame 70, when Florence asked Dowell for a divorce so she could go away with Edward and settle in California (p. 116). Why was Florence then not given a divorce, which would have made Dowell free to marry NR without Florence having to commit suicide?

Florence disguised prussic acid as amyl nitrate when she experienced Dowell's anger and consequently her fear of being murdered if found out. Following this, Florence went on to seek divorce, but Dowell did not grant this. This was because of Dowell's **dual personality**, his greed to inherit Florence's money to give Nancy a good life. On mapping all this information from the horizontal axis onto the hierarchical setting on vertical axis, Florence's fear in Frames 59–63 (65) logically instantiates the Bagshawe incident as the **trigger frame** for her to commit suicide. The narrative relations, both sequentially and then logically in Fig. 2.5 align with Dowell's motive as the median point in the narrative moment.

Conversely, in victim perspective, the revelation in the Bagshawe incident linked retrospectively the Florence–Jimmy affair (Frame 54) in the horizontal setting, which logically link back to Frame 65 (51) when Dowell was banned from his wife's bedroom due to her heart condition on their trip to Europe on *Pocahontas* (Frame 53). In retrospect, Dowell recognized this deception played on him by Florence and Jimmy in Frame 55. Frame 55 has the bidirectional function in the setting—a **backward function** with respect to Florence's conspiracy (her faked heart condition) to ban her husband from her bedroom to continue her affair with Jimmy when they were in Paris, and a **forward function** with respect to the Bagshawe incident, the **causal link** to Florence committing suicide.

The answer is also in Frame 103, where Dowell narrates that,

> *'he should have run up to her room and prevented her drinking the prussic acid* (p. 142). [Which Dowell did not, a **counterfactual incident** in **negation**] *But he couldn't do it, as Florence didn't matter, what mattered was his love for Nancy, his wish to give her a good life, and that* [he] *must get certain matters out of the way* [Florence dead] *smooth out certain fairly negligible complications* [the inheritance and Edward out of the way] *before* [he] *can go to a*

place that has, during all your life, been a sort of dream city? [To marry Nancy].' (p. 143)

Motive scenario

The use of **negation** is also noticeable, indexing a counterfactual scenario. Counterfactual construction is discussed more closely in Chap. 5. With motives at mid-points in the present, the relation formed in the setting is **bidirectional**; that is, the **temporal order** of events in the past and future now differs with reference to the mid-point in the present in respective narratives. In other words, in Fig. 2.5, the Frame 'Prussic acid for amyl nitrate' (Frames 84 (96)) is **temporally central** on the horizontal axis, however, positioned **to the right** in Fig. 2.6 relative to the Frame 79, Florence committing suicide. As an **Overlapping Frame**, Frames 84, 96 becomes part of the **consecutive arrangement** in the horizontal axis for Dowell's desire narrative. While the same frames in Fig. 2.6 are part of the **consequential relation** in the vertical axis for the victim of the secret affair in the victim perspective. This is also because, as Uprichard (in Williams and Vogt 2011: pp. 115–116) points out, in relation to narratives in the future,

'… *narratives share similarities insofar as the knowledge based is in present, and the present is always changing and so too the constructions of the past and future constantly shift according to the updated and emergent knowledge of the present.*'

As a second reading, the story, then, in the alternative narrative following the narrative relations in the setting in Fig. 2.5 is,

Florence sought divorce after she experienced Dowell's violent anger. Not achieving this, Florence disguised prussic acid as amyl nitrate in the fear that her husband might murder her if her affair with Jimmy was found out. However, because of the Bagshawe incident, Florence realized Dowell had found out about her affair in Paris, a **withheld frame** in the immediate context, and consequently her embedded locked-bedroom scenario to keep her husband away is now revealed; hence Florence committed suicide. This was also because, according to Dowell's **cognitive hypothesis**, Florence's mainspring of nature was vanity, her desire to be a great lady and retain Dowell's respect (Frame 97 and 98). This then logically links with Leonora (not Dowell) being aware of Florence's secret intention to commit suicide if Dowell found her out.

Florence did not commit suicide (Frame 79) simply because she discovered Edward's feelings for NR (Frame 92). The frame about the deception in Frame 76 is followed by Florence losing Edward to Nancy in Frame 92; they together become the deciding factors in the relational hierarchy in Fig 2.5 and become the cause of Florence's suicide in Frame 79 in Fig. 2.5. Dowell thus becomes an **abettor** in Fig. 2.5 who **affected** Florence in commiting suicide. In the **bidirectional axis** in Fig. 2.5, hence the central position of the frame *prussic acid for amyl nitrate* makes sense, and is therefore consequential to the negation of Frame 70 in the linear setting, where Florence sought divorce. While in Fig. 2.6, the secret about prussic acid (in reverse) is the causal link to Florence's death in Frame 79, directly formulating Dowell as a deceived husband, a **narrative object**.

The highlighted **overlapping frames** contribute to this **double reading**, which is possible with FA. In addition, the **discourse referent** as mid-point for each narrative discourse foregrounds a different cause and effect chain in the horizontal axis. Together with consecutive events in the vertical axis, the narrative levels produce **divergent consequential links** to the same mid-point for different narrative perspectives (PoR).

The above story logic also compels the realization of the offender orientation. By his own admission in Frame 99, Dowell was a *rather greedy man*, which Florence never discovered. Dowell confessed in Frame 81 and 102, of having a **dual personality**, [of] *one entirely unconscious of the other*. In **offender profiling**, this is interpreted as a **normal public self**, but opposed to an **abnormal self**. The abnormal self comes to the forefront due to trigger factors. The **trigger factor** in TGS is when Dowell's violent anger is foregrounded, when valet Julius dropped a leather grip containing drugs for Florence's heart condition in Frame 63, and *that was Florence's first idea of my* [Dowell's] *character* (p. 107).

According to Canter (1994: p. 5), this is a psychological trace connected to an offender. A telltale pattern of behavior that indicates the sort of person Dowell really is: not simply a trained poodle to his wife (p. 141) for 12 years (Frame 101), not a deceived husband, or a victim of circumstances (Frame 36). These **behavioral traces** cannot be dissected in the laboratory or examined under the microscope. They are shadows undoubtedly connected to the criminal (here an abettor) **who cast them**, shadows that indicate the abettor personality of Dowell.

Further, the **microcontext** relative to Dowell's **desire frames** (Frames 80, 85) and his **anger frame** (Frame 63), index to the **moral** in Frame 172 and link with Dowell's **self-gratification**, *the villains must be punished by suicide and madness*. Such **orientation** is akin to a person who has a personal goal to fulfil, to get rid of people who are 'undesirable' or unworthy to live with other human beings, a ***mission orientation*** (Sect. 5.4.1 in Chap. 5) according to serial killer orientation in Holmes and DeBurger (in Holmes and Holmes 1998: p. 12). In Dowell's eyes, Edward and Florence in the story are *villains*, who were to blame for his miserable outcome in Frames 162, 116, 160, where Dowell was left to look after Nancy who was unable to do anything ever again, as she went insane when she heard Edward committed suicide. Additionally, the guardian Leonora forewent the responsibility of taking care of Nancy; she married Rodney Bayham instead and brought her miserable life with Edward to a successful conclusion (Frame 173).

In linguistic analysis (**underlined**) of offender disposition, Dowell had professed (Frames 158, 172),

> '... Edward <u>must</u> die, the girl [NR] <u>must</u> lose her reason because Edward died [committed suicide]. (269) ... as *the villains in the story <u>must</u> be punished by suicide and madness.*' (Frame 172, p. 290)

The obligation sense evoked by the modal *must* in the utterance which, in the grammar of experience, formulates an **agent-oriented disposition** that is different from a **victim disposition** in the **here-and-now** of the narrative. This **agent-oriented** abettor disposition is distanced by use of the distal deictic *that* and by the use of the perfective *had never* and the imperfective aspect *was pimping* (underlined) in **Frame 36**,

> 'And I want you [the reader] *to understand that, from that moment* [when Maisie Maidan accidentally died] *until Edward and the girl and Florence were all dead together <u>I had never</u> the remotest glimpse, not the shadow of a*

suspicion, that there was anything wrong [the affair between E and F], *as the saying is ... How in the world should I get it? ... I was just a male sick nurse. ... I was a deceived husband. And that Leonora was pimping for Edward* [alluding to affairs with Maisie and Nancy].' (81)

The **negation** in, *I had never the remotest glimpse, not the shadow of a suspicion, that there was anything wrong*, and also in, '*I didn't pump him, I hadn't any motive. At the time I didn't in the least connect him with my wife.*' (p. 130) all alluding to the affair between Dowell's wife and Edward, a **textually created opposite** for **discoursal significance**, which simultaneously evoke Edward's affair with Florence, at the same time denying its existence, foregrounding Dowell again as an **unreliable narrator**.

Alternative narratives, such as Figs. 2.5 and 2.6, instantiate an alternative reading of the above kind in the story in TGS, where the protagonist is objectively argued as both an abettor as well as a narrative object. The analysis of alternative narrative relations based on the PoR, also helped to isolate different scenarios otherwise jumbled in a complex plot frame in TGS, which I now highlight.

2.6 Microcontexts: Scenarios (Case Study: *The Good Soldier*)

TGS being an unconventional story of crime and suspense, the scenarios forming microcontexts for Dowell as the victim and abettor are,

The victim scenario

Frame 13, ' *"I can't stand this,"* she [L said to D] ... *"don't you see what's going on ...* [F was] *Edward's mistress ... committing adultery in hired rooms."* (pp. 83–84). *The panic again stopped my* [D] *heart. ... don't you see of the eternal damnation of you* [D] *and me* [L] *and them* [E and F]. (p. 55)

Frame 36, 'Following L's revelation of the affair between F and E, '... *I want you* [the reader] *to understand that, from that moment until Edward and the girl and Florence were all dead together I had never the remotest glimpse, not the shadow of a suspicion, that there was anything wrong* [the affair between E and F], *as the saying is. ... How in the world should I get it?*

… *I was just a male sick nurse.* … *I was a deceived husband.* And that <u>Leonora was pimping</u> [alluding to affairs with Maisie and Nancy] <u>for Edward</u>.' (p. 81)

Frame 55, '*God, how they worked me! It was those two* [Florence and Jimmy] *between them who really elaborated the rules* [about how F needed sleep and privacy due to her heart condition]. *I must never enter her room without knocking, or her poor little heart might flutter away to its doom.*' (p. 103)

Flirtatious nature forewarned

Frame 50, '"*Don't do it John. Don't do it. You're a good man,*" and she [Miss Emily] *added* … "*We ought to tell you more. But she's our dear sister's child.*"' (p. 96)

The motive scenario

Frame 103, D narrated, '*he should have run up to her room and prevented her drinking the prussic acid.*' (p. 142)

Frame 87 and 116, '*But I just couldn't do it,* [as] *Florence didn't matter,* [what mattered was] *his love for NR, his wish to give her a good life,* [and that he] *must get certain matters out of the way* [Florence dead] *smooth out certain fairly negligible complications* [Edward out of the way] *before* [he] *can go to a place that has, during all your life, been a sort of dream city?*' (p. 143)

Frame 171, '*And he looked at me with a direct, challenging, brow-beating glare. I guess I could see in my eyes that I didn't intend to hinder him* [from using the pen knife he drew out]. *Why should I hinder him?*' (p. 294)

Trigger theme frame (the violent orientation)

Frame 63, '*I saw red, I saw purple. I flew at Julius.* … *I threatened to strangle him.* … *that was F's first idea of my character.* (p. 107)

Offender profiling

Frame 158 and 172, '… *Edward* **must** *die, the girl* [NR] **must** *lose her reason because Edward died* [committed suicide]. (p. 269) … *as the villains in the story must be punished by suicide and madness.*' (p. 290)

Victim disposition (The unreliable narrator)

'*And I want you* [the reader] *to understand that, from that moment* [when Maisie Maidan accidentally died] *until Edward and the girl and Florence were all dead together I had never the remotest glimpse, not the shadow of a suspicion, that there was anything wrong* [the affair between E and F], *as the saying is ... How in the world should I get it? ... I was just a male sick nurse. ... I was a deceived husband. And that Leonora was pimping for Edward* [alluding to the affairs with Maisie and Nancy].' (p. 81)

2.7 Conclusion

In order to cope with complicated plot structures, such as a **circular narrative** over a linear construction, the method of frame analysis representing events as *frames* (Rosenberg in Metzing 1980: p. 98)

- is supporting the matching of unconnected singularized events as part of dominant frame content;
- is supporting the narrative comprehension process for spotting asymmetry at the interpretive level of the concealer and the revelator.

Frame analysis also helped to work out the inexplicit entity representation encoded for narrative conflicts between curiosity and suspense in a narrative. For example, the cardinal function of a specific frame is similar to '*the predicate-based logical system within a declarative sentence*' (Minsky in Metzing 1980: p. 13). The processing of this logical system is achieved by the priming and focusing of microcontexts constructed in the plot form and formulating a bidirectional axis in the alternative storyworld for offender intention, in addition to the conventional horizontal and vertical axis of narrative relations. As a **reference resolution inferencing process**, in the forward- and backward-oriented bidirectional referential function of a discourse referent as the median point, it was possible in reorientation of discourse-based theme frames (microcontexts) to understand the three-dimensional representation of the perceptual processing of a narrative communication establishing a manipulated narrative context as the offender discourse.

In the layering of microcontexts, identified in the plot form, in the setting and then mapping them on to the vertical axis, this method of consecutive narrative relation based on PoR for manipulated contexts revealed a secondary layer, which is an **embedded storyworld** as discussed in Chap. 4, in the first story of crime. This **layer**, also termed as offender engagement discourse, is from a referential point of view of the concealer as opposed to the revelator. The processing of this layer is synonymous to Goffman's *framed activities*, '*the keying of fabrication*',[19] where the plotting of the cardinal point, is like the ostensible key, and in Goffman's terms reveals the nature of manipulation due to causal reversal of events in discourse. Firstly, the manipulation was cued in the forward and backward-oriented referential function, where the referential layer as surface reality for the DR at the cardinal point distinguished an underlying reality backgrounded in the plot form of the story. The **surface reality** as in Figs. 2.1 and 2.4 is apparent but illusory, authenticating an **underlying reality**, an intention which is hidden but authentic (such as the layered discourses of abettor Dowell and Dr. Sheppard different from the discourses of victim Dowell and of Ralph Paton as the framed narrative object).

Secondly, on mapping the intention (motive), which is the inexplicit discourse referent in the mediation point in each participant's narrative thread, showed distinct narrative relations when changing the temporal location of the event order at the level of description/setting. In the concealer perspective in *Ackroyd*, in the hierarchical narrative relation, the perpetrator Dr. Sheppard remembered a hypothetical scenario in Frames 21 (3) before he (doctor) executed the scenario of framing a suspect in Frame 15. As manipulation, a **causal** (logical) **fallacy** is formulated at the level of showing, when in revelator perspective narrative the fictional reality Frame 15 is before Frame 21. Consequently, due to causal fallacy implemented by the narrator/perpetrator, Ralph became the victim due to his chance meeting with the perpetrator in Frame 15. Ralph revealed to a prospective manipulator Dr. Sheppard, his secret marriage. Unknown to Ralph, this was later taken advantage

---

[19] Fabrication is, 'When an ostensible key is used to cover deception… [e.g.] a standard device for scouting nudity shows under the guise of an art class.' (Goffman 1975: p. 161)

of to frame him as a suspect in Frame 21, by the perpetrator as a **cognitive process** in the narrative.

Appendix 2a

Frame Analysis: *The Murder of Roger Ackroyd* (*Ackroyd*), 1993

Setting: King's Abbott a small village near Cranchester
Participants involved in the story
Roger Ackroyd (RA)—owner of Fernly Park
Ralph Paton (RP)—RA's stepson
Ursula—RP's wife, house parlor maid at Fernly Park
Flora Ackroyd (FA)—RA's niece (daughter of Cecil Ackroyd, RA's sister)
Mrs. Ferrars (Mrs. F)—a widow, rumored as RA's fiancé
Dr. Sheppard (Dr. S)—doctor at King's Abbot
Caroline (C)—Dr. Sheppard's sister
Miss Russell (Miss R)—housekeeper at Fernly Park
Ashley Ferrars—Mrs. F's husband, an alcoholic; dead when the story begins
Parker—RA's butler
Raymond—RA's secretary
Major Blunt RA's hunting friend (p. 33)

The story starts with the death of Mrs. F (a suicide), followed by the death of Roger Ackroyd (a murder). The way these deaths came about in the narrative was that, unable to stand the pressures of her alcoholic husband, Mrs. F poisoned him. Dr. S came to know of this, and blackmailed Mrs. F for large sums of money, narrated as the *legacy* that Dr. S came to possess (Frame 9). Mrs. F revealed her act of murder to her fiancé RA in a letter posted to RA (Frames 20, 22) before she committed suicide. In the letter, Mrs. F revealed the identity of her blackmailer and called for justice. This revelation leads to

RA's death (Frame 27), after which Poirot gets involved in solving the murder of his friend, RA.

The **counter narrative** is related to RP being framed as the suspect, who blackmailed Mrs. F leading to RA's murder. This is because; RP had a chronic condition with money (a tendency to overspend) (Frame 36). To save the family fortune, RA wanted RP to marry his cousin FA. But RP secretly married Ursula, the parlor maid, against his stepfather's wishes (Frame 8). The day RA was murdered; Dr. S met RP at the Three Boars (Frames 15, 32). According to the chronology of events, before frames 15 and 32, Dr. S speculated about RP's meeting with Mrs. F (Frames 3 and 11). He also speculated on the information about RP staying at the Three Boars and not at his family home in Fernly Park, when RP secretly met with *a girl* (Ursula) in the woods (Frames 4, 6, 8, 13), as volunteered by C.

In the second story of crime, Poirot reveals that Dr. S suggested RP should hide in a mental hospital until the investigation of RA's murder was over (p. 220). RP explains how he had agreed to this, as suspicion could not fail to attach to the facts that he was married and hence could not marry his cousin FA, aggravating his chronically bad financial condition (p. 219).

The narration in the story is in the first person by Dr. S, who is also the offender in the story.

Frame analysis (FA)

The theme frames as **episodes** are identified in FA. This gives the narrator gaze for reader focus in the plot structure before the second story of investigation. Though Frames 33–38 are from the second story of investigation, these frames form **episodic links** with the **cardinal point** in Frame 14 (3, 21) in the first story of crime.

The cardinal point is an utterance by the perpetrator/focalizer. The intention of the narrator/participant in these frames was relative to

- RP's secret marriage (Frames 8, 15);
- RP's financial situation (Frame 37);
- Dr. S be.ng the secret blackmailer of Mrs. F.

The first story of crime (Chapters 1–5)

Frame 1: Mrs. F found dead by Dr. S (p. 7)
Frame 2: Dr. S met Mrs. F a week before she died.
(implied) Blackmailing Episode

> '*Her manner had been normal enough considering—well—considering <u>everything</u>.*' (p. 15)

Frame 3: Dr. S remembered Mrs. F talking to RP the day before she was found dead (p. 15)
Recall and repeated in Frame 21   RP Episode

Frame 4: RA unaware that his stepson, RP, was at King's Abbott and not in London. Dr. S remembered seeing RP at King's Abbot talking to Mrs. F
Repeated Frame 11   RP Episode

Frame 5: Miss R visits Dr. S at his surgery
Miss R Episode

Frame 6: C informs her brother, Dr. S, that RP was staying at the Three Boars instead of Fernly Park, and met up with *a girl* (p. 19)
Repeated Frame 4   RP Episode

Frame 7: Dr. S came to know from RA that RP was engaged to FA (p. 25)
RP Episode

In this frame, Dr. S also came to know RP was married to Ursula, the parlor maid (p. 219) this was why he met RP at the Three Boars (p. 27). This information is **withheld** in prospective narration.

Frame 8: C overhears RP in the woods urging *a girl*, assumed to be FA (p. 26), but is Paton's wife Ursula the parlor maid at Fernly Park (pp. 203, 219). C overhears RP's concerns about his stepfather RA, how Ackroyd would cut off his inheritance if it was known that RP was secretly married to Ursula, when his stepfather wanted him to marry his cousin FA, and keep the inheritance within the family (p. 203).
Repeated Frame 6   RP Episode

Frame 9: Dr. S meets his neighbor Poirot and tells him how he came into a *legacy* (p. 22)

(Implied) **Blackmailing Episode**

Frame 10: C's assertion—Mrs. F's husband died over a year ago (Frame 1). He was an alcoholic and was poisoned by Mrs. F. Due to her guilt, Mrs. F committed suicide (p. 9)

(implied) **Blackmailing Episode**

Frame 11: Dr. S recalling RP and Mrs. F together the *day before* (the day is left unclear in prospective narration) walking along, side by side, and Mrs. F had been talking very earnestly. This tête-a-tête between RP and Mrs Ferrars the day before Mrs. F died struck the doctor as being odd,

'*I think I can safely say that it was at this moment that a foreboding of the future first swept over me.*' (p. 15)

The *future* is about RP being framed as the blackmailer (Frame 14). The reader focus in this frame is directed to the meeting between RP and Mrs. F due to the possibility implied that RP blackmailed Mrs. F.

Repeated Frame 3, 21   **RP Episode**

Frame 12: Miss R seeking information about drug habits, as her son, Charles Kent is an addict (p. 191), which is found out by Dr. S (p. 17)

Miss R Episode

Frame 13: RP at the local inn, the Three Boars and not at Fernly Park, but Dr. S insists of RP being in London according to RA. (19)

Repeated Frame 4 and 6   **RP Episode**

Frame 14: '*Could I do anything with the boy* [RP]*? I thought I could.*' (p. 27)

Cardinal point   **Desire Frame**   **RP Episode**

Frame 15: Dr. S met RP at the Three Boars and offers to help, but RP refuses help and acknowledges that he has to deal with his personal matters directly with his stepfather and reveal his secret marriage to Ursula the parlor maid. (p. 28)

In this frame RP shared with Dr. S his secret marriage to Ursula (p. 219) (Frame 8). RP was concerned that his stepfather would cut off his inheritance as he had secretly married the parlor maid at Fernly Park, when his stepfather wanted him to marry his cousin, FA, and keep the wealth in the family. This information is **withheld** in the first story of crime.

     Episodic link to Frame 8, 32 (Event C6)   **Withheld Frame**   **RP Episode**

Frame 16: Dr. S arrives at Fernly Park for dinner, when he meets Raymond, RA's secretary. She notices the ***black bag*** and asks if the Doctor's visit is a professional one. The Dictaphone was concealed in the *black bag* to manipulate the time of murder, making Dr. S <u>a premeditated murderer</u>

    Episodic link to Frame 17, 29 and A 5   **Murder Episode**

Frame 17: As he turned the door handle, Dr. S narrates he heard a sound like someone shutting a window in the drawing room. Later in the narrative, it becomes clear that the sound was from a table lid (a curio cabinet) being shut (p. 61), in which was displayed the murder weapon, a Tunisian dagger, gifted to RA by Major Blunt. Contrary to D S's narration, <u>Miss R later revealed that she closed the open table lid</u> when she came into the drawing room (61), also supported by FA that the dagger was not in the curio table when she joined Dr. S before dinner (A (Event 5); thus making the doctor an unreliable narrator about someone opening and shutting a window, when it was himself shutting the table lid to steal the murder weapon.

      Unreliable Narrator   **Murder Episode**

The frame sequence for this episode is thus:

A. **Sound episode for false trail**
 (Embedded within the master narrative frame (Frames 1–37))

Event 1: Dr. S coming into the drawing room hearing a sound like someone closing a window

                  Murder Episode

Event 2: Dr. S bumped into Miss R the housekeeper who explained that she had come in to check the flowers in the drawing room (p. 61), when in narrative reality she had returned from meeting her son Charles, the drug addict, and was running late to attend to the dinner.

                                                                                 Miss R Episode

Event 3: Dr. S realized the sound was someone gently and carefully shutting the silver table lid, in which was displayed the murder weapon, a Tunisian dagger.

Episodic link to Frame 17   **Unreliable Narrator**   **Murder Episode**

Event 4: FA asserted during the investigation that the dagger was not in the silver table when she found Dr. S before dinner looking at the contents of this silver table. (p. 31, 93)

                Episodic link to Frame 17   **Unreliable Narrator**

Dr. S at some point in this frame took the Tunisian dagger. This was used as the murder weapon. (p. 228)

                        Omitted Frame in first story   **Murder Episode**

Frame 18: FA announces to Dr. S her engagement to RP (p. 32)

                                                                                         RP Episode

Frame 19: Dr. S is in conversation with Mrs A (RA's sister), when Major Blunt enters the room and joins FA at the silver table, when FA notices the dagger is missing (p. 93)

                      Episodic link to Frame 17 (A 5)   **RP Episode**

Frame 20: Dr. S and RA leave the dining room after dinner for RA's study where RA shares his knowledge of Mrs. F having poisoned her husband (p. 38) and tells him how someone was blackmailing her for huge sums of money. He requests RA to punish the person who made her life hell for the last year. Dr. S narrates that the blackmailer was referred to in the letter as a person, and he took this to be a man. (pp. 37, 40, 108)

                                  Unreliable Narrator   **Letter Episode**

Frame 21: Dr. S recalls,

'*Suddenly before my* [Dr. S] *eyes there rose the picture of Ralph Paton and Mrs Ferrars side by side. .... I felt a momentary throb of anxiety. Supposing—oh! but surely that was impossible.*' (p. 37)

                                Repeated Frame 3, 14   **RP Episode**

As a **hypothetical scenario**, this frame is an **episodic link** to Frames 3 and 14. In retrospect, to **manipulate** the object's (RP) parameters, the reader's gaze is directed to *contextual frames* (information stored in the memory) 3, 7 and 8 to foreground the mystery surrounding RP in Frame 21. The object's parameters are made to appear as the agent responsible for blackmailing in Frame 20. Hence based on Frames 3, 14, and 20, this is a **hypothetical scenario.**

                          RP Episode
Frame 22: Parker enters study with the post containing the letter from Mrs. F. Dr. S insists that RA read the letter but he does not succeed. This frame contradicts Frame 20.

            Unreliable Narrator   **Letter Episode**
Frame 23: Dr. S narrates that the letter was brought in by Parker at 8.40 pm when RA read the letter to Dr. S. Ten minutes later the doctor leaves RA in his study to get back home. Before he leaves the study the doctor narrates,

'*I hesitated with my hand on the door handle, looking back and wondering if there was anything I had left undone, I could think of nothing.*' (p. 41)

Also in this frame, as a false trail the doctor sets up the Dictaphone to go off at 9.30 p.m., when Secretary Raymond heard RA talking to someone in his study. (Appendix 2b, screen grab @ 00.23.09.ff VII)

  At this point in the narrative, RA was murdered and the letter revealing the blackmailer was removed. This episode is withheld by the narrator in this immediate context.

Episodic link to Frame 29 Withheld (Murder Frame) Letter Episode

B. Murder Frame (embedded narrative)
Event 1: Parker brings the post at 9 p.m. when RA gets to know of Mrs. F's blackmailer
Event 2: the letter unread by RA   **Letter Episode**
Event 3: RA murdered (p. 45)   **Murder Frame**

Event 4: In fictional reality, Dr. S checks the study for *anything … left undone* and leaves the study by the open window, under which footprints of RP's shoes were discovered. It was later revealed by Poirot in the second story of investigation with the footprints that someone was deliberately trying to throw suspicion on RP. (p. 228)

Repeated Frame 34 in first story   **Withheld Frame (premediated murderer)**   **RP Episode**

Event 5: Dr. S visits RP at the Three Boars after murdering RA (p. 27), to suggest RP to hide (p. 219) at a mental hospital to save him from incriminating himself and his wife (Frame 8). This information was concealed in prospection.

Episodic link to Frames 8, 15, 32 and 37   **Motive Frame**   **RP Episode**

Frame 24: Dr. S leaves study and is startled to find Parker outside the study. He informs him that RA does not want to be disturbed.

Murder Frame

Frame 25: Dr. S collides with a man at the lodge gates, who asks for directions to Fernly Park, and whose voice (pp. 41, 172) sounds familiar. The man was Charles Kent, the housekeeper's son, a fact left undisclosed in the prospective narration—a minor event.

Miss R Episode

Frame 26: Dr. S receives phone call (from Parker)

Murder Episode

Frame 27: Parker is astounded to hear from Dr. S that he received a call from someone, who introduced himself as Parker, and requested him to come to Fernly Park where his master has been found murdered. (p. 43)

Murder Episode

Frame 28: Parker and Dr. S in the study find RA sitting on the armchair, his head had fallen sideways with the Tunisian dagger visible just below his collar. (p. 45)

Murder Episode

Frame 29: Parker leaves the study to ring the police. Dr. S, when alone in the study, narrates,

'*I did what little had to be done*' (45)

Dr. S removed the Dictaphone and moved back the armchair, and this act is withheld in this frame. The Dictaphone was placed to **distort** the time of murder.

Episodic link to Frame 16   **Withheld frame**   **Murder Frame**

Frame 30: Blunt and Raymond are in the study with Dr. S. Some letters were on the floor, when Dr. S notices Mrs. F's letter (the blue envelope) is missing, but does not disclose this to the others (p. 47)

Letter Episode

Frame 31: Inspector arrives at the scene.

Frame 32: FA wants to remove suspicion of RP being the murderer of RA. She questions Dr. S, as to why he went the Three Boars the night after, when RA was murdered (p. 66).

Episodic link to Frames 15 (C 5), 37   **RP Episode**

C. Ralph episode (embedded narrative)

Event 1 (Frame 3): RP at the Three Boars and found by Dr. S talking to Mrs. F the day before Mrs. F is found dead (p. 15), also confirmed by C in Frame 6 when RP was seen with a girl (p. 19), later revealed as his wife, Ursula in chapter 22.

RP Episode

Event 2: RP at King's Abbot and not in London as thought by RA, this found to be odd by Dr. S

Episodic link to Frame 4   **RP Episode**

Event 3: RA tells C about RP and FA being engaged (p. 25)

RP Episode

Event 4 (Frame 20): Mrs. F's confession revealed by RA to Dr. S in the study, how she poisoned her husband and there was one person who had known this all along. (pp. 37, 38)

Blackmailing Episode

Event 5 (Frame 8): RP talking to a *girl* (p. 26) overheard by C (thought as FA) when walking in the woods (p. 204)

RP Episode

Event 6 (Frame 32): FA questioned why Dr. S had been to the Three Boars last night. The night being when RA was murdered (p. 69)

RP Episode

2 Manipulated Context 81

D. Ralph Episode (Inferred fictional context)
Entity representation of character RP by Dr. S, relating to Frame 13 (the pro-representation)

Event 1: Dr. S's feelings relating to RP and Mrs. F talking earnestly in Frame 11.

> '… *That earnest tête-à-tête between Ralph Paton and Mrs Ferrars the day before struck me disagreeably.*' (p. 15)

Event 2: Dr. S's view of RP as having '*strain of weakness*' and his monologue in Frame 14, '*Could I do anything with the boy* [RP]*? I thought I could.*' (p. 27)

Event 4: Dr. S tells the Inspector why RP cannot murder RA (p. 71)
Inference to Dr. S as '*weak as water*' by C similar to RP, '*A weak nature*' (p. 167)

Episodic link to Frame 8

The second story of investigation (Chapter 6 onwards)

Parker framed as the second suspect by Dr. S

Frame 33: when asked by the inspector about a blackmailer, Dr. S narrated,

> '"*If Parker heard anything about blackmail,*" *I said slowly,* "*he <u>must have been listening</u> outside this door with his ear glued against the keyhole.*" …
> *Davis nodded.* …
> *I took an <u>instant</u> decision.* …
> *And then and there narrated the whole events of the evening as I <u>have</u> set them down <u>here</u>. The inspector listened intently, occasionally interjecting a question…*
> "*And you say that letter has completely disappeared? It looks bad—it looks very bad indeed. It gives us what we've been looking for—<u>a motive</u>. For the murder.*"' (p. 57)

Blackmailing Episode   **Motive Frame**

Frame 34: Inspector checks out the footprints under RA's windowsill and compares them with the shoes which belong to RP (p. 1). They matched the pattern in RP's shoes (pp. 73, 84)

RP Episode

Background on RP by the Inspector:

RP had not been seen in the neighborhood since 9.30 pm on the night when RA was murdered, and he had serious money difficulties. This was seen as the **motive** for murdering his uncle.

Frame 35: unknown to Dr. S, Mary Black had seen RP at 9.25 pm walking towards the house (Fernly Park), the night RA was murdered. **Alibi**

Frame 36: Poirot recovers a wedding ring inscribed, '*From R.* [RP], *March 13th*' (p. 95)

Frame 37: Lawyer tells Poirot that RP inherits RA's large fortune—Fernly Park and all the shares on his company, *Ackroyd and Son*, making RP a wealthy man. However, RP had a chronic condition, he spent money like water. (p. 97)   **Motive scenario**   **RP Episode**

Frame 38: . S asks C if she had revealed RP's secret meeting with *a girl* in the woods to Poirot (114).

Episodic link to Frame 8, 15, 32 (C 6)   **RP Episode**

The facts that reveal the murderer (p. 224)

- **The telephone call (the confusion)**

In the actual storyworld, Dr. S arranged with his patient, an American steward of a liner, to call him at a certain time (p. 115). This call was made to appear as made by Parker the butler (p. 42) informing RA had been found murdered, and gave the murderer (Dr. S) the chance to get back to the scene of crime before the others and recover the Dictaphone pre-set to frame RP. (p. 226)

2 Manipulated Context 83

In the first story of crime, the linear setting of the time of murder was—Parker bought the letter from Mrs. F for Ackroyd at 8.40 pm, when it was read to Dr. S. It revealed Dr. S as the person who blackmailed Mrs. F for having poisoned her alcoholic husband. Following this, Dr. S killed Ackroyd.

Omitted murder Frame

To conceal this act, Dr. S set up a false trail to conceal the real time of murder. He timed a recorder Dr .S bought with him in his *black bag* (Frame 16) when he joined Ackroyd and his family for dinner. This recorder was timed to start at 9.30 pm (pp. 49, 227). Dr. S then left the study at 8.50 pm, as was seen by Parker (Frame 24). Hence, RA's secretary Raymond, (SB 23.09.ffVII), heard RA dictating at 9.30 pm. In story reality it was the Dictaphone and not RA speaking, as was later revealed by Poirot in the second story of investigation. (p. 227)

- **The letter incident (Frame 20, 23)**

The letter written to RA by Mrs. F (p. 40) revealed how she was blackmailed (p. 38) for having poisoned her husband. Unable to live with this burden of guilt, she committed suicide. The blackmailer was revealed in the letter (p. 130), and consequently the second crime (RA murdered) took place (pp. 42, 146) in the narrative.

- **The chair and the Dictaphone incident (a false trail) (Frame 29)**

A secondary motive (RP framed being primary motive) is related to the incident when Parker noticed the armchair (p. 74) in the study, which was out of place and facing the door (p. 74). This was to hide the Dictaphone which was heard by Raymond, and not Ackroyd, who was already dead. (p. 227)

- **The footprints on the window ledge incident (Frame B4)**

A third motive was footprints under the windowsill of RA's study discovered by the inspector which matched RP's shoes (pp. 71, 84). In the final revelatory meeting, Poirot explains why he had concentrated on whether it was boots or shoes and their color (p. 140) instead of footprints. This way Poirot successfully obscured the real reason for his line of enquiry.' (p. 228)

The three facts framing RP as the murderer (p. 130)

- Theft of the blue envelope and its contents
- RP framed as the blackmailer
- RP's inheritance

The dominant episode in first story

In FA, the *frequency* (**text time** in Genette 1988) of repeated frames relates mostly to the RP episode in the narrative. *Prolepsis* (flash-forwards) in the narrative are noticed in RP episode, making this episode an embedded narrative in anticipation in the first story of crime.

Appendix 2b

Storyboard (SB)
 The Murder of Roger Ackroyd & *Lord Edgware dies* (2005) [DVD]. ITV Studios. Available: Part of a box set *Agatha Christie: Collection 5*.
 Note: The corresponding **Frames** from the novel are in **Appendix 2a**.

The first story of crime

Screen grab @ **00.07.13.ff1**
Poirot meets Ralph Paton at his friend, Roger Ackroyd's factory. Just before this scene, Roger Ackroyd informs Poirot of the forthcoming marriage to be announced in the newspaper on Saturday (between his stepson Ralph Paton and his niece Flora Ackroyd).
Ackroyd to Poirot:
"All in all this has been a good week for me. Read in your newspaper on Saturday morning Poirot of a forthcoming marriage."

screen grab @ **00.08.00.ff2**
Vera Ackroyd to her daughter Flora Ackroyd while parlor maid Ursula pours the tea,
"Isn't it exciting?"
"Tea!!!"
"No you goose, the forthcoming announcement, and not before its time either."
This mimetic narration is not present in the novel.

screen grab @ 00.08.42.ffIV
The conversation between stepfather and stepson about the announcement of Ralph's engagement to Flora went on for 15 minutes in the video clip, until interrupted by a telephone call from Mrs. Ferrars, Ackroyd's fiancée, which is another secret in the story. Ralph does not reveal to his stepfather his marriage to the parlor maid. Later in the video (01.12), Ursula revealed their secret marriage to Roger Ackroyd. Soon after this revelation, Ackroyd sacked her when she met Ralph at the summerhouse, as seen by Major Blunt in 00.22.32.ffVIII and 00.22.35.ffIX.

The conversation between Ralph and Roger Ackroyd,
"*I came down last night. I am staying at the White Hart.*
Look father, ..."
"*What's wrong with Fernly Park?*"
"*Look, I heard you are going to announce the engagement.*"
"*Flora is all for it.*"
"*Yes perhaps she is ...*"
Y"ou are putting it off, putting it off for now three months nearly ..."
"*I have been trying to look for a job father ...*" (interrupted by Raymond the secretary).

This mimetic narration is not present in the novel, but is presented as diegetic universe, as a description by. (Frame 7) relating to Ralph Paton and his whereabouts before the death of his stepfather, Rodger Ackroyd.

screen grab @ 00.08.11.ffIII
Parlor maid spills tea when she heard that Flora and Ralph were engaged. In story real time, the parlor maid is married to Ralph Paton. The marriage was a secret, as it was against Ackroyd's wish for his stepson Ralph to keep the money in the family and marry his cousin Flora.

Parlor maid to Flora:
"*Oh ... I am sorry ..., I'll get a cloth ...*" and she departs.
This mimetic narration, not present in the novel is the cardinal point in the audio-visual narrative, while in the novel this utterance (Frame 14) functions as the cardinal point, '*Could I do anything with the boy* [Ralph Paton]? *I thought I could*'. (p. 27). These frames are the point of departure for narrative option in the audio-visual and written narrative respectively.

Poirot is the narrator in TV version (third-person narration). Dr. Sheppard the murderer is the narrator/focalizer in the novel (first-person narration). This influences the nature of hinge points in the two versions of narrative discourse: a focalized utterance (Frame 14) in the written version versus a focalized event (00.08.11.ffIII) for the TV version of the same story.

The above hinge points (00.08.11.ffIII and Frame 14) give rise to alternative narrative path to delay the knowledge of the real perpetrator. Dr. Sheppard persuaded Ralph to stay at a mental hospital (Frame 15) until the investigation of his stepfather's death was over. This was to protect himself and his wife (in repeated frames 6 and 13 in written narrative) from being suspected for his stepfather's murder (Frame 36). Ralph's absence made him an obvious suspect for the murder, as he was to inherit his stepfather's estate. Dr. Sheppard took advantage of this situation (Frame 14).

Frame 15 becomes the cause for restricted (summerhouse) frames: SB ffVIII and ffIX, when Ralph met Ursula in the summerhouse, as seen by Major Blunt. It is to be noted, Frame 15 in written narrative is not present in the TV narrative.

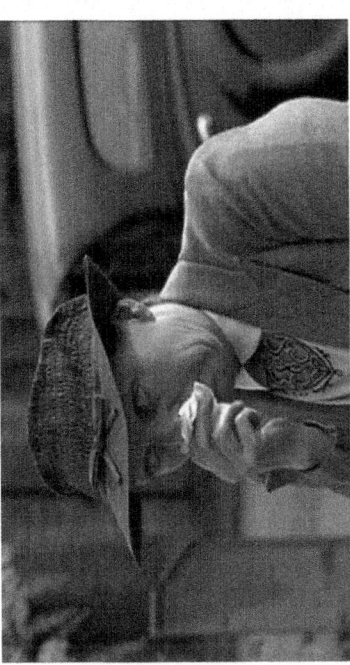

screen grab @ **00.14.25.ffV**

In this frame, Caroline (00.14.43.ffVI) found Ralph in conversation with a *girl*. Unknown to Caroline and others in the narrative, the girl was Ralph's wife, Ursula, in SB ffII pouring tea in SB ffIII.

Ursula was unhappy with Ralph for keeping their marriage a secret, and about his stay at the White Hart and not at his stepfather's house at Fernly Park. Ralph to Ursula,

"… Got to be patient"
"Oh for heaven's sake … "
"My dear girl, it's quite on the cards the old fellow will cut me off without a shilling"
"Of course he won't … "
"He is pretty fed up with me for last few years, a little will do it, we need the dibs. I will be a very rich man if the old fellow pops off, I don't want him to go off and alter his will."
"Why are you staying here and not Fernly Park?"
"Leave this to me, don't worry"
"Fine … "

This frame corresponds to Frames 6, 8 and 13 in the novel. Caroline in the novel overheard the couple in the woods, while in the film she finds Ralph at the local inn, earnestly in conversation with a girl, presumed as to be Flora since they were engaged (Frame 7)

screen grab @ **00.14.43.ffVI** (01 hr.12)

In the novel, this SB frame corresponds to Frames 7 and 8 in the novel

screen grab @ 00.22.35.ffIX
Episodic link to SB **00.08.11.ffIII**

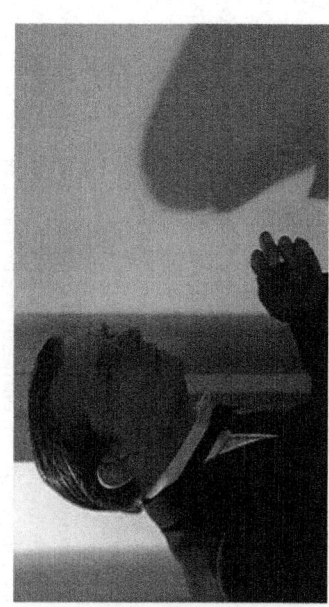

screen grab @ 00.23.09.ffVII
Raymond, Ackroyd's secretary was about to knock when he heard Ackroyd in conversation with someone. In real story time, this is a <u>post murder frame</u> in the narrative discourse. This frame is an episodic link to the concealed Dictaphone that confused the time of Ackroyd's murder, and led to Parker's death in SB ffXI.

screen grab @ 00.22.32.ffVIII
Episodic link to SB **00.08.11.ffIII**

screen grab @ 00.43.46.ffX
Episodic link to SB frame III
Poirot discovers a piece of linen stuck to the post in the summerhouse, which was from the parlor maid's uniform (revealed at video time 01.13.21). This frame is an episodic link to the SB ffVIII and ffIX above.

screen grab @ 00.51.26.ffXI
This additional murder did not take place in the novel.
This frame foregrounds the consequence of events in the story—1. the missing letter (Frame 23) to conceal the blackmailer of Mrs. Ferrars and 2. the Dictaphone incident in order to confuse the time when Ackroyd was alive in SB ffVII. In the written narrative, it is the focalizer utterance, Frame 37, which corresponds to this frame in the film version.

Difference in two versions (novel vs. the audio-visual)

The narrators are the murderer (Dr. Sheppard) in the novel, while Poirot, the detective, narrates in the TV version. Consequently it is a first-person narration versus a third-person narration. This influences the cardinal point for a secondary narrative path in the two versions. In the novel, it is the **focalizer's utterance**, Frame 14, when a mimetic (showing) action in SB ffIII is the mediation point in the video narration, mediation point being the middle position of the sequence of events before and after the crime. As a result, the narrative option as an alternative path centers round the utterance of the focalizer (Frames 11, 21, 23) in the novel, while in the audio-visual it is the **focalized event**, SB frame III.

The form of narration influences the hinge point in the narrative, which is a **focalizer utterance** in first-person narrative as opposed to an **event focalization** in third-person focalization. Additionally, in the video narration, by zooming into a participant action and expression, there is **mimetic narration** synonymous to the effect produced in the participant utterance in a written narrative form. This is also because of the voiceover technique in the film version instead of a **narrator or focalizer role** in the written form of the same story.

Appendix 2c

Frame Analysis (FA): *Cover Her Face* (CHF), 1974

Setting: Martingale house at Chadfleet
Participants involved in the story

Mrs. Eleanor Maxie (Mrs. M)—Lady of the Martingale House
Deborah Riscoe (Maxie) (DR)—Mrs. M's daughter and widow
Stephen Maxie (SM)—Mrs. M's son and doctor at St. Luke's Hospital (p. 27)
Miss Liddell (Miss L)—and Miss Pollock in charge of St. Mary's refuge at Chadfleet
Martha Bultitaft (MB)—the housekeeper at Martingale House
Sally Jupp (SJ)—the new house-parlor maid at the Martingale House (pp. 6–8), unmarried mother with child, Jimmy (p. 19)
Catherine Bowers (CB)—a nurse and daughter of Catherine (Katie) Bowers who went to the same school as Mrs. M, also keen on SM
Samuel Bocock—owner of the stables at Martingale House
Dr. Charles Epps (Dr. Epps)—the family doctor for the Maxies, and a widower at Chadfleet
Felix Hearne (FH)—an ex-soldier (pp. 24–25) and close friend of Deborah and the family (p. 26), who also owned the Hearne and Illingworth publisher (p. 26)
Bernard Hinks—the vicar of Chadfleet, a bachelor (pp. 5–6)
Detective Chief Inspector Adam Dalgliesh—in charge of the investigation

The story starts with Mrs. Maxie remembering a dinner party hosted for the annual church fete. This was three months before the death of the parlor–housemaid, Sally Jupp.

Upon Miss Liddell's recommendation, Mrs. Maxie employed Sally Jupp, an unmarried-mother-with-a child from the refuge, as extra help for their housekeeper Martha. Simon Maxie needed heavier nursing and Sally was capable as well as refined in comparison to the untrained, uneducated parlor–housemaids employed so far (p. 23). As Miss Liddell expressed, Sally Jupp was a grammar school girl (p. 8) a superior type to be a parlor–housemaid (Frame 3). However, Martha and Sally were not compatible kitchen mates. Following the Sally–Stephen situation (Frame 14), tension arose between Sally and Mrs. Maxie (Frames 8 and 13) and the rest of the household. Soon after this, Sally was found dead.

In the second story of investigation, it is clear that Sally had a **secret**; she loved mystery, which gave her power and control over others (p. 194). The secret was that **she was already married to James Ritchie**, Jimmy's father (p. 177). She led everyone to think that she had accepted Stephen Maxie's marriage proposal (Frame 14). She blackmailed her uncle for *being done out of her rights* (p. 191). She pried on Miss Liddell's account-keeping and threatened to accuse her of wrongdoing with charity fund accounts, as Miss Liddell was not very clever with figures and accounts (pp. 96, 108, and 183). Dalgleish explained,

'... *she enjoyed the feeling of power that this hidden knowledge gave her.*' (p. 195)

Frame analysis (FA)

Narration takes place through an omniscient narrator, and the Frames are mostly a cognitive construct of different participants for inferred and intended contextual effect relating to Sally. The theme frames as **episodes** are identified in FA. The **cardinal point** in the narration in CHF is Frame 1 (clause 10) and Frame 4 (clause21). Unlike *Ackroyd*, the omnipresence in Frames 1 and 4 (clauses 10, 20 and 21) is additionally foregrounded in the narration through the eyes or the mind of Mrs. Maxie and Miss Liddell.

The first story of crime (Chapters 1–3)

The concrete external context
Frame 1: Mrs. M remembered the ritual gathering of her guests for the summer church fete that took place three months before the killing of SJ

1. 'Exactly three months before the killing at Martingale, Mrs Maxie gave a dinner party. 2. Years later, when the trial was a half-forgotten scandal and the headlines were yellowing on the newspaper lining of cupboard drawers, Eleanor Maxie looked back on that spring evening as the opening scene of tragedy. 3. Memory, selective and perverse, invested what had been a perfectly ordinary dinner party with an aura of foreboding and unease. 4. It became, in retrospect, a ritual gathering under one roof of victim and suspects, a staged preliminary to murder. 5. In fact not all the suspects had been present. 6. Felix Hearne, for one, was not at Martingale that week-end. 7. Yet, in her memory, he too sat at Mrs Maxie's table, watching with amused, sardonic eyes the opening antics of the players.

8. At the time, of course, the party was both ordinary and rather dull. ... 9. Mrs Maxie had just employed one of Miss Liddell's unmarried mothers as parlor–housemaid and the girl was waiting at the table for the first time. 10. <u>But the air of constraint which burdened the meal could hardly have been caused by the occasional presence of Sally Jupp who placed the dishes in front of Mrs Maxie and removed the plates with a dextrous efficiency which Miss Liddell noted with complacent approval.</u>' (p. 5)

Recalled Frame   **Cardinal Point**   **SJ Episode**

Frame 2: Mrs. M employed SJ from St. Mary's Refuge on Miss L's recommendation.

SJ Episode

Frame 3: The abstract internal context on morals (social consequences of illegitimacy) and *death* (pp. 5–13)

Dr. Epps' moral scruples are unimportant when it's a case of another pair of hands at the kitchen sink (p. 7)

Miss L concerned about moral standards and *'society getting too soft with these girls.'* [becoming a mother out of wedlock, like SJ]

SM's liberal view on the principle of moral code that SJ had broken, when not many representatives of modern youth accept it in practice

SJ Episode

Frame 4: SJ's sudden and brief change of attitude from *Sally the submissive to Sally the enigma*, as Miss L noticed,

2 Manipulated Context   93

11. *'Miss Liddell watched Sally Jupp as she moved about the table. ...* 12. *Suddenly Miss Liddell was visited by an irrational spasm of affection.* 13. *Sally was really doing nicely ... Suddenly their eyes met.* 14. *For a full two seconds they looked at each other. Then Miss Liddell flushed and dropped her eyes. ...* 15. *Confused and horrified she tried to analyse the extraordinary effect of that brief contact. ... she had read in the girl's eyes, not the submissive gratitude which had characterizes Sally Jupp. ... but amused contempt, a hint of conspiracy and a dislike which was almost frightening in its intensity.* 16. *Then the green eyes had dropped again and Sally the enigma became once more Sally the submissive, the subdued, ... She had recommended Sally without reserve. ...* 17. *The girl was a most superior type. ...* 18. *The decision had been taken.* 19. *It was too late to doubt its wisdom now.'* (p. 10)

SJ Episode

- the omniscient narrator

20. *'Miss Liddell was aware for the first time that the introduction of her favourite to Martingale might produce complications.* 21. <u>*She could not be expected to foresee the magnitude of those complications nor that they would end in violent death.*</u>' (My emphasis) (p. 10)

Cardinal point   SJ Episode

Frame 5: SM and his sister DR, following dinner, converse in his bedroom about various issues:

SM's affair with CB the nurse
  Family responsibilities (Simon Maxie, their father being bedridden),
  Keeping the house running by SM marrying someone with money to preserve his inheritance, Martingale House

Simon Maxie Episode

Frame 6: DR's cognitive world relative to her father's long-term illness and his impending death (21)

'*...waiting for a death*' [concerning her long term bedridden father] *came suddenly into her mind she* [Deborah] *told herself firmly that her father was no worse, ...* (p. 21)

DR's preoccupation with death,

'... *she watched Felix writing under Saturday's date* [the day of the summer church fete] *in his cramped meticulous hand as if he were making a date with death.*' (p. 27)

Simon Maxie Episode

Frame 7: When waiting for her brother at the hospital waiting room, DR saw SJ and SM (28), she later found out from her brother that SJ had come to see him and return the tablets (Sommeil) she found in their father's bed. According to SM, SJ made the effort to find out what was going on in their father's mind (p. 29). This did not go down well with DR as she felt that her brother was accusing her of not looking after their father well, and failing to recognize SJ's sincerity,

'... *She's very devoted to Father.*' (p. 31)

Following this incident, DR's thoughts about her brother are interesting, as they highlight SJs presence and the effect on each individual in the house,

'Never since the death of Edward Riscoe [Deborah's late husband] *had she felt so alienated from Stephen; never since then had she been so in need of HIM.*' (p. 32)

Tablet episode (SJ Episode)

Frame 8: Mrs. M's reaction when she found out aboutSJ's discovery of the tablets and the heated conversation that followed between Mrs. M and SJ which revealed Mrs. M's feeling about her,

'*If you had to lie there, year after year, perhaps you might like to know that you had something, a few ... tablets maybe that would end all the pain and tiredness. Something that nobody else knew about, until a silly bitch, no better than she should be, came ferreting them out. ... I'll have you out. You and that brat. I'll find a way, never fear!*' (p. 33)

Tablet Episode (SJ Episode)

Frame 9: SJ's remark to Mrs. M's reaction,

> '... *I'd like to see Stephen's face if I told him that you knew all the time!*' (p. 33)
> **Tablet Episode (SJ Episode)**

Frame 10: MB overheard this conversation (Frames 8 and 9) and her cognitive world of disgust for Sally was,

> '... *She* [Martha] *indulged in phantasies of Sally disgraced, Sally and her child banished from Martingale, Sally found out for what she was, lying, wicked and evil. And, since all things possible, Sally dead.*' (p. 34)
> **Tablet Episode (SJ Episode)**

At the summer fete at Martingale House (Chapter 3)
Frame 11: SJ overslept on the morning of the summer fete, as CB observes,

> '... *Catherine remembered that there had been some trouble that morning* [the day of the annual church summer fete at Martingale House] *with Martha because the girl* [Sally] *had overslept. ... she had to rush to make up the lost time for she looked flushed and was, Catherine thought, <u>concealing some excitement behind an outward air of docile efficiency</u>.*' (p. 36)
> **Sally's secret**

Frame 12: C and DR went back to the house for a break from manning the stalls when SJ's uncle (identity concealed in prospection) brushed past them *looking for the toilet* (p. 39)
> **SJ Episode**

Frame 13: SJ appears at the fete wearing the same dress as DM (p. 39/40)
> **SJ Episode (the dress)**

Frame 14: SJ appears with SM and announces, when asked to change into her uniform,

> '*Would that be appropriate madam* [Mrs. M], *for the girl your son has asked to marry him?*' (p. 43)
> **SJ Episode (the dress)**

Frame 15: On the following day, in the early hours of morning, CB comes into Mrs. M's bedroom for an aspirin when,
Frame 16: MB comes into Mrs. M's bedroom to say that Sally had overslept again,

'It's Sally madam, she said. 'She's overslept again I suppose.' (p. 45)
Murder Episode

Frame 17: FH and SM got the ladder to climb into Sally's bedroom and found SJ dead,

'... the killer's hands had choked the life from her.' (p. 47)
Murder Episode

The second story of investigation

Frame 18: Post murder thoughts of Mrs. M and DR about SJ, the victim,

'...A mother murdered and a father he'll [Sally's son] *never know now. That was <u>one secret</u> she kept. One of many probably. ...'*
'Deborah thought, "I ought to dislike her [Sally] *loss now that she's dead, but I can't. She always did make trouble. She would enjoy watching us like this, sweating on the top line. ... Perhaps she can ... I mustn't get morbid. ... Felix knows that Sally was doped. Well, if she was, it was in my drinking mug. Let them make what they like of that."'* (57, 100)

Overall **cognitive contexts** (a construct) as an underlying propositional content in the Frames of reference are,

A. **The Surprise**
  SM's surprise relating to the tablets prescribed for their father;
  SJ's tidiness as a surprise to Dalgliesh
  SJ had been a wife (Sally Ritchie) as well as a mother (Jimmy Ritchie) (p. 176).

B. The motive

"'...Stephen Maxie had proposed to Sally Jupp. You could call that *a motive for the family, I suppose.*'" Manning to Dalgleish. (p. 50)

Mrs. M in reply to Dalgleish's question, "'...*from your* [Dalgleish] *point of view it provides a motive for several people, myself* [Mrs. M] *particularly.*'" (p. 77)

Mrs. M wanted her son SM to marry someone with money, who could help to protect the house, his inheritance, as remarked by DR,

"'... *You ought to get married. Mummy would like it really. Someone with money if you can find her. Not stinking, of course, just beautifully rich.*'" (p. 15)

C. The death [in anticipation]

... '*waiting for a death*' [of her long term bedridden father] *came suddenly into her mind she* [Deborah] *told herself firmly that her father was no worse,* ...' (p. 21)

'...*as if he* [FH] *making a date* [Saturday's dinner after the fete] *with death*' (p. 27)

'... *She* [Martha] *in phantasies of Sally disgraced,* ...*Sally found out for what she was, lying, wicked and evil. And, since all things are possible, Sally dead.*' (p. 34)

The dominant episode in first story

In the FA, SJ episode or episodes (the dress and Sommeil tablet) related to her provocations before she was murdered is the dominant episode over the murder frame in the first story of crime.

Appendix 2d

Frame Analysis (FA): Moser (2008)

Setting: Town of Nauheim (near a Spa for heart cure (p. 57), Hotel Regina (p. 28), the dining room of Hotel Excelsior (p. 31) and the Branshaw estate (p. 37)

Principal participants involved in the story
The Dowells (American couple 1): **Florence Hurlbird** (F) from Connecticut/New England and **John Dowell** (D) from Philadelphia
The Ashburnhams (English couple 2): **Captain Edward** (E) from England (Branshaw Manor) and **Leonora** (L) from Ireland
Nancy Rufford (NR), the Ashburnhams took her on as their (adopted) child; she was from the same convent as Leonora (p. 87)

Edward's affairs of the heart (p. 69)
The Kilsyte Case for kissing a servant girl in a railway train (pp. 59, 72, 113, 175); Maisie Maidan (MM) affair (pp. 60/61, 68); Nancy Rufford (Part III)
Affairs that cost Edward money: the Spanish courtesan affair (Grand Ducal Lady) at Monte Carlo (65, 186); Mrs Basil affair with the wife of a brother officer (pp. 68, 198); numerous other infidelities (p. 66)

Significant dates
August 4, 1899—F set out with her uncle for the tour round the world
August 4, 1901—F married D
1903—F sick of Jimmy and taken on E   (p. 105)
August 4, 1904—MM died
Sept. 4, 1904—E accompanied F and D to Paris   (p. 117)
1905–1906—between this period E was in Paris visiting D and F three times
August 4, 1913—*the last day of my absolute ignorance* [revelation of F and Jimmy's affair by Bagshawe)   (p. 117)

Frame Analysis (FA)

When frames corresponding to a theme frame are displaced with respect to its sequence in the story, the scenario is marked out in parentheses at the end of each frame. This is to distinguish and also draw attention to these displaced events of a theme frame (episode) embedded within another dominant theme frame. Most of the frames are 'mimesis of action' narrated by the narrator Dowell, except quotes which are mimesis of the character or the narrator as the character.

Dowell is telling their story (the two couples) and their time at Nauheim. The Dowell's and Ashburnhams met once a year at Neuheim. Their time at Neuheim is the master narrative. The narratives embedded in the story are presented as the story of three triangles: Florence, Edward and himself; Florence, Edward and Leonora; Edward, Leonora and Nancy.

In total, there are 176 Frames in the four-part narration of three triangles in the story in TGS.

Part 1/I

Location: Fordingbridge, the Ashburnham's place (p. 9)
Year: 1913
Setting: town of Nauheim and Fordingbridge (Connecticut)
Episode: Florence, Edward and Dowell

Frame 1: D took his Swedish baths at Nauheim when F met (*'protracted negotiations'*) E and his wife who never spoke a word to each other at the time because of his affairs which led to vast debts. (p. 12)

Episodic link to Frame 27

Frame 2: L's outburst to D about her attempting to have a lover when travelling from a *hunt ball* but unable to do so (p. 13)

Frame 3: D's perception of men in smoking rooms like E,

> '... perhaps all men are like that [Edward]. .... *They'd be offended if you suggested that they weren't the sort of person you could trust your wife alone with ... suggestion that they might make attempts upon your wife's honour.*' (p. 15)

Frame 4: F carried off the ship at Le Havre when the ship doctor made D aware of F's heart condition (p. 21).
(**Florence and Jimmy affair scenario**)   **F's conspiracy**

Part 1/II

Location: country cottage at Fordingbridge, Dowell narrating his time with his wife Florence who is now dead (p. 19)
Year: 1901 (1913)
Setting: Las Tours, Beaucaire (p. 17), New York, Fourteenth Street (p. 20), New England (p. 20), Waterbury (p. 22)
Episode (s): Florence–Jimmy affair scenario and **NR scenario**

Frame 5: year 1899 (p. 91), F accompanied her retired uncle John (Hurlbird) on a trip around the world. Jimmy was to guard the old man's heart and keep him from any political discussions. (p. 24)
Frame 6: F died five days after her uncle died of bronchitis, aged 84, and D inherited the money left to F. He had to go to Waterbury to appoint trustees to handle the money (p. 24)
D's inheritance

Following Florence's death
Frame 7: D receives an extraordinary cable from E

> '*begging* [him] *to come back* [to England/Branshaw Telegraph house] *and have a talk with him* [Edward]' (25). E wanted NR to return to her father. L came to know of this decision made by E from *the girl* (Nancy) (34)
> **Restricted Repeated Frame:** *the girl*   **NR Episode**

Restricted because, in prospection the name of *the girl* as NR is not revealed at this point in the story, until later in Frame 66.

Frame 8: D arrives in England/Branshaw Telegraph house from Waterbury, and L greets D (p. 25). D's account of E's reaction,

2 Manipulated Context 101

'The girl [Nancy Rufford] *was out with the hounds. ... And that poor devil* [Edward] *beside me was in an agony'* (26)
   Restricted Repeated frame: *the girl*   NR Episode

Part 1/III

Location: Town of Nauheim (p. 28)
Year: summer of August 1904
Setting: Hotel Regina (p. 28), dining room of Hotel Excelsior (p. 31), the Branshaw estate (p. 37)
Episode: The Ashburnhams arrive at Hotel Excelsior

Frame 9: D walking F to the baths and narrating about the way she dressed for these visits

'Yes, that is how I most exactly remember her, in that dress, in that hat, looking over her shoulder at me so that the eyes flashed very blue—dark pebble blue ... For whose benefit did she do it? For that bath attendant? Of the passers by? I don't know.' (p. 29)

This allusion to F as *characterized by flirtations* is repeated in the narrative (p. 96)
               F's flirtatious nature

Frame 10: The Ashburnhams' arrival at Nauheim (p. 31)

'There were gun cases, and collar cases, and shirt cases, and letter case, and cases each containing four bottles of medicine; and hat cases and helmet cases.' (32)

About how the couples came to sit at the same table in the dining hall, and the start of a nine-year long friendship,

'... Florence saying: "Why shouldn't we all eat out of the same trough—..."And then Florence said: "And so the whole round table is begun."' (p. 40)

Part 1/IV

Location: Town of Nauheim (p. 42)
Year: 1904
Setting: excursion to the city of M—(pp. 46, 49)
Episode: The Protest scene

Frame 11: D senses F was up to something,

> *'But on this occasion I knew that something was up.* (p. 49) ... *I must say that, until the astonishment came* [the Protest scene] *I got nothing but pleasure out of the little expedition.* (p. 50) *I was aware of something treacherous, something frightful, something the evil in the day* (p. 53)

Frame 12: F was being sarcastic to L, who was an Irish Catholic, unlike E and herself who were Protestants. In the museum at city of M—, F explains the letter about the Protest and compliments E,

> *"'It's because of that piece of paper* [draft of the Protest drawn up by Luther and others] *that you're honest, sober, industrious, provident and clean-lived. If it weren't for that piece of paper you'd be like the Irish or the Italians or the Poles, but particularly the Irish..."'* (p. 53)

Frame 13: L reveals to D (or indicates) the affair between E and F,

> *"'I can't stand this," she said* [to Dowell] *with a most extraordinary passion; "I must get out of this. ... Don't you* [Dowell] *see?" she said, "don't you see what's going on* [Florence was Edward's mistress ... committing adultery in hired rooms. (pp. 83–84)]*?" The panic again stopped my heart. ... "Don't you see, ... of the eternal damnation of you and me and them"* [alluding to Florence and Edward who lack constancy]' (p. 55)

       Episodic link to Frame 36 **E and F affair**

Part 1/V

Location: Nauheim (p. 58)
Year: one afternoon at Nauheim
Setting: Hotel Excelsior corridor just before dinner
Episode: Maisie's death scenario

Frame 14: D's interest in L, not in the way of love, L *a good actress*, and according to D, L treated him as a *patient*, or a mother to a *child* (58) and as an *invalid—a poor chap in a bath chair* (p. 40)

Frame 15: F could *run* (despite heart condition) for the connection to Brussels to get to Nauheim, *a good actress,*

'The Belgian state railway trains [had the] *trick of letting the French trains miss their connections at Brussels. ...And even if the French trains are just on time, you have to run—imagine a heart patient running! ... My wife used to run—she never ... tried to give me the impression that she was not a gallant soul. Well, she was a good actress* [this alluding to F having a heart condition] (p. 58)

Episodic link to Frame 4   (Florence and Jimmy affair)
                                                    F's conspiracy

Frame 16: E did not have a heart condition,

'There was nothing the matter with Edward Ashburnham's heart—... and had left India and come half the world over in order to follow a woman [Mrs. Maisie Maidan] *who had a "heart" to Nauheim.'* (59)
        Episodic link to Frame 18   **E's heart condition**

Frame 17: D's view of E,

'... for years he [Edward] *was my wife's lover, since he killed her, since he broke up all the pleasantness that there were in my life.'* (p. 59)
                                                           E and F affair

Frame 18: E's *mad passion* for MM; he followed her from Burma to Nauheim.

Frame 19: F accused by D of playing with *adultery*, for playing a trick on MM by not leaving alone the affair between E and MM, when MM overheard F and E below her bedroom window,

'[MM] *soaked her noon day pillow with tear whilst Florence, below the window talked to Captain Ashburnham about the constitution of the USA... left a better taste... if Florence had let her* [MM] *die in peace.*' (p. 62)
   In her letter to Leonora MM expressed herself further:
   And I heard Edward call me a poor rat to the American lady. He always called me a little rat in private, and I did not mind. But, if he called me it to her, I think he does not love me anymore (82). Soon after this she accidentally died (p. 88)]

The trick by F on MM

Frame 20: L boxed Mrs. M's ears (pp. 63, 75) when she found Mrs. M coming out of E's bedroom and wondered if Mrs. M had been her husband's mistress (p. 64)

Frame 21: L opened the letter she took to be from Colonel Harvey who was coming to stay with them. However, on reading the letter she found that E was being blackmailed for £300 a year because of an affair at Monte Carlo with the mistress of a Russian Grand Duke (p. 65)

Edward's affairs and debts Episode

Frame 22: L forced E to let her manage the family business to save them from bankruptcy. E was '... *ashamed of himself, ... he hated—he ... revolted at the thought that she* [L] *should know that sort of thing that he did* [as an afflicted fool chasing women] *existed in the world.*' (p. 67)

Edward's affairs and debts scenario

Frame 23: E revealed his frame of mind to D during his long walks with D '*while the girl was on the way to Brindisi*' (p. 67)

Restricted Repeated frame: *the girl*   **NR Episode**

Frame 24: E and L bitterly quarrelled for those three years (p. 68)

Episodic link to Frame 1   **Edward's affairs and debts Episode**

Frame 25: L succeeded in sorting out the debts of E and reopened Branshaw Manor (England) when she agreed that MM could join them in England, as she trusted MM would not blackmail E for several thousand pounds. (p. 74) She paid for M's treatment at Nauheim (pp. 74, 85)

Edward's affairs and debts Episode

Frame 26: E treated MM like a father with a child (p. 74)

Frame 27: L discovered a letter from a brother officer (Major Basil) when E was serving in the army in India. Basil threatened E for having an affair with his wife, and blackmailed E for £300 or £400 a year (pp. 68, 75, and 198)

Episodic link to Frame 23   **Edward's affairs and debts Episode**

Frame 28: Following the letter from Major Basil, and trying to convince L there was nothing else against him, E left for the post office to send a telegram to his solicitor to take out a warrant against the blackmailing brother officer(p. 76)

Frame 29: L found MM coming out of E's room and thought E was with MM for the two hours since the letter was discovered (p. 76). She boxed MM's ears

E and MM affair

Frame 30: On seeing E leaving for the post office from her window, MM went into E's room to return the scissors (p. 77)

E and MM affair

Frame 31: L struck intimacy (friendship) with F and appeared hand in hand with her into the dining room (p. 77)

Frame 32: L ran up to MM's room to beg her pardon (for boxing her ears) and asked E to take MM out to the Casino

E and MM affair

Frame 33: L waited with D for the pair [E and MM] to return from the Casino (p. 78)

Frame 34: D realizes that MM died as they returned from the museum at city M—.

MM's accidental death

'We found her dead when we got back—pretty awful, that, when you come to figure out what it all means ...' (p. 78)

Frame 35: D requests L to accept F's view on Irish Catholics (Frames 12, 13) (p. 78)

                Repeated Frame 13   **The Protest scene Episode**

Part 1/VI

Location: contd. from Part IV excursion to the city of M—
Year: August 4, 1904 following L's reaction to F's comment about Irish Catholics (Frame 12)
Setting: archives of the Schloss in city M—
Episode: Maisie's death scenario contd.

Frame 36: D reminiscing L's reaction to F's comment (Frame 12) on the draft drawn up by Luther and others (p. 81)

"'It would be better if Florence said nothing at all against my co-religionists, because it is a point that I am touchy about."
    That was the hint that, accordingly I conveyed to Florence when, shortly afterwards, she and Edward came down from the tower. And I want you [the reader] *to understand that, from that moment until Edward and the girl and Florence were all dead together I had never the remotest glimpse, not the shadow of a suspicion, that there was anything wrong* [the affair between E and F], *as the saying is. ... How in the world should I get it? ... I was just a male sick nurse. ... I was a deceived husband. And that Leonora was pimping* [alluding to the affairs with Maisie and Nancy] *for Edward.'* (p. 81)
    The Protest scene   **Victim: deceived husband**   **Unreliable Narrator**

Frame 37: D accusing F of trying to reunite E and L when she was E's mistress.

'She should not have done it. She should not have done it.' (83)

F tried to convince L that her affair with E was of spiritual kind, and tried to reunite E to his wife, when L accused her,

"'You come to me straight out of his bed to tell me that is my proper place.'"
(p. 84)

                  Episodic link to Frame 19   **E and F affair**

Frame 38: L in her bedroom doing her hair when she reminded F of how L and F murdered MM.

"'You and I murdered her [Maisie Maidan] *between us.'"* (p. 84)

Maisie Maidan's death scenario (pp. 85–88)

Frame 39: L went up to MM's room on returning from the trip to M—
Frame 40: L found a letter addressed to her by M— expressing how L could buy her as an *adulteress* from her husband,

"'You paid money [to Bunny, her husband] *for me to come here* (74). ... You should not have done it, and we out of the same convent ... '"* (p. 86)

Frame 41: L found MM's boxes packed
Frame 42: Manager confirmed M— had paid her bill; she went up to the station to find out her way back to Chitral (Burma) (p. 86)
Frame 43: L decided to leave E to F and look after and provide for MM as her own child (MMonly 23 years of age)

'... *with an atmosphere of love until she could be returned to her poor young husband.*' (p. 87)

Frame 44: D narrates,

'[MM wandered in the hall] ... *sat down beside a screen that had Edward and Florence on the other side* ...[when MM overheard] *Florence was ... warning* [E] *as to the ravages he might be in making in the girl's heart.* ... *and Edward would have sentimentally assured her* ... *Maisie was just a poor little rat whose passage to Nauheim his wife had paid out of her pocket. That would have been enough to do the trick.*' (p. 86)

                                          F's manipulative nature

Frame 45: D narrates; L panicked and ran to see if MM had returned to her room. L wanted to take MM away from the *hideous place* [Nauheim] and *play the part of the mother*, when she found MM dead when attempting to strap up a great portmanteau,

> '*Maisie had died in the effort to strap up a great portmanteau. She died so grotesquely that her little body had fallen forward into the trunk, and it had closed upon her, ... The key was in her hand.*' (p. 88)

Frame 46: D narrates how L thought MM had committed suicide, L did not disclose the letter from MM to L, and how E thought that MM died of natural causes. E soon got over the death of MM and *never felt much remorse* (p. 88)

Part 2/I

Location: Nauheim
Year: August 4, 1901
Setting: Hotel Excelsior (p. 109)
Episode: Florence's heart condition: the conspiracy
   Jimmy episode: the fix
   Julius episode: for locked bedroom arrangement
   (F and D's marriage, the voyage on *Pocahontas*)

Frame 47: D describes his days in Stamford, Connecticutt and how he came to marry F (p. 92)
Frame 48: F's plan about Europe and marriage (pp. 93, 94)

> '*If I never so much as kissed Florence, she let me discover ... her simple wants. .... She wanted to marry a gentleman of leisure; she wanted a European establishment. She wanted her husband to have an English accent, an income of fifty thousand dollars a year from real estate ... And—she faintly hinted—she did not want much physical passion in the affair.*' (p. 93)
>   **F's marriage of convenience**

Frame 49: D narrates F's travels to Venice, and then to England, where she spent time at Stratford as paying guest to an aristocratic family called Bagshawe and stayed there for two months. They had to return to Stamford because of her uncle's business matters, but Jimmy stayed in Europe, and later joined the Dowells in Paris, when he stayed with them for 2 years.

Episodic link to Frame 4   **Florence Jimmy affair scenario**

Frame 50: F declared to her aunts her wish to marry D. F's aunts were not keen that F and D were planning to go away to Europe and thought of a *European career*. They also wanted to warn D of F's life being characterized by flirtations,

"'Don't do it, John. Don't do it. You're a good young man,' and she [Miss Emily] *added, ...* 'We ought to tell you more. But she's our dear sister's child.'" (p. 96)

D engaged berths on the *Pocahontas*, found that F had gone to visit her uncle in Waterbury to give him the news of her wish to marry D. However, her uncle was also not keen and D found that

'... *family* [Florence's uncle and aunts] *simply did not intend t her to marry ever in her life.*' (p. 97)

F's flirtatious nature

Frame 51: For the first time, D gets to know of F's heart condition, just as they were to go away for their voyage,

"'I wanted to know, so as to pack my trunks. ... I may be ill, you know. I guess my heart is a little like Uncle Hurlbird's. It runs in families.'" ...
  Now I wonder what had passed through Florence's mind during the two hours that she kept me waiting at the foot of the ladder. ... Till then, I fancy she had no settled plan in her mind. She certainly never mentioned her heart till that time.' (99, 101)

F's heart condition

Frame 52: F and D were married and sailed for Europe on the *Pocahontas* (p. 100)

Frame 53: Ship doctor warning D about F's heart,

'Florence went down into her cabin and her heart took her. An agitated stewardess came running up to me, and I running down. I got my directions how to behave to my wife. Most of them came from her, though it was the ship doctor who discreetly suggested to me that I had better refrain from manifestations of affection. ... I wonder, though, how Florence got the doctor to enter the conspiracy—the several doctors ... Anyhow, she and they tied me pretty well down—and Jimmy, of course, that dreary boy—...' (p. 101)

F's heart condition

The Jimmy (J) episode: F's bad fix   **Florence and Jimmy affair**

Frame 54: J joined F and D at Havre and lived with them in Paris for two years (p. 102)

Frame 55: J and F made rules for D about entering her bedroom,

'It was those two between them who really elaborated the rules. ... that fellow [Jimmy] impressed upon me that Florence needed most of all were sleep and privacy. ... So at ten o'clock at night the door closed upon Florence, ... And ten o'clock of the next morning she would come out of her door ... because she was nervous about thieves; ... It was pretty well thought out, you see.' (p. 103)

Deception Frame in retrospect

Frame 56: F later wanted to return to Fordingbridge, but was tied to Europe, as D was unwilling to let her cross the channel due to her heart condition,

'For the young man rubbed it so well into me that Florence would die if she crossed the Channel—... It fixed her and it frightened her.' (p. 104)

The fix

Frame 57: (1903) F sick of Jimmy and had taken on E (pp. 105, 108)

E and F affair

Frame 58: E got rid of J for *blackmailing* F (pp. 105, 108)

E and F affair

The Julius (Ju) episode (p. 107)

Frame 59: D narrates, F frightened for her life (107)
  Repeated Frame 56 **D's anger**   **Trigger factor**
Frame 60: Ju (aged 60, and valet for D) was to accompany D and F to Paris from Waterbury on the ferry and was to be in charge of the leather grip that contained the drugs for F.
Frame 61: F refused to let D take Ju to Paris.
Frame 62: overcome with grief that he (Ju) might not accompany F and D, Ju dropped the leather grip containing the drugs
Frame 63: D was furious,

'I saw red, I saw purple. I flew at Julius. ... I threatened to strangle him. ... that was Florence's first idea of my character. It affirmed ... to conceal from me the fact that she was not "a pure woman." For that was ... the mainspring of her fantastic actions [locked bedroom door arrangement, and heart condition]. *She was afraid that I should murder her.'* (p. 107)
  D's anger   **Trigger factor**

Frame 64: This made F conceal her true intentions, 'of not being a *pure woman*' (p. 107)
  F's secret
Frame 65: F feared D would murder her and thus made up the possibility of heart attack (p. 108)
  D's anger   **Trigger factor**
Frame 66: D narrates, *the girl* was NR, and lived with the Ashburnhams since the age of 13. L was her guardian and friend, while NR was like her child. E always called her '*the girl*' and described the affection they had for each other

'... *the evident affection he had for her and she for him.*' (p. 110)
  E and NR affair

Frame 67: D's testimonial to his friend E when he described how E never looked at any other woman, and '... *he talks of you* [Leonora] *as if you were the angels of God.*' (p. 112)
  Unreliable Narrator

Part 2/II

Location: Nauheim
Time: August 4, 1913
Setting: Hotel Excelsior (117)
Episode: Florence and Jimmy affair contd.

Frame 68: December 1904, E knocked J's teeth down his throat. (p. 114)
   Episodic link Frame 58   **Florence and Jimmy affair**
Frame 69: F called for more attention from E as time went on (p. 115)
                     E and F affair
Frame 70: F told D, her situation was too unbearable and she wanted to divorce him and go with E and settle in California (p. 116)
                     F sought divorce

Bagshawe incident (revelation of F's **conspiracy**)
August 4, 1913 *the last day of my absolute happiness* (p. 117)

Frame 71: D with Bagshawe at the hotel lounge at Excelsior (p. 117)
Frame 72: F first wanted to stay with L and D, while E and NR (*the girl*) went off to the concert at the Casino (p. 117)
Frame 73: L wanted NR to be chaperoned with E and wanted F to join them
Frame 74: D and L sat in the lounge waiting until 10pm
Frame 75: D came to know Bagshawe was from Ludlow Manor near Ludbury
    Repeated Frame 49   **Florence and Jimmy affair**
Frame 76: D saw F running. F rushed in through the swing doors, looked round to see Bagshawe speaking to D

'She saw the man who was talking to me. She stuck her hands over her face as if she wished to push her eyes out.' (118)
                     Bagshawe incident

2 Manipulated Context

Frame 77: Bagshawe surprised to find F, remarked,

"'By Jove: Florry Hurlbird. ... Do you know who that is?" he asked. "The last time I saw that girl she was coming out of the bedroom of a young man called Jimmy at five'oclock in the morning. In my house at Ledbury.'" (p. 118)

                   F and J affair

Frame 78: D pulled himself up to go up to F's room
Frame 79: August 4, 1913

First night F does not lock her room, lying dead,

'She had a little phial that rightly should have contained nitrate of amyl, in her right hand.' (p. 119)

       Episodic link to Frame 6   **F commits suicide**

Part 3/I

Location: Nauheim
Time: August 4, 1913
Setting: Hotel Excelsior
Episode: D's secret desire   **Cardinal point**

Frame 80: L reminded D of his remark,

"'Now I can marry the girl [Nancy].*" To which L replied, "of course you might marry her," and, when I asked whom, she answered: "The girl.'"* (123)
            Cardinal Point   **D's desire Frame**

Frame 81: D evaluating his remark above as having *dual personality,* one entirely unconscious of the other' (123)

D's dual personality

Location: Branshaw Manor (124)
Time: a month after E's funeral
Setting: L's study (125)
Episode: NR and Edward affair

Frame 82: L persuades D to stay at Branshaw (following E's death)
Frame 83: L said how it was stupid of F to commit suicide
Frame 84: D was not aware of F committed suicide, was not aware of the brown flask supposed to have amyl nitrate, containing prussic acid, and therefore thought that her heart would have been unable to stand the strain of running, therefore causing the heart attack. D narrates that E was not aware of F's intention, and believed F died of heart failure. Only L, the head of the police and hotelkeeper knew that F committed suicide. (p. 127)

        Prussic acid for amyl nitrate: Deception Frame
Frame 85: D's remark, *'Now I can marry the girl'.* (p. 129)
              Cardinal Point D's desire Frame

Year: August 4, 1913 (130)
Setting: Hotel Excelsior
Episode: NR and Edward affair contd.

Frame 86: E led NR up the alley to the Casino
Frame 87: E told D,

> "'... in his final outburst. I didn't pump him, I hadn't any motive. At the time I didn't in the least connect him with my wife.'" (p. 130)

Frame 88: E and NR go to the park and not to the Casino
Frame 89: E swore to D that he never had the slightest notion to enfold his arms around NR. They sat at one end of the bench (p. 132)
Frame 90: NR was glad, seemed that all bitterness of her father and mother were in the past and she had been rewarded. She did not make out any other meaning when E said that NR was the person he cared

about most. D realized this as the most monstrous thing: 'It is, I have no doubt, a most monstrous thing to attempt to corrupt a young girl just out of a convent', and E was anything but straight, upright and honorable. (pp. 133, 134)

D's cognitive hypothesis

Frame 91: D saw NR as the last woman with whom E would settle for good,

'... *this was the case with E.*' (136)

D's cognitive hypothesis

Frame 92: F heard E from behind the trees as N being the person he cared most (p. 137)

F's realization of E's feelings

Frame 93: E and N went out and F followed them immediately

E and NR affair

Frame 94: F ran back to the hotel with pallid face, clutching her dress over her heart; her face fell upon Bagshawe and D

E and NR affair

Frame 95: D speculating that Bagshawe was the determining influence in her suicide (p. 137)

D's cognitive hypothesis

Frame 96: L had known for many years, the flask contained prussic acid and not amyl nitrate and F would use it if her true relationship with J was ever discovered (p. 138)

Prussic acid for amyl nitrate: Deception Frame

Frame 97: D speculated, F's *mainspring of nature* was vanity

D's cognitive hypothesis

Frame 98: F wanted to be a *great lady* and retain D's respect (p. 138)

D's cognitive hypothesis

Frame 99: D's **secret,** that he was a rather greedy man, never discovered by F

D's dual personality   Dowell: **The motive**

Frame 100: D evaluated F as a person and her affair with J and this revelation as the factor to commit suicide (p. 140)

D's cognitive hypothesis

Frame 101: The significance of August 4, for F, D's repression of instinct, playing the trained poodle (p. 141)

Deceived husband: Victim

Frame 102: D's dual personality (p. 142)

D's dual personality

Frame 103: D in love with NR (Age: D 45 and NR 22)

'But, from that moment until her worse than death, I do not suppose that I much thought about anything else. ... Do you understand the feeling—... that you must get certain matters out of the way, smooth out certain fairly negligible complications before you can go to a place that has, during all your life, been a sort of dream city?' (p. 143)

Dowell: The motive

Frame 104: NR did not want to be nun (p. 143)

Frame 105: D could make NR happy

D's concealed desire

Frame 106: D did not want to present himself as *an old maid* (a nurse) to NR and left for USA after F's death (p. 144)

Frame 107: E's assurance
E regarded NR as his daughter
E had no motive (p. 132)

Repeated Frame 23   **Episodic link** to Frame 118

Frame 108: They sat at one end of the bench

Frame 109: NR said E was like father, a model of humanity

Frame 110: E realized what he was doing and D narrates,

'... wicked thing E ever did in his life. (p. 133) *... to corrupt a young girl just out of a convent'* (p. 134)

Frame 111: But E loved NR and had no idea of corrupting NR

Unreliable Narrator (Episodic link to Frame 110)

Repeated Frame 23   **E and NR Episode**

Part 3/II

Location: Branshaw Manor (Leonora's account)
Time: August 4, 1913 evening
Setting: Hotel Excelsior, three weeks after E's death D left for States
Episode: NR and Edward affair contd.

Frame 112: NR tried to go off alone with E. L kept NR under leash following the Casino event,

'She had guessed what had happened under the trees near the Casino.' (p. 145)

Frame 113: NR described to D her days at a convent, about her parents, and about her saturnalian nature. This frightened D (p. 147)
Fourth tale
Frame 114: NR received news of her mother's death (p. 149) but later NR received a letter from her mother in Glasgow (p. 243)
Unreliable Narrator
Frame 115: NR's father, Major Rufford, went away to India, and NR lived with Edward and Leonora
Frame 116: D narrating,

'Why she was like the sail of a ship, ... and to think she will never ... Why, she will never do anything again. I can't believe it...' (p. 150)
Restricted Repeated Frame 23: *the girl* Dowell: **The motive**
Frame 117: D gets back to the story of L stopping NR from going off alone with E (p. 152)
Repeated Frame 112

Frame 118: E started to drink a great deal every evening long after L and NR had gone to bed (p. 153). E excused himself and went to bed early, as he thought L had reproached him for trying to corrupt NR (p. 155)
Frame 119: L found E holding the image of a blessed virgin presented by NR. L slept for the first time, narrator eluding this as L started to trust her husband, and came round to believe E was not having an affair with NR (p. 157)

Part 3/III

Location: London (Branshaw Telegraph)
Year: 1913
Setting: Branshaw Manor house
Episode: NR and Edward affair contd.

Frame 120: L could now trust E with NR and she knew that NR could be trusted, L slackened in her vigilance of E and N being together, which was a mistake,

'This is perhaps the most miserable part of the story.' (p. 158)

Frame 121: D's summary of L's family, how L came to marry E, how L and E drifted apart

(pp. 159–173)

Frame 122: The Kilsyte case—how it came about. E was desperately unhappy as the estate affairs were not going well, partly due to his mad generosity and partly because he had too much responsibility,

'… to take upon his own shoulders the burden of his troop, of his regiment, of his estate and of half of his country.' (p. 174)

E saw a nursemaid crying in the train and tried to comfort her by kissing this pretty girl of nineteen. This led to E being tried in court. L supported E's actions, which eased immediate tension between E and L, but the case *did mentally a good deal of harm* (pp. 176, 183)
                    Edward's affairs and debts episode (Kilsyte case)

Part 3/IV

Year: 1907
Setting: Dowell in Paris (179), Philadelphia (181), E in London, Monte Carlo (p. 185)
Episode: Edward's other affairs (Grand Duke's mistress)

Frame 123: the Kilsyte case gave E's first realization of being capable of unfaithfulness,

'... *that girl* [nurse-maid in Kilsyte case] *appeared desirable to him—and Leonora completely unattractive.*' (p. 183)

E's visit to Monte Carlo relieved him from work and being a workaholic, but he got involved with the Spanish dancer, which cost him money, and L came to know of his affair

(pp. 186–190)

Part 3/V

Location: London
Year: 1904
Setting: Shimla, Chitral/India, Branshaw Manor
Episode: Edward's other affairs contd.
Edward's side of story

Frame 124: L and E left for India renting out Branshaw for seven years. L sold portraits of E's ancestors to pay off E's creditors (p. 195)
Frame 125: E and L in Shimla for their health where E had an affair with Mrs Basil (p. 196)
Frame 126: Major Basil discovered his wife's affair and blackmailed E for £300 or £400 (p. 200)
Frame 127: E in Chitral where he met Maisie Maidan (p. 201)
Frame 128: letter from Mrs Basil's to L enquiring about E's death (p. 201)
Frame 129: Ashburnhams at Chitral settled down as the model couple but did not speak to each other speak in private (201)
Repeated Frame 1
Frame 130: E keen to take MM to Europe from India and then to Nauheim for her heart, E a sentimentalist—the Maidan affair in Chitral (pp. 201–206)
Episodic link to Frames 25 and
Frame 131: L proposing to get back to Branshaw Manor (London) as the financial situation at the Manor house was sorted (p. 203)

Frame 132: E resigned from the army, hated L for trying to get E to be the dummy Lord (205)
Frame 133: L paid MM's husband to take his wife to Europe, E hated L for this

Leonora's side of story
Frame 134: L starved herself to save the house, and their fortune, while making sure E had his financial liberty. However, all her efforts went unnoticed by E,

'... did none of the good deeds that she did for her husband ever come through to him, or appear to him as good deeds. By what trick of mania could not he let her be as good to him as Mrs Basil was?' (p. 208)

L was afraid of scandals due to E's affairs and tried to keep MM's husband unsuspicious, L's desperate attempt to get back her husband from his string of affairs. She realiszed by making him happier, she would get back his love (p. 210)

Part 4/I

Dowell summarizing L and E's marriage
Year: September 1, 1913
The Protest scene (Frame 135)
According to D, it would have been good for L to get E back to Branshaw after MM died, not kept him on tight rein and threatened to take his bank account away from him (p. 226)

Frame 135: L trying to warn D about F making eyes at her husband,

"'Your wife is a harlot who is going to be my husband's mistress ..."'... A week after Maisie Maidan's death she was aware that Florence had become Edward's mistress.' (p. 221)

F's flirtatious nature

2 Manipulated Context   121

Frame 136: L's passion to get E to love her (pp. 215, 216)
L tried to believe E did not seduced M (p. 217)
E made advances to L (p. 218)
L took F's advice on dress sense (p. 218)
L's happiest moment was when E complemented her about her tight rein with money, when he spent money without giving a thought (p. 218)
   (Repeated Frame 139, 151) Reference to **E's generosity**
L realized, to keep E happy was to keep him well supplied with money and pretty girls (219)
Frame 137: F's attempt to bring L to a better frame of mind about E (pp. 223, 225)
Frame 138: F confessed to L about her affair with J. L was outraged,

> '*You* [Florence] *want to tell me that you are Edward's mistress. You can be. I* [Leonora] *have no use for him.*' (p. 222)
>
> E and F affair

F chose to confess to L,

> '"*She was afraid her spiritual advisers would blame her for deceiving me* [Dowell]. ... *I rather imagine that she would have preferred damnation to breaking my heart.*"' (p. 223)

F acknowledged E had mistreated L (p. 223)
   E wanted to be polygamist

Frame 139: NR (the girl) was on her way to India (34, 67, 226), when E bailed out a gardener from being acquitted for murder (p. 226)
   Restricted Repeated Frame 23: *the girl*   NR episode
Frame 140: D's frame of mind about F—F's *contaminating influence, was vulgar, unstoppable talker* (p. 214)
Frame 141: L should have taken E back after Maisie's death, *she acted wrongly* (215)

Frame 142: D requesting readers to consider *the Luther- Protest and L's agonies*
Frame 143: L's view of matrimony (p. 216)
Frame 144: Mental deterioration of L due to F (p. 222)

Part 4/II

Year: September 1, 1913
Setting: Waterbury, Branshaw
Episode: D in Waterbury to sort out his inheritance

Frame 145: D received an urgent cable from E to come to Branshaw (pp. 227, 25)

Repeated Frame 7
Frame 146: D in Waterbury to sort out his inheritance

D's inheritance
Frame 147: Unknown to D, F's aunts knew about E and F from a letter written by F before she died, which L had posted, (p. 229)

F's secret
Frame 148: D wanted to marry NR and give her a good life (230)

D's Desire Frame
Frame 149: At Branshaw, D realizes that NR was to be sent back to India to her father, as L realized,

'He [Edward] *was, she realised, gone from her for good.'* (233)

What happened is this:
Frame 150: On their return from Nauheim, NR nursed L for her headaches
Frame 151: The Selmes incident reported by NR to L which caused tension for L when E gave away an old Irish cob to one of the stable worker) (p. 241)

E's generosity

Part 4/III

Year: 1913
Setting: Branshaw House
Episode: E and NR affair contd.

Frame 152: NR's realization of E's love for her aunt L (p. 250)
Frame 153: NR realized E may love her, if he did not love L (p. 253)

> '... she gave way to the thought that she was in Edward's arms; that he was kissing her on her face that burned; on her shoulders that burned, and on her neck that was on fire.' (p. 259)

Frame 154: NR received letter from her mother in Glasgow (p. 260)

Part 4/IV

Year: 1913
Setting: Branshaw House
Episode: The triangle: E, NR affair and L

Frame 155: E dying of love for NR, and NR for E (p. 262)
Frame 156: L wanted NR to stay in Branshaw to save E, though it was decided NR should return to her father in India (p. 262)
Frame 157: L proposed divorce, if E wanted to marry NR (p. 263)

Part 4/V

Year: 1913
Setting: Branshaw House
Episode: The triangle E, NR and L contd.

Frame 158: The quote below sums up the way things end in the final part of the story

'*The end was plain ... <u>Edward must die, the girl must lose her reason because Edward died</u>—... that end, on that night, whilst Leonora sat in the girl's bedroom and Edward telephoned down below—that end was plainly manifest.*' (p. 268)

Abettor disposition

Frame 159: L marries Rodney Bayham (p. 269)
Frame 160: NR goes mad when she read the news of Edward's suicide.
    The miserable outcome: NR and Dowell   **Fourth tale**
Frame 161: It was decided that NR was to go back to England, as it was best for her to be with her father (270, 271)
    Episodic link Frame 7
Frame 162: D in England (Branshaw House) took care of NR
    The miserable outcome: NR and Dowell   **Fourth tale**
Frame 163: L and NR drove E mad (275)
Frame 164: E remembered the night when

'*the girl, in dim light, rising up at the foot of his bed. ... I am ready to belong to you—to save your life.*'
He answered: '*I don't want it; I don't want it; I don't want it.*' (278)

Part 4/VI

Year: 1913
Setting: Branshaw House
Episode: The triangle E, NR and L contd.

Frame 165: D arrived at Branshaw in the midst of the disagreement between E and L over N
    Episodic link to Frame 7
Frame 166: D realized NR was to return to India and to accompany E to witness her departure,

2 Manipulated Context 125

'Look here, old man [Dowell], *I wish you would drive with Nancy and me to the station to-morrow.'* (p. 287)

Frame 167: D wished to marry NR, but L was of the opinion that,

'... the girl ought to see a little more of life before taking such an important step.' (284)

                                                                   D's Desire Frame

Frame 168: following NR's return to India, E gets back to managing the Manor House

                                                                         (p. 289)

Frame 169: L happy to see that the NR affair was a passing phase (p. 293)

Frame 170: E in the stables one afternoon talking to D, a stable-boy brings a telegram, which reads,

'Safe Brindisi. Having rattling good time. Nancy.' (p. 293)

Frame 171: E got out a penknife from his waistcoat pocket, asked D to take the telegram to L, D realized E's intention but did not interfere with it

                                                                    E commits suicide

'And he looked at me with a direct, challenging, brow-beating glare. I guess I could see in my eyes that I didn't intend to hinder him. Why should I hinder him?' (p. 294)

Frame 172: D's summary of the story—the **villains** punished by suicide and madness
(p. 290)

                                                  D's Self-gratification: The moral

Frame 173: Heroine L was married to Rodney Bayham (p. 276), and became a happy wife (p. 290)

     The miserable outcome: NR and Dowell   **Fourth tale**

Frame 174: D's admission of being like E (p. 291)
Frame 175: D became the owner of Branshaw Manor. When NR went mad on hearing news of E's death, it was left for D to take care of her (p. 292)

Fourth tale
Frame 176: L's child to be brought *up by a Romanist* (p. 292)

Appendix 2e

Manipulated Contexts (murder mystery)

a. MC: *The Murder of Roger Ackroyd*
Frame 2: Dr. S met Mrs. F a week before she died,

> *'Her manner had been normal enough considering—well—considering every-thing.'* (15)

Frame 14: *'Could I do anything with the boy* [RP]*? I thought I could.'* (27)
Frame 21: Dr. S recalls,

> *'Suddenly before my* [Dr. S] *eyes there rose the picture of Ralph Paton and Mrs Ferrars side by side. .... I felt a momentary throb of anxiety. Supposing—oh! but surely that was impossible.'* (37)

Frame 29: Parker leaves the study to ring the police and Dr. S is alone in the study and narrates,

> *'I did what little had to be done'* (45)

Frame 33:

> *'If Parker heard anything about blackmail,* 'I said slowly, *'he must have been listening outside this door with his ear glued against the keyhole.'* ...
> Davis nodded. ...
> I took an *instant* decision. ...

And then and there narrated the whole events of the evening as I have set them down here. The inspector listened intently, occasionally interjecting a question.

... 'And you say that letter has completely disappeared? It looks bad—it looks very bad indeed. It gives us what we've been looking for—a motive. For the murder.' (57)

b. **MC:** *Cover Her Face*
Frame 1: Mrs. M remembered the ritual gathering of her guests for the summer church fete that took place three months before the killing of SJ

1. Exactly three months before the killing at Martingale Mrs Maxie gave a dinner party. 2. Years later, when the trial was a half-forgotten scandal and the headlines were yellowing on the newspaper lining of cupboard drawers, Eleanor Maxie looked back on that spring evening as the opening scene of tragedy. 3. Memory, selective and perverse, invested what had been a perfectly ordinary dinner party with an aura of foreboding and unease. 4. It became, in retrospect, a ritual gathering under one roof of victim and suspects, a staged preliminary to murder. 5. In fact not all the suspects had been present. 6. Felix Hearne, for one, was not at Martingale that week-end. 7. Yet, in her memory, he too sat at Mrs Maxie's table, watching with amused, sardonic eyes the opening antics of the players.

8. At the time, of course, the party was both ordinary and rather dull. ... 9. Mrs Maxie had just employed one of Miss Liddell's unmarried mothers as parlor-housemaid and the girl was waiting at the table for the first time. <u>*10. But the air of constraint which burdened the meal could hardly have been caused by the occasional presence of Sally Jupp who placed the dishes in front of Mrs Maxie and removed the plates with a dextrous efficiency which Miss Liddell noted with complacent approval.*</u> (5)

Cardinal point (underlined)
Frame 4: SJ's sudden and brief change of attitude from *Sally the submissive* to *Sally the enigma*, as Miss L noticed,

11. Miss Liddell watched Sally Jupp as she moved about the table. ... 12. Suddenly Miss Liddell was visited by an irrational spasm of affection. 13. Sally was really doing nicely ... Suddenly their eyes met. 14. For a full two seconds they looked at each other. Then Miss Liddell flushed and dropped her eyes. ...

15. *Confused and horrified she tried to analyze the extraordinary effect of that brief contact. ... she had read in the girl's eyes, not the submissive gratitude which had characterizes Sally Jupp. ... but amused contempt, a hint of conspiracy and a dislike which was almost frightening in its intensity.* 16. *Then the green eyes had dropped again and Sally the enigma became once more Sally the submissive, the subdued, ... She had recommended Sally without reserve. ...* 17. *The girl was a most superior type. ...* 18. *The decision had been taken.* 19. *It was too late to doubt its wisdom now.'* (10) 20. *'Miss Liddell was aware for the first time that the introduction of her favorite to Martingale might produce complications.* 21. <u>She could not be expected to foresee the magnitude of those complications nor that they would end in violent death.</u>' (10)

Cardinal point (underlined)

Frame 11: Sally overslept on the morning of the summer fete, as CB observes,

22. '*... Catherine remembered that there had been some trouble that morning* [the day of the annual church summer fete at Martingale House] *with Martha because the girl* [Sally] *had overslept. ... she had to rush to make up the lost time for she looked flushed and was, Catherine thought,* <u>concealing some excitement behind an outward air of docile efficiency</u>.' (36)

Sally's secret (conspiracy)

c. MC: *The Good Soldier*

The Protest scene

Frame 11: Dowell senses Florence was up to something,

'But on this occasion I <u>knew</u> that something was up. (49) ... I <u>must</u> say that, until the astonishment came [the Protest scene] *I got nothing but pleasure out of the little expedition.* (50) *I was aware of* <u>something treacherous, something frightful, something the evil</u> *in the day* (53)

Frame 12: At the museum in the city of M— Florence explains the letter about *the Protest* and compliments Edward,

'*It's because of that piece of paper* [draft of the Protest drawn up by Luther and others] *that you're honest, sober, industrious, provident and clean-lived. If it weren't for that piece of paper you'd be like the Irish or the Italians or the Poles, but particularly the Irish...*' (53)

Frame 13: Leonora reveals to Dowell the affair between E and F,

'"*I can't stand this,*"' *she said* [to Dowell] *with a most extraordinary passion; "I must get out of this. ... Don't you* [Dowell] *see?*" *she said,* "<u>*don't you see what's going on*</u> [*Florence was Edward's mistress ... committing adultery in hired rooms.* (83–84)]*?*" *The panic again stopped my heart. ... "Don't you see, ... of the eternal damnation of you and me and them*" [alluding to Florence and Edward who lack constancy] (55)

Episodic link to Frame 18, 20

Frame 36: D narrating L's reaction to F's comment in Frame 12,

'*It would be better if Florence said nothing at all against my co-religionists, because it is a point that I am touchy about.*'
  That was the hint that, accordingly I conveyed to Florence when, shortly afterwards, she and Edward came down from the tower. <u>*And I want you*</u> [the reader] <u>*to understand that, from that moment until Edward and the girl and Florence were all dead together I had never the remotest glimpse, not the shadow of a suspicion, that there was anything wrong*</u> [the affair between E and F], <u>*as the saying is. ... How in the world should I get it? ... I was just a male sick nurse. ... I was a deceived husband. And that Leonora was pimping*</u> [alluding to affairs with Maisie and Nancy] *for Edward.*' (81)

Frame 135: following the Protest scene, L warned D about F making eyes at her husband,

'"*Your wife is a harlot who is going to be my husband's mistress...*"'... *A week after Maisie Maidan's death* <u>*she was aware*</u> *that Florence* <u>*had become*</u> *Edward's mistress.*' (221)

The conspiracy

Frame 51: just as they were to go away for their voyage, D got to know of F's heart condition for the first time,

> "'I wanted to know, so as to pack my trunks. ... I may be ill, you know. I <u>guess</u> my heart is a little like Uncle Hurlbird's. It runs in families. ... "
> Now <u>I wonder what had passed</u> through Florence's mind during the two hours that she kept me waiting at the foot of the ladder. ... Till then, I fancy she had no settled plan in her mind. She <u>certainly never mentioned</u> her heart till that time.' (99, 101)

Frame 53: The ship doctor warned D about F's heart,

> 'Florence <u>went down</u> into her cabin and her heart took her. An <u>agitated stewardess came running up</u> to me, and I <u>running</u> down. I <u>got my directions</u> how <u>to behave</u> to my wife. Most of them <u>came</u> from her, though it was the ship doctor who <u>discreetly suggested</u> to me that I <u>had better refrain</u> from manifestations of affection. ... I <u>wonder</u>, though, how Florence <u>got the doctor to enter</u> the conspiracy—the several doctors ... Anyhow, she and they <u>tied me pretty well down</u>—and Jimmy, of course, that dreary boy—...' (101)

<u>Bagshawe incident</u>: revelation of F's conspiracy   (<u>Florence and Jimmy affair</u>)
August 4, 1913 *the last day of my absolute happiness* (117)

Frame 71: D with Bagshawe at the hotel lounge at Excelsior (117)
Frame 73: L wanted NR to be chaperoned with E and wanted F to join them
Frame 74: D and L sat in the lounge waiting until 10 p.m.
Frame 75: Bagshawe, from Ludlow Manor near Ludbury, joined D at the hotel lounge
Frame 76: D then saw F running back into the hotel lounge. F rushed in at the swing doors, looked round to see Bagshawe speaking to D

> 'She saw the man who was talking to me. She stuck her hands over her face <u>as if she wished to push her eyes out</u>.' (118)

Frame 77: Bagshawe surprised to find F, and remarks,

"'*By Jove: Florry Hurlbird.*'... '*Do you know who that is?*' he asked. '*The last time I saw that girl she was coming out of the bedroom of a young man called Jimmy at five'oclock in the morning. In my house at Ledbury.*'" (118)   (Florence and Jimmy affair)

Frame 78: D pulls himself up after this to go up to F's room
Frame 79: August 4, 1913, first night F does not lock her room, lying dead,

'*She had a little phial that rightly should have contained nitrate of amyl, in her right hand.*' (119)
Episodic link to Frame 6

F's intention according to character D in narrative

Frame 37: D accusing F of trying to reunite E and L when she was Edward's mistress.

"'*She should not have done it. She should not have done it.*'" (83)

F tried to convince L about her affair with E was of spiritual kind, and tried to reunite Edward to his wife, when L accused her,

'*You come to me straight out of his bed to tell me that is my proper place.*' (84)
Episodic link to Frames 1, 25

Frame 38: L in her bedroom doing her hair when reminded F of how L and F murdered MM.

'*You and I murdered her* [Maisie Maidan] *between us.*' (84)

Frame 140: D's **frame of mind**—F's *contaminating influence, was vulgar, unstoppable talker* (214)

The cardinal point

Frame 80: L reminded D of his remark,

> "'*Now I can marry the girl* [Nancy].' To which L replied, "of course you might marry her," and, when I asked whom, she answered: "The girl."'" (123)

Frame 85: D's remark, '*Now I can marry the girl*'. (129)

Cardinal point for D

Frame 87: D's retrospective narration on E's actions in the Casino Park with NR,

> 'And it appears that Edward Ashburnham *led the girl* not up the dark trees of the park. Edward Ashburnham *told me* all this in his final outburst. I *have told* you that, upon that occasion, he became deucedly vocal. I *didn't pump* him, I *hadn't* any motive. At the time I *didn't* in the least connect him with my wife.' (130)
> (The motive: Dowell)

Frame 92: F heard E from behind the tress as NR being the person he cared most (137)

Cardinal point for F's storyworld

Frame 110: E realizes what he was doing and D narrates,

> '... wicked thing E ever did in his life. (133) ... to corrupt a young girl just out of a convent (134)

Frame 116: D narrating,

> 'Why she was like the sail of a ship, ... And to *think she will never* ... Why, she *will never do anything* again. I *can't believe* it...' (150)

Restricted context   (The motive: Dowell)

Frame 120: L could trust E with NR and she knew that NR could be trusted, L slackened her vigilance of E and NR being together, which was a mistake,

> 'This *is perhaps* the most miserable part of the story.' (158)

Frame 158: The quote below sums up the end to come in this final part of the story.

'The end <u>was</u> plain ... Edward <u>must</u> die, the girl <u>must lose her reason</u> because Edward died—... that end, on that night, whilst Leonora <u>sat</u> in the girl's bedroom and Edward <u>telephoned</u> down below—that end was plainly manifest.' (268)

Frame 170: E in the stables one afternoon talking to D. A stable-boy brought a telegram, which read,

'Safe Brindisi. Having rattling good time. Nancy.' (293)

Frame 171: E got out a penknife from his waistcoat pocket, asked D to take the telegram to L, D realized E's intention but did not interfere with E's intention to **commit suicide**

'And he <u>looked</u> at me with a direct, challenging, brow-beating glare. I <u>guess</u> I could see in my eyes that I <u>didn't intend</u> to hinder him. Why <u>should I hinder him</u>?' (294)

The hierarchical perspective at integrational level thus accounted for the **intention** behind the narration of the story. Intentionality relative to the desire or motive served as the cardinal point in respective sub narratives in the embedded storyworld, which affected the discourse of offender participant's narrative thread. Real motive behind the deaths or crimes thus becomes evident which would otherwise be lost in the intended gaze in a mixed-up chronological sequence of events in the plot summary of the story.

Bibliography

Texts

James, P.D. 1974. *Cover Her Face*. 3rd ed. London: Penguin Books.

Sources cited: Chapter 2

Barthes, R. 1977. *Image Music Text*. Trans. Stephen Heath, 81–124. London: Fontana Press.
Bloor, T., and M. Bloor. 2013. *The Functional Analysis of English*. 3rd ed., 95–96. London: Routledge.
Bock, J. Kathryn, and Richard K. Warren. 1985. Conceptual Accessibility and Syntactic Structure in Sentence Formulation. *Cognition* 21: 47–67.
Boltanski, L. 2014. *Mysteries and Conspiracies*. Trans. Catherine Porter, 3, 49, 77, 102, 123, 132–133, 144–145. Cambridge: Polity Press.
Brown, G., and George Yule. 1983. *Discourse Analysis*. Cambridge, New York, Melbourne: Cambridge University Press.
Canter, D.V. 1994. *Criminal Shadows: Inside the Mind of the Seriel Killer*. London, UK: Harper Collins.
Chatman, Seymour. 1978. *Story Discourse: Narrative Structure in Fiction and Film*. Ithaca, NY: Cornell University Press.
Clark, B. 2014. Stylistics and Relevance Theory. In *The Routledge Handbook of Stylistics*, ed. Michael Burke, 155–174. Oxon: Routledge.
Coulthard, Malcolm, and Alison Johnson. 2007. *An Introduction to Forensic Linguistics: Language in Evidence*. London and New York: Routledge.
Cowburn, Malcolm. 2005. Confidentiality and Public Protection: Ethical Dilemmas in Qualitative Research with Adult Male Sex Offenders. *Journal of Sexual Aggression* 11 (1): 49–63.
Danesi, Marcel. 2014. *Signs of Crime: Introducing Forensic Semiotics*. Berlin: De Gruyter Mouton.
De Beaugrande, Robert-Alain, and Wolfgang Ulrich Dressler. 1981. *Introduction to Text Linguistics*. London and New York: Longman. Translation (1981), German edition (1972).
Emmott, Catherine. 1992. Splitting the Referent: An Introduction to Narrative Enactors. In *Advances in Systemic Linguistics: Recent Theory and Practice*, ed. Martin Davis and Louise Ravelli, 221–228. London: Pinter Publishers.
———. 1997, 1999, reprinted 2004. *Narrative Comprehension: A Discourse Perspective*. Oxford: Oxford University Press.
———. 2014. Schema Theory in Stylistics. In *The Routledge Handbook of Stylistics*, ed. M. Burke, 268–289. London and New York: Routledge.
Genette, G. 1988. *Narrative Discourse Revisited*, 13–19, 21–77. Ithaca, NY: Cornell University Press.

Glenn, A.L., and A. Raine. 2014. Neurocriminology: Implications for the Punishment, Prediction and Prevention of Criminal Behaviour. *Nature Reviews Neuroscience* 15 (1): 54–63. doi:10.1038/Nrn3640.

Goffman, E. 1975. *Frame Analysis. An Essay on the Organization of Experience.* Harmondsworth: Penguin Books.

Grice, H.P. 1975. Logic and Conversation. In *Syntax and Semantics III: Speech Acts*, ed. P. Cole and J. Morgan. New York: Academic Press. Reprint, A. Jaworski and N. Coupland, eds. *The Discourse Reader*, 2nd ed., 66–77. London: Routledge.

Herman, D. 2007. Cognition, Emotion, and Consciousness. In *The Cambridge Companion to Narrative*, ed. David Herman, 245–259. Cambridge: Cambridge University Press.

Holmes, Ronald M., and Stephen T. Holmes, eds. 1998. *Contemporary Perspectives on Serial Murder*. London and New Delhi: Sage Publications International Educational and Professional Publisher.

Howard, Richard, and Jonathan Culler. 1977. *Tzvetan Todorov: The Poetics of Prose*. Ithaca, NY: Cornell University Press.

Lemert, Charles, and Ann Branaman. 1997. *The Goffman Reader*. USA, UK, Australia: Blackwell Publishing.

Metzing, Dieter, ed. 1980. *Frame Conceptions and Text Understanding*. Berlin and New York: Walter de Gruyter.

Minsky, M. 1980. A Framework for Representing Knowledge. In *Frame Analysis: Text Understanding*, ed. D. Metzing. Berlin: Walter de Gruyter.

Moser, Thomas C. 2008. Introduction. In *The Good Soldier*, ed. Ford Madox Ford, 3rd ed. Oxford: OUP.

Palmer, Alan. 2004. *Fictional Minds*. Lincoln and London: University of Nebraska Press.

Prince, Gerald. 1982. *Narratology: The Form and Functioning of Narrative*. Berlin, New York, and Amsterdam: Mouton Publishers.

Quirk, Randolph, Sidney Greenbaum, Geoffrey Leech, and Jan Svartvik. 1985. *A Comprehensive Grammar of the English Language*. London: Longman.

Rimmon-Kenan, S. 2002. *Narrative Fiction: Contemporary Poetics*, C2. London: Routledge.

Rosenberg, St.T. 1980. Frame-based Text Processing. In *Frame Analysis: Text Understanding*, ed. D. Metzing. Berlin: Walter de Gruyter.

Schank, R.C., and R. Abelson. 1977. *Scripts, Plans, Goals and Understanding*. Hillsdale, NJ: Lawrence Erlbaum.

Scott, Jeremy. 2009. *The Demotic Voice in Contemporary British Fiction*. New York: Palgrave Macmillan.
Short, Mick. 1996. *Exploring the Language of Poems, Plays and Prose: Learning About Language*, 306–325. London and New York: Routledge.
Sperber, Dan, and Deirdre Wilson. 1986. *Relevance: Communications and Cognition*. Oxford: Basil Blackwell.
Sternberg, M. 2003. Universals of Narrative and Their Cognitivist Fortunes (I). *Poetics Today* 24 (2): 395.
Todorov, T. 1987. *The Poetics of Prose*. Trans. Richard Howard and Jonathan Culler, 43–52. Ithaca, NY: Cornell University Press. Reprint, 1977.
Van Dijk, T.A. 1977. *Text and Context. Explorations in the Semantics and Pragmatics of Discourse*. London: Longman.
Van Gelder, Jean-Louis, and Stijn Van Deale. 2014. Innovative Data Collection Methods in Criminological Research: Editorial Introduction. *Crime Science a Springer Open Journal* 3 (6): 1–6. Accessed 24 September 2014. http://www.crimesciencejournal.com/content/3/1/6
Weizman, E., and M. Dascal. 1991. On Clues and Cues: Strategies of Text-Understanding. *Journal of Literary Semantics* XX (1): 19–29.
Widdowson, H.G. 2004. *Text, Context, Pretext: Critical Issues in Discourse Analysis*, 36–57. Oxford: Blackwell.
Williams, Malcolm, and W. Paul Vogt. 2011. *The Sage Handbook of Innovation in Social Research Methods*. Los Angeles, London, New Delhi, Singapore, Washington, DC: Sage.
Wilson, Deirdre. 2011. UCLWPL 2011. 01. 70, 69–80. Available at: https://pdfs.semanticscholar.org/0b0d/a8c9faf335310d08d2fc78db8341eb0c2318.pdf (Accessed 28 February 2017)

3

Double Function

3.1 Introduction

At the micro level, criminality is investigated in a functional environment called the **double function** (DF). DF, as a performed act by a speaker or narrator in fictional context, is a process by which participants create vantage points for participant disposition, which is not obvious in prospective or in retrospective narration. DF takes advantage of the cluster of internal *analeptic* or *proleptic* **references**[1] for deliberate misrepresentations in a discourse-based frame slot. DF enables tellers to encode information at multiple levels as *hypothetical scenarios* or *alternative storyworlds*, as in Herman (2009) and Polanyi (1982) respectively. These **scenarios** or **storyworlds** in the prospective and retrospective narration are simultaneous constructions, and are in

---

[1] *Anachronies*—Departure from the order in which events occurred in the story is termed by Genette (1988) as *anachrony*. An achronological earlier incident is related later in text; it is a movement back in time and is an *analepsis* (flashback). An achronological future event is related textually before its time; it is a movement forward in time before the presentation of intermediate events and is a *prolepsis* (flashforward). (Toolan 2001: p. 43)

anticipation. As a result, there is ambiguity, indeterminacy or *polysemy*[2] of information produced for the narrative interest of conflict between curiosity and suspense. In the alternation of time in tense, DF enables speakers to manipulate causality in the sequence of events, while DF is also a means for the story recipient, or for an analyst, to decode the polysemantic properties of the tense-alternation technique. The DF of the participant role for an **implicit post-murder participant disposition** is argued by Flanders (2014) in her article on the perpetrator Dr. Sheppard, 'Concealment and Revelation: An Interdisciplinary Approach to Reader Suspense'.

In this chapter, the dichotomy of **narrating discourse** from that of the **narrated** is analyzed for participant disposition in anticipation, as opposed to a disposition in retrospection and in prospection.

Frames carry thematic facts in the narrative discourse and can be **episodic** (unchronological). On distinguishing them as types of frames: recall, repeated, withheld beside a restricted frame (as in Emmott and Minsky), it was possible in Chap. 2 to monitor the manner of event representation, which can be a major event, an action, or a happening that advances the plot and changes its state. Therefore these frames as microcontexts become significant in the long and complex plot form of crime narratives.

In frame analysis it is also possible to evaluate constructed microcontexts. For example, the **iterative focus** in repeated frames, the **omissions** (gaps) between frames otherwise missed in narrative prospection, the **cause and effect** in episodic links formulated or left unconnected in the overall plot form for illusion, and finally the formed **narrative relation** based on a different **agentive parameter**. This processing of manipulation causes **manipulated scenarios** (a referential layer at the point where narrative options arose) and creates alternative narratives based on the PoR of the concealer and the revelator. It was also found in Chap. 2 that the narrative option(s) that arise are centered round an inexplicit discourse referent with bidirectional functionality and double functionality of a cardinal function. Its bidirectional functionality, when processed

---

[2] *Polysemy*—Poses the question of meaning, to choose some and ignore others from a floating chain of meaning/signified in signifiers.

in the **priming** and **focusing** of narrative **events**, and when **mapped** on to the telling and showing axis of a narrative thread, surface **primed events** (Chap. 2, note 14) relative to a concealed agent parameter, their **motive**(s) behind the reality as a secondary narrative, which was distinct from the actual frame sequence in the first story of crime.

These *primed events* form the referential layer for MC and center round a **bidirectional discourse referent** in the participant utterance constituting a **post-offence** vantage point of the offender. As argued in Chap. 2, an MC is not a restricted frame. It is where **frame modification** is withheld or is omitted to alter the frame sequence of a specific event in prospection, and the narration here is in anticipation. All this is because of the first crime committed and consequently a new logical consecution of events being constructed (the **logical fallacy**). In the second crime that consequently follows, a victim suspect is instantiated, as in a whodunit crime narrative. The readers are restricted to this modification in the narrative's **concrete external time and place**. However, readers are provided with a text condition for a desired contextual effect (meaning) such as the simultaneous concurrence of temporal sequences in anticipation (duality) in which events are dynamic, but manipulated in the way that events unfold, and found in the linguistic analysis of stylistic functions using,

- Genette's (1988) model on anachrony,
- alternation techniques (as a functional environment)
- the concept of storyworlds in Palmer (2004) Herman (2009) and Polanyi (1982)

Analysis of this functional environment is carried out in the MCs (Appendix 2e) analyzed in Chap. 2. The context is the frames of the referential layer of DR for MCs in Figs. 2.1, 2.4 and the short extract adopted from CHF.

The order in Genette (1988: p. 14) is: *story* (the completed events) as in an historical narrative, *narrating*/**discourse** (the narrative act of the historian), and *narrative*/plot form (the product of that that act). This chapter is concerned with the **issue of narrating** in the narrative. In plot form, in Chap. 2, the degree of complexity employed in telling the story was examined. This chapter takes up this degree of complexity in MC and examines the desired **transformation**[3] through the study of language and narrative situations.

The model of **anachrony** in narrative situation (Genette 1988: p. 31) is the study of the temporal order of events (flashback/*analepsis* or flashforward/*prolepsis*) relative to perspective/**focalization: who sees** (the question of mood) and **who tells** (a question of who tells/ speaks/ voice). The functional role of *analepsis* in retrospection is for exposition, simultaneity, digression or delaying in narrative discourse. *Prolepsis* as a narrative function in prospection is for advance notice whether immediate or long-range. Genette in *Narrative Discourse* (1988: p. 66) is also concerned with alterations of these anachronic structures within the dominant modal course of the narrative such as *paralipsis* (the holding back of information that would be logical in the focalization selected at the point of narration) or *paralepsis* (excess of information relative to the type of focalization selected). These types of **focalizations** distinguished in Genette are narrative with a vision from behind for **omniscience** and termed *zero focalization*; narrative with point of view, *a reflector* with selective omniscience, and restricted vision termed *internal focalization*; or a biased behaviorist for an objective narrative with the possibility of excluded thoughts, and termed as *external focalization*.

Genette's observation is interesting when the author comments that

'... *two types of focalizations cannot be confused unless the author has constructed (focalized) his narrative in a manner that is not only incoherent but chaotic.*' (p. 75)

in examining the manipulated plot forms in their nonlinear structure and in the themes as microcontexts, the *incoherent and chaotic* manner of **episodic links** is evident in the narrative frame of each story. Especially, when participants are reconsidered as **focalizers**, the telling and showing of the narrative relations in the narrative axis (Figs. 2.2, 2.3, 2.5 and 2.6) displayed difference in the logical sequence of constructed events when

---

[3] *Transformation*—A transition from an earlier state to a later and resultant state e.g. *I walk* implies and is contrasted to a state of departure and a state of arrival. (Genette 1988: p. 19)

based on the cardinal point relative to the motive behind the death and not the actual crime that took place.

These secondary narratives are for the narrating participant who is the **object**[4] and based on the principle of (participant) reference, and treated as a *fictive subject*.[5] At the micro level of the narrative, the agentive role framed as fictive subject creates an **implicit post-murder participant disposition** with a double function for simultaneous reporting, narrating and evaluating a **three-dimensional (re)reading** of clauses in MCs. This makes the narration in MCs resort less to **retrospection** (accommodates the full scope of a storyworld's history) than to **prospection** (narratorial commentary that inhibits drawing connections among earlier and later events or prospection into the future of the respective narrative world) and to **anticipation** (characteristic of the authorial narrative type). The authorial role is **omnipresent**, and with **paraliptic focalization** holds back information that would be logically produced under the dominant modal position of a homodiegetic or heterodiegetic narrator of the moment.

As an embedded narrative, a MC entails concurrence of two temporal sequences (duality) in which the events that happened are dynamic. However, MC is manipulated in the way that, at the cardinal point, the narrative content relates to the '*displacement* [or change] *of focus* ... [for the] *embedding of* [participant motive] *but not of focalizations*. ... [As Genette] *do*[es] *not believe the focus of the narrative can be at two points simultaneous* [that is, the] *embedding of focalizations* ... [of the] *focalized in the second degree, by the focalizer who is focalized*' (Genette 1988: p. 77). At a cardinal point, the narrative then is **simultaneous** in the **merger** of the **focalizer** with the **focalized**, and the **merger** is of the participant disposition at that point in the narrative, which displays in a deep grammatical distinction (agent, patient, instrument, beneficiary or as an instrument) the motivation to achieve a certain goal, therefore,

---

[4] *Object*—Refers to a person or other entity involved in the situation (Huddleston and Pullum 2005: p. 23). In criminal context, the person is an object (a narrative object, NO) of the criminal narrative.

[5] Fictive subject is the narrative focus [which] coincides with a character, who then becomes the fictive "subject" of all perceptions, including those that concern himself as object. (Genette 1988: p. 74)

(indirectly) initiating sequences of actions; manipulating them by design or by action in the order of the plot. For example,

> '... [as] *types of agent in the deep grammatical distinction: a rogue is not always in control of his actions—he is often manipulated as instrument or patient;* [while] *a villain is definitely agent, but often covertly so, working through an instrument, and always a persecutor of patients.*' (Fowler 1977: p. 31)

The discourse of the embedded narrative in MCs is thus an assertion of the **fictive consciousness** of reality distinct from real subjects. The inner transparency in the discourse is in the way of conveying the words or thoughts of the fictive subject both in first- and third-person narratives, allowing flexibility for the break between fiction and assertion. The point subsequently made by Ricoeur, translated by Kathleen McLaughlin and David Pellauer (1985: p. 88) is,

> '*The question will then be to determine by which special narrative means the narrative is constituted as the discourse of a narrator recounting the discourse of the characters. The notions of point of view and of narrative voice designate two of these means.*'

The discourse of the narrator conflates with the character's changed disposition in the narrative, such as a post-murder participant disposition, where the participant is in the modal position of the moment. Following Genette (1988: p. 74), there will be then,

> '... *alterations of the dominant modal course of a narrative like paralipsis (reduced information that would be logically produced under the types of focalization selected)* [or] *paralepsis (information in excess of what is called for by the logic of the type selected).*'

The above modal positions are based on the **principle of focalization**, and using this principle, form the study of participant disposition in this chapter. Following narratologies in Genette (1988: p. 16), this is ***thematic*** (an analysis of the story or the narrative content) rather than *modal* (an analysis of narrative as mode of representation of stories) as in Chap. 2.

In characterizing a narrative as *thematic* with a *mode of representation*, the narrative is, with its own spatiotemporal parameters, designated in a character/ participant's (perpetrator) thoughts and **outside** the diegetic narrative in retrospection. A storyworld, as an '**interdiegesis space**' (Chap. 4, note 1), is formulated in narrative in the **dual function** of linguistic aspects based on the offending participant disposition. The **spatiotemporal universe** of this storyworld is relevant to the modal position of the participant moment in the narrative, which is simultaneously in prospection and in anticipation. This **micronarrative** is formed from the chains of actions and events at the horizontal and vertical axis of the interdiegesis space, where the narrative comes with its own language of suspense. In linguistic dysfunctions like **functional contrast** and in the **deviation from the norm**, when analyzed in its functional environment of the dual function in tense aspect and modality and within the context of distortion, form a **secondary universe** generated for the narrating-I, or the narrating-he. This is a **performed narrative**, where there is **merger** of the spatiotemporal diegetic universe of the 'focalizer-I' or 'focalizer-he' with the focalized in the **simultaneity of narrating, reporting and evaluating** for re-reading of the Narrator-offender's present with the past and to its future.

This chapter is concerned with this form of **narrative act** in the MCs, which are **utterances** in prospection (an outlook, a view over a scene) and an **authorial foresight** in anticipation (advance notice whether immediate or later), in the **interdiegesis space** of the secondary narrative formulated within the first story of crime. Prospective narration here is regarded as distinct from the narration in anticipation. In Genette (1988: p. 31), the traditional position of *analepses* is in retrospection while *prolepsis* is in anticipation (Genette 1988: p. 30). **Utterance** in Ricoeur (1985: p. 88) becomes the **discourse of a character**, where the shift from the **narrated action** is towards the **mimesis of the character** and is accounted for in Riceour by stylistic features like point of view and narrative voice. However, in this chapter, this shift is accounted for in the tense aspect, and then in Chap. 4 in the linguistic dysfunctions for simultaneity of omission and restricted revelation in the **metanarrative**.[6]

Before the shift analysis from **narrative action** to **character discourse** of the **narrative object** in transitivity and modality, the principle of dual function is made clear which is necessary to understand the shift in the discourses.

3.2 The Double Function (DF) Principle

DF is based on the principle of conversational historical present (CHP) (Wolfson 1982), where the CHP tense alternates with simple past tense in such a way that simple past tense is substitutable for CHP without change in referential meaning. For example, there is referentially no difference between the underlined particle verbs in the excerpts below.

> '*It came about six months later and the guy is picking up one hundred pounds now ....*'
> and
> '*So about a year went by. I was picking up two hundred pounds off the floor, you know, ...*'

This is a characteristic of **performed narratives**. In Wolfson, CHP refers only to the time at which the narrated event took place and not to the moment of speaking, or to the moment at which the narrative is told. This makes CHP restricted in its function. Characteristically in performed narratives, CHP is not necessarily found in all verbs where it might be used. For example, in a simple past tense form could substitute a verb in simple CHP. The following underlined verb from Wolfson (1982: p. 4) is in CHP progressive,

> '*A couple of years ago I'm going to Miami from New York.*'

---

[6] *Metanarrative*—Is an overarching intellectual scheme, which claims to help us understand some aspect of modern life in order to legitimate their own knowledge (e.g. Darwinism evolutionism). (Wales 2001: p. 264)

3 Double Function   145

This may be transformed into past progressive tense with no change in referential meaning:

'A couple of years ago I was going to Miami from New York.' (My emphasis)

In this use, the present progressive is equivalent to past progressive; similarly, the present perfect is also the equivalent of its past form without a change in referential meaning,

'All of a sudden, I get a letter that I've been accepted.'   Versus
'All of a sudden I got a letter that I had been accepted.' (Wolfson 1982: p. 4).

Narrative discourse in fiction is not similar to that of performed stories. There are other past tense forms in the narratives which are not CHP and do not have the characteristics of substitutability with past tense. The CHP perfect form is rare in conversational narrative, but not in fictional narrative. The choice made in an **utterance** in narration is for **reported actions** (narrated event), or the **action of reporting** causing two **reference points** (Benveniste, 1956 in Wolfson, 1982: 5) in narration. The **default tense** in written narrative is related to the narrated event. Historic Present (HP), like CHP, may contrast with past tense in conversational narratives. Similarly, depending on the **situational context** of the speaker, the addressee, the goal and the spatiotemporal parameter of the interaction in fictional narrative, the **reference time** in the story narrative may contrast with other uses of tense depending on the **intentionality** of the writer.

For instance, for a situational context like **distortion**, certain linguistic features are used for stylistic effects to create realism, and to affect reader anticipation in prospective narration. Like in CHP, categories of present tense may be related to the moment of speaking for giving an opinion, for making a comment or for explaining something which is a general truth or an aside. Similarly, a past tense verb form may express the judgment of the speaker related to the moment of speaking, where it is not the narrated event. As in the example from Wolfson (1982: p. 7) below, when the speaker expresses opinion towards the behavior of the subject in the relative clause,

'She was standing in the rain, which wasn't smart.' (My emphasis)

Here, the text as an utterance contains **two processes** in verb tenses respectively:

(a) the **reported action** or the narrated event, according to Jacobson,
(b) the **action of reporting**, according to Benveniste in Wolfson (1982).

In addition, like functioning *shifters* (*last night* would refer to the *night before* the moment of speaking) and *connectors* (the *night before* the event, which is the subject of the narrative), the utterance constitutes a **form-meaning relationship** in language. Functioning shifters and connectors are time place co-ordinates in Brown and Yule (1983). In the above **discourse markers** thus, an **interdiegesis space** is conditioned within the situational context of the detective narrative, where in the **merger** of the focalizer with the focalized, a formulated **fictive subject** (Chap. 4) has duality of role with **simultaneous reference points** in verb tenses as the grammar of **character discourse**. As internal focalization, the focus here coincides with a character, who then becomes the *fictive subject* (Genette 1988: p. 74) of all perceptions, including that concern himself as object.

As events in fictional narratives are not necessarily told in the order in which they occurred, and can be recapitulated, an **alternation technique** as a **narrative act** is particularly effective in such discourses. In alternation, the participant as the speaker in the narrative restructures the recapitulation of past events to allow the individual's way of looking at the world to come through, as seen in Chap. 2 with the same utterance as the mediation point in the participant's respective narrative thread (Figs. 2.1–2.6).

Furthermore, the **switch** or the shift in story-oriented verbs comes at the crucial point in the narrative, for narrative options. This functional device as a narrative act is also employed to partition events at the most dramatic point in the narrative (Wolfson 1982: p. 51), and in the offender context to switch to another verb tense which also focuses attention on the different roles or entities of the same participant in the story. The discourse function of tense switch (as alternation) is not neces-

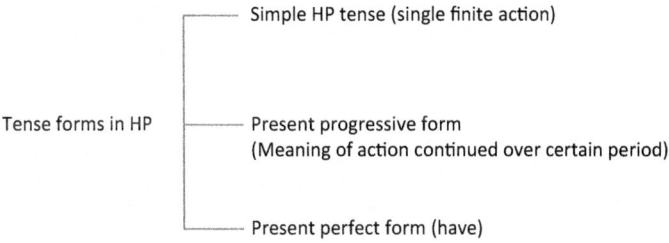

Fig. 3.1 Tense forms in HP

sarily limited between the CHP and past tense, but also includes tense relevant to the dominant modal position in the narrative and **intentionality induced** tense form relevant to the participant disposition at the moment of narration. This is **distinct from the moment** related to the narrated event. Note that, the functional environment for DF is relevant to the participant (character) discourse set in the moment of narration. This function is similar to Benveniste's (narrative) **connector** connecting the action of reporting, with other storyworlds enabling a **three-dimensional** re-reading of a narrative situation in retrospection, where there is **distortion** in prospection by manipulating the reader in anticipation. This **intersequencing** of narration emulates a narrative circumstance in tense forms (Fig. 3.1) for the storyworld as an interdiegesis space for a fictive subject, distinct from the storyworld of participant as retrospective character in the story narrative. The concept of storyworlds (Herman 2009 and Polanyi 1982) is discussed further below.

3.3 Storyworlds: Inter diegesis Space in the Narrated World

Herman states,

> '*Storyworld* (SW) *evoked implicitly or explicitly is a mental model of situations and events recounted. As global representations storyworld enables analysts and interpreters alike, to frame inferences about situations, characters, and occurrences mentioned implicitly or explicitly—who did what to and with whom, when, where, why and in what manner.*' (My emphasis) (2007: p. 107)

The multifacetedness of SW is indicated as representational practices in microstructural approaches such as *textual cues* (the deictic center, the contextual effects) and *textual markers* (modal auxiliary verbs and preposition) which typically encompass **the given world, the private world** or **sub-world** consisting of desires, beliefs, fantasies, intentions, and imaginative projections. Readers this way can **sift** out the domain of factual occurrences from the elliptical or distorted versions of events in the microstructure of the narrated world (e.g. a **sub-world** of **desire**).

From a pluralist stance, in both narrative and non-narrative contexts, Goodman (in Herman 2009: p. 110) identifies five **world-making** procedures, for constructing worlds out of other worlds. One of which, the *deformation* procedure, is about corrections or **distortions** according to a participant point of view, and is of importance in relation to MCs. By **mapping** textual cues on to the sub-world occupied by the narrator of the storyworld it is possible to realize the surface vantage point of the **experiencing-I** from the **narrating-I**. For example, as **internal focalization**, perceptual verbs, spatial prepositions and adverbs encode a perceptual position of the experiencing-I (**story-NOW**) or the narrating-I (**discourse-NOW**) (chapter 1: 96). The time frame encoded in perceptual verbs is centered round the time of telling, and is **motivated** according to the narrative purpose of obscuring the real hierarchy of events, and prompting the listener not to **recenter** to the fictional world, but **relocate** (in prospection) to the alternative **re-created** storyworld in retrospection.

This **definition** of **SW** is concerned with inference making of the **represented world**; **how** the narrator says it from **how** it really is. According to Polanyi (in Tannen 1982) this represented SW has its own spatiotemporal parameter and **enactor** (different versions of participant) and is not wedded to one vantage point, but the **enactor** as teller switches from one vantage point to other to recount tales of other worlds. Sometimes an enactor speaks from two worlds at once. There is **collapse** of viewpoints which is foregrounded by textual cues, as *discourse-shifters*, like the deictics, demonstratives and pronouns also mentioned above. This switch is relative to a character in the story (Polanyi 1982: p. 157), index to a disposition like the fictive subject in the secondary narrative embedded in the primary narrative.

This **alternative storyworld** indexed in tense forms (Fig. 3.1) is relative to the **teller** in the SW, whose **backgrounded disposition** has **affected** the merger of the SWs, demonstrating the relevance of the second embedded story to the offender circumstances in the moment of telling. Here there is **movement between worlds** in the **simultaneous encoding and decoding** taking place in the **real 'now'**, in which telling takes place in a **real 'here'** and the **real 'I'** who is speaking to the (fictive) listener in the fictional narrative. This is unlike Polanyi's conversational narrative embedded in the conversation, but a **sub-world** which has an embedded participant disposition in anticipation.

No part of literary text actually takes place in the real world, but **model** the **moment of speaking** and an **embedding context**. To capture the simultaneous encoding and decoding, the relationship formed between sentences for semantic representation in the SW, Polanyi (1982: p. 166) suggests **discourse markers** which enable the analyst to distinguish whether the teller is reporting or commenting, if a **modeled persona** is operating as 'I' in the world of the story in literary text. The analyst might want to identify this persona, by assigning a semantic representation to every sentence in the alternative storyworld (like the MC), to capture the relationship between the **constructed** and the **actual storyworld**. Like Polanyi's discourse shifters, an *exit talk*, a *swing phrase*,[7] there are linguistic dysfunctions (Chap. 4) which enables the speaker to merge discourse worlds with the main SW; making distinct the **enactor disposition** from the **default narrator** or the **indexed character** as the **teller**.

---

[7] *Discourse shifters*—Swing phrase and exit talk are **discourse shifters** manipulating the speaker's way back and forth from the storyworld and inserted back into the embedding conversation. **Exit talk** elicits 'acceptance talk' on the part of the listeners. Events of the **storyworld** are ended and the teller has begun to elicit responses and remarks from the listeners, giving them the chance to demonstrate their understanding and appreciation of the story. **Swing phrase** on the other hand, effects the movement between worlds: the **storytelling world** and the **storyworld**. For example, after having narrated an incident of being held at gunpoint, the speaker explains to other listeners her inability to remember the person who was holding the gun to her head, and says, 'If it ever happens to you …'. As continuation of *exit talk*, the speaker is making it clear her inability to remember what her assailant was wearing. But in the context of the story, in this **swing phrase** the speaker switches the talk back into the story in the pronoun **you** (the listeners) instead of the general you in the Storytelling world. (My emphasis) (Polanyi, in Tannen 1982: pp. 165–166)

3.4 Narrative Act: Narrating Discourse and Narrated Discourse

In the light of created storyworlds based on the switch from the default narrative tense as the functional device, the analysis below addresses the question posed in Ricoeur (1985: p. 88) about the narrative means to recount the **discourse of the characters** (**mimesis** of characters) from the **narrative action**. To recount discourse from action, Ricoeur suggests the need for another narrative technique which is necessary in addition to voice and point of view. The **alternation technique** as another **narrative act** is here suggested to report the **'goings on'** in the story, to determine where the narrator is standing when switching between narrating positions of the teller in the narrative. Traditionally, narrators speak from one vantage point at a time. This gets complicated when there is conflation of participant disposition, the **'here' and 'I' and 'this' of the characters** with the **'here' and 'I' and 'this' of the narrator**. This switch is studied by analysis of tense and aspect to work out and distinguish the vantage points in storyworlds.

Tense alternation technique as a narrative means also sets a functional environment for the operation of the **narrative conflict** between suspense and curiosity or conflict between mystery and suspense for gaps in crime narratives. The following quote from Sternberg explains and subsequently illustrates these functional operations within the narrative's overall **intersequencing** of retrospection, prospection, recognition, and (I argue) anticipation.

> 'Suspense arises from rival scenarios about the future: from the discrepancy between <u>what the telling lets us readers know about the happening</u> (e.g. the conflict....) at any moment and what lies ahead, ambiguous because yet unresolved in the world. Its fellow universals [surprise and curiosity] rather involve manipulations of the past, which the tale communicates in a sequence discontinuous with the happening. ... for curiosity: for knowing that we do not know, we go forward with our mind on the <u>gapped antecedents</u>, trying to infer (bridge, compose) them in retrospect. For surprise, however, the narrative first unobtrusively gaps or twists its chronology, then unexpectedly discloses to us our misreading

3 Double Function   151

and enforces a corrective rereading in late re-cognition.' (My emphasis) (Sternberg 2003: p. 327)

The three narrative universals accordingly fulfil the possibilities of a **complicating action** in the narrative: from an early-to-late development with its untimely openness, as seen in **microcontexts** in Chap. 2. The **intentionality (concealed motive)** in the story, as untimely openness affected the **episodic links** in the plot form of the story, where re sequencing of the narrative order produces **narrative gaps** or twists in which past events occur. MCs are such discourses and are akin to Sternberg's narrative *surprise*; where the MC is an index for false understanding and which call for realignment. However, *curiosity* throws the reader forward into the opacity of opaqueness, while narrative *suspense* in MC signals that the past has been deformed into an alternative formation. The alternative chronological sequence indicated in the logical fallacy is the narrative curiosity answered, while MC is a narrative suspense where there is accounting of the false understanding deliberated in the episodic links of the narrative form.

The alternation technique as a functional environment then enables the linguistically informed reader to understand the realignment that takes place at the micro-level (clausal level) in the embedded storyworld (**sub-world**) which is parallel to the default modal position of a homodiegetic or heterodiegetic narrator of the moment. In relation to genre, and with respect to literary criticism, the parallel narration is described by Sussex as,

'… *the story of crime takes a polygenetic approach, in which the literary evolution of a new type of writing takes place.*' (2010: p. 6)

The *polygenetic approach* as the new type of writing is achieved in the flexibility gained in collapsing vantage points for inner transparency as in the **embedding of focalizations**. For instance, in Mieke Bal a *focalization in second degree*, Genette argues is *a displacement of focus*. This difference of opinion, as seen in the example cited below, is due to **participant status**. Participants can be voluntary agents of their actions, reported in the material and mental process respectively and...; hence there is **displacement of focus**, rather than the vantage points of the same participant in a **narrating disposition**, separate from the **narrated discourse**, due to the embedding of different storyworlds at any one point in the narration. This is evident when we compare the following underlined material.

1. '*She watched him drink and felt a sudden pang of desire at the sight of his mouth pressing against the rim of the glass. But he felt so weary that he refused to share that pang*'. (My emphasis) (Genette 1988: p. 76)
2. '*But the air of constraint which burdened the meal could hardly have been caused by the occasional presence of Sally Jupp who placed the dishes in front of Mrs Maxie and removed the plates with a dextrous efficiency which Miss Liddell noted with complacent approval.*' (p. 5) (CHF)
3. Parker <u>leaves</u> the study to ring the police; Dr. S is alone in the study and narrates,

'*I did <u>what little</u> had to be done.*' (p. 45) (Ackroyd)

If a single teller, for example the perpetrator in crime fiction, made all the utterances in above three sentences, in 1 the **displacement of focus** is from the participant *she* to participant *he*, but the **modal position** remains unchanged unlike the verb phrases underlined in 2 and 3. In 2, the vantage position of the teller in a third-person narration shifts from a **reflector** with selective omniscience to **zero focalization**, while it is the **reverse** in 3, from zero focalization to a **reflector** with first-person narration. In *could hardly have been caused*, the time and space as context co-ordinate of the teller is **outside the utterance**, and joins with the focalized *Sally Jupp* and *Miss Liddell*. Following Polanyi's (1982: p. 158) the **deictic discourse shifter** '*here*' joins the participants' **space** in the telling, as well as in time, 'The *new apartment'll be better for her since it costs $300. Here she pays $450.*' In the shift from the default narrative past tense to tense aspect, there is a **collapsing** of the reference points of the teller, which effect a **merger** in tense aspect. As well as the **dichotomy** of storyworlds (Fig. 3.2 below) caused by tense alternation within the conversation in which the narration is embedded, tense alternation also

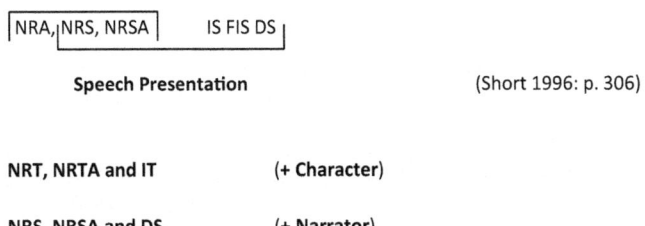

Fig. 3.2 Narrator intervention

demonstrates the relevance of the story to the **circumstance** in, 2. '... *the air of constraint which burdened the meal*'; and in 3. '... *what little had to be done*,' obtained at the moment of telling in the narrative. The presence of the teller in 2 and 3 has a **double disposition** of the principal narrator and an **inexplicit disposition** (intermediary status in Chap. 4) embedded within the principal disposition in order to move forward the narrative in tense aspect in 2 and 3, which constitutes a **narrative curiosity** for story suspense (not narrative universal suspense in retrospection) by the sudden shift in tense form. Notably, this suspense constituted in the tense shift is without the narrative content to go with it. The **withheld** circumstance is indexed in the tense shift; linguistically aware readers then become aware of this **content gap** due to tense alternation, constituting a **narrative conflict** between narrative universals, suspense and curiosity.

Alternation as a technique is a **narrator intervention** device. In **simultaneous narration**, the present is given value against the backgrounded contrast in the past tense, where the past does not give the reader the same heightened feeling, as does the present. The 'narrator in **diegesis**' (Genette 1988: p. 83) then makes linguistic choices in the utterance **affected** by this process of **simultaneous** retrospection and prospection in anticipation in the narrative. A **secondary fictional time** (such as future tense in past) is constituted in this technique to create a dichotomy of storyworlds, to obtain credibility and accuracy for the evaluation of an event, instead of obtaining veracity (truthfulness) of a story. As an **internal evaluation device**, the alternation technique is a marked form, the participant narrator undertakes the crucial task of articulating the point of an event in the story and its tellability. This effect is achieved in functions affected by the tense alternation like,

- Simultaneity of narration (*homodiegeticization*) in both homodiegetic and heterodiegetic modal course of a narrative, which has atemporal (**transitory**) value for tipping over into character discourses from narrative actions, and vice versa.
- Like a discourse shifter, the point of alternation shifts the vantage point for distinct participant disposition, which would be otherwise blurred.
- Important events or points are partitioned off from each other in the story (Schiffrin (1981) in Toolan 1988: p. 167).

The time framework for the alternation technique is the temporal distance manifested between **narrating the discourse** and the **narrated discourse (actions)**. In this **double system of variations**, the boundary between narrator and character in a particular modal discourse (B(N)+be, A(N)+ve narrative modes in Chap. 4) is maintained by grammatical distinctions concerning the persons and the verb tenses. Consistency of a tense type is the unmarked option. In the structures of the historic tense (HP) form, the double system of narration also includes the progressive and perfect aspect. Such as,

In tense and aspect the reference points for SWs are,

Table 3.1 Storyworld reference points

Following the definition of SW in section **3.3**, with classification of three types of narration on p. **141** and corresponding function (distortion for manipulation) on p. **138**, the different **storyworlds** in relation to the **double system of narration** are,

- **SW a**–The storyworld in relation to the **reference points** of the **modal narrator**
  –The storyworld (a i in retrospection)
  –The 'now' of time of speaking (a ii in prospection)
- **SW b**–The storyworld in relation to the reference points of a **character** (in retrospection)
- **SW c**–The storyworld constructed in relation to the reference points of **participant** positioned **outside** the storyworld **in anticipation** (narrator as **reflector** commenting, acting in anticipation). For example, *Ackroyd*: '*Could I do anything with the boy?*'

3 Double Function 155

In the alternation from the default narrative tense, the narrator is **not to be wedded** to one viewpoint but speaks from different standpoints to attain a **displacement of focus** in the narrative, such as in the simultaneity of,

- The **omniscient narrator** who knows everything, who can see everywhere.
- A **restricted, external narrator** who reports what an uninvolved character (such as an **offender**) present in the scene might reasonably notice.
- A **character** in the story involved in the action at the time it occurred.

The choices in Table 3.2 represent a participant in speech or thought in SWs. As semantic structuring, this stylistic means help us further to analyze the character discourse, distinct from narrator intervention, the **utterance statement dichotomies** in narrated discourse.

DS and DT contrast can bring out the external and internal world distinctions of characters, such as,

'You think too much, old man,' he said. (**Participant external world**)

As opposed to the character internal world in,

But you enjoyed killing the dentuso, he thought. (**Character internal world**)

Within a narration, it is also felt that the narrator was taking on the character's viewpoint. Authors have choices to represent character speech affecting meaning and viewpoint, and therefore **affecting** the focus from where the narration takes place. In adopting the Speech and thought discussion from Short (1996: chapter 10),

Table 3.2 The character in speech (S) and thought (T)

Direct focus	(towards character)
Direct speech (DS)	Direct thought (DT)
'Oliver, you will be late', she said.	'He will be late', she thought.
(External world)	(Internal world)

(Hemingway, *The Old Man and the Sea*, Triad Panter edition. (1976), p. 61 in Short 1996: p. 313)

Indirect focus	(towards character)
Indirect speech (IS)	Indirect thought (IT)
She said that Oliver will be late.	She thought that he would be late.

From 'towards Character', DS and DT form, the move in free (F) forms is 'towards **narrator**' (**N**) **control** and **N viewpoint**. **Free indirect thought (FIT)** and **Free indirect speech (FIS)** as **mixed forms**, have markedly different effects. For instance,
Free indirect speech (FIS) underlined   (towards narrator)

'So that was the first part of the story. Czech troops out, Russian troops in. Got it?' <u>Smiley said yes, he thought he had his mind round it so far.</u>
(John Le Carré, *Tinker, Tailor, Soldier, Spy*, Chapter 28, in Short 1996: p. 307)

As we see in the example for FIS, as a **mixed form** there is initial verbal response, *yes* and the informal lexis, *had his mind round it so far*, which is typical of DS features, while subordination, tense, pronoun and deictics is typical of IS. There is **narrator filtration** in textual cues, distancing from the original speech for a **muted, guarded and ironic tone** of the **narrating-I** in discourse-Now in the narrative.
Free indirect thought (FIT)   (towards character)

He was bound to be late!

Conversely, in **FIT** we feel **close** to the character, this *close effect* is opposite to FIS, where in FIS there is a **distancing effect**, which influences one to feel distanced from the character. This is often a vehicle for **irony**.
Event narration: narration of actions and events
As we move along the scale from DS to NRS the control and **influence of the narrator's viewpoint** over the reporting of what the character said gets stronger and stronger. **Narrative report of act (NRA)** and **speech act (NRSA)** are the speech equivalents of the narration of actions and events, and are closer to the character in thought presentation, while report of speech is more akin to narrator intervention.

3.5 Storyworld Analysis

In the notion of storyworld and the speech and thought of participants for the displacement of focus, the analysis in Tables 3.3, 3.4 and 3.5 below is about the **multilevel** and **multifunctional semantic structuring** of SWs in the MCs from Chap. 2. In tense alternation and in participant thought, the analysis is about the several points of view peeking through the **utterance** as the cardinal point in the story narrative. Here, the **semantic structuring** of the SW in respect to the double function in storyworlds is first worked out, and then in Chap. 4 this understanding is taken up for the analysis of **polysemantic properties of suspense** in linguistic ambiguities in stylistic functions such as in,

- Functional contrast
- Deviation from norm

In tense alternation the temporal SW organization (Table 3.1) are identified along with the speech and thought presentation at a clausal level to work out the **close-up focus** from the distancing effect created by the same participant (perpetrator) in three MCs.

3.5.1 Case Study: Storyworld for Offender Dr. Sheppard

Frames constituting the MC in *Ackroyd* are,

Frame 2: Dr. S met Mrs. Ferrars a week before she died,

> 'Her manner had been normal enough considering—well—considering everything.' (p. 15)

Frame 14:

> 'Could I do anything with the boy [Ralph Paton]? I thought I could.' (p. 27)

Cardinal point
Frame 21: Dr. S recalls,

'Suddenly before my [Dr. S] eyes there rose the picture of Ralph Paton and Mrs. Ferrars side by side. .... I felt a momentary throb of anxiety. Supposing—oh! but surely that was impossible.' (p. 37)

Frame 29: Parker leaves the study to ring the police. Dr. S is alone in the study and narrates,

'I did what little had to be done.' (p. 45)

Frame 37:

*"'If Parker heard anything about blackmail," I said slowly, "he must have been listening outside this door with his ear glued against the keyhole. ... "
Davis nodded. ...
I took an instant decision. ...
And then and there narrated the whole events of the evening as I have set them down here. The inspector listened intently, occasionally interjecting a question.
... "And you say that letter has completely disappeared? It looks bad – it looks very bad indeed. It gives us what we've been looking for – a motive for the murder."'* (p. 57)

Storyworlds in *Ackroyd*

Note: Time orientation markers are marked tense, modality and adverbials as circumstances/ complements are <u>underlined</u>; the default narrative tense is past tense form.
Explanation

There is alternation of SWs. The teller creates an alternative re-created SW in anticipation (clauses 1, 2, 3, 4) for a prospective narrative in clauses 5, 6 and 7. Frames 2, 14 and 21 are **authorial foresight** in anticipation alternating with utterance in prospection (clause 6 and 7) conveying a view on the scene reflecting Parker as the possible perpetrator due to the information about the letter in retrospection in clause 9, Frame 37. In **textual cues** like the deictics there is merger of vantage points of

Table 3.3 Storyworlds in *Ackroyd*

Frames	Storyworlds (reference points)	Time orientation markers
Frame 2	FIT + Character SW c, narration in anticipation (Narrator/reflector positioned outside the past storyworld) **Collapse** of narrator with **offender** standpoint with respect to progressive aspect	1. Her *manner had been normal enough <u>considering</u>—well—<u>considering everything</u>.* (p. 15)
Frame 14 **Cardinal point**	FIT + Character SW c, narration in anticipation (Narrator/reflector positioned outside the past storyworld, when evaluating an event in anticipation but restricted in anticipation) (**modality**) for an involved participant **Merger** of narrator and **offender**, framing RP as a suspect, the blackmailer of Mrs. F	2. *'Could I **do** <u>anything</u> with the boy [Ralph Paton]? I **thought** I <u>could</u>.'* (p. 27)
Frame 21	FIT + Character SW c, narration in anticipation (Narrator/reflector positioned outside the past storyworld relative to the moment of narration). **Collapse** of standpoint with respect to progressive aspect *supposing*. **Merger** of **offender** and narrator.	3. *'Suddenly before my* [Dr. Sheppard] *eyes there **rose** the picture of Ralph Paton and Mrs Ferrars side by side. ..... I **felt** a momentary throb of anxiety. <u>Supposing</u>—oh! but surely that **was** impossible.'* (p. 37)
Frame 29	NRA + Narrator SW a ii, narration in retrospection. Narrator positioned in the past relative to the moment of narration. A **post-murder event**, when *what little... done* refers to the removal of the Dictaphone, it was placed to go off at 9.30 pm long after Dr. S murdered RA at 9 pm. This was to create a confusion; RA was talking to someone when he was actually dead. This information is **withheld** in clause 4. **Merger** of the character/offender's past perfective with the narrator in past tense.	4. *'I **did** <u>what little</u> **had to be done**.'* (p. 45)

Frame 37

DS + Character	5. "'If Parker heard anything about blackmail," **I said** slowly. "he <u>must</u> <u>have been listening outside this</u> <u>door with his ear glued against the</u> <u>keyhole." ...</u> Davis nodded. ...	
SW a i, narration in retrospection (Narrator positioned in the past relative to the moment of narration).	6. **I took** an instant decision. ...'	
6. NRA + Narrator		
SW a ii, narration in prospection (Narrator relative to the moment of narration).	7. 'And <u>then</u> and <u>there</u> narrated the whole events of the evening as I <u>have set</u> them down <u>here</u> [the journal written by Dr. Sheppard whilst in prison]. 8. The inspector listened <u>intently</u>, occasionally interjecting a question.'	
7. NRA + Narrator		
SW a i, narration in **retrospection**, deictic **then** and **there**, and SW a ii, narration in **prospection**, deictic **here** with **present perfective have set**.	... 9. "'And you say that letter <u>has</u> <u>completely disappeared</u>? It <u>looks</u> <u>bad</u>—it looks very bad indeed. It <u>gives us what we've been looking</u> <u>for</u>—a <u>motive</u>. For the murder."' (p. 57)	
Merger of **post-conviction** standpoint, *here* and *have set* with **offender** standpoint, *then* and *there*.		
9. DS + Character		
SW b, narration in retrospection (Mimesis of inspector).		

3 Double Function   161

Table 3.4 Storyworlds in CHF

Frames	Storyworlds (reference points)	Time orientation markers
Frame 1	NRA + **Narrator** SW i a, narration in retrospection	10–19. *gave, was a half-forgotten scandal, were yellowing, looked back, invested what had been, became, had been present, was not, he too sat….watching, had just employed, was waiting, burdened … could hardly have been caused, placed, removed, noted*
Cardinal point	burdened … <u>could hardly have been caused</u> FIT + **Character** SW c, narration in anticipation. **Merger** of character and narrator **(modality)** as an involved participant.	
Frame 4	NRA + **Narrator** SW a i, narration in retrospection <u>could not be expected to foresee, would end</u> FIT + **Character** (SW c, narration in anticipation) **Merger (modality)** as an involved participant **Merger** of character and narrator. *might produce, could not be expected to foresee, would end* (SW c, narration in anticipation)	20–21. *watched, moved, was visited, was really doing, flushed, dropped, tried, had read, was almost frightening, had dropped, became, had recommended, was, had been taken, was too late to doubt, was aware, might produce, could not be expected to foresee, would end*
Cardinal point		
Frame 11	NRA + **Character** (anticipation in aspectual verb form) (SW c, narration in anticipation).	22. *remembered, had been some trouble, had overslept, had to rush to make up, looked flushed and was concealing*

Table 3.5 Storyworlds in TGS

Frames	Storyworlds (reference points)	Time orientation markers
Frame 11	*knew, came, was aware* – FIT + **Character** Deictic *this* SW c, narration in anticipation *this, must say* SW c, narration in anticipation	23. 'But on *this* occasion I <u>knew</u> that something was up.' (p. 49) … I *must* say that, until the astonishment <u>came</u> [the Protest scene] I got nothing but pleasure out of the little expedition.' (p. 50) I was aware of something treacherous, <u>something</u> frightful, <u>something</u> the evil in the day' (p. 53)
Frame 12	*is because, are honest, If it weren't for that piece of paper you'd be…* DS + **Character** SW b, narration in retrospection (mimesis of character Florence).	24. '"It's because of that piece of paper [draft of the Protest drawn up by Luther and others] that you're honest, sober, industrious, provident and clean-lived. If it weren't for that piece of paper you'd be like the Irish or the Italians or the Poles, but particularly the Irish…"' (p. 53)
Frame 13	*can't stand, must get out of this, don't you see what's going on, committing adultery, stopped* DS + **Character** SW b, narration in retrospection (mimesis of character Leonora). *stopped my heart* … NRT + **Narrator** SW b, narration in retrospection (narrator positioned in the past)	25. '"I can't stand this," she said [to Dowell] with a most extraordinary passion; "I must get out of this." … Don't you [Dowell] see?" she said, "don't you see what's going on [Florence was Edward's mistress … 'committing adultery in hired rooms'. (pp. 83–84)]?"' 26. 'The panic again <u>stopped</u> my heart. … "Don't you see, " … of the eternal damnation of you and me and them [alluding to Florence and Edward who lack constancy]' (p. 55)

(continued)

3 Double Function   163

Table 3.5 (continued)

Frames	Storyworlds (reference points)	Time orientation markers
Frame 36	DS + **Character** SW b, narration in retrospection (mimesis of character Leonora). 28. *was, conveyed, came down* NRA + **Narrator** SW a i, narration in retrospection (Narrator reflecting in adverbial *accordingly*). 29. *want you* [reader] *to understand, that moment, had never the remotest glimpse, as saying is …* IS + **Character** SW c, narration in anticipation (In deictic *that* narrator positioned in the moment of speaking). 30. *was a male sick nurse, was a deceived husband* FIT + **Character** SW c, narration in anticipation. 31. *was pimping* SW c, narration in anticipation. **Merger** of character (deceived husband) and narrator.	27. '"It would be better if Florence said nothing at all against my co-religionists, because it is a point that I am touchy about."' 28. 'That was the hint that, accordingly I conveyed to Florence when, shortly afterwards, she and Edward came down from the tower.' 29. 'And I want you [the reader] to understand that, from that moment until Edward and the girl and Florence were all dead together I had never the remotest glimpse, not the shadow of a suspicion, that there was anything wrong [the affair between E and F].' 30. 'as the saying is. … How in the world should I get it? … I was just a male sick nurse. … I was a deceived husband.' 31. 'And that Leonora was pimping [alluding to Maisie and Nancy affair] for Edward.' (p. 81)

Frame 135	32. going to be	32. '"Your wife is a harlot who is going to be my husband's mistress …."'
	DS + **Character**	
	SW a i, narration in retrospection (mimesis of character Leonora).	
	33. was aware, had become	33. 'A week after Maisie Maiden's death she <u>was aware</u> that Florence <u>had become</u> Edward's mistress.' (221)
	NRA + **Narrator**	
	SW a i, narration in retrospection (teller/narrator positioned in the past).	
Frame 51	34. wanted to know, may be ill, you know, I guess my heart is, runs	34. '"I wanted to know, so as to pack my trunks." …. I may be ill, you know. I guess my heart is a little like Uncle Hurlbird's. It runs in families. …"'
	DS + **Character**	
	SW b, narration in retrospection (mimesis of character Florence)	
	35. Now, wonder what had passed, kept me waiting, then, had no settled plan, certainly never mentioned	35. '<u>Now</u> I <u>wonder</u> what <u>had passed</u> through Florence's mind during the two hours that she <u>kept me waiting</u> at the foot of the ladder. ….'
	FIT + **Character**	36. 'Till <u>then</u>, I fancy she <u>had no settled plan</u> in her mind. She <u>certainly never mentioned</u> her heart till <u>that time.</u>' (p. 99)
	SW c, narration in anticipation (Teller/narrator reflecting in adverbials, certainly and DS verb fancy).	
	Merger of narrator and character.	

(continued)

Table 3.5 (continued)

Frames	Storyworlds (reference points)	Time orientation markers
Frame 53	37. went down, agitated stewardess came running, running down, got my directions, to behave, them came from her, was the ship doctor who discreetly suggested, had better refrain NRA and NRT + **Narrator** SW a i, narration in retrospection (narrator positioned in the past). 38. wonder, got the doctor to enter, tied me pretty well down NRT + **Narrator** SW c, narration in anticipation (Narrator reflecting in adverbials anyhow, mental process wonder).	37. 'Florence <u>went down</u> into her cabin and her heart took her. An agitated stewardess <u>came running</u> up to me, and I <u>running</u> down. I <u>got</u> my directions how to behave to my wife. Most of them <u>came</u> from her, though it <u>was</u> the ship doctor who discreetly <u>suggested</u> to me that I <u>had better refrain</u> from manifestations of affection. ...' 38. 'I <u>wonder</u>, though, how Florence got the doctor to enter the conspiracy—the several doctors ... <u>Anyhow</u> she and they tied me pretty well down—and Jimmy, of course, that dreary boy—.' (p. 101)
Frame 76	39. saw the man ... was talking to me, stuck her hands NRA + **Narrator** SW a i, narration in retrospection (Character reflecting in subordination).	39. 'She saw the man who was talking to me. She stuck her hands over her face <u>as if she wished</u> to push her eyes out.' (p. 118)
Frame 77	saw ... she was coming out ... called DS + **Character** SW a i, narration in retrospection (Mimesis of character Bagshawe).	40. '"By Jove: Florry Hurlbird." ... "Do you know who that is?" he asked. "The last time I saw that girl she was coming out of the bedroom of a young man called Jimmy at five o'clock in the morning. In my house at Ledbury."' (p. 118)
Frame 79	had ... that rightly should have contained NRA + **Narrator** SW a i, narration in retrospection (modality). **Merger** of narrator and character in modality.	41. 'She had a little phial that <u>rightly should have contained</u> nitrate of amyl, in her right hand.' (p. 119)

Frame 37	42. *should not have done it, should not have done it* FIT + **Character** SW c, narration in anticipation (Narrator reflecting in modality *should*).	42. 'She should not have done it. She should not have done it.' (p. 83)
Frame 38	43. DS + **Character** SW a i, narration in retrospection (mimesis of character Leonora). DS + **Character** SW b, narration in retrospection	43. '"You come to me straight out of his bed to tell me that is my proper place."' (p. 84) 44. '"You and I murdered her [Maisie Maiden] between us."' (p. 84)
Frame 80 **Cardinal point**	45 and 46 DS + **Character** Dowell and Leonora SW a i, narration in retrospection (mimesis of character Dowell and Leonora)	45. '"Now I can marry the girl [Nancy]."' To which L replied, "of course you might marry her," and, when I asked whom, she answered: "The girl."' (p. 123)
Frame 85 Frame 87 The motive: Dowell	47 and 48. *led the girl, told me, that occasion, at the time* FIT + **Character** SW a i, narration in retrospection (Narrator reflecting in adverbial *appear*) 49. *didn't pump him, hadn't any motive, didn't in the least connect* NRT&A + **Narrator** SW c, in anticipation (Narrator reflecting in **negation**).	46. D's remark, '"Now I <u>can</u> marry the girl."' (p. 129) 47. 'And it appears that Edward Ashburnham led the girl not up the dark trees of the park.' 48. 'Edward Ashburnham told me all this in his final outburst.' 49. 'I have told you that, upon that occasion, he became deucedly vocal.' 50.' I didn't pump him, I hadn't any motive.' 'At the time I didn't in the least connect him with my wife.' (p. 130)
Frame 110	*ever did in his life, to corrupt* NRT + **Narrator** SW c, narration in anticipation Narrator reflecting in evaluative adjectives *wicked*.	51. '… wicked thing Edward ever did in his life.' (p. 133)' … to corrupt a young girl from convent' (p. 134)

(continued)

3 Double Function 167

Table 3.5 (continued)

Frames	Storyworlds (reference points)	Time orientation markers
Frame 116 Restricted context Narrative conflict of suspense and curiosity	52. *was like the sail of a ship* NRT + **Narrator** SW c, narration in anticipation (Narrator reflecting in evaluative adjectives *sail of a ship*). 53. *think she will never, think she will never do anything again, can't believe it* NRT + **Narrator** SW c, narration in anticipation (Narrator reflecting in negation, in futurity).	52. '*Why she was like the sail of a ship,*' … 53. '*Why, she will never do anything again. I can't believe it*…' (p. 150)
Frame 120	NRT + **Narrator** SW a ii, narration in anticipation (Narrator reflecting in adverbial *perhaps*).	54. '*This is perhaps the most miserable part of the story.*' (p. 158)
Frame 158	*was plain, must die, must lose her reason* NRT + **Narrator** SW c, narration in anticipation (Narrator reflecting in futurity and in obligation *must*). *died* NRA + **Narrator** SW a i, narration in retrospection (Narrator positioned in the past). *sat, telephoned down below* NRA + **Narrator** SW a i, narration in retrospection (Narrator positioned in the past).	55. '*The end was plain* … *Edward must die, the girl must lose her reason because Edward died*—… *that end, on that night whilst Leonora sat in the girl's bedroom and Edward telephoned down below—that end was plainly manifest.*' (p. 268)

Frame 170	**FIS + Character** SW a i, narration in retrospection (Mimesis of character Nancy).	56. *"Safe Brindisi. Having rattling good time. Nancy."*
Frame 171	*looked at me with a direct, challenging ... gaze* **NRA + Narrator** SW a i, narration in retrospection (Narrator positioned in the past). *I guess I could see, didn't intend to hinder him* **NRT + Narrator** SW a i, narration in prospection (Teller/narrator reflecting in modal *could*, in rhetorical question, in negation).	57. *'And he looked at me with a direct, challenging, brow-beating glare.'* 58. *'I guess I could see in my eyes that I didn't intend to hinder him. Why should I hinder him?'* (p. 294)

a pre and post-murder participant relocating the listener to the process of framing RP and (clause 2, 3 and 4) then Parker (clauses 5 and 6) as the possible perpetrators (the blackmailer relative to the letter episode in clause 9). In perfective aspect and present tense, the narrator intervention is undercut, as we shall see in Chap. 4 with respect to verb aspects as static syntax, to create an **intermediary status**, and therefore an **'interdiegesis space'** in tense form for a post-crime narrative. In the overall MC from *Ackroyd* (also in the analysis of other offenders below) free indirect representation of thought captures the impromptu nature of the change of circumstances in anticipation or in prospection, and narrative report of act in the storyworld reflects the clauses as narrator intervention. This causes the simultaneous thoughts and actions of the narrator, with respect to textual cues like tense aspect and deictic shifts, which functioning as a **post-offence character** at the time of the event that took place in the narrative, tipping it over to an **offender-character** discourse from the default first-person narrator narrating retrospectively. The **close effect** in FIT (+Character) is opposite to NRA (+Narrator). The character disposition in anticipation is created by the use of the modal *could* in Frame 14. FIT and SW in anticipation, such as in Frame 14, fits in with the concealer-participant perspective analyzed in Fig. 2.2. The offender disposition is supported in the sequential setting in Fig. 2.2, where the utterance relative to RP as the blackmailer in Frame 14 occurred before Dr. S met him at the Three Boars in Frame 15, soon after the doctor had murdered RP's stepfather RA, making the doctor a **premeditated murderer**. Thus the SW in anticipation together with + Character sematic structure in textual cues supports a **post-murder SW scenario**; a three-dimensional re-reading of the utterance in Frame 14 from a **post-murder standpoint**.

In the use of the perfect tense, the retrospective narrator is not simply the family doctor in the MC, but the teller of the story from the standpoint of a post-murder-participant. The narrative tense in *story logic* (Herman, 2004) should be in past tense form when made in retrospect. The alternation to perfect tense, from the default narrative past form is not just a literary style, but serves a functional purpose. Perfect tense is a **compound tense** (Huddleston and Pullum 2005: p. 46), which encodes past time meaning in relation to the moment of speaking. Hence, the narrative act of alternation to perfect tense from the default narrative past tense does not allow the narrator to be wedded to any one-participant role, but be able to speak from different SW standpoints, as in Table 3.2. Dr. S is accounting in anticipation (SW c) how to manipulate the past circumstances that led to the chain of events resulting in the second death (murder) of RA, following on from the first crime of the doctor blackmailing Mrs. F because she poisoned her alcoholic husband.

The **double disposition** in perfect tense is also ideal for the purpose of focusing narrative interest of conflict between curiosity and suspense. in the futurity of tense in modal probability (such as '*could*' in Frame 14), where the participant tells the reader about situations and events which are to happen in the prospective narrative, the act of framing RP as blackmailer by offender-doctor is a retrospective event, as the story in *Ackroyd* was written as an autobiography by the doctor following the revelation that he the murderer. To illustrate this, in Table 3.2, the narrative contrast in the participant standpoint in reference time, such as in Frame 37 (clauses 6 and 7) is different from Frame 14. In clause 6, the participant reference point *took*, is from a character involved in the action, and is in the retrospective storyworld of the narrative. Then in 7, the standpoint in spatial deictics *then and there*, shifts to the 'here' and 'I' and 'this' of the narrator **outside** the retrospective storyworld of the narrative where, from an **external disposition**, the decision in anticipation was to frame Parker for the missing suicide note/letter from Mrs. F. To illustrate this further, the shift in speaker perspective as an **internal construct** in clauses 2 and 4 is relative to a post-murder-participant, who in the use of the perfective aspect and adverbials in 2, is providing an anticipation about RP as a possible suspect who blackmailed Mrs. Ferrars. This **internal construct** is evident in the **withheld** reporting in 4, '*I did what little had to be done*', which contains embedded information, revealed in retrospective reading, about the Dictaphone being removed from the murder scene, which Dr. S used to distort the time of RA's death. In fictional reality, RA was dead before his secretary heard him talking to someone in the study at 9.30 p.m. Deictic *here* and present perfect *have set* in clause 7 determine the participant's position to report in retrospection the 'goings on' in the story about a storyworld; where there is **merger** of the focalizer doctor-character in anticipation with himself as an **focalized offender** in story prospection. The offender-doctor's (+ character) alternative **logic** indexed in tense aspects is relative to the narrator-doctor's past tense form of narration in Table 3.3. In FIT and NRA an involved participant viewpoint over reporting is distinguished. In viewpoint a **close effect** index towards an involved participant over default first-person narrator representation.

In FIT, readers witness a character without narrator intervention. In tense aspect, the post-murder-participant disposition is embedded in a SW, which merges a post-murder point of view with the story telling. In tense alternation, the embedded participant as a speaker has multiple functions, where he is able to speak from a retrospective SW, also getting involved in the story action in NRA or NRT, while making a spatiotemporal leap and joining the readers' world in the moment of narration. This **multilevel function** highlights Frame 14, 29 and 37 (6) as climactic moments in the story, realized as cardinal points in Chap. 2, where the narrative forks, as shown in Fig. 2.2, causing alternative narrative paths and subsequently creating a delay in solving the mystery in *Ackroyd*.

Below, in the extract from CHF, the dichotomy of storyworlds also highlights a post-murder-participant disposition in the narrative act of tense alternation.

3.5.2 Case Study: Storyworld for Offender Mrs. Maxie

Frames constituting the MC in CHF is,

Frame 1: Mrs. M remembered the ritual gathering of her guests for the summer church fete that took place three months before the killing of Sally Jupp.

10. *'Exactly three months before the killing at Martingale Mrs Maxie gave a dinner party. 11. Years later, when the trial was a half-forgotten scandal and the headlines were yellowing on the newspaper lining of cupboard drawers, Eleanor Maxie looked back on that spring evening as the opening scene of tragedy. 12. Memory, selective and perverse, invested what had been a perfectly ordinary dinner party with an aura of foreboding and unease. 13. It became, in retrospect, a ritual gathering under one roof of victim and suspects, a staged preliminary to murder. 14. In fact not all the suspects had been present. 15.*

Felix Hearne, for one, was not at Martingale that week-end. 16. Yet, in her memory, he too sat at Mrs Maxie's table, watching with amused, sardonic eyes the opening antics of the players.
17. At the time, of course, the party was both ordinary and rather dull. ... 18. Mrs Maxie had just employed one of Miss Liddell's unmarried mothers as house-parlourmaid and the girl was waiting at the table for the first time. 19. <u>But the air of constraint which burdened the meal</u> **could hardly have been caused** *<u>by the occasional presence of Sally Jupp who placed the dishes in front of Mrs Maxie and removed the plates with a dextrous efficiency which Miss Liddell noted with complacent approval.</u>* (p. 5)'

Frame 4: Sally's sudden and brief change of attitude from *Sally the submissive to Sally the enigma*, as Miss L noticed,

20. '*Miss Liddell watched Sally Jupp as she moved about the table. ... 21. Suddenly Miss Liddell was visited by an irrational spasm of affection. 22. Sally was really doing nicely ... Suddenly their eyes met. 23. For a full two seconds they looked at each other. 24. Then Miss Liddell flushed and dropped her eyes. ... 25. Confused and horrified she tried to analyse the extraordinary effect of that brief contact. ... she had read in the girl's eyes, not the submissive gratitude which had characterizes Sally Jupp. ... but amused contempt, a hint of conspiracy and a dislike which was almost frightening in its intensity. 26. Then the green eyes had dropped again and Sally the enigma became once more Sally the submissive, the subdued, ... She had recommended Sally without reserve. ... 27. The girl was a most superior type. ... 28. The decision had been taken. 29. It was too late to doubt its wisdom now.*' (p. 10)

20. 'Miss Liddell was aware for the first time that the introduction of her favourite to Martingale might produce complications. 21. <u>She **could not be expected to foresee** the magnitude of **those complications** nor that **they would** end in violent death.</u>' (p. 10)

Frame 11: Sally overslept on the morning of the summer fete, as CB observes,

22. '... *Catherine remembered that there had been some trouble that morning* [the day of the annual church summer fete at Martingale House]

with Martha because the girl [Sally] *had overslept. ... she had to rush to make up the lost time for she looked flushed and was, Catherine thought, concealing some excitement behind an outward air of docile efficiency.*' (p. 36)

Storyworlds in CHF

Unlike Table 3.2, due to space constraint the frames are not re-quoted in following Tables 3.3 and 3.4. The marked tense is given in column 3 as reference points in SWs.

Explanation

The narration in the extract is in the third person. The story in CHF, unlike *Ackroyd*, does not announce a murder or a death at the outset, but is an event to follow. Similarly to *Ackroyd*, the narrator in the extract above is more **omnipresent (authorial)** than omniscient. Omnipresence of an involved participant in SW c construct a secondary narrative embedded within the primary narrative forming an **interdiegesis space** for Mrs. Eleanor Maxie the murderer, and for other participants, Deborah Maxie and Martha, relative to Sally Jupp's action in Frame 14.

According to the speech and thought continuum, NRA falls within the domain of event narration and is characteristic of narrator intervention. In the switch from default past tense to perfective tense form, as in *Ackroyd*, there is **restricted focalization**, where the perspective is limited to the participant status of Mrs. Eleanor Maxie; a **murderer in retrospect** narrating for the narrative interest of curiosity formulating narrative suspense encircling the victim, Sally Jupp. For instance, in the time place co-ordinates as **context of the situations** below, narration is through the mind's eye of Miss Liddell.

Clause 19, 'But *the air of constraint which burdened the meal* **could hardly have been caused** *by the occasional presence of Sally Jupp who placed the dishes in front of Mrs Maxie and removed the plates with a dextrous efficiency which Miss Liddell noted with complacent approval.*' (p. 5)

Clause 21, '*She* **could not be expected to foresee** *the magnitude of* **those complications** *nor that* **they would** *end in violent death.*' (My emphasis) (p. 10)

The narrator in clause 19 (who is not the character Miss Liddell) in anticipation negates Sally's challenging manner of serving at the table. Sally's manner was not the cause of complications that ended in her violent death, but the cause is inferred in retrospect to clause 13,

> Clause 13, '*It became, in retrospect, a ritual gathering under one roof of victim and suspects, a staged preliminary to murder.*'

In other words, in linguistic aspects, the context of the situation in clauses 19 and 21 reveals a **futurity** (in bold) in prospection in tense markers (as future time in bold), that gives away the standpoint of the participant, which is different from that in the rest of the extract. The difference is in transition from **omniscience** (distant focus), to an **omnipresent** character (**close-up focus**). An **omnipresent status** with limited or restricted omniscience in clauses 19, 21, imply that in the story narrative the events in Frames 8 (the Tablet episode), 13 and 14 (the Dress Episode) which are to follow (Appendix 2c), in reality these events as provocation episode (see Appendix 2c) cause Sally's death (Murder episode). The mystery constructed in linguistic modal probability (underlined in Table 3.4) forms narrative **suspense gaps** in retrospection, while **curiosity signals** are constructed in the **textual cues** such as temporal shift from futurity to present tense, … *foresee* [of what, which] *magnitude of complications* throws the readers into **suspense gaps** by failing to make explicit the episodic link in above frames to the complications that consequently link to the murder episode in the story. The events embed a secondary narrative within the primary narrative forming an **internal construct**, an **interdiegesis space**, for the murderer, Mrs. Eleanor Maxie, relative to Sally Jupp's actions in Frames 8, 13 and 14 (Appendix 2c).

The participant status in clauses 19 and 21 is of a **concealer** in the story realm, who is standing to report events and situations to follow as a third-person narrator in the primary storyworld (the discourse-NOW of the narrating-I) where information is withhold as a conflict of interest in the 'here' and 'I' and 'this' of the third-person narrator. The teller/participant thus speaks from the storyworld of an omniscient narrator whilst also **performing** as a restricted participant embedded in the dominant omniscient mode. This **restricted status** is not of an omniscient narrator, but a **close-up focus** of a post-murder-participant, who is aware of the circumstances that lead to the murder in the story, and wants to share the initial ambiguity of herself, who is now evaluating, post-murder, the circumstances that surrounded the death of Sally. This **alternative status** is foregrounded in the perfective aspect in anticipation (clauses 19 and 21), where the aspectual tense like a **discourse shifter** determines the meaning in the tense marker by reference to its context in the mimesis of each character in the story and is relative to Eleanor: Frames 8, 9, 14, relative to Martha: Frames 10 and relative to Deborah: Frame 13.

Also in the futurity in the past form of narration, there is secondary disposition, realized as an **intermediary status** in Chap. 4, and is for **focalization in anticipation.** Such narrative act in alternation evokes narrative curiosity relating to *the* [inexplicit] *magnitude of complications* (Frames 8, 13 and 14) in clause 21 that lead to Sally's death, and in futurity throw the readers forward in the narrative. Another noteworthy aspect is in the **negated** present tense form of the VPs, *could hardly have been, could not be expected to foresee.* In omniscience the vantage point is negated to index another possibility for the forthcoming complications in the story. To reinforce the deduction, this disposition is not simply of an omniscient narrator narrating through the characters of Miss Liddell or Mrs. Eleanor Maxie, but is a **participant disposition in anticipation** positioned in the perfective tense *had been taken* in sentence 28, and *now* in clause 29. The grammatical significance of negation is taken up further in the analysis of MC in *The Good Soldier* (TGS) below.

3.5.3 Case Study: Storyworld for Abettor Dowell

D—Dowell, F—Florence, L—Leonora, E—Edward
Frames constituting the MC in Ackroyd are,
The Protest scene

Frame 11: Dowell senses Florence was up to something,

'But on this occasion I knew that something was up. (p. 49) ... I must say that, until the astonishment came [the Protest scene] *I got nothing but pleasure out of the little expedition. (p. 50) I was aware of something treacherous, something frightful, something the evil in the day.'* (p. 53)

Frame 12: At the museum in the city of M— Florence explains the letter about *the Protest* and compliments Edward,

"'It's because of that piece of paper [draft of the Protest drawn up by Luther and others] *that you're honest, sober, industrious, provident and clean-lived. If it weren't for that piece of paper you'd be like the Irish or the Italians or the Poles, but particularly the Irish...'"* (p. 53)

Frame 13: L reveals to D the affair between E and F,

"'I can't stand this," she said [to Dowell] *with a most extraordinary passion; "I must get out of this." ... "Don't you* [Dowell] *see?" she said, "don't you see what's going on* [Florence was Edward's mistress '... *committing adultery in hired rooms.'* (pp. 83–84)]*?" The panic again stopped my heart. ... "Don't you see," ... of the eternal damnation of you and me and them* [alluding to Florence and Edward who lack constancy]*'"* (p. 55)

Frame 36: D narrating L's reaction to F's comment in Frame 12,

"'It would be better if Florence said nothing at all against my co-religionists, because it is a point that I am touchy about."
That was the hint that, accordingly I conveyed to Florence when, shortly afterwards, she and Edward came down from the tower. And I want you [the reader] *to understand that, from that moment until Edward and the girl and Florence were all dead together I had never the remotest glimpse, not the shadow of a suspicion, that there was anything wrong* [the affair between E and F]*, as the saying is. ... How in the world should I get it? ... I was just a male sick nurse. ... I was a deceived husband. And that Leonora was pimping* [alluding to Maisie and Nancy affair] *for Edward.'* (p. 81)

3 Double Function   177

Frame 135: following the Protest scene, L warned D about F making eyes at her husband,

"'Your wife is a harlot who is going to be my husband's mistress ..."... A week after Maisie Maiden's death she was aware that Florence had become Edward's mistress.' (p. 221)

The conspiracy

Frame 51: as they were to go away for their voyage, D got to know of F's heart condition for the first time,

"'I wanted to know, so as to pack my trunks. ... I may be ill, you know. I guess my heart is a little like Uncle Hurlbird's. It runs in families. ..."
   Now I wonder what had passed through Florence's mind during the two hours that she kept me waiting at the foot of the ladder. ... Till then, I fancy she had no settled plan in her mind. She certainly never mentioned her heart till that time.' (pp. 99, 101)

Frame 53: Ship doctor warned D about F's heart,

'Florence went down into her cabin and her heart took her. An agitated stewardess came running up to me, and I running down. I got my directions how to behave to my wife. Most of them came from her, though it was the ship doctor who discreetly suggested to me that I had better refrain from manifestations of affection. ... I wonder, though, how Florence got the doctor to enter the conspiracy—the several doctors ... Anyhow, she and they tied me pretty well down—and Jimmy, of course, that dreary boy—...' (p. 101)

Bagshawe incident: revelation of F's conspiracy   (Florence and Jimmy affair)
August 4, 1913 *'the last day of my* [Dowell] *absolute happiness'* (p. 117).

Frame 71: D with Bagshawe at the hotel lounge at Excelsior (p. 117).
Frame 73: L wanted NR to be chaperoned with E and wanted F to join them.
Frame 74: D and L sat in the lounge waiting until 10 p.m.

Frame 75: Bagshawe from Ludlow Manor near Ludbury joined D at the hotel lounge.
Frame 76: D then saw F running back into the hotel lounge. F rushed in at the swing doors, and looked round to see Bagshawe speaking to D.

'She saw the man who was talking to me. She stuck her hands over her face as if she wished to push her eyes out.' (p. 118)

Frame 77: Bagshawe surprised to find F, and remarks,

'"By Jove: Florry Hurlbird." "... Do you know who that is?" he asked. "The last time I saw that girl she was coming out of the bedroom of a young man called Jimmy at five o' clock in the morning. In my house at Ledbury."' (p. 118)

Frame 78: D pulls himself up after this to go up to F's room.
Frame 79: August 4, 1913, first night F does not lock her room, lying dead,

'She had a little phial that rightly should have contained nitrate of amyl, in her right hand.' (p. 119)

Florence's intention
Frame 37: D accusing F of trying to reunite E and L when she was E's mistress.

'"She should not have done it. She should not have done it."' (p. 83)

F tried to convince L that her affair with E was of a spiritual kind, and was trying to reunite E to his wife, when L accused her,

'"You come to me straight out of his bed to tell me that is my proper place."' (p. 84)

Frame 38: L in her bedroom doing her hair when she reminded F of how they both murdered Maisie Maiden.

'"You and I murdered her between us."' (p. 84)

The cardinal point
Frame 80: L reminded D of his remark,

> "'Now I can marry the girl [Nancy].' To which L replied, "of course you might marry her," and, when I asked whom, she answered: "The girl."' (p. 123)

Frame 85: D's remark, *"Now I can marry the girl."* (p. 129)
Cardinal point for Dowell's SW

Frame 87: D's retrospective narration on E's actions in the Casino Park with NR,

> 'And it appears that Edward Ashburnham led the girl not up the dark trees of the park. Edward Ashburnham told me all this in his final outburst. I have told you that, upon that occasion, he became deucedly vocal. I didn't pump him, I hadn't any motive. At the time I didn't in the least connect him with my wife.' (p. 130)
>   (**The motive**: Dowell)

Frame 92: F heard E from behind the trees as saying N is the person he cared for most. (p. 137)

Frame 110: E realizes what he was doing and D narrates,

> '... wicked thing E ever did in his life. (p. 133) ... to corrupt a young girl from convent. (p. 134)

Frame 116: D narrating about Nancy,

> 'Why she was like the sail of a ship, ... And to think she will never ... Why, she will never do anything again. I can't believe it...' (p. 150)
>   **Restricted context, conflict of suspense and curiosity**

Frame 120: L could trust E with N and she knew that Nancy could be trusted, L slackened her vigilance of E and N being together, which was a mistake,

> 'This is perhaps the most miserable part of the story.' (p. 158)

Frame 158: The quote below sums up what is coming in this final part of the story.

'The end was plain ... Edward must die, the girl must lose her reason because Edward died—... that end, on that night, whilst Leonora sat in the girl's bedroom and Edward telephoned down below—that end was plainly manifest.' (p. 268)

Frame 170: E in the stables one afternoon talking to D. A stable-boy bought the telegram, which read,

"'Safe Brindisi. Having rattling good time. Nancy.'" (p. 293)

Frame 171: E got out a penknife from his waistcoat pocket, asked D to take the telegram to L, D realized E's intention but did not interfere with E's intention to commit suicide.

'And he looked at me with a direct, challenging, brow-beating glare. I guess I could see in my eyes that I didn't intend to hinder him. Why should I hinder him?' (p. 294)

Storyworlds in TGS
Explanation

The extract from TGS is a first person narration. In the speech–thought continuum, NRT or NRA is close to the character. The displacement focus in the extract is towards a + Character perspective than + Narrator, indicated by the DS reporting of what the character said.

In tense perspective, the switch to perfective tense and to futurity in modal assertions (like *must*, and *could*) points towards the **merger** (conflation) of participant disposition. This effect is ***narrational***; the act of narrating merges with the present situation diminishing the prominence of the **metadiegetic content**. It is also ***thematic*** (the contrast or the similarity is between the **narrative levels: extradiegetic, intradiegetic and metadiegetic**) rather than ***explanatory*** as there is no explicit link of direct causality between events (Coste and Pier 2014: p. 2). Hence, in anticipation, and in the + Narrator following thought continuum conflated with the Character Dowell (as deceived husband profile) in retrospection, there is merger of the participant disposition manipulated in aspectual tense as discourse shifters and in the narrative act of the alternation technique. The alternative world of belief or intent in the form of retrospective interpretations of the past, in other words, can merge with the projections about the future relational to the actual storyworld carried out in **textual cues** like tense aspect, modality or futurity in clauses.

Conflation of the standpoint of a retrospective narrator in anticipation, for example, in Frames 11, 36, 51, 53 and 87, is possible for evaluating the significance of episodes in these frames. The episodes relate to the Protest scene and to Florence's conspiracy about her heart condition which **background** (diminish) the **content** (reason for the act) over the narrative acts (who said what to whom as DS) in the frames for the **thematic foregrounding** (integration) of Dowell's ignorance of his wife Florence's affairs with Edward and Jimmy, and the subsequent deception in Frame 79.

In above *homodiegeticization* (simultaneity of SW narration), there is a **dual relation** in the extract between Dowell the **person** and the homodiegetic **narrator** present in the narrated world, and in the *diegesis* (narrator discourse) and *autodiegetic* (identical with protagonist) in *rhesis* (character discourse). For example, in Frame 135 when Leonora was trying to warn Dowell about Florence making eyes at her husband,

"'Your wife is a harlot who is going to be my husband's mistress ..."... A week after Maisie Maiden's death she was aware that Florence had become Edward's mistress.' (p. 221)

                        F's flirtatious nature

The protagonist Dowell, as a speaker, stands in relation to the character Leonora's discourse in the perfective aspect '*had become*', when as a homodiegetic narrator Dowell could have used the simple past tense form instead, '*became*'.

Also in negation, as in futurity (underlined below), the retrospective homodiegetic narrator shifts from his narrating disposition to a participant status who anticipates the outcomes of events in the *story telling*, and not the veracity of events that take place in the actual *storyworld*.

Frame 116: D narrating about Nancy,

'Why she was like the sail of a ship, ... and to think she <u>will never</u> ... Why, she <u>will never</u> do anything again. I <u>can't believe it</u>...' (p. 150)

Frame 158: The following quote sums up the way things end in the final part of the story,

'The end was plain ... Edward <u>must die</u>, the girl <u>must lose her reason</u> because Edward died—... that end, on that night, whilst Leonora sat in the girl's bedroom and Edward telephoned down below—that end was plainly manifest.' (p. 268)

Abettor disposition

Frame 171: E got out a penknife from his waistcoat pocket, asked D to take the telegram to L, D realized E's intention but did not interfere with it.

E commits suicide

'And he looked at me with a direct, challenging, brow-beating glare. I <u>guess he could see</u> in my eyes that I <u>didn't intend</u> to hinder him. Why <u>should I hinder him?</u>' (p. 294)

The intermediary status is further illustrated in Frame 87 as well as in Frames 116 and 171 quoted above,

Frame 87: E told D,

... in his final outburst. I <u>didn't pump</u> him, I <u>hadn't</u> any motive. 'At the time I <u>didn't in the least connect</u> him with my wife. (p. 130)

This **autodiegetic narrator** Dowell is also an **unreliable narrator** in his negated SWs, *didn't pump him* [about Edward having affair with his wife], *she* [Nancy] *will never do anything* [because she became mad], and in *didn't intend to hinder* [stop Edward from committing suicide]). **Negation** has an overall **semantic effect** on an utterance or statement in a clause (Huddleston and Pullum 2005: p. 149); in this way the

truth-value of the clause is foregrounded in its **negative polarity**. Based on this observation, Dowell, while **hedging** in textual **cues** like futurity and modality, is also negating the **veracity** of the utterance made in negated clauses. Consequently, in these clauses, the participant disposition is not a protagonist in retrospection, or a protagonist in prospection, but it is a **participant in performance** in anticipation.

3.6 Conclusion

The MCs above have homodiegetic (MC 2.4.1 and 2.4.2) and heterodiegetic narrators (MC 2.4.3). Depending on the narrator's relation (presence or absence) to the story, the first-person narrator indicates its presence as a character in the story whom mention is made, and in third person its absence as a narrator. Narrative also distinguishes, by means of language (textual cues), Narrator position conflated with Character disposition.

As in a conversational narrative, the teller (person) is narrating a past event while sharing the same spatiotemporal parameters with the receiver. In fictional narratives, such as analyzed above, the spatiotemporal parameter standpoint of the teller and listener in the context of story *diegesis* are the same, but it is different in the context of *rhesis* when taking into account the tense in aspect which cause different storyworlds in relation to the reference points of the teller as person narrator,

- The storyworld (a)
    - In retrospection (i. The **default** storyworld)
    - In prospection (ii. The '**now**' of time of speaking)
- The storyworld (b)
- In relation to the **reference points of a character** in the storyworld (in retrospection)
- And also alternative storyworld (c) The **restricted** storyworld
- In relation to the **reference points of participant in anticipation** (narrator as reflector)

SW a ii, is a narration by the teller in prospection. In deictic now this is the **external** construct of the narrator as an involved participant. In SW c, in which a comment or action in anticipation is also **external** to the retrospective narration. For instance, Dr. Sheppard in *Ackroyd* in anticipation comments, '*Could I do anything with the boy* [Ralph Paton], *I think I could.*' In this utterance, he is a post-murder **involved** participant, and as such is **restricted** to the disposition as post-murder character in the discourse-Now when making the utterance. For instance, the post-retrospective teller in TGS is evaluating in modal *must* an obligation in anticipation in Frame 158, '*The end was plain ... Edward must die, the girl must lose her reason because Edward died*'. Edward did die and the girl Nancy became mad in the actual SW. The epistemic modal *must* causes anticipation in story prospection, rather than reporting in retrospection.

In accounting for the reference points of the teller there is thus participant disposition in the *homodiegeticization* (simultaneity of narration) of a narrative, where the narrator is not wedded to any one standpoint. Alternation as a functional device index speaker switches relative to the types of narration (retrospection, prospection or in anticipation), providing flexibility for shifts in vantage points, and for the merger of participant dispositions for **embedding focalization** like beliefs, intentions, motives are otherwise unnoticed in the narrative comprehension. Furthermore, tense aspect and modality as discourse shifters and the tense alternation as a narrative act show dichotomy of storyworlds (SWs a-c), where the teller tackles types of indeterminacy (e.g. restriction, withheld information in authorial and close-up omnipresence), floating points of view in omniscience, and the reporting (NRA) of 'the goings' on in an alternative world for an (internal) interdiegesis space, whilst at the same time fulfilling the role of the narrator in the dominant modal discourse.

Tense alternation as a narrative means sets a functional environment for the interplay of multiple dispositions of the protagonist in narrative discourse. This multilevel entity is addressed in the next chapter in stative syntax.

Bibliography

Sources cited: Chapter 3

Brown, G., and George Yule. 1983. *Discourse Analysis*. Cambridge, New York, Melbourne: Cambridge University Press.
Coste, Didier, and John Pier. 2014. Narrative Levels. In *The Living Handbook of Narratology*, ed. Peter Huhn et al. Hamburg: Hamburg University Press. Available at: http://www.lhn.uni-hamburg.de/article/narrative-levels-revised-version-uploaded-23-april-2014 (Accessed 16 December 2014).
Flanders, Reshmi D. 2014. Concealment and Revelation: An Interdisciplinary Approach to Reader Suspense. *Style* 48 (2) (summer): 219–242, 257–259. Available at: https://www.questia.com/library/p1129/style/i3785709/vol-48-no-2-summer (Accessed 23 October 2015).
Fowler, Roger. 1977. *New Accents: Linguistics and the Novel*. London and New York: Methuen.
Genette, Gerard. 1988. *Narrative Discourse Revisited*. Ithaca, NY: Cornell University Press.
Herman, David. 2009. *Basic Elements of Narrative*. Chichester: Wiley-Blackwell.
Huddleston, Rodney, and Geoffrey K. Pullum. 2005. *A Student's Introduction to English Grammar*. Cambridge: Cambridge University Press.
Palmer, Alan. 2004. *Fictional Minds*. Lincoln: University of Nebraska Press.
Polanyi, Livia. 1982. Literary Complexity in Everyday Storytelling. In *Spoken and Written Language: Exploring Orality and Literacy. Vol IX*, ed. Deborah Tannen, 155–169. Norwood, NJ: Ablex Publishing Corporation.
Ricoeur, Paul. 1985. *Time and Narrative: Vol 2*. Trans. Kathleen McLaughlin and David Pellauer, 88–99. Chicago: The University of Chicago Press.
Schiffrin, Deborah. 1981. Tense Variation in Narrative. *Language* 57 (1): 45–62.
Short, Mick. 1996. *Exploring the Language of Poems, Plays and Prose*. London and New York: Routledge.
Sternberg, M. 2003. Universals of Narrative and Their Cognitivist Fortunes (1). *Poetics Today* 24 (2): 297–395.
Sussex, L. 2010. Creative Writing and Stylistics. In *The Routledge Handbook of Stylistics*, ed. M. Burke, 423–438. London and New York: Routledge.

Toolan, Michael. 1988. *Narrative: A Critical Linguistic Introduction (Interface)*. 1st ed. London and New York: Routledge.
———. 2001. *Narrative: A Critical Linguistic Introduction*. London: Routledge.
Wales, Katie. 2001. *A Dictionary of Stylistics*. Edinburgh, Harlow, Essex, UK: Pearson Education Limited.
Wolfson, Nessa. 1982. *CHP: The Conversational Historical Present in American English Narrative*, 3–53. Dordrecht - Holland/Cinnaminson - USA. Foris Publications.

4
Disposition

4.1 Introduction

The participant disposition characterizes the relation between entities. They are based on specified goals, and are associated with the set of events that are expected from these entities. All other events outside the related entity are valueless or penalized in terms of social science. An individual's attachment to an entity in social science is an object of explicit procedure, and schemas are constructed in which these recognized entities appear, for instance, doctor–patient schema. However, there is plurality of relations within an entity, which can cause a **conflict of interest**. In the plurality of an individual's entities, at any one given point, new types of entities emerge such as a post-murder participant disposition in a situation of utterances such as in the manipulated context in Chap. 3. The situation of utterance in MCs is where asymmetries are constructed when holding multiple positions termed as *double dipping* in Boltanski (2014). In Boltanski, the problem of ***multipositionality*** or ***double dipping*** (p. 251) is due to a multiplicity of connections between entities, which is grounded to the different objectives an individual needs to fulfil. Linguistics is a means of studying the conflict of interest created due to

© The Author(s) 2017
R. Dutta-Flanders, *The Language of Suspense in Crime Fiction*,
DOI 10.1057/978-1-137-47028-7_4

this multipositionality. In crime discourse, multipositionality is for the conflict of interests between suspense and curiosity, or between suspense and surprise. The asymmetries grown out of multipositionality for a new entity are explained at the micro level in the **linguistic dysfunctions** in clauses like,

- the deviation from the norm in circumstantial elements;
- the functional contrast constructed in the default narrative mode;
- the degree of Narrator intervention in narrative mode.

Staging the order of events, as in Chap. 2, is based on the principle of relevance of participants in the story. This relevance may be a secret desire, and is related to a concealer's or a revelator's motive in the plot. In the staging of events and descriptions, the significance of a microcontext in the way of repeated or recalled frames in a plot form are foregrounded in the discourse-based frame analysis (Appendix 2a, c, d). As well as being foregrounded in the microcontext, the cognitive restructuring of an utterance based on the crime is related to the motive of the concealer and the revelator's PoR as shown in Figs. 2.1 and 2.4.

In Chap. 3, it was proposed that an agentive role is framed which has a **post-murder participant disposition** with **double function** for simultaneous reporting, narrating and evaluating in three dimensional (re)reading of clauses in a MC. This made the narration in MCs resort less to retrospection than to prospection and more to anticipation; a characteristic of the **authorial narrative** type. This authorial role is **omnipresent**, and with *paraliptic focalization* can hold back information that would be logically produced under the dominant modal position of a homodiegetic or heterodiegetic narrator of the moment. As a result, this three-dimensional focalization causes narrative gaps where readers are left in **suspense** in prospect and projected forward into the story with *curiosity gaps* such as in manipulated causal links in retrospection in Appendix 2a, 2c and 2d. At the micro level, these gaps reveal linguistic dysfunctions in the grammar of a clause, and as linguistic properties of suspense, inform the multipositionality of a post-murder perpetrator in the offender discourse. This form of narration calls for consideration of a participant disposition, which is analyzed in the functional properties of transitivity, passivity, and modality and in the referential and evaluative function in narrative clauses.

As stated in Fowler (1977: p. 42) all language is modalized, and abounds in constructions which express or draw attention to the utterance representing an individual voice, drawing attention to the performed or required action, and to the attitudes displayed and desired by the participant in the act of communication. A communicative act may be unidirectional, from sender to receiver. However, a speaker as a participant has many ways of indicating their involvement in this act, such as in the positioning of a speaker-actor as an active or passive agent in clauses, as well as in the linguistic constructions signaling the speaker's degree of commitment to the truth proposition, and in the manner of doing and saying clauses. There is a linguistic **counterpositioning** of a narrator-actor for different goals in a *master narrative* (culturally the dominant narrative—the criminal narrative), as agents can manipulate other characters by design or by some accidental action which may not be entirely their responsibility or will. Fowler (1977: p. 31) provides an interesting example in the grammatical distinction between *rogues* and *villains* in which the former is not always in control of his actions, being often manipulated as an instrument or patient, while the latter is definitely an agent.

The problem of **multipositionality** is at a manifestational level. In the *story logic*, a post-murder participant disposition as entity is formulated in the narration alongside the conventional narrative dispositions such as the **character** (in direct or indirect discourse), or as the **narrator** (as first person, or third person) or a *focalizer* (the focal position of one who perceives or the locus of the perceptual focus). For example, in the surface structure of the clause, '*Peter tried to pull down the sails, but felt the mast give way and the boat caught up by enormous wave*', (Chatman 1980: p. 45). Peter is the *effector* and is the subject of many actions in the narrated event. However, at the deep story level, Peter is not the *effector*, but the **narrative object** that is **affected** by the enormous wave, an entity represented in the deep grammatical structure of clauses. When considering Bals' (cited in Genette 1988) **embedded focalization** to Genette's *displacement of focus*, Genette (1988: p. 73) comments,

'... *narrative sometimes places its focus at a point so* [far out from the immediate context] *that it cannot coincide with any character.*'

Such focus in Genette proposes a narrative constraint termed as *prefocalization* (1988: p. 78). *Prefocalization* is the restriction of the field in the selection of narrative information; it is *a situated focus* in omniscience authorized by the situation to prompt either a breach of trust as *paralepsis* (information in excess by the logic of the narrative type) or *paralipsis* (holding back of information by the logic of focalization or the perspective selected). As was seen earlier in the MCs from heterodiegetic and homodiegetic stories, the consequence of unchronological episodic links for the selected information in Appendix 2a and c from *Ackroyd* and TGS respectively, submitted a modal restriction in the selected focus, which was sidestepped by **infraction** (breach) or by **cognitive** (perceptive) distortion. The **modal restriction** is specific to the narrative purposes of suspense and curiosity in the discourse, and the claim is that it results in an **intermediary disposition** such as a post-murder-participant disposition in linguistic dysfunctions treated as the properties of suspense. The restriction is analyzed further in Chap. 5 by the **orientation** of an Agent, or a Speaker, or a-state-oriented utterance provided in the utterance.

The framework (Sect. 4.4) used for participant disposition analysis combines the functional linguistics of Halliday (1974) on the experiential function in transitivity. The framework also combines stylistics and critical linguistics in Simpson (1993) on point of view, and Simpson's typology of the narrative modes for the articulation of a narrative as a social structure with the structural properties of the referential and evaluative functions in clauses from Toolan (2001). The analyzed extracts are from thrillers where the crime is resolved or the criminal is revealed as in a whodunit.

4.2 Story Resolved, a Criminal Revealed

Narrative texts comprise elements like *events* (actions or happenings) and *existents* (a sense of an existence of things) caused by or being **affected** by the evocation of the narrative voice. In the function of narrative discourse, selected affairs are *resolved* or *revealed* in the story. In the discourse function of a revealed plot form, the state of affairs is revealed in the story. There is a strong sense of a chronological order present in the narrative form, where deaths in the first story of crime are unraveled, displaying the way deaths came about in the second story of investigation, evident in *Ackroyd* and CHF. Conversely, in the resolved plot (Chatman 1980: p. 48), the function of discourse is about events resolved happily or tragically. For instance, events turn out as tragic in TGS, when Dowell the principal character was unable to marry Nancy Rufford and the circumstances lead him to become her nurse instead, as he was for his wife Florence. TGS is at once revelatory and a resolved narrative, while Ackroyd and CHF have the plot form of revelation, a state of affairs revealed relative to the crime. As a resolved narrative, there is more than one principal character involved in TGS. There is **simultaneous** forward and backward causality (a cause and effect relation) for ideological reasons, for instance in TGS the repeated microcontext related to Nancy Rufford narrated intermittently by abettor/protagonist Dowell alongside other tales in the narrative discourse (Frames 7, 8, 23).

The narrative in *Ackroyd* like TGS is also ***circulatory***, where events become simultaneous with the multilinear story line. In circular narratives, there is thus structure reversal and a linear rearrangement, (Prince in Pavel 2014: p. 301) that is constituted for a major change is triggered by human action, goal and conflict. As seen in the repeated frame about *the girl* [Nancy Rufford] in TGS. The Nancy Rufford episode in the story involved all the principal characters in the story and was pre requisite to a concealed fourth tale in the TGS discourse. On the other hand, the ideal chronological order, a strict succession called '*natural chronology*' in Todorov (1966: p. 127) is in single-line stories where other characters are relative to the principal character in the thriller stories (For example, Ripley in *The Talented Mr. Ripley*, Raven *in A Gun for Sale* and Bud Corliss in *A Kiss Before Dying*).

Unlike the *rogue* in classic 'whodunit' detective stories, the villain is revealed at the outset in the above thrillers. The stories in the thrillers are about the outrageous wickedness of the villain. The state of affairs—the villainy—is resolved in thrillers when the villain dies, unlike the murderer who is revealed in a murder mystery and taken to justice. Taking the logic in Fowler,

... *a villain is definitely an agent,* ... *a rogue is not always in control of his actions.* (1977: p. 31)

The *villain* in the story logic is then an active agent (the anti-hero) in the narrative world unlike the *rogue* (the character/ murderer) in a murder mystery. The villain is the *effector* of many actions in the event narrated. For the analysis of a disposition shift from an **effector/actor** to an **affected *narrative object* (NO)**, three thrillers are selected that realize the villain disposition from an embedded rogue in MCs (Appendix 4g). The narrative outcomes of villainy are different from a rogue, and developed in the linguistic dysfunctions (Sect. 4.5).

The focus of analysis is on the ***prefocalization***, a narrative constraint in the linguistic properties of the dominant participant disposition in a linear plot form in thriller stories. The focalization in linear plot form is then compared to the offender disposition in the multilinear plot form in murder mystery. In multilinear plot form the narrating character as an agent, such as Dr. Sheppard and Dowell, occupies multiple positions in the formulated space as an **interdiegetic**[1] universe and is based on the offender agent's spatiotemporal parameter or storyworlds like the ***online*** and ***offline*** deictic universe of the narrating speaker. In the example, this simultaneous universe is understood following Jahn in Herman as, '*And now I see* [narrator's **offline perception** of] *the outside of our house ... We are playing in the winter twilight ... I watch her* [mother] winding *her curls round her fingers* [**online perception** of the narrator as the child] ...' (2007: chapter 7). The offline and online alternation is in bold for emphasis. Offline perception is synonymous to the ***discourse-Now*** (pp. 26, 97) and on line perception to ***story-Now*** (p. 97).

The principal agents like Raven and Ripley occupy a singular role as a villain in a linear plot form of the story, and do not have the problem of multipositionality like the offender Dr. Sheppard in a murder mystery. Readers are aware of the villain in the story, and the reader expectation fits with the character actions to complete the task as the police track down the person responsible for the criminal act. On the surface, the

---

[1] Interdiegetic space—an *online perception* in static syntax and modal reading of unmodalized assertions (categorical assertions) is embedded on to narrator's *offline perception* in proximity within an interdiegetic space.

suspense in the story is in the unfolding of the sequence of events revealing the villainy in the story, but suspense is not in the way of multipositionality in narration. The spatiotemporal parameters of a multiple position participant have a linguistically complex disposition in narration. In a single role participant narration, **the analyst** encounters an evaluation of a situation for asymmetries grown out of **pre- and post-murder** *multipositionality* for a new entity. This results in an alternative storyworld based on the offender spatiotemporal parameter and generally forms a post-murder disposition. This **offender reflector** is residing within an **interdiegesis space** constructed for the narrative purpose of illusion, delay or even distortion in the simultaneity of revealing or persuading the readers in the discourse. A transposition of perception is formulated in this intermediary space, where there is an *online perception* embedded on to narrator's *offline perception*. In the analysis of this *multiperspectivism* in a participant disposition, there is linguistic dysfunctions developed in clauses for a **dual narrative act**.

Linguistic dysfunctions, such as in circumstantiation are formulated to foreground the background to the clause, or functional contrast in static syntax for the **simultaneity** of omission or restricted revelation in the **metanarrative** (a narrative about a narrative). The metanarrative in thrillers is in the resolution, while in murder mysteries the metanarrative is embedded as a circulatory affair in the plot form of the narrative. Before undertaking a comparative analysis of the offender discourses from selected detective thrillers (Appendix 4g), the background of the villains is realized. This is then selected to identify an intermediary post-murder disposition in the offender narrative in the linguistic dysfunctions stated above.

4.3 Villains: Their Contextual Background

Raven in Greene's *A Gun for Sale* is a hit man contracted by Mr. Davis and Sir Marcus to kill the Czech Minister of War to trigger a global conflict. They double-cross Raven when the agent Mr. Davis, also known as Cholmondeley, pays Raven in stolen bank notes. The police (Detective-Sergeant Jimmy Mather and his junior, Saunders) are on Raven's trail for a *safe robbery*, when he uses the stolen notes from this safe to buy a dress for Alice, the cleaner at the German café where he also rented a room. Bent on revenge, Raven tracks Mr. Davis down to the Midlands city of Nottwich. In no time, there is double pursuit in the story with a narrative twist, when Raven kidnaps Anne Crowder, the sergeant's girlfriend, in order to use her ticket to Nottwich, as he is unable to buy one with the stolen notes. The sequential events in the story are carried forward in two pursuits alternating in the narrative—Raven following Cholmondeley to Nottwich with detective-sergeant Mather on his trail.

In the story, Raven is identified as a killer, *'Murder didn't mean much to Raven'* (p. 1). Raven is a cold-blooded killer '... [who] *had been fed the poison from boyhood drop by drop: he hardly noticed its bitterness now'* (p. 11). He was contracted to kill the War Minister which he did not know by name. However, he understands pain, when he narrates, *my father hanged* (pp. 15, 39), his *mother cut her throat* and committed suicide (p. 122). Conversely, his concern for his pet cat is distinctive of his character, ' *"It's not a dark secret. It's a cat I left back in my lodgings in London when they* [police] *chased me out"'* (p. 114). In response to Dr. Yogel's fear of being revealed by Raven (p. 24) for working on his harelip, we glimpse Raven as a man of principle and a man of trust when Raven replies, *"'I don't go back on a fellow who treats me right,"* (p. 24) then again, *"I wouldn't shoot, ... I'm not all that crazy,"* he said. *"If people go straight with me, I'll go straight with them."'* (p. 114).

Though a contract killer, he knew pain when he was betrayed by the chaplain in the orphanage and by Dr. Yogel at Charlotte Street (p. 165). This betrayal theme is emphasized when Raven was double-crossed by Davis when he was paid with the stolen money in order to frame Raven for the safe robbery.

> '... *There was no one outside your own brain whom you could trust: not a doctor, not a priest, not a woman.'* (p. 164).

Alice (p. 10) further betrayed Raven when she revealed his identity as the person who had gifted her a dress using the stolen cash (p. 13). Raven who was on the run to avoid the police, visited Dr. Yogel to conceal his distinctive harelip (pp. 23–25), and was for the third time in the narrative, double-crossed by this doctor and his secretary,

> 'These people [Dr. Yogel and his secretary] were of his own kind … for the second time in one day he had been betrayed by the lawless' (p. 25).

Raven's final betrayal in the narrative was when, 'the girl in skirt' (Anne Crowder) betrayed him by giving away his location (p. 134) and by revealing his other killings (p. 123) to the sergeant. She was someone Raven confided in at his emotional moments when hiding from the police.

> 'How could he [Raven] have expected to have escaped the commonest <u>betrayal</u> of all: to go soft on a skirt [Anne]? They all went soft at some time or another: Penrith and Carter, Jossy and Ballard, Baker and the Great Dane.' (My emphasis) (p. 165)

Sir Marcus and the harelipped Raven are symbolically bound together as villains with similar scars. However the difference between the characters is Marcus' greed and vice (p. 161), while Raven was a cold-blooded killer, who could kill for the simplest of reasons, '*I cut his* [Kite] *throat*', [because Kite bumped off his former boss on the race course] (p. 123). In Raven there is depiction of villainy, while the figure of Marcus is a '*spiritless but deadly destroying angel, for whom spilt blood is as nothing compared to a rocketing share price* …—*about the killing* [by Raven] *which is to be made in munitions shares*' (Macfarlane in *A Gun for Sale* 2009: p. ix). This contrast in the **direct discourse**[2] when Raven regrets that he had killed a man that Marcus could make money from out of his death.

> '"I wouldn't have done it," Raven said, "if I'd known the old man* [Czech Minister] *was like he was. I smashed his skull for him* [Marcus]. *And the old woman, a bullet in both eyes,*" *He shouted at Sir Marcus,* "*That was your doing. How do you like that?*"' (p. 161)

In the introduction to the novel MacFarlane (2009: pp. v–x) comments,

---

[2] Direct discourse as defined by Abbott in Herm an (2007: p. 42) is *a recorded speech or thought (dialogue, monologue, interior monologue).*

'... *fear preoccupies the characters of* A Gun for Sale. *The moral world in Greene's novels is mixed, where the bad and the good are not opposed, but shade into one another by fine degrees.*'

Contextually, Raven is preoccupied with fear in the narrative discourse. The modalized alternative world relative to the good will in Raven is linguistically opposed with the world of action and evil. The character of Raven is portrayed as a victim of pain that does not mind the killing, but has standards when it comes to double crossing which he does mind (p. 117). He is then overpowered by the thrill of villainy. With respect to the film, McFarlane adds,

'... *Hollywood had begun to spawn a dark filmic alter ego. ... dialogue was terse. There were few verbs, and no happy endings. Action drove character, not the other way round. Everything was cast in extravagantly stylised greyscale, with sudden Caravaggio-contrasts of light and grey.*'

In a story context as described by McFarlane, Raven appears as an instrument in his world of villainy who becomes a bystander in the story, though an agent in the narrative. Text relative to the events discussed above is selected to analyze the Agent–Patient linguistic reality constructed of an agentive villain.

The plot form in *Ripley* in the second selected thriller, *A Talented Mr. Ripley*, is also sequential and linear, with Tom Ripley as the villain in the story. However, he is driven by sexual jealousy, greed, and vice (unlike Raven) making him more akin to Marcus in *A Gun for Sale*. Like Raven, the contrast is drawn when Tom kills his friend, Dickie, to take on his identity, driven by his homosexual jealousy. In the second part of the story, he lives off Dickie's trust money, for which he has to commit further killing to preserve his identity.

The killer Tom Ripley is the narrator in the story. The extract selected for the analysis from the *Ripley* text is at the point in the narrative when Tom and his friend Dickie are preparing for their trip to San Remo, where Ripley kills his friend. Dickie, son of Herbert Greenleaf, an owner of a shipbuilding company, is living in Mongibello, south of Naples.

4 Disposition

Greenleaf approaches Tom to persuade his son, Dickie, to come back to America, as he was unwilling to do so at his parent's request. Tom wants the good life of Dickie and his money; he is struggling to keep away from his creditors, hence he takes up the offer of Dickie's father, Mr. Greenleaf, to persuade his friend to return to America and in pretext gets away to Europe, as the narrator puts it,

> '*He was starting a new life. … he felt as he imagined immigrants felt when they left everything behind in some foreign country, left their friends and relations, and their past mistakes,* [implying Tom's larceny and theft] *and sailed to America. A clean slate!*' (p. 31)

In the story, unknown to the other characters, Tom is a homosexual. The book was first published in 1955 when to be a gay or a lesbian was an illegal act. Keeping to its time, Tom's homosexuality is implied in the narrative when Bud, Tom's housemate comments, when Ed Martin's girlfriend jokingly requests,

> '*Tommie, take me?*' … *I can fit in here* [the cabin], *Tommy, said the girl …*' [to which Ed replied] '*I'd like to see Tom caught with a girl in his room!*' *Ed Martin said laughing.*' … [This comment was not received well by Tom] '*Tom glared at him* [Ed] (p. 29)

Tom's homosexuality is the motive in the story. Driven by his sexual jealousy, he is possessive and selfish, and unable to understand any other perspective besides his own. Thus on seeing Dickie kissing Marge,

> '*That kiss—it hadn't looked like a first kiss.*'

Tom runs back to Dickie's place, throws a fit, and starts throwing around paintbrushes, a palette and other painting stuff from Dickie's studio. This anger becomes a **trigger factor** for his suppressed disposition. Tom tries on Dickie's clothes, a Tyrolean hat and realizes *how much he looks like Dickie with the top part of his head covered* (p. 69). In his storyworld of fantasy, he imagines himself as Dickie telling Marge,

"'Marge, you must understand that I don't love you." Tom said into the mirror in Dickie's voice.' (p. 68)

He **imagines** grabbing Marge's throat, and twisting until she is limp on the floor. An imaginary dialogue follows and again Tom addresses Marge in the mirror,

"'You know why I had to do that ... You were interfering between Tom and me—No. not that! But there is a bond between us!'" (p. 69)

A jealous, possessive character emerges, who wants money, success and the good life for which he is willing to kill.

Tom's imagined act of violence towards his aunt (p. 35) is evident when he was brought back every time he tried to run away, which reveals Tom's violent disposition from a very young age. His aunt Dottie brought up Tom, as his own mother abandoned him. Tom tried to escape his aunt's strict upbringing, and her taunts that *"'He's a sissy from the ground up. Just like his father!'"* (p. 34). This **imagined world** of violence is repeated in his **imagined world** of killing Marge when Tom feels rejected and Dickie wants him to know that,

"'Another thing I want to say, but clearly," he [Dickie] *said looking at Tom, "I'm not queer. I don't know if you have the idea that I am or not.'"* (p. 70)

In the text discourse, an **evolving killer** is evident, who imagines the act of violence, which then turns into an imagined act of killing in the monologue by the killer (p. 68), followed by the actual act of killing. The transition from an imagined killer to a confident murderer is a process, which can be linguistically traced as an **imagined world**, distinct from the **sub-world** and then the **actual world** of the killer in the experiential and interpersonal functions at the micro level of these worlds.

The third text, Levin's thriller, *A Kiss before Dying*, is a hybrid construction where the perpetrator is not revealed until the end of chapter 11, (total 15 chapters). The story is resolved in the end when Marion is saved from marrying the killer of her two sisters, Evelyn and Dorothy. In line with the revealed plot structure, the cardinal point in the story provides narrative options to the killer to delay his criminal identity. The narrative option arises when Evelyn writes to her boyfriend Bud (who, unknown to her, is the murderer) about her doubts that her sister Dorothy committed suicide. Ellen's attempt to reclassify her sister's suicide as an unsolved murder and find the murderer starts the second story of investigation in a whodunit style in the novel. Ellen doubts her sister's suicide, arising from unexplained facts in the first story of crime, related to a borrowed belt, a cheap pair of gloves, a blue shirt and a suicide note copied by the murderer (p. 41). The anomaly was that, in the suicide letter Dorothy addressed her sister as *Darling*, contrary to her usual *dear or Dearest Ellen* (p. 93). Annabelle Koch (a girl from the same dormitory) also found another anomaly when Dorothy, her roommate, borrowed her belt on the day she died, and the police later found a perfectly fine belt of similar style in her room. Dorothy also had on her a cheap pair of (new) gloves, when she had expensive handmade white cloth gloves to go with her dress given by her younger sister, Marion. On recounting these facts, Ellen realizes that Dorothy was in the Municipal Building not to commit suicide, but to get married (pp. 62–65). The above facts then make sense: Dorothy selected them to get married to,

'... the man who made her [Dorothy] pregnant ... the handsome blue-eyed blond [Bud Corliss] of her fall English class ... [and therefore she got] something old, something new, something borrowed and something blue' (p. 95).

In the story logic of a detective thriller, all three participants, Raven, Bud and Tom, as villains, are active agents who drive the narrative forward in the story. This is in contrast to *rogues* (the character/murderer) like Dr. Shephard and Mrs. Maxie who are **narrative objects** affected by the *events* (story composed of actions) and *existents* (characters and entities) in the story, while Raven, Bud and Tom are *effector* of many actions in the story. They are the dominant voice in the thriller narrative. The anti-hero in the thrillers is a conscious initiator of actions, while the participating character as a murderer is an **anticipatory participant** functioning also in an **epistemic sub-world** in the story. As narrators, the principal characters as the villain or the murderer are closer to the action (the murder committed) either retrospectively or in anticipation. As well as a participating character in the story, they have the privilege of anticipating the narrative outcome and consequently as events in the plot structure, are able to rearrange the order of clausal structure for a disclosure privileging their **intentionality** for the kind of disclosure they intend.

The **change of disposition** from an actor/effector to a *narrative object* is in the linguistic dysfunctions developed in the offender discourse. Extracts selected are from the direct discourse of murderer and villains in the stories.

4.4 Framework: The Grammar of Experience

The framework for shift analysis in participant disposition is to tackle the problem of ***multipositionality*** in linear and multilinear texts and to analyze at micro level in clauses the **dual narrativity** in discourse. Linguistic features for the dual narrativity are in the circumstantial elements (prepositional, adjectival and the adverbial phrases), in the passivity in modal assertions, and in the referential and evaluative functions in clauses.

4.4.1 Experiential Function: Transformational Outcome

As a concept for construing our experience, circumstance is associated with a process (material, mental or relational) and is significant for assigning an indirect participant role. For instance, in 1a and 1b below, the Actor–Goal relationship is reversed. The nominal element *train* occupies a Goal position (directed at/receives the action) in 1a, but in 1b occupies a subject position in the experiential notion of one not doing the deed or bringing about the change.

1a. *I* (Subject) *take* (Process) *the train* (Goal).
1b. *The train* (Subject/circumstance) [takes] *me*. (The experiential notion)
2. *The bridge was built by the army*. (Halliday 1994: p. 117)

Circumstantiation of *The train*, as a concept, is transitive in 1a; however, in 1b, the nominal element in the grammar of experience constructs a semantic space for a participant role in circumstance (C); in 1a, *the train* is the **expansion of the process** of takes. Circumstance in 1b, as a fact or a process, is as an **expansion of an entity**. These elements in Halliday (1994: p. 50) occur freely in all types of processes, and are expressed not as nominal group, but either as an adverbial group or a prepositional phrase (PP).

Circumstantial is thus a minor process, and is subsidiary to the main process. Instead of standing on its own, the circumstantial element (in 1b) is parasitic on another process and is typically **indirect**. Example 2 is a **hybrid construction**, the participant *army* in the PP (underlined) is indirectly linked into the main process, *built*, via the PP. A direct participant in the nominal group inside the PP expresses an **indirect disposition** through whom the Process came into being. An **indirect agency disposition** is instantiated for *the army* by positioning the effected nominal element *the bridge* in subject position. The entity in subject position is not the **thematic** agent through which the process came into existence. This property of the PP as a circumstantial element formulates *bidirectionality*[3] of the agentive participant, a direct agent with **indirect disposition**, or a focalized in the narrative; like in a dream or a fantasy, as in Toolan (2001: p. 62), in criminal context for an entity in transition.

In the experiential function of clauses such as in (3), a **restricted client**, or a **scope-entity** or an **agent** involved in the process as **participant roles** is also significant in re surfacing an **indirect disposition** in clauses (Halliday 2004: chapter 5). Unlike a Goal as a participant, Recipients and Clients benefit from the process. For instance, in (3a), *for Mary* is the cause formulating a **Client role**, which is more restricted in contrast to the **Recipient role** *for his wife* in (3b). While *to Los Angeles* is functioning as **circumstance** and not Recipient in (3c).

---

[3] Bidirectionality—Participant role is presented simultaneously as a Medium (The <u>tourist</u> ran) versus a Recipient (The lion chased the <u>tourist</u>). Simultaneity is due to multipositionality of participant, such as Medium disposition created of a Recipient element functioning as circumstance (C/scope). All this is due to the experiential function represented in clauses, and due to the semantic change brought about by causation, emphasizing the participant role as an entity associated with the process.

Linear and non-linear model

The transitive model (5b)	The ergative model (5a)
(**Direct** causation)	(**Manipulative** causation)
Actor Goal	Instigator (Is) Medium (Me)

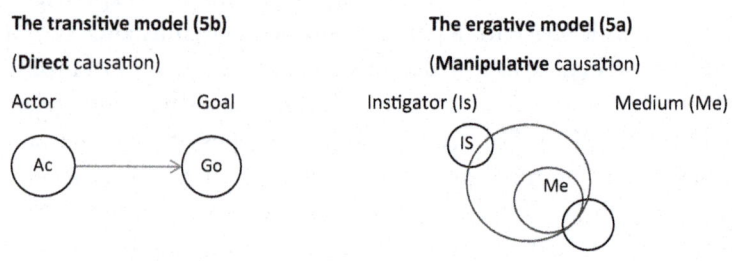

Davidse (in Davies and Ravelli 1992: p. 118)

Fig. 4.1 Linear and non-linear model

3a. *I* [Client] *am doing all this **for Mary**.*
3b. *Fred brought a present **for his wife** (Recipient).*
3c. *She sent her luggage **to Los Angeles*** (Circumstance/Location). (My emphasis)

4.4.1.1 Semantic Change: Causation

Causation in the experiential function could be one of *deed-and-extension*. As a process it may be brought about by entity and may not be a direct participant engaged in the process. This can also be achieved by use of a passive construction reversing the cause and effect linear chain of the process, with an additional option of suppressing the role of the agent.

Such as in the pattern in (4a) below, the object, *the tourist* in **Medium** role is a **Recipient** due to the act, *chase*. The act of running in 4a is a situation that **came into being** as an effect of the *chase*, an **analytical causation** where the primary Agent Ag$_1$ (the lion) is the **instigator** of the action *chase*. The *tourist* then becomes the **object** of lion's *chase*, functioning as an entity, a meal for *the lion*. There is **double function**[4] (Flanders

---

[4] Double function (DF)—DF is simultaneity of participant disposition for simultaneity of reporting, narrating and evaluating in narrative discourse. For instance, in, *I opened the front door with my latch key, and purposely delayed a few moments in the hall, hanging up my hat and the light overcoat that I had deemed a wise precaution against the chill of an early autumn morning.* (Ackroyd 1993: p. 7), there is Intentional Agent in past tense but an Engaged Agent in progressive and perfective dispositions (*hanging up* (C), *had deemed*) (Flanders 2014: p. 220).

Table 4.1 Double analysis

Standard analysis (based on extension):	Actor	Process	Goal
Ergative analysis (based on causation):	Agent	Process	Medium
4a. *The lion* (Agent) *chased* (Process)		*the tourist* (Recipient)	
4b. *The lion* (Agent) *chased* (Process)		*the tourist* (Medium)	

2014: p. 220) instantiated for a participant in subject position, which is (1) a Medium role through which the act of *running* came into existence, and (2) making the tourist an entity **instigated** by an Agent in the clause formulating an ergative reading of causation in 4b. Such double analysis of transitivity function is significant in the criminal discourse, where Agent and Object status is for the same participant in criminal context, and the examples and the examples below show the way agency and causation relate to process for contextual implications as stated in Simpson (1993: pp. 92, 94) are,

Furthermore, the transitive structure in the table above has only **one processual layer**, while there are **two processual layers**, such as in 5a, for **manipulative causation** (Davidse in Davies and Ravelli 1992: chapter 5). They are,

Function 1. The Medium is hosting the process, as well as
Function 2. Something is being done to the Medium.

For instance in,

5a. *John* (instigator) *opened the door.* **Manipulative causation**

(Schema a: **Instigator–Medium**)

5b. *John* (Actor/Agent) *threw the ball* (Goal). (Analytical causation)

(Schema b: **Actor–Goal**)

5c. *Mary* (instigator) *changed John* (Medium), *but it took her a whole lifetime to bring it about* (C).

(Schema c: **Actor–Affected**)

Schema C: The coming about of Ag$_2$, as a narrative object created in the Medium and C/scope of the Process.

In 5a, **instigator** *John* manipulates the door by **instigating** its opening. This situation in 5a is explained as a ***manipulative causation*** by Shibatani (1976: p. 31) in Davies and Ravelli (1992: p. 119), where the **Causer** *John* must physically **manipulate** the cause in **affecting** (influencing) the **caused** event of opening the door. The **instigation** of the process and the **instigated** process **co-exist**. However, in clause 5b, the Actor *John* does the throwing, but the *ball* does not co-participate in the process unlike *the door* in 5a, where there is **change of state**—a closed door is now open, and thus **object** door co-participated in the process of opening. The significant point is about a **change of state**. When the **Causee** in a Medium role is related to a perpetrator, a **non-volitional object entity** is instantiated in a **Medium–Process constellation**, which is argued below as a **secondary Agent, Ag$_2$** in **analytical causation**, such as in clause 6a below.

In 5b, the *energy input* in the **transitive model** is of the actor at *one level*, and can only be extended to the **right** to include a circumstance (to-phrase, John walked *to the shop*) or a recipient. In the **ergative model** the *energy input* is at ***two levels***, that of **Instigator** (Is) within the outer ring and that of the **Medium** (Me) within the inner ring, where the **Medium–Process** constellation is opened up to the **left** to incorporate the **instigator** and is **external** to the clause. To explain this **external disposition** further, such as in clause 5c, there is no reference item for *John changed* to allow the independent meaning to be picked up in the Circumstance (C) by reference to the grammatical wording *so*, but it does allow an **independent** meaning *John changed*. It is possible for the C element to **modify** the Medium–Process complex and to some degree to provide grammatical independence as an **ergative: effective** structure, although this independence is less strong than the **cause–process** constellation, where the C (scope) element necessarily **modifies** the entire Actor–Process–Goal nucleus.

In **transitive clauses**, the actor **intentionality** is **agent-centered**, but the **ergative paradigm** is **medium-centered**, where the **instigation** of the process is optimally realized. With the instigator lacking in the ergative system, as in clause (6a), the shift is towards the transitive paradigm with the general schema, **agent-affected** rather than an **actor–goal** (6b) or an **instigator–medium schema**.

6a. *John* (superventive) *fell into the pool.*
Analytical causation Agent-Affected Schema
6b. *Peter* (Actor) *made John* (Medium) *fall into the pool.*
Instigator–Medium Schema

Analytical causation is structurally realized (6a) by adding the **feature of agency**: causative Agent + causative process, but not a true Agent. The Causer role in subject position is **superventive** (action not engendered by the participant in 6a) and implies an **indirect** transitional participant (Ag_2) different from a direct participant (Ag_1) in the ergative: effective causation (7c below). Ag_2 as a **secondary Agent** (Ag_2) is thus brought into the constellation.

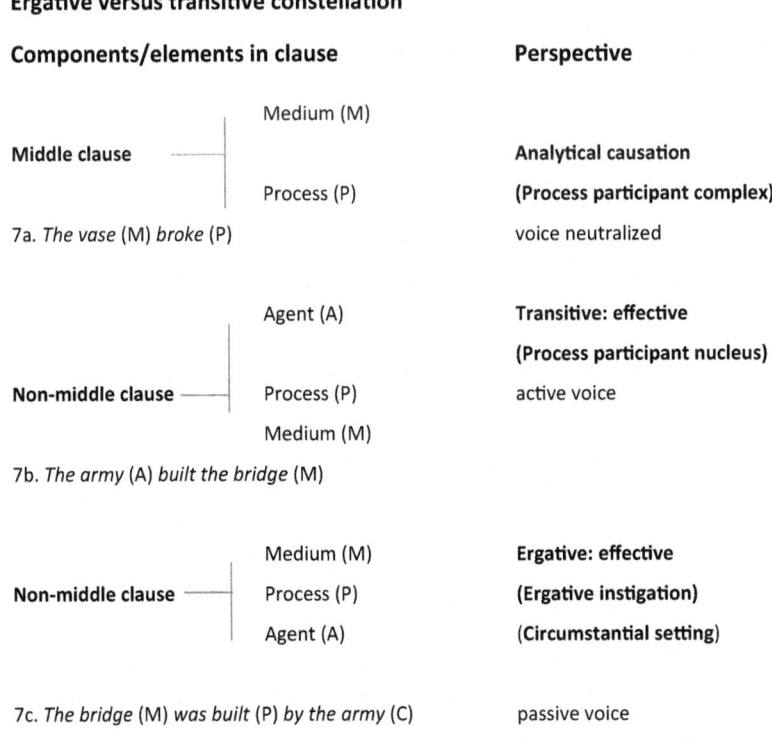

Fig. 4.2 Ergative transitive constellation

The **analytical and ergative difference** is also between **circumstantial settings** versus the **process–participant nucleus**. This distinction, as in Fig. 4.2, is based on the crucial principle of ergative structure **altering** the inherent voice of the Medium-Process complex, while analytical causation (7a) does not alter the inherent process-participant complex to which it adds a feature of causation (Halliday 1998: p. 198 in Davies and Ravelli 1992: p. 119). On the other hand, a **dual function** is instantiated in the circumstantiation of an indirect participant such as in the clause complex (7c). The instigator in (7c) is an indirect participant in the complex, and as the scope of the process, the nominal element is a circumstance, which modifies the process.

The **difference** between the transitive ergative systems are,

- The actor participates in the process, but the Medium in non-middle clause does not actively **co-participate** in the action.
- The 'who by' probe applies to all clauses below except the Medium–Process complex (7a)
- The instigator affects the medium by instigating its Process (7b). The process is one of instigation: **self-instigated** (7b) or an **externally-instigated** (7a) process.

4.4.1.2 Semantic Change: Deed-and-extension Relation

Entity transformation is also instantiated in the **scope**[5] of a participant role in the C element. For instance in Halliday (2004: p. 194),

Scope entity: 8a. *The dormouse* [actor] *crossed* [process: material] *the court* [**entity**/location].

---

[5] Scope—Halliday (2004: chapter 5), scope as participant exists independently of a doing process that takes place, it is a domain over which the process takes place, like specifying a range of tourist climbing: 'You will be crossing some lonely mountains, so make sure you have enough petrol.' Scope is restricted to intransitive clause consisting of syntagm 'nominal group + verbal group + nominal group, or Actor + Process + Goal or Actor + Process + scope. Scope cannot be a personal pronoun, cannot be probed by do to, do with. Scope can become subject of the clause, but in obvious sense is not directly involved in the process by bringing it about.

Scope process: 8b. *The whole country* [Medium] *is paying* [process: material] *a heavy price* [**process/scope of the Process**].
Scope-receptive (passive) clause: 8c. *This mountain* [Medium] *has never been climbed*, are common, but rare.
Scope-receptive clause with Actors: 8d. *What he did do to the cubby horse* [Medium] *was make it*; scope here is asserted but is odd. The 'do to' *manipulative construction* must **presuppose** the prior existence of the 'done to' construction in the intransitive construction (8d), where the Actor–Medium participant roles, *Lion chased the tourist*, exist prior to the unfolding of the process in, *The tourist ran*. The **outcome** of **transformation** in above examples is of a change of state also seen in logical relationship created in **Reverse Circumstantiation**.

4.4.1.3 Logical Relationship: Reverse Circumstantiation

As stated above, the **transformational** outcome is fulfilled by a *logical relationship* related by dependency rather than experientially to the remainder of the clause. For instance,

10a. *He drove quickly.*	(**Elaboration**)
10b. *He drove upstream.*	(**Extension**)
10c. *He left before the debate.*	(**Enhancement**)

Quickly is **logically** related and closer to the verb *drove*, whereas *upstream* **modifies** the whole situation referred to by the clause. Similar to this **dependency relationship**, McGregor in Davies and Ravelli (1992: p. 144) argues that **C elements** are not experientially identifiable parts, but are **experiential entities** as experiential roles, hence appear as Medium roles or C (scope) elements. That is, C/scope elements are an **extension** of the Process or elements **that modify the Process** in the clause, as in examples 8b and 8c above. This is the case for the offender disposition as **Narrative Object** (NO) with **intermediary status** in offender discourses analyzed (Sect. 4.5).

If an Actor–Goal relationship (clause 11a, 11b below) is at the level of the organization of elements in a clause, there is another underlying semantic level retrieved by *backward retracing transformational process* (Rimmon-Kenan 2002: p. 10). For instance, *thief* is a direct object in 11a, a subject in 11b, and *Flying planes* an **entity** that modify the Process in 11c,

11a. *The police killed the thief* (subject + predicate + **direct object**)
11b. *The thief was killed by the police* (Subject + predicate + **indirect object**)
11c. *Flying planes can be dangerous* (**entity** + predicate + complement)

The meaning in 11c is an entity, *flying planes* and an assignable property of being dangerous. The **circumstantial entity**, *Flying planes* is also in clause-initial position, **marked for focus**, where the clause-initial nominal element as the **scope** of the process, or in Medium role is not in control like a typical agent in clause initial position. In this process, termed as **Reverse Circumstantiation (C)**, a clause is linguistically marked for deviating from a norm. An entity here (11c) in reverse C is instantiated with a disposition, not as an *effector* of actions (such as, I sailed the boat), but as a *narrative object* that is (may be) *affected* by clause-initial circumstantiation of a circumstance, *flying planes*, and is relative to an entity formulated in the context. In *circumstantiation* thus, a semantic **space** is constructed for an indirect participant entity in the Reverse C element, which is in thematic relation an **expansion** or as the **scope** of the Process in clause. **Expansion** of an Actor–Goal schema to an entity as Medium–Process construct for a primary Agent (Ag_1) is relative to the **multiplicity of connections** with different objectives an individual needs to fulfil, such as a perpetrator participant from an Actor-offender.

One way of tackling this multiplicity of connections is in the **analytic overlap** such as the nominal element, *thief* in 11a and 11b. Additionally, the order of event recapitulation in the linear positioning of thematic relations is also significant for the cause and effect relation established between events, like in the ***Reverse Circumstantiation*** (Circumstance (C)/Actor/Process/Medium), **deviating from the norm** (Actor/Process/Medium/Circumstance). This marked focus is significant for an additional **post-murder participant disposition as entity**, which is formulated in the narration alongside the conventional narrative dispositions such as the **character** (in direct or indirect discourse), the **narrator** (as first person, or third person) or a *focalizer* (the focal position of one who perceives or the locus of the perceptual focus)

4.4.2 Interpersonal Function: Passivity and Modality

Modality
Whilst transitivity addresses the experiential function of language, modality is concerned with the interpersonal or the attitudinal feel of an utterance in text and is relative to the point of view of the speaker. In modality in clauses, there can be an **overlap** in the inferences available to the role of an actor in an event. For the interplay of participant dispositions, and for the conflict of interest in multiple positions of a participant, the modal commitments in interpersonal functions in clauses can surface a space in the dual function for restricted narration. For instance, modal meanings generated in the modality provide the reader with the means by which the emotional presence of a person is felt, a voice expressing feelings, needs, uncertainties or doubts. It is a powerful indicator of a narrator point of view. Modality fosters **interactivity** (connection) between the speaker and the receiver, where the reader is given the possibility of taking on the modalized claims of the speaker. This **modalized telling** (in modal system) creates a textual effect distinct from an unmodalized epistemically non-modal categorical assertion.

The schema in Fig. 4.3 summarizes the function of the modal system above, and is utilized for analysis of narrative modes (Fig. 4.4, Table 4.2) employed by the offender in its discourse. This **interpersonal function** of language based on four modal systems is the deontic system closely related to the boulomaic system, and the epistemic modality with its subsystem of perception modality. As stated in Simpson (1993: p. 51), *the boxed enclosures capture the interrelatedness of categories, and the non-linguistic concepts which each category represents are explained to the right.*

Modal system
Non-linguistic concepts represented
Deontic
Obligation, duty and commitment
Boulomaic
Desire
Epistemic
Knowledge, belief, and cognition (knowing, perceiving)
Perception
Human perception, normally visual perception

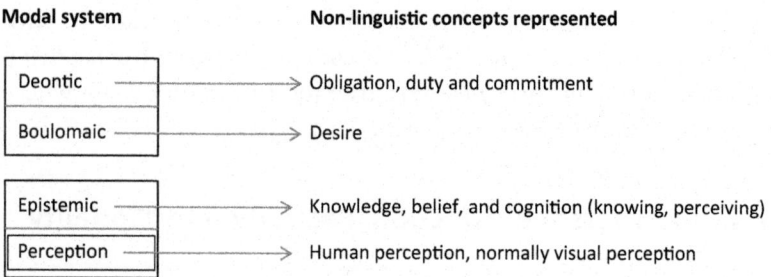

Fig. 4.3 Modal system

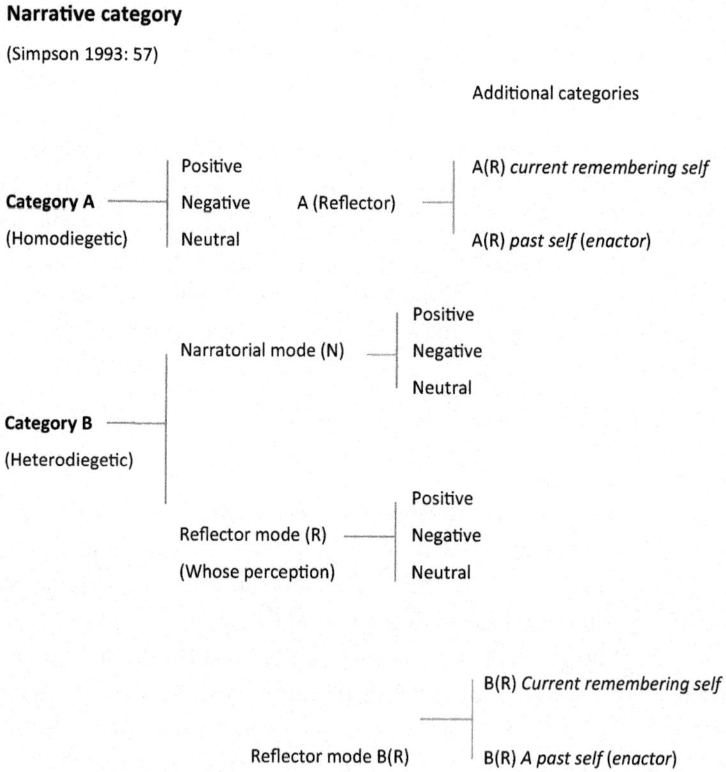

Narrative category
(Simpson 1993: 57)
Additional categories
Category A
(Homodiegetic)
Positive
Negative
Neutral
A (Reflector)
A(R) current remembering self
A(R) past self (enactor)
Category B
(Heterodiegetic)
Narratorial mode (N)
Positive
Negative
Neutral
Reflector mode (R)
(Whose perception)
Positive
Negative
Neutral
Reflector mode B(R)
B(R) Current remembering self
B(R) A past self (enactor)

Fig. 4.4 Narrative categories

4.4.2.1 Narratorial Modes in Story Telling

Narratorial modes direct reader attention to the narrator, or reader attention to the narration, deriving a **tentative** narrator characterization. In the transposition between **I-narration, they-narration** and **s/he-narration**, or modulating from an **involved first person, external**

Table 4.2 Modal tendencies in narrative categories: A (homodiegetic) B (heterodiegetic); **N**—narrator, **R**—reflector

N+ve	R+ve	N-ve	R-ve
Floating omniscience: inside + outside the character position	Mediated through third person single perspective	Limited knowledge: concerning the thoughts of the character	Limited knowledge: consciousness of the participating characters
Floating omniscience	Restricted omniscience	Alienation and bewilderment e.g., *Someone must have been telling lies...*	Words of estrangement e.g. *seemed*
Invisible non-participating narrator	Through the consciousness/ knowledge of Reflector	Epistemic and perception modal expressions	Disorientating effect
outside character position	Proximal deictics	–	Epistemic and perception modal expressions
Birds-eye panoramic view	Epistemic and perception modal expressions	–	–
Deontic boulomaic modal expressions	Restricted omniscience	–	–
Evaluative adjectives and adverbials	–	–	–
Highly modalized discourse	–	–	–
Action suspended for causality	–	–	–

or reflector-narrator, can render gaps in the narrative. As observed in Toolan,

> '... *intercategory* [I-narration, they-narration, and s/he-narration or A, B(N), B(R)] *transpositions are significantly more problematic. Transforming ... an unmodalized account into a modalized one ... can be done, but not the reverse.*' (2001: p. 73)

Table 4.3 Syntactic devices to undercut agency (Kies in Davies and Ravelli 1992: pp. 231–242)

Passives Where agentive NP occurs out of thematic, sentence-initial position in an optional agentive by-phrase at the end of the sentence	**Presentational 'there' structure** Where agentive subject is de-emphasized in sentence-medial position by using presentational there structures
Nominalized verbs Supplied through the optional presence of an agentive by-phrase creating overt mention of agency	**Subjunctive mood** (conditional 'if') Possible world with no necessary suggestion of action in the real world expressed as conditional 'if'
Intransitive use of verbs Suggest that events arise or occur beyond the control of characters by suppressing an agentive participant role	**Linking verbs like 'seem'** Casting doubt on the agency of the grammatical subject
Depersonalization Part of a person is used to represent figuratively the whole person	**Impersonal 'one'** **Point of view shifts** to undercut clear sense of agency and responsibility for any conclusion
Perfect aspect of verb Suggests completed activity in the remote past, undercutting thereby any sense of action that might have any relevance to the activity of the present	**Modality shifts** Where modal or quasi-modal auxiliary (e.g. ought to) undercuts the agency of the transitive verb
Negation Highlighting the meanings of 'not possible' and 'certain that not', undercutting the statement and thereby directly undercutting agency	**Existential 'it' and other cleft sentences** Allow information focus on one constituent, a divided focus, effectively undercutting the agency of the grammatical subject
Stative verbs (resultative verbs) Verbs whose meaning denote lack of motion, suggests an outside agency	**Patient as subject** Where the grammatical subject as patient is the goal of the prediction (passives)
Aspectual verbs Verbs whose meaning is more state-oriented than agent or speaker-oriented **An additional device added to Kies' syntactic categories to undercut agency**	

If narration is **reversed** when transiting from the default first- or third-person narrative mode, such as in syntactic devices (Table 4.3) to undercut Narrator Agency, this proposes a conflict of narrative interest at the point of narration (storytelling). In modal assertions, the **new profile** instantiated is an <u>emotional state</u> of an embedded and dynamic participant separate from the **narrating narrator** (first or third person) or a **focalizer/reflector**. For these dispositions, the narratorial modes (Fig. 4.3) are a way of categorizing and assessing the visibility of a narrator from a new entity formulated for a narrative purpose.

Simpson's (1993: chapter 3) schema makes one think about the degree to which different narratorial stances are expressed and are demonstrated through aspects of grammar in the construction of each mode. The framework from Simpson in Fig. 4.4 distinguishes narratives as *category A* (a participating character as I- narrator) and *category B* (mainly corresponding to Genette's invisible, disembodied, non-participating omniscient heterodiegetic narration). Another viewing position outside the character as **Reflector** of the fiction can move into the active mind of a particular character (category B Reflector mode) *'through whom situations and events told about by a heterodiegetic or third-person narrator are refracted'* (Herman in *The Cambridge Companion to Narrative* 2014: p. 245).

These narratorial modes are suitable for **multiperspectivism** in modal assertions in offender narrative. Category A (homodiegetic) and B (heterodiegetic) modes are subdivided based on the negative, positive or neutral shadings, and appear as in Fig. 4.4.

The narratorial mode in Fig. 4.4 is distinct from the Reflector mode. The distinction of (N) and (R) mode for Category B narratives is also extended to A narratives, where the participating character transposes to a **role outside** the first person participating character anchored in the **primary text-world** in the present tense distinct from an **enactor** in the default past tense.

In the A(R) mode, the point of perceptual origins hover between two coordinates, the **narrating-I** (current remembering self, e.g. *now I see*), and the **experiencing-I** (the past self/the other/enactor), **focalized** through the protagonist *I watch her*). In the B(R) mode, the **remembering reflector** may also split into a current and a past self (Jahn in Herman 2007: p. 100).

Modality further has the tendency in narrative categories to add positive or negative shading (Fig. 4.3), compared to those with the absence of modalization that are mainly flat and non-subjective categorical assertions (CA). This is summarized in Table 4.2, where in **B(N)+ve mode** the narrating **position is outside the participating character** functioning as an invisible and non-participating entity, that has a birds-eye panoramic view of the narrated event. This discourse is highly modalized, where the action is suspended for causality. Evaluative adverbials and adjectives, deontic modalities of obligation and desire (Fig. 4.4) are the features characteristic of this mode. This position contrasts with the **B(N)-ve mode** where there is **lack of detail** concerning the thoughts of the character in the epistemic and perceptual modality. The effect is one of alienation and bewilderment e.g. *Someone must have been telling lies*. Notice the stative form in tense aspect.

While in B(R)+ve and B(R)-ve modes, the narration is mediated through the **consciousness** of the participating character as a Reflector, who has a restricted omniscience from a single character perspective in epistemic and perception modal expressions, and is also anchored in the proximal deictics.

In A-positive (A+) narratives, deontic and boulomaic (Fig. 4.4) modal systems are prominent, foregrounding the narrator's desire, obligation, duties, and opinions about events and characters. By contrast, the epistemic and perception modal system with negative shading (-ve) is more alienating. An instance of bewilderment and estrangement derives from the participating character's consciousness and highlights the uncertainty about characters and events.

In the A-neutral narrative, the narrator withholds subjective evaluation, and the story is told through CAs. There is a neutral point of view, with no psychological development due to straightforward descriptions. A-neutral point of view characterizes the hard-boiled detective novel (Simpson 1993: p. 61).

4.4.2.2 Stance in Transition

In the transition or oscillation from one mode to another, the **point-of-view** perspective is adjusted according to the position of a participating character as the narrator, or a narrator-reflector in the discourse. The epistemic system is important for the analysis of the transition of point

4 Disposition

of view. Epistemic modal auxiliaries *could, may be* or lexical verbs *think, suppose* and epistemic modal adverbs *sure to be, certain that* (be…to, be… that constructions), *arguably, perhaps* render speaker's commitment to the **truth factuality** of propositions dependent on the speaker knowledge. Modal auxiliaries used in an epistemic sense convey varying degrees of epistemic commitment to the basic categorical/unmodalized assertion, *you are right*, which is epistemically stronger than assertions like, *you could, may be, must be, might have been right* (Simpson 1993: p. 49). Schema for the basic proposition with modal assertions adopted from Simpson and Butler in Nash (1990) are shown in Fig. 4.5.

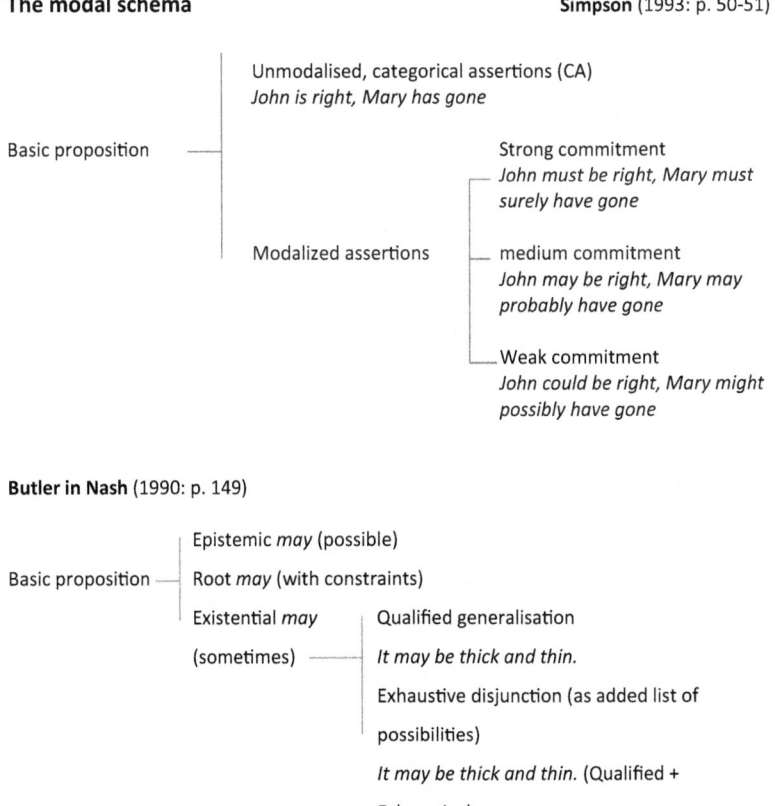

Fig. 4.5 The modal schema

It is evident from the figure that, not only at the level of plot (Chap. 2) but also at the level of language, the readers can appreciate the powerlessness of the embedded characters. In the above modal scheme, the modal forms may appear in a dominant unmodalized discourse (CAs), for example, **verba sentiendi** (verbs of physical and mental perception of participating participant, e.g. see, hear, taste, learn) of a participating narrator, or in modality expressing uncertainty or doubt (**evidentiality**). In addition, a sudden transition from a positive to negative orientation in a category A or B can have a disorientating effect for the reader where events presented are no longer seen as tangible or palpable before the transition occurred. In detective discourse, this effect is for ***interactional evidentiality*** (Biber and Finegan 1989), or as concluded in Opas and Tweedie (2000) in Opas-Hanninen and Seppanen (2010: p. 274),

'...*detective stories seem to mark evidentially, that is, the character expresses their certainty and doubt.*'

Passivity: Point of View

Chatman (1978: p. 154) summarizes that **point of view** is the perspective or stance, which is in the story with respect to the characters, while **voice** is the medium through which point of view, perception, conception, and interest is communicated and is external to the narrative discourse. For instance, **stance** is made external in static syntax (Table 4.3) for suppressed agency to foreground a conflict of interest in multipositionality. The **agency** in static aspects, *had been running, was going to* (Corliss clause 1 below) is minimized, when compared with conscious assertion in VP such as, *sat* (Corliss clause 23 below). Formulating a **functional contrast** in discourse for *multiperspectivism* in participant disposition, created in static syntax like aspectual verb, whose meaning is more state-oriented than agentive for the narrating-he, such as in clause 23. The aspectual form draw up a conflict of interest for participant Bud Corliss who in clause 1 is in a state of transition,

Corliss 1. '*His plans had been running so beautifully, so goddamned beautifully, and now she was going to smash them all.*'   Versus a conscious-initiator of actions in

Corliss 23. *'He sat at the back of the room, in the second seat from the window.'* (My emphasis)

In Quirk et al. (1972: p. 801),

> *'The active–passive relation involves two grammatical levels: the verb phrase and the clause. ... At the clause level passivization involves rearrangement of two clause elements and one addition.'*
> A. *The active subject becomes the passive agent*
> B. *The active object becomes the passive subject*
> C. *The prepositional by is introduced before the agent.'* (My emphasis)

Kies (1992) agrees that passives as a grammatical device *undercut* agency,

> '... *by writing in the passive voice, eliminating the agentive by-phrase, Orwell* [in his style of writing] *was able to suggest that his characters are not conscious initiators of action.* (1992: p. 231)

The fourteen syntactic devices in Table 4.3, from Kies (in Davies and Ravelli 1992: chapter 12), can suppress or undercut agency to suggest how the writer in scientific discourse is not made a conscious initiator of actions, when it should be agentive, where a conscious experimenter is summarizing its findings.

4.4.3 Referential and Evaluative Function: Truth-Value

Besides narratorial modes for modal restrictions and for narratorial stance in narration, the manner of event recapitulation is also significant for further analyzes of stance. A narrative clause (NC) is a sequential clause. The fixity (order) of a true NC is crucial. Evaluative clauses (EC) convey the point and tellability of the story in narrative clauses. These clauses are identified in the linguistic-structural properties that relate to two broad functions identified in the **referential function** (also termed as NC) (recapitulating experience in the order that matches the temporal sequence of the original experience) and in the **evaluative function**

(Toolan 2001: chapter 6). In contrast, a **free clause** (FC) is a **circumstance** relating to the fixed sequence of events in the narrative clauses and has the potential to be moved anywhere as a wholly FC (clause 12) in the text, relative to the NCs that the FC relates to (clauses 13–17), while NCs are locked in their given interrelated positions. The examples below from Labov (1997) in Toolan (2001: p. 146) put into context these functional differences in the narrative below, where clauses are separated to distinguish the different types when explained.

12. *John got this urge to be the star of the party.* (Restricted FC/comment parallel to main action)
13. *He had two large whiskies,* (NC)
14. *performed a standing somersault on the embankment wall,* (NC)
15. *fell in the river,* (NC + coordinated to NC 16)
16. *got very cold* (NC)
17. *and ruined his suit.* (NC + coordinated NC to 14)
18. *This happened when he was still at school.* (FC/narrative report (NR))

(Toolan 2001: p. 147, chapter 6).

Clauses 12 and 18 as FCs are distinct from each other. Clause 12 is a comment on NCs 13–17, a perspective (as opinion) from someone's standpoint. In the FC/narrative clause (clause 18), deictic *this* points to the proximity of the speaker's temporal location with respect to the past narrated event. With reference to **frame analysis**, the characterization of events, such as the statement in 12, as a **framed activity** from an individual's point of view, generates **motivational relevancy**; a sarcastic comment on NCs 13–17. This is **restricted clause** in the sequence of events, as it must appear before the actual narrative is reported, and is not a reported clause like 18. Clause 12 is then a **cognitive prefocalization** of events that is to follow in 13–17, revealing the disposition of the speaker relative to the reported event. There is a **double dipping** (multiple positions) in the evaluative stance (perspective) in proximal deictic *this urge* in clause 12, unlike FC/narrative report 18, *This happened*, also with syntactical properties of being in simple present tense. Furthermore, in clause 12 there is direct speaker/listener constellation in the context of the situation, where the speaker is direct but positioned **outside** the events described in the narrative discourse. This is unlike the indirect participant disposition associated with *the army* in the PP underlined, *The bridge was built <u>by the army</u>*, in which *the bridge* as an entity (Medium) in the subject position is not the agent who performed the Process *was built*.

The status in reality or the truth-value of a narrative action or sayings is also informed in the definite and indefiniteness of elements as circumstance alongside referential and evaluative functions in clauses. As seen in restricted FC 12, there is juxtaposing of evaluative properties (in **tense alternation**) with the basic narrative syntax. Deictic *this* in clause 18 indicates a temporal and spatial proximity to the speaker, which is in opposition with the definite temporal and spatial past of the narrative in 12–18. The alternation manifests a **narrator intervention** in clause 12 about the narration in clauses 13–17. In contrast, FC 18 locates the event in time. If it were to be placed at the start of the narrative, FC 18 would not alter the comprehension of the narrative. Spatial, temporal or scope (circumstantial adverbials, adjectival) elements are used alongside aspect and syntactic devices to undercut agency narration (Table 4.3). This is relevant for the differences in participant dispositions in the **transformation** between the narrator and narration in narrative discourse.

On accounting a narrative function **(what is done)** as one distinct from an evaluative function **(what is said)**, the following linguistic devices can render a narrative (NC) as evaluative.

Clause types (reclassification)
Bare narrative/Sequential recapitulation function (NC)
Narrative clause (NC) (fixed type)
Narrative circumstance

> Free clause (FC/narrative report)
> Free clause (Restricted FC/comment parallel to the main action)

Syntactical properties in (independent) NCs clauses with main clause finite verbs. Clauses occur in,
Simple present or past
Progressive aspect (performing), perfective aspect (**had performed**) are **rare** in NCs

Evaluative clause (EC)
Types: external EC and internal EC
Internal evaluation (NC-internal-evaluation)

Intensifiers (repetition, gestures, accompanied by deictic that)
Comparators (negation)
Correlatives (bring together events, be + v-ing forms for simultaneity of actions)
Explicatives (subordinate clauses although, while, since, because)

External evaluation

Wholly external
Embedded evaluation (comment reported)
Embedded evaluation (comment by teller)
Embedded evaluation (from another participant)
Evaluative action

The above classification is adopted from Toolan (1988: p. 157) with slight variation.

Additional evaluative properties

Narration time in tense alternation (external/outside the fixed position of NC)
Subordination altering temporal sequence of NC (external/outside the fixed position of NC)
Static aspect for narrator intervention (internal evaluation)

To summarize, the above framework adopted for the analysis of **multiperspectivism** in **multipositionality** is thus in:

- The grammar of experience (ergative vs. transitive constellation)
- The transformational outcome (for experiential entities into experiential roles)
- The point of view or stance (in passivity and in modality for tentative characterization)

- The distinction between the narrative action from an evaluative saying in referential (NC) and evaluative function (EC) in clauses (C)

The tables for analysis of **multiperspectivism** in **multipositionality** are based on three functions,

1. Experiential function in,

- **Transitive perspective**

Transitive clauses are non-middle clauses (Fig. 4.2) where the agency is **overt** (clause 7b) and is **one of deed-and-extension**.

Type a. Agent (A)/Process (P)/Medium (M)/Circumstance (C)
                                                (Transitive reading)

Ripley, 18. *Dickie and Marge* (A) *began to talk* (P) *about the changes* … (C)

Type b. Agent/Process/Circumstance   **(Transitive reading)**

Ripley, 13. *Tom* (A) *swore* (P) *to himself* (C).

Type c. *C/Agent/Process/Medium   **(Reverse circumstantiation)**

Ripley, 25. *That* (C) *he* (A) *wanted* (P) *more than anything else* (C).

Transitive clauses are generally goal-oriented non-middle clauses, whose function is **one of extension**. It indicates an intentional **agent** or one who is **engaged**[6] in a mental process.
The **transitive reading** is **linear** (Fig. 4.1),
    Actor → Goal

- **Ergative perspective**

---

[6] Engaged Agent: Not a mere senser, but also involuntarily involved in the process like an experiencer, e.g., '*He knew he smelled cheese*'; Ackroyd: '*I had deemed a wise precaution*'; Ripley: '*Tom swore.*'

Ergative clauses are middle clauses, where the medium in subject position is the element through which the process came into being.

Type d. Medium (M)/Process (P)/Circumstance (C)
                                              (Intransitive reading)

Raven, 2. *You* (Medium) *had to be careful.* (Process)

Type e. Medium/Process/Circumstance   (Intransitive reading)

Ripley, 29. *Tom* (M) *slowed* (P) *as he climbed* (C) (something triggered to slow down)
Ripley 7. *Tom* (Experiencer/M) *had a pang* (P)

Type f. Agent/Process/Circumstance   (Intransitive reading)

Raven 9b. *she;* (Medium) *moaned* (Process) at *him* (C/location)

Type g. Circumstance/Medium/Process
                                         (Reverse Circumstantiation)

11. TGS Frame 158. *The end was plain* (C/scope), *Edward* (Medium) *must die* (Process).
*Type h. Unusual structures   (C/Scope clauses)

i. **C/P/C**   e.g.   Raven 1. *Murder* (C) *didn't mean much* (P) *for Raven* (C)
ii. **M/P/M**   e.g.   Ripley 10. *He* (M/C) *might become* (P) *a representative* (M)
iii. **C/P/M**   e.g.   Raven, 54. *It* [not a word about Anne] (C) *shook* (P) *him* (M)

The **causative reading** (ergative) is **circular** (Fig. 4.1). The causative perspective is at **two processual layers** causing a circular ergative reading of clauses where, the Medium is **hosting** the Process and **something is**

4 Disposition

being done to the Medium (Ripley clause 22) to **instigate a change of state.** Such as,
John (**instigator** + **instigating** the opening) *opened the door*.
Ripley 22. *Tom* (Medium) *wondered* (**instigator** + **instigating** the wondering) *if* [they] *were having an affair* (Circumstance imagined).

(Double dipping)

Circumstance (C) encodes the **background** against which the process takes place. The C element is an indirect participant in the complex, and as the scope of the Process, the nominal element is a circumstance, which modifies the Process, instantiating an Affected-Actor disposition.

C elements: Scope of the process/range (e.g. adverbial, adjectival), *location* (time/when, space/where), *manner* (how), *extent* (duration, distance), *cause* (because), *contingency* (despite, although), *accompaniment* (who, what with), *matter* (what about), *product*, and *angle* (point of view) (Thompson 1996: pp. 104–107)

Voice (passivity): for **plurisignification** of perception, cognition outside the discourse in syntactic devices (Kies 1992) and tense aspect that undercut agency,

Undercut agency in static syntax (Kies 1992) undercut agency; it is also in tense aspect.

Double dipping is in **analytical overlap** of the standpoint of Narrator in different narratorial modes.

2. Interpersonal function: transition in perspective/stance for interactional evidentiality **Modal assertions** (Fig. 4.5):

- **Modal Assertions (MA)**
- **Categorical Assertions (CA)**

Narrative modes (Narrator/N or Reflector/R): (Fig. 4.4 and Table 4.2)

- **A+ve, A-ve, A neutral**
- **B+ve, B-ve, B neutral**
- **R+ve, R-ve, R neutral**

3. Referential and Evaluative function informing truth-value (Section: clause types: reclassification)

Truth-value: A status in reality in Narrative (NC) and Evaluative Clause (EC)

- **Narrative clauses**/NC (Fixed Referential/function) (what is done)
- **Evaluative Clauses**/EC (Evaluative/Tellability function) (what is said)
- **Fixed Comment Clauses** (FC/Comment)
- **Fixed Narrative Clauses** (FC/Narrative)

Following the above three functions in linguistics features, an '**intermediary state**' as an embedded disposition is distinguished for the primary Agent in the discourse and subsequently the intermediary state as the backgrounded stimulus of the perpetrator (the embedded second story) for the offending act (the first story of killing or murder,) in crime story.

The table header below is for analysis of **experiential function 1**.

Clause no.	Transitive	Ergative	Devices undercut agency	Background condition

The table header below is for analysis of **interpersonal function** 2, and referential, evaluative function 3, for **truth-value**.

| Clause no. | Assertions | Narrative modes | Truth value | | Devices undercut agency |
			NC (what is done)	EC (what is said)	

4.5 Findings: Linguistic Dysfunctions

The view here is that the offender who is also the narrator has three functions in the story from three simultaneous dispositions:

4 Disposition   225

- The Narrator,
- The character, and also
- An **intermediary participating character**, which lies between these two dispositions, and who is an *indirect participant* (Secondary Agent/ Ag_2). As expressed in Davidse, the distinction is tied up,

With *the grammar that makes direct participants in the Process, Circumstantial elements attendant on it and some transitional category like 'indirect participant' that lie between these categories.* (1992: p. 119)

Following the **experiential function** analysis in Appendix 3a–g, the intermediary position is in the differences in meanings encoded in clause structures with the Reverse Circumstantiation (type c, C/A/P/M) **deviating** from the standard transitive and intransitive perspective (type a. A/P/M/C and type b. A/P/C). In type C clauses, there is **analytical causation** more than **direct causation**. Analytical causation, unlike **ergative: effective structures** (Fig. 4.2) do not alter the inherent voice of the process–participant complex (7a). The clause complex adds a feature of external causation by indirectly adding a secondary Ag_2 in the constellation, where the action is **not engendered** (caused) by this subject position Ag_2, but is **supervened** (to take place or occur as something **additional** or **extraneous**) as in clause 6b, *John* (superventive) *fell into the pool*. As a **deep structure analysis**, the reverse circumstantiation in middle and non-middle clauses, as deviations from the norm in the analyzed discourses, provide analytical focus on the offender circumstance.

Following the **interpersonal function** in narrative mode, the *double dipping* for multiperspectivism is in the alternation from B(N)+ve to B(R)-ve and in an unmodalized narrative mode (Categorical Assertions) with static syntax (Figs. 4.3 and 4.4), formulating a **functional contrast** for an effector disposition of a villain or an offender. Static syntax in an otherwise unmodalized narrative assertions undercut the Narrator intervention in offender discourses. The functional contrast is asserted in unmodalized assertions, when the discourse is juxtaposed with static aspects for stative orientation, this instantiate a participant state, a condition of being passive. This state when correlated with the evaluative and referential functions for truth-value at the clause level, where the FC/comment clauses as circumstance also inform the evaluative enactment of the **perpetrator experience**, in the narrative stance the experience related to the backgrounded sub-themes of the perpetrators.

Offending is an enactment (Presser in Youngs and Canter 2012: p. 290), where offending experience is always known and is acted upon. These roles in the criminal context in Youngs and Canter (2012) are *Hero*,[7] *Victim*,[8] *Professional*[9] and *Revenger*.[10] However, the backgrounded perpetrator experience is linguistically conceptualized in the **linguistic dysfunctions** like Reverse C **deviating from the norm**, and in **functional contrasts** when there is static syntax in Narrator omniscience for limited intervention. Additionally, **FC/comment clauses** as NC are circumstances that are outside the fixed narrative sequence, and like above linguistic features instantiate a secondary disposition in addition and **external** to the narrating-I as participant in the default narrative mode. The above linguistic dysfunctions thus provide an analytical focus, where the **victim enactment** in the discourses analyzed is an **externally instigated backgrounded circumstance**, which as the scope or Medium role modify the Process, where the criminal is an **entity** than an effector in the offending process. In the discourses analyzed below, the enactor as an entity in Reverse C/scope or as Medium role is for an affected (victim) **status**, which is the stimulus for the offending act in default effector role of a criminal.

The **process of enactment** is analyzed in the experiential and interpersonal functions found in the narration, juxtaposed with truth-value in the deep clausal structure of each offender/perpetrator's discourse. It is to this analysis that we now turn to.

---

[7] The *Hero* role describes an offending experience where the role is about focus on proving oneself and being part of a greater mission, about overcoming obstacles in pursuit of pure and joyful objectives.

[8] The *Victim* role, a narrative irony is a life story underpinned by a sense that nothing makes any sense, there are no rules and nothing matters.

[9] *Professional* is a role that emerges from an underlying life narrative of adventure. The story is about the protagonist's victorious mastery over his or her environment.

[10] *Revenger* role—Taking together all the offending experience the offender sees himself or herself as acting out the role of *Revenger*. Like the story in Tragedy narrative, the story is of an extraordinary victim, an individual who must respond to the wrong or deprivation they suffered.

4.5.1 Perpetrator: Bud Corliss

Experiential Function (Appendix 4a)
A Kiss before Dying is a hybrid construction. Unlike the Raven and Ripley stories, Bud Corliss is not revealed as the perpetrator until near the end of the story. Bud Corliss is an **anticipatory** participant functioning in a sub-world as a post-murder participant. The **sub-world context** is developed in Reverse Cs. It is about the background conditions for Bud Corliss as the grammatical subject *he*, projected as the third -person Narrator in the story. For instance, the new information in Reverse C (C/scope) in clauses 1–3 below set up a relationship with Medium Dorothy who was responsible for smashing *his plan*, where the Medium is really the C of the Process. Unlike the norm (clause 4), the nominal elements, *the plan*, *she* (Dorothy) and *hate* in circumstantial roles are not in the predicate position. Reverse C in subject/thematic position in the clauses below is thus marked for to picalization (high topicality) of the new information, as in newspaper reports,

> '... given the thematic progression as the discourse pattern New information is fronted in the larger unit of the sentence followed by information which is given in the smaller unit of the sentence.' (Flanders 2012: p. 275)

Clause no.	Transitive	Ergative	Undercut agency	Background condition Clause type
1a. *His plans had been running so beautifully, so goddamned beautifully, and now she was going to smash them all.*		*His plans (receptive/ Medium) had been running so eautifully, so oddamned beautifully,* (Process)	Progressive aspect	M/P/C **Intransitive reading Type d**

(continued)

228   The Language of Suspense in Crime Fiction

(continued)

Clause no.	Transitive	Ergative	Undercut agency	Background condition Clause type
1b. and now she was going to smash them all.		... and now (C/scope) she (Medium) was going to smash (Process) them all (C/scope)		*Reverse C/M/P/C Intransitive reading Type g
2. Hate erupted and flooded through him, gripping his face with jaw-aching pressure.	Hate (C/scope) erupted and flooded (Process) through him (Medium), [hate] (Agent) gripping his face (Medium) with jaw-aching pressure (C/scope)		Depersonalization Depersonalization Progressive aspect	*Reverse C/P/M Unusual structure (undercut) Inanimate A/P/C Intransitive reading
3. That was alright though, the lights were out.	That [the eruption of his hate] was alright though (C/scope entity)	the lights (Medium) were out. (Process)		C (Scope) C (Scope)
4. He closed his eyes and spoke dreamily, intoning the words in a sedative chant.	He (Agent) closed (Process) his eyes (Medium) and [he] spoke dreamily, intoning the words in a sedative chant. (C/scope)			Intentional A/P/M Transitive reading Type a [Intentional A]/P/C Intransitive reading Type b
10. You would have told me what he's interested in, what he likes, what he dislikes-' he stopped short, then continued.	DS he (Agent) stopped short, then continued. (Process)			Intentional A/P Transitive reading

4 Disposition   229

(continued)

Clause no.	Transitive	Ergative	Undercut agency	Background condition Clause type
16. When he called her 'baby' and held her in arms he could get her to do practically anything.	When he called her 'baby' and held her in arms (C/scope) he (Agent) could get her to do (Process) practically anything. (C/scope)		Modality shift (Modality signal possibility *could*)	*Reverse C/ (undercut) Intentional A/P/C Intransitive reading Type b
18. What angered him most was that in a sense the responsibility for the entire situation rested with Dorothy.	What angered him most (C/scope) was (Process) that in a sense the responsibility for the entire situation (C/scope) rested (Process) with Dorothy. (Medium)			*Reverse C/P/C Unusual structure
20. It was Dorothy, with her gently closed eyes and her passive, orphan hunger, who had wished for further visits.		It was Dorothy, with her gently closed eyes and her passive, orphan hunger, (C/scope) who (Medium) had wished (Process) for further visits. (C/scope)	Perfective tense	*Reverse C/M/P/C Intransitive reading Type e
24. The seat on his left, the window seat, the empty seat, was hers.		The seat on his left, the window seat, the empty seat, (C/scope) was (Process) hers. (Medium)		*Reverse C/P/M Unusual structure

(continued)

(continued)

Clause no.	Transitive	Ergative	Undercut agency	Background condition Clause type
25. It was the first class of the morning, a daily Social Science lecture, and their only class together this semester.	It was the first class of the morning, a daily Social Science lecture, and their only class together this semester. (C/scope)		Existential it	C(scope)
30. The important thing was to get time, time to think.	The important thing was to get time, time to think. (C/scope)			C(scope)
40. The earliest Ellen could get the note would be—three o' clock.	The earliest (C/scope) Ellen (Agent) could get (Process) the note (Medium) would be— three o' clock. (C/location)		Modality shift (Modality signal possibility could)	*Reverse C/(undercut) hypothetical A/P/M/C Transitive reading Type c
41. Five hours and forty minutes.	FIT			
42. No step by step planning now.	FIT			Temporal deictic now
43. It would have to be quick, positive.	FIT			
44. No trickery that counted on her doing a certain thing at a certain time.	FIT			
45. No poison.	FIT			
46. How else do people kill themselves?	FIT			

(continued)

Clause no.	Transitive	Ergative	Undercut agency	Background condition Clause type
47. In five hours and forty minutes she must be dead. (55)	FIT	In five hours and forty minutes (C/scope) she (Medium) must be dead. (Process)	Modality shift (Modality signal obligation must)	Reverse C/M/P Intransitive reading Type g

In Reverse C, as a feature of causation, an external secondary Agent (Ag_2) is brought about formulating an **Actor-Affected schema** (Table 4.1). That is, as a 'done to' construction Reverse C is an entity which corresponds to *His plans* in clause 1, instantiates *hate* in clause 2, equates to the *that* clause in clause 3, and to the situation relating to a letter (clauses 24, 25, 30 and 40) from Dorothy to Ellen to fake Dorothy's murder as a suicide. This implied Ag_2, such as in clauses like 47, is an external Causer who manipulates the circumstance in clauses 40 and 41 that did not go to plan in clause 1, and also had to manipulate the cause in effecting the caused event in clause 47. In the background provided in Reverse C, an **anticipatory participant** is embedded in the discourse. As the **sayer** in these utterances, it is an **affected participant** in anticipation. This anticipatory disposition of the third -person default narrator in the world of an **offending participant** withheld in clauses like 4, is also a reporting participant of the direct and indirect discourses grounded in the proximal deictic universe as *offline* narration of the default narrator in its offender engagement discourse.

As observed earlier, multiple positions of a third person narrating-*he* is established according to different objectives that the individual *he* (Bud Corliss) needs to fulfil. Clauses with Reverse C leave intact the inherent active voice of the process–participant constellation in clauses. Following the linearity of the transitivity model in Fig. 4.1, the energy input in direct (DS) and indirect (IS) discourse is linear in clauses such as 10, where the participant position in the utterance, *he stopped short, then continued*, is from the Actor *He* to the implied hearer Dorothy. Conversely, in the Medium role in clauses like 1, 2 and in the C/scope clauses 3,

25, 30 in the discourse, the offending participant is an instigator who co-participates in the process of instigating the scope entity in these clauses. This instigator is non-direct and **external** (yet to be revealed as the offender) in the clausal context. Circumstantiation of the implied causer *he* in clauses 2, 3, 16, 18 and the narrated circumstance relating to the victim Dorothy in clauses 20, 24, 25, 30 are thus **non-volitional thematized entities** of an Ag_2 in the clauses.

Thematized circumstantiation is an emotional state of the **offending participant** [Bud], who is constructed as a background in Reverse Cs for the forthcoming murder in clause 47 in the offender's internal narrative. This **affected participant** is a narrative object (NO) in the entity representation in Reverse C, and the disposition embedded in Reverse C is marked in the **deviation from the norm**: Agent/Process/Medium/Circumstance in the clause structure. Such an **affected intermediary role** for **interactional intentionality** is also marked in the temporal proximity to the *now* of the default speaker/Narrator in clause 1, distinct from the speaker in direct discourse, as in clause 10.

The Interpersonal Function

When accounting for the deictic *now* (clause 1) and the adverbial *today* (clause 27) in restricted FC/comment clauses in the table below, there is a temporal proximity to the speaker situated in the **primary textworld** in present tense, projecting a **cognitive prefocalization** of events reported in the NCs (FC/narrative in clauses 23, 24 and 25). However, FC/comment clauses as speaker circumstance reveal the evaluative stance of the speaker relative to the event reported. As a framed activity from an individual's point of view, FC/comment clauses generate **motivational relevancies** and are therefore restricted in the sequence of NCs, setting a **binary distinction** between the *real* and **fixed** NCs, from the *irrealis* FC/comment NCs in transition, formulating a **binary opposition** in the same **offending discourse**. In FC/comment clauses, the participant is **anticipating** the narrative outcome and consequently is mentally re calculating (for instance the letter event in clause 40); privileging **intentionality** for the disclosure that the **intermediary** *he* intends. Contextually, the 'perpetrator in transition' in clause 40 wanted the letter to reach the recipient (Ellen) after the victim (Dorothy) was dead in order to manipulate the murder as a suicide. An **intermediary discourse** of the

4 Disposition   233

third -person perpetrator *he* in clause 3 is formulated in Reverse Cs significant for marked focus. This is also marked in FC/comment clauses for the evaluative stance in transition, and these functions are distinct from the direct discourse of a reported character as in clause10 in the story.

Clause no.	Assertion	Narrative modes	Truth value NC (what is done)	EC (what is said)	Devices undercut agency
1. *His plans had been running so beautifully, so goddamned beautifully, and now she was going to smash them all.*	B(R)+ve	Proximal deictic *now*	FC/comment		Perfective aspect Progressive aspect Proximal deictic *now*
2. *Hate erupted and flooded through him, gripping his face with jaw-aching pressure.*	B(N)+ve	Evaluative adjective	FC/comment		Deperson-alization Progressive aspect
3. *That was alright though, the lights were out.*	B(N)+ve	Evaluative adverbial *alright though*	FC/comment		
4. *He closed his eyes and spoke dreamily, intoning the words in a sedative chant.*	B(N)+ve	Evaluative adverbial *dreamily*)		Internal Correlative	Progressive aspect
10. *You would have told me what he's interested in, what he likes, what he dislikes-' he stopped short, then continued.*	DS				Modality shift
23. *He sat at the back of the room, in the second seat from the window.*	CA		B neutral	FC/narrative	

(continued)

(continued)

Clause no.	Assertion	Narrative modes	Truth value NC (what is done)	EC (what is said)	Devices undercut agency
24. The seat on his left, the window seat, the empty seat, was hers.	CA	B neutral	FC/narrative		
25. It was the first class of the morning, a daily Social Science lecture, and their only class together this semester.		B(R)+ve	Proximal deictic *this*	FC/narrative	
27. Today of all days she could have made an effort to be on time.		B(R)+ve	Proximal adverbial *today*	FC/comment	Modality shift Proximal adverbial *today*
40. The earliest Ellen could get the note would be—three o' clock.	FIT	B(R)+ve	Proximal time adverbial	FC/comment	Modality shift
47. In five hours and forty minutes she must be dead. (p. 55)		B(N)-ve	Epistemic perception modality *must*	Embedded evaluation (comment by participant)	Modality shift

Additionally, modalized discourse with evaluative adverbials and adjectives render Bud Corliss' narration primarily as a B(N)+ve narrative mode. However, in static aspects like the progressives and perfectives, and in other syntactic devices (Table 4.3) that undercut the agency of B(N)+ve Narrator, a **functional contrast** is constructed by appending a static world with floating omniscience. The static syntax in the discourse undercuts the omniscience of this intervening offender/narrator in process, formulating an **authorial omnipresence** over **omniscience** to drive the story forward in prospection like a thriller narrative. This is because there no explicit qualification of the commitment to its factuality of propositions. The assumption then is that the full *epistemic warrant*

(Lyons 1977: pp. 808–809 in Simpson 1993: p. 52) for what the speaker *he* says in the FC/comment clauses 1 and 47 is of an **affected participant**. Unlike the speaker of DS, the modal and temporal remoteness conceptualized for the affected participant in perfective aspect and in modality shift is to formulate a predicated proposition, predicated on the limited knowledge of the **intermediary Agent (Ag$_2$) in anticipation**. This epistemic distance is **metaphorical** in nature and involves transition between two domains of conceptualization; the transition from unmodalized neutral diegetic narrator, from the reported mimetic narration of direct discourse, to a **disposition** grounded in static aspects. Perfective aspect syntactically denotes a lack of action and suggest **outside agency**. This domain of cognition in static aspects provides epistemic narration of an omniscient B(N)+ve mode. Like the entity representation in Reverse C, in the epistemic reading of the static aspects, the concrete world of B(N)+ve is associated with a narrator who is not centrally omniscient, and the narration is also not mediated through a third person Reflector. This disposition of the narrating participant *he* is made limited in the static syntax for an intervention minimized in anticipation to explain the circumstance involving the killing of Dorothy and her sister Ellen in the prospective narrative, distinct from the narrative shifts between modalized bird's eye view of B(N)+ve mode to a Reflector mode. In other words, a **plurality of relations** for the same entity with overall omniscient disposition presents a conflict of interest for the character as narrator in evaluative elements, *dreamily, though* as in clause 4 in table below, with an embedded character/ Reflector disposition in clause 51, who is justifying the killing of privileged individuals like Ellen. The narrative B(N)+ve mode of desire and obligation associated with the static syntax for an epistemic distance successfully accommodates the actual first-person narration with a presented third-person pronoun in the offender discourse. Linguistically, third-person narration is also used for formulating distance from the crime.

Clause no.	Assertion	Narrative modes	Truth value NC (what is done)	EC (what is said)	Devices undercut agency
4. He closed his eyes and spoke dreamily, intoning the words in a sedative chant.		B(N)+ve Evaluative adverbial *dreamily*	Internal Correlative		Progressive aspect

(continued)

236 The Language of Suspense in Crime Fiction

(continued)

			Truth value		Devices
Clause no.	Assertion	Narrative modes	NC (what is done)	EC (what is said)	undercut agency
51. He told her these things with irritation and contempt;		B(N)+ve Evaluative adverbial irritation and contempt +			
this girl with her hands over her mouth in horror had had everything given her on a silver platter; she didn't know what it was to live on a swaying catwalk over the chasm of failure, stealing perilously inch by inch towards the solid ground of success so many miles away. (175)		B(R)+ve Proximal demonstrative this, these	FC/comment		Perfective aspect Progressive aspect Negation

Ira Levin cleverly presents a first person narration with the third person pronoun *he* for an involved character narrator in the fictional reality. Levin then introduces the FIT and DS of the reporting narrator/character, but conceptualizes an **intermediary position** in the temporal remoteness, who is involved as an **anticipatory participant** and who is foregrounded as an entity in Reverse C, that is preparing to murder his girlfriend Dorothy, then her sister Ellen. In the modal system, the CAs are dynamic and event-related predicates (B neutral mode), but with static syntax bordering on an epistemic reading for **functional contrast** in participant role. Such illustrates an **intermediate stage** for an **involved** character, separate from the default third -person narrator in the **functional** (stylistic) **contrast**, where epistemic commitment in the

4 Disposition   237

static context constitutes limited ability for an omniscient narrator with floating omniscience.

4.5.2 Villain: Raven

Experiential Function (Appendix 4b)
In contrast, villain Raven is a bystander in his world of villainy in *A Gun for Sale*; an instrument in the offender engagement discourse related to the character's sub-theme of betrayal and trust. At the micro level of offender's discourse (Appendix 4b), Reverse C alongside the unusual C/scope clausal structures also present the background conditions for Raven as a bystander.

In *A Gun for Sale*, the sub-theme of pain, betrayal by *skirt* [mother], Anne's love and her treachery towards Raven (pp. 122, 178, 180), are backgrounded to Raven as a villain. The backgrounded sub-themes are the **narrative gaps** as **suspense** in the contrasting Raven-Anne narrative, where Anne loathes Raven, *Anne felt desperate hatred for Raven* (p. 126)], but this contrasts with the situation where Anne regrets her betrayal to Raven, *I've failed* (pp. 179, 180). She then goes on to narrate how '*she had lost the only man* [villain Raven] *she cared a damn about*' (p. 178)] due to her betrayal of revealing Raven's hiding location to the police.

In the sub-theme of betrayal, the role of Raven, in the table below, is of a bystander set against the conception of Raven as an agentive villain. For instance, the circumstance in Medium role and the C/scope clauses below, provide an intransitive background for the narrating participant. Reverse C in the clauses in Raven's discourse encode a background against which the process of *Murder* takes place. For example, the Medium *you* as an entity of C/scope *murder* in clauses 1–4 below, encode an ergative (causative) perspective of the *murder* as a process related to the villain Raven. In Reverse scope Raven is an indirect *oblique participant*, not directly related to the process of a primary Agent, Ag_1 such as in clause 9 below.

238 The Language of Suspense in Crime Fiction

Clause no.	Transitive	Ergative	Devices undercut agency	Background condition
1. *Murder didn't mean much to Raven.*		*Murder (C/scope) didn't mean much (Process) to Raven. C/scope*	Negation	C/P/C Unusual structure
2. *You had to be careful.*		*You (Medium) had to be careful. (Process)*	Perfective aspect	M/P Intransitive reading Type d
3. *You had to use your brains.*		*You (Medium) had to use (Process) your brains. (C/scope)*	Perfective aspect	M/P/C Intransitive reading Type e
4. *It was not a question of hatred.*		*It [Murder] (C/scope) was not (Process) a question of hatred. (C/scope)*	Existential *It*	C/P/C Unusual structure
5. *He had only seen the Minister once: he had been pointed out to Raven as he walked down the new housing estate between the small lit Christmas trees, an old grubby man without friends, who was said to love humanity.* (p. 1)		*He (Experiencer/Medium) had only seen (Process) the Minister (Medium) once: (C/scope)* ... *he (Medium) had been pointed out (Process) to Raven (C(scope) as he walked down the new housing estate between the small lit Christmas trees, (C/location) an old grubby man without friends, who was said to love humanity. (C/manner) (C/scope)*	Perfective aspect	M/P/M/C Unusual structure M/P/C/C Intransitive reading Type e Complex Cs

9. Then he turned on the secretary; she moaned at him; she hadn't any words; the old mouth couldn't hold the saliva.	Then he (Agent) turned (Process) on the secretary; (C/location)		Intentional A/P/C **Transitive reading Type b**
	b. she; (Medium) moaned (Process) at him (C/location)	Negation	M/P/C **Intransitive reading Type e**
	she (Medium) hadn't any words; (C/scope)		M/P/C **Intransitive reading Type f**
	the old mouth (Medium) couldn't hold (Process) the saliva. (C/scope)	Depersonalization Modality shift Negation	M/P/C **Intransitive reading Type e**
19. Raven was satisfied.	Raven (Medium) was satisfied. (Process)		M/P **Intransitive reading Type d**

(continued)

(continued)

Clause no.	Transitive	Ergative	Devices undercut agency	Background condition
31. *Raven could never realize other people; they didn't seem to him to live in the same way as he lived* [*to play fair* (16), *Raven did not go back on a fellow who treated him right* (24), *he kept a promise* (41)]; *and though he bore a grudge against Mr Cholmondeley, hated him enough to kill him, he couldn't imagine Mr Cholmondeley's own fears and motives.*		*Raven (Medium) could never realize (Process) other people; (C/Scope)*	Negation	M/P/M/C (Scope) Unusual structure
		they (Medium) didn't seem (Process) to him (C/scope) to live in the same way as he lived; (C/manner)	Stative verb *seem*	M/P/C/C Intransitive reading Type e
		c. and though (C/concession) he (Medium) bore a grudge (Process) against Mr Cholmondeley, (C/scope)		Reverse Cs/ intentional M/P/M Transitive reading Type a
		[*he*] *hated (Process) him enough (Medium) to kill him, (C/scope)*	Negation	P/M/C
		he (Medium) couldn't imagine (Process) Mr Cholmondeley's own fears and motives. (C/scope)		M/P/C
34. *It was normality* [*human feelings*] *he couldn't cope with.* (39)		*It was normality (C/scope) he (Medium) couldn't cope with. (Process)*	Negation	*Reverse C/M/P Intransitive reading Type d

39. She never knew, he thought, that he had meant to kill her; she had been innocent of his intention as a cat he had once been forced to drown; and he remembered with astonishment that she had not betrayed him, although he had told her that the police were after him.	a. She (Agent) never knew, (Process)		Negation	Negated Engaged A/P Intransitive reading
	b. he (Medium) thought, (Process) that he had meant to kill her; … (C/scope)		Perfective aspect	M/P/C Intransitive reading
	c. she (Medium) had been innocent (Process) of his intention as a cat (C/scope) he had once been forced to drown; (C/manner)		Perfective aspect	M/P/C/ Intransitive reading
	d. although (C/concession) he (Agent) had told (Process) her (Medium) that the police were after him. (C/matter)		Perfective aspect	*Reverse C/ intentional AP/M/C Transitive reading
	e. and he (Medium) remembered with astonishment (Process) that she had not betrayed him, (C/scope)		Perfective aspect	M/P/C Intransitive reading

(continued)

(continued)

Clause no.	Transitive	Ergative	Devices undercut agency	Background condition
44. His mother had borne him when his father was in gaol, and six years later when his father was hanged for another crime, she had cut her throat with a kitchen knife; afterwards there had been home.	His mother (Agent) had borne him (Medium) when his father was in gaol, (C/time)	... and six years later when (C/time) his father (Medium) was hanged (Process) for another crime, (C/scope)	Perfective aspect	Intentional A/P/M/C Transitive reading
				C/M/P/C Intransitive reading
	she (Agent) had cut (Process) her throat (Medium) with a kitchen knife; (C/accompaniment) afterwards there had been home. (C/scope)			Intentional A/M/C/C Transitive reading

Example	Analysis	Perfective aspect	Modality shift Conditional *if*	Modality shift (modality signal obligation *must*)	M/P Intransitive reading	Obligatory A/P/M/C/C	Double dipping Medium also as Agent
46. He had a sudden terrified conviction that he must be himself now as never before if he was to escape.	He (Medium) had a sudden terrified conviction (Process)						
	... that he (Agent) must be (Process) himself now (Medium) as never before (C/scope) if he was to escape. (C/cause) **Double dipping**						
47. It was not tenderness that made you quick on the draw. (62) ...	It was not tenderness that made you quick on the draw. (C/scope)				Negation	C(scope)	
48. He thought: give her time and she too will go to the police.	IT						
49. That's what always happens in the end with a skirt, (63)	That [betrayal by skirt] 's what always happen in the end with a skirt, (C/scope)					C (scope)	

Moreover, syntactic devices such as the use of perfective aspect limit the agency role to the moment of the narrated event as in clause 5. In which Raven *had seen* the Minister and not *saw* the Minister in its simple past form. Synonymous to clause 9b (an unintentional Agent *she moaned*), the perfective aspect foregrounds an **external force** that brought about the action, due to contract killing, and is not an intentional action unlike clause 9a. The Medium disposition in clauses 5, 19, 31a, 34 and 39 b, c, and e in the table above, with static syntax that undercut the agentive villain disposition foregrounds the backgrounded betrayal when Raven was astonished of not being betrayed; contrary to his experience in clauses 31 and 39. The **cognitive prefocalization** in Medium role, together with syntactic devices to undercut agency as a **functional contrast**, project the agentive villain Raven as a **NO** who is a bystander in the discourse; a victim of his circumstance imposed on him as a contract killer, although contextually Raven is an *effector* in the story who willingly killed as a profession.

In the grammar of experience, the overall intransitive reading of clauses in Reverse C foregrounds an instrument disposition of the bystander who is in opposition to a contract killer disposition in his world of villainy. There is linguistic **counterpositioning** of an agentive effector projected as an **instrument/patient** in the intransitive reading of clauses clause-initial circumstantial element modifying the Agent-Actor role of Raven, who is **affected** by the entity in C/scope, despite his Actor/effector disposition of a villain in the story logic. In addition, the static syntax as a device to undercut the intervention as Narrator Agency restricts the relevance of past actions to the activity in the present. Harding also supports this in the observation,

> '*In describing counterfactuals, speakers have at their disposal … cues that indicate the counterfactual nature of an utterance, including if/then constructions, negatives and modal verbs.*' (2007: p. 266)

In addition to *if/then constructions, negatives and modal verbs* linguistic cues, past perfective verb constructions in modality shift (as an interpersonal function) also mark offender engagement discourse as a *counterfactual alternative*, where scenarios related to Raven's trust in women are narrated as foreclosed possibilities unrealized in the main story line which is a **counterfactual** background in the villain context.

The Interpersonal Function

As stated earlier, past perfective verb constructions in modality shift reinforce the alternative counterfactual texture of the dominant narrative mode B(N)+ve mode in stance analysis. As in Corliss' discourse, action is suspended in static aspect for **causality**. The modalized B(N)+ve narrative alternates with restricted omniscience of a Reflector, who is participating as a participant in B(R)+ve and B(R)-ve mode for *online narration* in stative verbs, and in *offline narration* formulated in proximal deictics alongside unmodalized neutral mode as in hard boiled thriller narratives. This online narration is an **internal construct** of the default narrating-I, as in the evaluative FC/comment in clause 47, and is relative to the sub-theme of betrayal. A state of affairs is constructed for the narrating-he Raven in online narration, where the willful contract killer Raven is minimized and restricted by undercutting his agency role in static aspects as **linguistic cues**, to place him as a participant who is not in control of his circumstances grounded in the *double dipping* presented below.

			Truth value		
Clauses	Assertions	Narrative modes	NC What is done	EC What is said	Devices undercut agency
12. *He pressed the trigger again; she staggered under it as if she had been kicked by an animal in the side.*	CA	B neutral + B(N)+ve Action suspended for causality Double dipping	NC (fixed)	Embedded evaluation (comment by teller)	Perfective aspect

(continued)

(continued)

Clauses	Assertions	Narrative modes	Truth value NC What is done	EC What is said	Devices undercut agency
...31. Raven could never realize other people; they didn't seem to him to live in the same way as he lived [to play fair (16), Raven did not go back on a fellow who treated him right (24), he kept a promise (41)]; and though he bore a grudge against Mr Cholmondeley, hated him enough to kill him, he couldn't imagine Mr Cholmondeley's own fears and motives.		B(N)+ve Modalized discourse B(R)+ve Perception modality seem Double dipping		Embedded evaluation (comment by teller)	Modality shift Negation
44. His mother had borne him when his father was in gaol, and six years later when his father was hanged for another crime, she had cut her throat with a kitchen knife; afterwards there had been home.		B(N)+ve Action suspended for causality		Wholly external (in subordination)	Perfective aspect
47. It was not tenderness that made you quick on the draw. (62) ...		B(N)+ve Action suspended for causality	FC/ comment	Embedded evaluation (comment by teller)	
49. That's what always happens in the end with a skirt,... (63)		B(N)+ve moralizing		Embedded evaluation (comment by teller)	

Following the analysis of the clauses cited above, in the transposition to different narrative modes in Appendix 4b, the dominant third-person omniscient narration is suspended for selective information. That is, the functioning Narrator-Actor in B(N)+ve discourse alternates with the character-Reflector disposition for a *cognitive refocalization* in the proximal deictic universe, in aspectual verb and in perception modality. This is also reinforced in the referential reading of FC/comment clauses, showing stance as an evaluation from the point of view of Raven as a character-Reflector. However, the **situated focus** for constructing a **NO**, Raven as a bystander, and also a victim of betrayal and trust, becomes evident with the suspended narration of B(N)+ve mode, when Raven's backgrounded pain and betrayal has agentive narration such as in clause 44. The background in clause 44 contrasts with Cs in the experiential function in clauses 47 and 49 in the table above, which are the outcomes of the agentive process in clause 44, and that form a causal link with the proximal *now* in clauses 46 and 47. This disposition of betrayal is developed further in the **functional contrast** of the static syntax appended with omniscient B(N)+ve narrative features to provide **causality** for the villainy in betrayal **behind** the criminal process. As a result, the **counterfactual** nature of the villain in clause 39, and clauses 46–49 in table above starts making sense to the readers.

4.5.3 Perpetrator: Ripley

Experiential Function

Unlike Raven, perpetrator Tom Ripley in *The Talented Mr. Ripley*, is not a hardened well-rooted killer; he first imagined the act of violence, which turned into an imagined act of killing followed by the actual act of murder. In the transition from an **imagined killer** to a **confident murderer** in linguistic cues like the C/scope clauses and in functional contrast in narrative mode surfacing as the **imagined circumstance** (clauses 35–50; 55–57), the **epistemic sub-world** (clauses 72–74; 77–92) and then the **actual world** in CAs (clauses 71, 75 and 93–97) of the killer in Appendix 4c. Appendix 4c is not included for copyright reasons, and the non-chronological numbering of selected clauses in the tables below corresponds to the complete analysis of perpetrator Ripley discourse in Appendix 4c.

The dysfunctions in the Ripley discourse are similar to the discourses of Bud and Raven. Reverse C in clause 17 (table below), foregrounds Ripley's naiveté about the workings of the real world. This foregrounding also occurs in clause 24 in the circumstantiation of Tom's decision to get Dickie to like him. Also in clause 33 below, Tom's disgust relative to Dickie being a heterosexual is foregrounded with his sexual status being reduced to an existential *it*. Further, on, in clause 69, One thing Tom was sure of: Dickie was glad to have him here the reverse C is relative to Tom's internal construct about Dickie being glad to have Tom with him which is contrary to Dickie's outburst in clauses 63–67 about not being a *queer* like Tom. The next context in Reverse C is Dickie's ring (clauses 76–79), which later in the story plays an important role in relation to Tom being responsible for Dickie's death in clause 93 (clauses 72, 88).

Clause no.	Transitive	Ergative	Undercut agency	Background condition
17. *And it was astounding and pitiful how naïve he had been, how little he had known about the way the world worked, as if he had spent so much of his time hating Aunt Dottie and scheming how to escape her, that he had not had enough time to learn and grow.* (35–36)	*And it was astounding and pitiful* (C/scope) *he had been,* [*naïve*] (Process)	*how little* (C/scope) *he* (Medium) *had known* (Process) *about the way the world worked,* (C/matter) *as if* (C/scope) *he* (Medium) *had spent* (Process) *so much of his time hating Aunt Dottie* (C/Scope) *and scheming how to escape her, that he had not had enough time to learn and grow.* (C/scope) **Double dipping**	Perfective aspect Perfective aspect Conditional if Perfective aspect Progressive aspect	**Reverse C/Engaged A/P Ergative reading** (a psychological process, one of causation) **Reverse C/M//P/C Intransitive reading Reverse C/M/P/C Intransitive reading** C (scope) **Double dipping:** Medium as **Engaged Agent**

4 Disposition 249

(continued)

Clause no.	Transitive	Ergative	Undercut agency	Background condition
... 24. The first step, anyway, was to make Dickie like him.		The first step, anyway, (C/scope) was to make (Process) Dickie like him. (C/scope)		Reverse C/P/C Unusual structure
33. What disgusted him was the big bulge of her behind in the peasant skirt below Dickie's arm that circled her waist. And Dickie -! Tom really wouldn't have believed it possible of Dickie ! (67)	FIT And Dickie -! Tom (Agent) really wouldn't have believed it possible (Process) of Dickie ! (C/scope)	What disgusted (Process) him (Medium) was the big bulge of her behind in the peasant skirt below Dickie's arm that circled her waist. (C/matter)	Negation	Reverse C/P/M/C Unusual structure The bulge ... as **trigger** for the process disgust Engaged A/P/C agency **triggered** by his orientation Intransitive reading
63. Dickie snapped in a way that shut Tom out from them. ...		Dickie (Agent) snapped in a way that shut Tom out from them. (C/scope)		(Dickie) Intentional A/P/C Transitive reading
'Another thing I want to say, ... looking at Tom, 'I'm not queer. I don't know if you have the idea that I am not.'	DS			The theme of queer

(continued)

(continued)

Clause no.	Transitive	Ergative	Undercut agency	Background condition
64. 'Queer?' Tom smiled faintly. 'I never thought you were queer.'	DS			
... 65. 'Well Marge thinks you are.'	DS			
... 66. 'Why should she? What've I ever done?' He felt faint. Nobody had ever said it outright to him, not in this way. ...	DS	He (Medium) felt faint. (Process) Nobody had ever said it outright to him, not in this way.(C/scope)	Perfective aspect	M/P Intransitive reading C(scope)
... 67. 'Dickie, I want to get this straight,' Tom began. 'I'm not queer either, and I don't want anybody thinking I am.' ...	DS			
72. Dickie was in a slightly more cheerful mood, but the awful finality was still there, the feeling that this was the last trip they would make together anywhere.	the feeling that this was the last trip they would make together anywhere. (C/scope)	Dickie (Medium/ experiencer) was (Process) in a slightly more cheerful mood, but the awful finality was still there, C(scope)	Proximal deictic this	M/P/C Intransitive reading C (scope)

4 Disposition   251

(continued)

Clause no.	Transitive	Ergative	Undercut agency	Background condition
76. *Tom sat opposite him, staring at his bony, arrogant, handsome face, at his hands with the ring and the gold signet ring.*	*Tom* (Agent) *sat* (Process) *opposite him,* (C/ location) *staring at his bony, arrogant, handsome face, at his hands with the ring and the gold signet ring.* (C/location)		Progressive aspect	Intentional A/P/C **Transitive reading** Complex C (location + scope + location)
77. *It crossed Tom's mind to steal the green ring when he left.*		*It* (C/scope) *crossed* (Process) *Tom's mind* (Medium) *to steal the green ring when he left.* (C/scope)	Existential *it*	**Reverse C/P/M/C Unusual structure**
78. *It would be easy: Dickie took it off when he swam. ...*		*It would be easy:* (C/scope) *Dickie* (Agent) *took it off* (Process) *when he swam. ...* (C/scope)	Modality shift (Modality signal obligation *would*)	**Reverse C/A/P/C Transitive reading**
79. *He would do it the very last day, Tom thought.*	FIT			

(continued)

(continued)

Clause no.	Transitive	Ergative	Undercut agency	Background condition
88. *Dickie was just shoving him out in the cold.*	*Dickie* (Agent) *was just shoving out* (Process) *him out in the cold C/* scope + location)		Progressive aspect	Dickie Intentional A/P/C *Ergative reading Complex C (scope + location)
If he killed him on this trip, Tom thought, he could simply say that some accident had happened.	IT *he* (Agent) *could simply say that* (Process) *some accident had happened.* (C/scope)		(Modality signal obligation *could*)	A/P/C **Transitive reading**

In these contexts, the background in Reverse Cs as a represented entity about the Narrator Tom provide extra specification for Tom as the grammatical subject. With Tom being the grammatical subject, his background entity has the marked focus in Reverse C, which would otherwise be unnoticed. As a linguistic environment, Reverse C foregrounds the sub-theme of Tom's homosexuality; thereupon situating the **intentionality** in an action-oriented thriller.

Taking on the context of pervert in Reverse Cs (**in bold**) (related to the theme of homosexuality) creates sexual jealousy as the narrative focus in the offender Ripley discourse. In the table below, a queer orientation implied for Tom in Reverse Cs is present at the outset in clauses 2 and 3. The queer disposition, thematized in **negation**, is a counterfactual utterance. Further, the Medium role of Ripley in clauses like 45c, suppress the agentive feature of control in his imagined world, where a Tom murderer-to-be narrates the process of murdering Marge which stems from his sexual jealousy in the intransitive reading of Reverse C clauses, where the represented circumstance is of a **victim** of his homosexual

4 Disposition 253

disposition. In clause initial Medium role, the Process in clauses are not engendered but superventive due to a homosexual orientation, and initiates an agentive imagined world such as in clause 45c.

Clause no.	Transitive	Ergative	Undercut agency	Background condition
1. My God, what does he want?	FIT			
2. He certainly wasn't a pervert, Tom thought	IT			
For the second time, though now his tortured brain groped and produced the actual word, as if the word could protect him, because he would rather the man be pervert than a policeman.		a. for the second time, though now (C/scope) his tortured brain (undercut Agent) groped and produced (Process) the actual word, (Medium)	Depersonalization Proximal deictic *now*	*Reverse C/(undercut) A/P/M/C Transitive reading
		b. **C/cause clause:** as if the word (Agent) could protect (Process) him, (Medium)	Conditional *if* Depersonalization Modality shift (Modality signal possibility *could*)	(Undercut) A/P/M Transitive reading
		c. **C/cause clause:** because he [the man] (Medium) would rather (Process) be pervert than a policeman. (C/angle)	Modality shift (Modality signal intentionality *would*)	**C/cause:** M/P/C **Intransitive reading** concealed theme of homosexuality as '*pervert*'

(*continued*)

(continued)

Clause no.	Transitive	Ergative	Undercut agency	Background condition
3. To a pervert, he could simply say, 'No thank you,' and smile and walk away.	DS To a pervert, (C/scope) he (Agent) could simply say, (Process) 'No thank you,' and smile and walk away' (verbiage)		Modality shift (Modality signal possibility *could*)	Reverse C/ (undercut) Hypothetical A/P/verbiage Intransitive reading a concealed theme of homosexuality as '*pervert*' in verbiage
45. He shook her, twisted her, while she sank lower and lower, until at last he left her, limp, on the floor. He was panting.	He (Agent) shook (Process) her, (Medium) twisted (Process) her, (Medium) while she sank lower and lower, (C/scope)			Intentional A/P/M/P/M/C Transitive reading
	until at last (C/scope) he (Agent) left (Process) her, (Medium) limp, on the floor. (C/scope)	He (Medium/ Experiencer) was panting. (Process)		C/intentional A/P/C Transitive reading M/P Intransitive reading

4 Disposition   255

Furthermore, Reverse C and the C/scope clauses alike in Ripley discourse are marked contextually for the realm of thought provided in the *discourse-now* (a narrating-I) in the story. Like the Corliss and Raven discourse, Reverse C as a realm of thought encodes Tom as an **affected participant** with a backgrounded homosexual state in the discourse. Thus, in the analytical causative reading of clauses with Reverse C and the clause initial Medium role of Tom in the discourse, the Process is modified by the homosexual circumstance. As Reverse C, the entity thus functions as an indirect instigator for the grammatical subject Tom in Medium role. In such linguistic counterpositioning of the default Narrator-Actor Tom, the affected grammatical subject in an analytical causative reading of clause-initial Medium roles and non-Middle clauses with Reverse C, such as clauses like 2, 3 and 45c, construct an intermediary position for a **NO**. An **Affected-Actor schema** is thus developing for the **effector** Ripley.

The Interpersonal Function

Like Corliss and Raven discourses, B(N)+ve is also the dominant narrative mode in Ripley's discourse (Appendix 4c) and alternates with the B(R)+ve mode (Appendix 4c). As is the characteristics of B(N)+ve mode, the **narrating position** is outside of the participating character Tom and is relative to Tom's secret about being a homosexual. In this modalized discourse, for example in the clauses below from Appendix 4c, the narration suspended for causality relative to his childhood (clauses 14–17 above), relative to Tom making up his mind to kill Dickie to take on his identity (clauses 93–95 above) foreground an entity in **linguistic cues** that is otherwise backgrounded in the story.

Clause no.	Assertion	Narrative modes	Truth value NC	Truth value EC	Devices undercut agency
2. He certainly wasn't a pervert, Tom thought for the second time, though now his tortured brain groped and produced the actual word, as if the word could protect him, because he would rather the man be pervert than a policeman.		B(R)+ve Evaluative adverb *certainly*, B(R)+ve proximal deictics *now*		Embedded evaluation (Comment reported)	Depersonalization Conditional *if* Modality shift
3. To a pervert, he could simply say, 'No thank you,' and smile and walk away.	FDT	B(N)+ve Modalized discourse B(R)+ve Reported clause **Double dipping**		Embedded evaluation (Comment reported)	Modality shift
8. When Mr. Greenleaf's money was used up, he might not come back to America.		B(N)+ve Modalized discourse		Embedded evaluation (comment by teller)	Modality shift
9. He might get an interesting job in a hotel, for instance, where they needed somebody bright and personable who spoke English.		B(N)+ve Modalized discourse		Embedded evaluation (comment by teller)	Modality shift
10. Or he might become a representative for some European firm and travel everywhere in the world.		B(N)+ve Modalized discourse		Embedded evaluation (comment by teller)	Modality shift

4 Disposition   257

(continued)

Clause no.	Assertion	Narrative modes	Truth value		Devices undercut agency
			NC	EC	
11. Or somebody might come along who needed a young man exactly like himself, who could drive a car, who was quick at figures who could entertain an old grandmother or squire somebody's daughter to a dance.		B(N)+ve Modalized discourse		Embedded evaluation (comment by teller)	Modality shift
14. Aunt Dottie had hated him when he had a cold; she used to take her handkerchief and nearly wrench his nose off, wiping it. ...		B(N)+ve Evaluative adverbial used to	Internal evaluation (Correlative)		Perfective aspect Modality shift used to
15. He remembered the vows he had made, even at the age of eight, to run away from Aunt Dottie, the violent scenes he had imagined— Aunt Dottie trying to hold him in the house, and he hitting her with his fists, flinging her to the ground and throttling her, and finally tearing the big brooch off her dress and stabbing her a million times in the throat with it.		B(N)+ve Action suspended for causality	Internal evaluation (Correlative)		Deperson- alization Progressive aspect

(continued)

(continued)

Clause no.	Assertion	Narrative modes	Truth value NC	EC	Devices undercut agency
16. He had run away at seventeen and had been brought back, and he had done it again at twenty and succeeded.		B(N)+ve Action suspended for causality	FC/narrative report		Perfective aspect Existential *it*
17. And it was astounding and pitiful how naïve he had been, how little he had known about the way the world worked, as if he had spent so much of his time hating Aunt Dottie and scheming how to escape her, that he had not had enough time to learn and grow. (35–36)		B(N)+ve Action suspended for causality	Internal evaluation (intensifier *that*)		Perfective aspect Conditional *if* Progressive aspect Conditional *if*
… 41. He reparted his hair and put the part a little more to oneside, the way Dickie wore his.	CA		NC (fixed)		
42. 'Marge you must understand that I don't love you,' Tom said into the mirror in Dickie's voice, with Dickie's higher pitch on the emphasized words.	IS				
43. With little growl in his throat at the end of the phrase that could be pleasant or unpleasant, intimate or cool, according to Dickie's mood.		B(N)+ve Modalized discourse	Internal evaluation (Intensifier *that*)		Modality shift

4 Disposition   259

(continued)

Clause no.	Assertion	Narrative modes	Truth value NC	Truth value EC	Devices undercut agency
44. 'Marge, stop it!'	FIT				
45. Tom turned suddenly and made a grab in the air as if he were seizing Marge's throat.		B(N)+ve Evaluative adverbial *suddenly* + B(R)+ve Progressive aspect *were seizing* **Double Dipping**	NC (fixed)	Internal evaluation (Correlative)	Progressive aspect Conditional *if*
46. He shook her, twisted her, while she sank lower and lower, until at last he left her, limp, on the floor.	CA		NC (fixed)		
50. 'You know why I had to do that,' he said, still breathlessly, addressing Marge, though he watched himself in the mirror.	IS				
51. 'You were interfering between Tom and me—No, not that! But there is bond between us!'	FIS				
52. He turned, stepped over the imaginary body, and went stealthily to the window.		B(N)+ve Evaluative adverbial *stealthily*		Evaluative action	
93. He could—He had just thought of something brilliant: he could become Dickie Greenleaf himself.		B(N)+ve Modalized discourse		Embedded evaluation (comment by teller)	Perfective aspect Modality shift

(*continued*)

(continued)

Clause no.	Assertion	Narrative modes	Truth value NC	Truth value EC	Devices undercut agency
94. *He could do everything that Dickie did. ... receive Dickie's cheques every month and forge Dickie's signature on it.*	B(N)+ve	Modalized discourse		Embedded evaluation (comment by teller)	Modality shift
95. *He could step right into Dickie's shoes.*	B(N)+ve	Modalized discourse		Embedded evaluation (comment by teller)	

B(N)+ve mode is contextually a world of desire and obligation in a narrative, however in the Ripley discourse the world is modalized as a hypothetical context in epistemic modalities. This epistemic **storyworld** oscillates with the storyworld of a **Reflector** Tom with the use of proximal deictics related to Tom's **mind style** such as his uncertainty of the stranger being a pervert rather than a policeman (clauses 2 and 3). It is also related to his prospective financial situation in clauses 8–11 when the money runs out from his sponsor, Dickie's father. Such a suspended act of narration is also related to the centering of Tom's childhood as an entity; his **imagined** violence towards aunt Dottie (clauses 14–17) and then for Marge (41–46; 50–52). Contextually a storyworld for the killer **profile** emerges, where the violence narrated in the aunt sub-theme is the **trigger factor** for the forthcoming murder by Ripley. In the **imagined world** of violence, Tom is also an agent in control unlike the intransitive reading of the clause-initial Medium role, where the **narrative voice** remains active but without an Agent-Actor.

As with other offender discourses, static syntax is the overall B(N)+ve narrative mode that undercuts the agency role of Narrator-Actor Tom. This occurs when a further storyworld as a **sub-world** is formulated for a **constrained narrator** disposition. Perfective, continuous aspect and modal auxiliaries: *could, might, would* for modality shift, all undercut agency disposition when expressing probability. This narrator discourse is associated to Ripley's sexual jealousy when Dickie favours Marge over

Ripley in clauses 55, 56 (imagined circumstance), and consequently stems Tom's disgust, and compels him to revenge when Tom goes on to steal Dickie's identity following Dickie's murder in clauses 89, 91–92 (**epistemic sub-world**) and in clauses 93–95 (**actual world**). Influenced by disgust and revenge, the epistemic sub-world positions Tom as a **constrained** narrator, intervening in **anticipation** in the goings on before the actual world of murder. This constrained stance in epistemic mode is distinct from the disposition in the proximal or distal deictics, and is relative to the Reflector Ripley in proximity, constituting within an *offline* B(N)+ve narration an *on line* character proximity, who is constrained in static syntax by undercutting its narrational agency. (B(N)+ve narrative mode as a mode for desire and obligation is dominant in Ripley discourse. However, the mode is minimized in static syntax as an internal construct for Ripley as an affected participant and foreground the **experiencing-he** Ripley's homosexual stance and connecting this stance to the main story line of Ripley killing his friend to steal his identity, when in story context, homosexual stance was the real **stimulus** behind the murder. This minimized world in static syntax is Ripley's **desired world**, and is juxtaposed within an action-oriented B-neutral mode (un-modalized assertions/CA) in offender Ripley discourse, where participant has full epistemic commitment in CAs, such as in the clauses 96–97, which is in the **actual world** of villainy.

4.5.4 Offender: Mrs. Maxie

Experiential and Interpersonal Functions (Appendix 4d)
Resembling the sub-narrative in Raven's discourse, a sub-theme focus for the criminal process is also found in CHF. At the outset, the retrospective focus in Mrs. Maxie's discourse is on the victim Sally, and not on Mrs. Maxie, the perpetrator, a characteristic of a murder mystery stories. (For example, in *Ackroyd*, where the retrospective narration starts with the perpetrator and a death in consecution at the outset). The situated focus in CHF is on the characterization of the victim Sally, unlike the focus on the perpetrator Dr. Sheppard in *Ackroyd*. In addition, in Reverse circumstantiation, the social and financial context related to Sally is foregrounded, as this was the real **stimulus** that led to an accidental murder of Sally. For instance,

Experiential Function

Clause	Transitive	Ergative	Undercut agency	Background condition
10. *But the air of constraint which burdened the meal could hardly have been caused by the occasional presence of Sally Jupp who placed the dishes in front of Mrs Maxie and removed the plates with a dextrous efficiency which Miss Liddell noted with complacent approval.* (5)		*But the air of constraint which burdened the meal* (C/scope) *could hardly have been caused* (Process) *by the occasional presence of Sally Jupp* (Medium, C/scope)	Perfective aspect	**Reverse C/P/M + C Intransitive reading** (blending of Medium with C)
The median point	*who* [Sally] (Agent) *placed* (Process) *the dishes* (Medium) *in front of Mrs Maxie* (C/location)			Intentional A/P/M/C **Transitive reading**
	and [Sally] (Agent) *removed* (Process) *the plates* (M) *with a dextrous efficiency* (C/manner)	*which Miss Liddell* (experiencer/ Medium) *noted* (Process) *with complacent approval.* (C/manner)		A/P/M/C **Transitive reading** M/P/C **Intransitive reading**

4 Disposition   263

(continued)

Clause	Transitive	Ergative	Undercut agency	Background condition
21. *She could not be expected to foresee the magnitude of those complications nor that they would end in violent death.*' (10) **Cardinal point**		*She* (Medium) *could not be expected* (Process) *to foresee the magnitude of those complications nor that they would end in violent death.*' (C/scope) **Double dipping**	Negation Modality shift (Modality signal obligation *could*)	**Sally M/P/C** (Sally) **Sally presented as the scope of the process *Double dipping**

Interpersonal Function

Clauses (Frames)	Assertions	Narrative modes	Truth value		Devices undercut agency
			NC (what is done)	EC (what is said)	
21. *She could not be expected to foresee the magnitude of those complications nor that they would end in violent death.*' (10)		B(N)+ve Panoramic view of the magnitude of those complications B(R)+ve Distal deictic *those*	Internal evaluation		Modality shift Negation

The static syntax in the third-person narration, like **negation** and **modality shift** undercuts the agency of the transitive verb as seen in clause 21, foresee and *would end in violent death*. Additionally, restricted *omniscience* of the post-murder Narrator Eleanor Maxie creates **suspense** in **prospection**. The **victim focus** for the post-murder-participant Mrs.

Maxie at clause level is foregrounded in narrating Sally as the C/scope of the Process, or the Medium (Sally's secret) through which the offence/murder came into existence.

In the transition from omniscience to a Narrator in Reflector mode, the circumstance as the **intention** behind the murder is thematized. Contextually this intentionality was related to Mrs. Maxie's financial situation and her desire for a marriage of convenience for her son Stephen, to save the family house. For instance, in Frame 21 (table above) B(N)+ve mode turned to B(R)+ve indicated by the distal deictic *those*; distal to the speaker's proximal deictic *these*. The speaker in **prospection** is positioned in Frame 21 outside Miss Liddell's consciousness. This externality in distal deictics creates a bird's eye view of the withheld outcome of the *introduction of* [Sally] *to Martingale* [that] *might produce complications ... that ... would end in* [Sally's] *violent death*. Contextually, this is a **restricted view** of the real mystery centering on Sally. The **withheld** outcome was that Sally was already married, and she deliberately led the Martingale family to believe that she was going to marry her son Stephen. This was contrary to Mrs. Maxie's desire for her son to marry into money to save the family mansion, and besides her upper class pride about having a daughter-in-law who lives below their station. In circumstantiation, this sub-theme is foregrounded as the cause for the accidental murder of Sally in prospection; Sally is made the background entity in Reverse C and in Middle clauses. In linguistic cues, the **multipositionality** of the participant Sally is thus evident in the discourse. In Medium role Sally is hosting the process in Middle clauses, as well as something (murdered) being done to the Medium, Sally. As in **manipulative causation** (Fig. 4.1), Sally is an **instigator** of her own accidental death who is **co-participating** in being murdered. In other words, in **retrospective** narration, the represented entity of Sally in Reverse circumstantiation at the outset, projects a two way process for Sally the enigma and Sally the victim in the story. In the entity where Sally the enigma withholds her background (being already married and her child being legitimate contrary to the knowledge of perpetrator Mrs. Maxie's and others in Martingale House) this secret of Sally **instigates** a **consequential action** resulting in her own (accidental) death. If Mrs. Maxie were aware of Sally's secret marriage, this knowledge would have prevented Sally's death. However, static syntax in the B(N)+ve mode of desire and obligation, provide a **restricted prefocalization** in retrospective narration. This sub-theme is then the **suspense** in **retrospection** formulated with the help of linguistic cues in the offender discourse.

In following the above mode of circumstantiation of Sally as a background to the murder process, this concealed theme is brought to focus especially in the Medium role, where Sally's concealed circumstance **instigated** her own fate in the story. For linguistically informed readers, linguistic dysfunctions foreground an entity where Sally becomes the **stimulus** for the crime to take place in **prospection**. This stimulus as a cue in linguistic dysfunctions is set up before the readers become aware of the secret *that Sally had been a wife* (p. 176). Thus, with Sally becoming a victim in the first story of crime, she also becomes the cause of her own murder as revealed in the second story of investigation.

The mystery thus in the story in CHF is not about 'who' is the murderer. It is about the revelation of the narrative gap as **suspense** constructed in retrospection by taking advantage of Sally's secret marriage that took place before the story begins, thereby enabling the floating omniscient Narrator to play with Mrs. Maxie's ignorance and fear which then became the *curiosity gap* in retrospection in the second story. The making of Mrs. Eleanor Maxie as a **victim of Sally's secret** and consequently forms the circumstance that lead to her murdering Sally. This is also the act of *doubling*, where the victim is the **instigator** for her own fate, just as in the TV series, *The Fall*, when the killer stalks the female detective on his trail. This was possible to unravel through the analysis of the linguistic cues as dysfunctions in the discourse.

4.5.5 Offender: Dr. Sheppard

Experiential Functions (Appendix 4e)
The theme of **double dipping** (holding multiple positions) is also in simultaneous narration found in *Ackroyd*. For instance in Frames 29 and 37,

Clause no.	Transitive	Ergative	Devices undercut agency	Background condition
Frame 29: [Parker leaves Ackroyd's study to ring the police. Dr. Sheppard alone in the study narrates,] '*I did what little had to be done*' (p. 45)	FDT *I* (Agent) *did* (Process) *what little had to be done* (C/scope)		Perfective aspect	Intentional A/P/C **Intransitive reading** **(Ellipted)** *What little* Dr. Sheppard did was to remove the Dictaphone that framed Ralph Paton as the blackmailer, and put back the armchair that concealed it.
Frame 33: a. '*If Parker heard anything about blackmail,* '*I* [Sheppard] *said slowly,* '*he must have been listening outside this door with his ear glued against the keyhole.*' ... *Davis nodded.* ...	IS			IS
Frame 33*b*. *I took an instant decision.*	NRA *I* (Agent) *took* (Process) *an instant decision* (C/scope)			Intentional A/P/C **Transitive reading** about what? **(Ellipted)** The *instant decision* was to frame Ralph Paton as the blackmailer.

(continued)

Clause no.	Transitive	Ergative	Devices undercut agency	Background condition
Frame 33c: c. And then and there [I] narrated the whole events of the evening as I have set them down here.	NRA And then and there (C/scope) [I] (Agent) narrated (Process) the whole events of the evening as I have set them down here. (C/scope)	Proximal deictic *here*		**Reverse Cs** C/[intentional A]/P/C **Transitive reading**
d. The inspector listened intently, occasionally interjecting a question.	The inspector (Agent) listened intently, (Process) occasionally interjecting a question. (C/scope)			Inspector Engaged A/P/C **Transitive reading**

Interpersonal Functions

Frame no.	Assertions	Narrative modes	Truth value		Devices undercut agency
			NC (what is done)	EC (what is said)	
Frame 29: [Parker leaves Ackroyd's study to ring the police. Dr. Sheppard alone in the study narrates,] *'I did what little had to be done'* (45) [remove the evidence: the letter and Dictaphone]		A(R)+ve Perfective aspect under-cutting Narrator inter-vention			Perfective aspect **Double dipping** Juxtaposing the Reflector *I* with the Narrator-*I*

(continued)

(continued)

Frame no.	Assertions	Narrative modes	Truth value NC (what is done)	EC (what is said)	Devices undercut agency
Frame 33: a. 'If Parker heard anything about blackmail,' I said slowly, 'he must have been listening outside this door with his ear glued against the keyhole.' ... Davis nodded. ...	IS	A(N)+ve Evaluative adverbial slowly			

Similar to the ones discussed above, the Narrator position is also undermined in the static syntax for a **constrained participant disposition** where the relevance of a past action undercut in relation to the activity of the present. An **intermediary, secondary Agent**, Ag_2, is brought into the process–participant constellation in the experiential function in clauses. For example in Frame 29, the perfective aspect undercuts narrator intervention to encode a **post-murder Reflector** who removed the evidence that would incriminate Dr. Sheppard as the murderer. The 'I' Narrator in the Frames omits this fact. However, in tense aspect, an embedded activity for **intentionality** is revealed in the discourse which is to undercut relevance of a past action; the blackmailing of Mrs. Ferrars that might have relevance to Dr. Sheppard in the *discourse-Now* in present following the second murder in Frame 29.

Following the Reflector, Narrator distinction, the Narrator-Actor is distinct from the Reflector in modal shifts (*would, could* to undercut the agency of transitive verb), in de-emphasis of the agentive subject as presentational *there* structures, and when presented as a **hypothetical** world with *if*, and with no suggestion of action in the real world. The participant disposition in the above frames is simultaneous with that of a **Reflector** (knowledge of participating character) and a **Narrator** (a floating position from both inside and outside the character position). The participating character/narrator Dr. Sheppard, in the category A narrative, takes on a floating omniscient position to relate **retrospectively** to events in his discourse both from **outside** as Narrator, and from **inside** the consciousness of Sheppard as the participating character. This *'license of omniscience'* (Simpson 1993: p. 55) invokes a (positive) Narrator in the evaluative adjectives and adverbs, and is similar to a category B, third -person Narrator, foregrounding the post-murder participant's desires, duties, obligations and opinions in relation to the events and characters in the clauses, as in Frames 29 and 33.

For the purpose of the perpetrator's intention in Frames 29 and 33, the participating character takes on the **double positions** of both Narrator and Reflector. This **double dipping** in the narrative act of alternation is from the default narrative past tense to the aspectual tense, and in the evaluative adverbials about thoughts and feelings of the Narrator oriented towards the implied reader. While the proximal deictics *here* as opposed to distal *'then and there'* in Frame 33c, encode proximity to a **post-murder** speaker's location in relation to the an **intermediary disposition** positioned between the Reflector and a Narrator.

4.5.6 Abettor: Dowell

Experiential Function (Appendix 4f)
In our final piece of the offender engagement discourse, victim Dowell in the story is the narrator and a principal character in the story. The **situated focus** in Reverse Cs in Frame 51 in table below, is about the conspiracy related to his wife Florence with a fake heart condition to deceive her husband Dowell. Then Frame 87f, is about Edward and Dowell's wife, Florence having an affair, while Edward was interested in Nancy Rufford, a withheld fourth triangle is thus running concurrently as a deception scenario as the Edward Nancy scenario in the discourse (see Appendix 2d).

In the withheld fourth triangle, Dowell wanted to marry Nancy (Frame 80). In **negation** in Frame 87 g, Dowell reveals a motive. The negation in Frame 87 f also relates to Dowell's **intended** ignorance regarding Edward Florence affair. In story context, Edward committed suicide, and as claimed in Frame 171, Dowell did not stop his friend from doing so. Presented as Reverse C in Frame 158, Dowell's obligatory desire related to Frame 171, is made circumstantiated, *'The end was plain ... Edward must die ...'* this subtheme of Dowell's desire is additionally foregrounded by the epistemic reading of modal *must* in Frame 158. A **negated motive** in Frame 87g is related to his jealous disposition of being deceived by his wife and friend Edward, countered in the epistemic reading in Frame 158, *Edward must die.*

Frame no.	Transitive	Ergative	Devices undercut agency	Background condition
The conspiracy **Frame 51:** Now I wonder what had passed through Florence's mind during the two hours that she kept me waiting at the foot of the ladder. ... Till then, I fancy she had no settled plan in her mind. She certainly never mentioned her heart till that time." (99, 101)	She (Agent) certainly never mentioned (Process) her heart (C/matter) till that time." (C/scope)	Now (C/scope) I (Medium) wonder (Process) what had passed through Florence's mind during the two hours that she kept me waiting at the foot of the ladder. ... (C/ scope) Till then, (C/scope) I (Medium) fancy (Process) she had no settled plan in her mind. (C/matter)	Proximal temporal deictic now Presentational what Perfective aspect Negation Negation Distal demonstrative that	Reverse C/M/P/C Intransitive reading C/M/P/C Intransitive reading Florence **(negated)** intentional A/P/C + C **Transitive reading** **Complex Cs**
Withheld fourth tale **Frame 80:** [Leonora reminded Dowell of his remark,] 'Now I can marry the girl [Nancy].' To which Leonora replied, "of course you might marry her," and, when I asked whom, she answered: "The girl." (123)	DS (by Dowell) 'Now I can marry the girl' IS To which Leonora replied, "of course you might marry her," and, when I asked whom, she answered: "The girl."		Proximal deictic now	C/Dowell intentional A/P/M **Transitive reading** Fourth tale revealed IS

4 Disposition 271

(continued)

Frame no.	Transitive	Ergative	Devices undercut agency	Background condition
The motive: Dowell Frame 87: [Dowell's retrospective narration on Edward's actions in the Casino Park with Nancy Rufford,] 'And it appears that Edward Ashburnham led the girl not up the dark trees of the park. Edward Ashburnham told me all this in his final outburst. I have told you that, upon that occasion, he became deucedly vocal. I didn't pump him, I hadn't any motive. 'At the time I didn't in the least connect him with my wife.' (130)	And it appears that (C/scope) Edward Ashburnham (Agent) led (Process) the girl (Medium) not up the dark trees of the park. (C/location) Edward Ashburnham told me all this in his final outburst. I have told you that, upon that occasion, he became deucedly vocal. I didn't pump him, f. 'At the time I didn't in the least connect him with my wife.'	e. I hadn't any motive	Negation Existential it	C/intentional A/P/M/C Transitive reading Intentional A/P/M/C Transitive reading Intentional A/P/M/C Transitive reading Dowell Negated intentional A/P/M Transitive reading Negated M/P/C Intransitive reading Reverse C/Dowell negated intentional A/P/C Transitive reading

(continued)

(continued)

Frame no.	Transitive	Ergative	Devices undercut agency	Background condition
The motive: Dowell Frame 158: [The quote below sums up the end to come in this final part of the story,] 'The end was plain ... Edward must die, the girl must lose her reason because Edward died—... that end, on that night, whilst Leonora sat in the girl's bedroom and Edward telephoned down below—that end was plainly manifest.' (268)	*whilst Leonora (Agent) sat (Process) in the girl's bedroom (C/scope)* and *Edward (Agent) telephoned down below (Process) —that end was plainly manifest (C/scope)*	*The end was plain ... (C/scope) Edward (Agent) must die, (Process)* *the girl (Agent) must lose her reason (Process) because Edward died— (C/cause) ... that end, on that night, (C/time)*	Modality shift Modality shift Distal demonstrative *that*	Reverse C/M/P Transitive reading M/P/C + C Transitive reading Reverse C/ Intentional A/P/C Transitive reading Intentional A/P/C Transitive reading

4 Disposition 273

(continued)

Frame no.	Transitive	Ergative	Devices undercut agency	Background condition
Frame 171: [Edward got out a penknife from his waistcoat pocket, asked Dowell to take the telegram to Leonora, Dowell realized Edward's intention but did not interfere with Edward's intention to **commit suicide,**] 'And he looked at me with a direct, challenging, brow-beating glare. I guess I could see *in my eyes that I didn't intend to hinder him. Why should I hinder him?*' (294)	*And he looked at me with a direct, challenging, brow-beating glare.*	*I guess* (Process) *I could see in my eyes* (C/location) *that I didn't intend to hinder him. Why should I hinder him?* C(scope)	Progressive aspect Modality shift (Modality signal possibility *could*)	Intentional A/P/C **Intransitive reading** M/P **Intransitive reading** M/P/C **Intransitive reading** Complex C (Location + scope)

Interpersonal Function

Frame no.	Assertions	Narrative modes	Truth value		Devices undercut agency
			NC (what is done)	EC (what is said)	
The conspiracy: Florence **Frame 53**: [Ship doctor warned Dowell of Florence's heart,] *'Florence went down into her cabin and her heart took her. An agitated stewardess came running up to me, and I running down. I got my directions how to behave to my wife. Most of them came from her, though it was the ship doctor who discreetly suggested to me that I had better refrain from manifestations of affection. ... I wonder, though, how Florence got the doctor to enter the conspiracy— the several doctors ... Anyhow, she and they tied me pretty well down—and Jimmy, of course, that dreary boy—...'* (101)	CA	+ A+ve (N) Evaluative adverbials discreetly, Anyhow, pretty well down + A-ve (R) Suppressed limited knowl- edge wonder, though **Double dipping**		Embedded evaluation (comments by teller)	
The motive: Dowell **Frame 158**: [The quote below sums up the end to come in this final part of the story,] *'The end was plain ... Edward must die, the girl must lose her reason because Edward died—... that end, on that night, whilst Leonora sat in the girl's bedroom and Edward telephoned down below—that end was plainly manifest.'* (268)		A+ve (N) Obligation modality must die		Embedded evaluation (comment by teller)	Modality shift

Dowell's disposition as a deceived husband is made prominent following the stance in interpersonal function. Like in the Dr. Sheppard discourse, the perspective stance in the Dowell discourse in Appendix 4f, corresponds to the dominant A(N)+ve narrative mode, undercutting agency in passivity, in modal shift, and in negation. This undercut narrative mode is alternated with the A(R)-ve mode, where Dowell as Reflector anchors his limited knowledge in perception, *I wonder* alongside his obligation and desire, *she certainly never mentioned her heart until that time*. Within the same discourse, there is also the neutral mode in CAs, (Frame 53), and there is indexing between these modes, which creates an **intermediate disposition** in static syntax for the narrative purpose in establishing the fourth tale of Dowell, Edward and Nancy which is left implicit in the main story.

The Dowell discourse in static syntax characterizes a restricted disposition for limited omniscience. Such **narrative act of alternation** for a restricted disposition at the micro level resurfaces the abettor–Narrator disposition in the Dowell discourse. This surfaces a narrative gap about the fourth triangle as a sub-theme related to Dowell, where Dowell wishes to marry Nancy in Frame 80. On accounting for this backgrounded fourth triangle of Nancy, Edward and Dowell, with its episodic links in Frames 80 and 158, these events are then thematized in Reverse C (Florence's conspiracy, Edward's affair with Nancy, Dowell's desire to marry Nancy), as discussed in Chap. 2 for Fig. 2.4. Consequently, following the motive as the DR, these thematized events provide the context for the abettor–Dowell disposition in passivity; contrasting with a transitive Goal oriented Narrator narrated as a deceived husband in Fig. 2.6. The sequence of events in the narrative thread lead up to a vertical concatenation of one who is a victim of circumstance.

4.6 Conclusion

Reverse Circumstantiation in the experiential function encodes a backgrounded entity against which the offending process is justified. The status of circumstantial elements in the clause is not as a real participant, but a state relative to the offender who is the grammatical subject. In **binary formalization**, Reverse C is in opposition with the norm: Agent/Process/Medium/Circumstance. Consequently, there is switch in information focus, where the information in Reverse C receives a marked focus, and foregrounds the backgrounded circumstance. Thus, sub-themes contextualized in Reverse C, are embedded as an entity of an offender and made concurrent alongside the dominant narrative purpose of the villain in the thriller and the perpetrator in the murder mystery. In other words, in circumstantiation of the offender setting in clauses, there is reorientation and reconnecting of the backgrounded entity as sub-themes modifying the offending process. This was observed in the Raven discourse: Anne's love and betrayal of the villain Raven, in the Ripley discourse: Ripley's sexual jealousy over his financial greed being the trigger factor for murder in Ripley offender discourse, and in CHF: the concealed marital status of Sally as manipulative causation making Sally the instigator of her own death. All of this create a NO where the murderer is intended to be interpreted as the victim in their respective discourses. This is termed as the *doubling* (mentioned above) act by pathologist Reed Smith in the TV drama, *The Fall*. In the TV drama, Reed tells the female detective Gibson, 'The older I get, the more I have two selves', to which Gibson explains—'There's a name for it. It's called doubling. I do the same. And so does the killer'. The killer at the end of the first season tells the detective on the phone, 'We're very alike you and me' [the **doubling** of perpetrator disposition as the victim and vice versa]

A recent paper (Jermyn 2015), 'The Fall *as the most feminist show*,' takes up this theme of **doubling** where she explains,

> [The] *doubling takes place ... in terms of creating an abstract sense of a relationship between* [the detective] *Gibson and* [the killer] *Spector, one where each of them at one time intimates they understand themselves as being linked to the other, drawing directly on the notion of "the double".*'

The notion of *doubling* in the offender discourses analyzed here is with reference to an intermediate disposition of the murderer when turned victim in the intransitive ordering of active participant roles in clauses, and when the victim as the offender is foregrounded in aspectual syntax for a constrained disposition within a default Narrative mode in criminal discourse. Simpson (2014: p. 7) observes,

> *... actions and events need to be anchored in the deictically proximal cognitive reference point that is the main story, and not in ... a negated or counterfactual sub-world.*'

However, in the offender engagement discourses analyzed, the actions and events in the personal story of the perpetrator in **anticipation** is anchored indirectly in linguistic cues such as deviation in Reverse C. Actions and events of the personal story are also maintained in the modalized as well as the negated world of the perpetrator, by forming a secondary Agent in the functional contrast in static aspect to minimize the relevance of past action into the present. The thematic content in linguistic dysfunctions is in contrast with the deictically proximal, or in distal cognitive references with reference to the Narrating disposition in the primary text world, to which the story is anchored for the *narrative urgency to be sustained*. This is also in contrast with the factual texture of the perpetrator/offender discourse provided in the unmodalized (CA) assertions, where propositions are in raw form, as it was before the retrospective narration began with linguistic dysfunctions for an **intermediary (post-murder) disposition** in the story.

Also revealed in this analysis is the counterfactual **discourse world** in static syntax, to which the factual CA mode as well as the **deictic world** of the Narrator and Reflector in the discourse is anchored. *Counterfactual events are scenarios not realized* (Harding 2007: p. 263); they are desired in the crime stories, such as the **imagined sub-theme** of Ripley. In other words, in the discourses analyzed, the propositions with static syntax are made *contrary to* [the] *known facts* [in CA]… (Ziegeler 2000: p. 15). In this counterfactual world, the participant is not in charge of events, but a **justification** of the offending actions are realized; that is, how it was the only thing to do. As a *post-offence verbalization* (Youngs and Canter 2012: p. 297) the statements in this world are evident in Reverse Cs, in C/scope clauses and in the functional contrast, where static syntax undercut Actor Narrator intervention to project a constrained, minimized omniscience in both the narrative world of desire in A(N) and B(N) diegetic modes. If the world of CAs is relational to the offender who was in control, the static counterfactual world is a **post-offence rewriting** and is about the related **stance** the offending participant brings to the criminal issues at hand. The offender discourses, with reference to stance, are further analyzed in participant orientation in Chap. 5, taking into account the counterfactual versus the hypothetical nature of the discourses adopted from true crime narratives.

Appendix 4a

Perpetrator Bud Corliss: *A Kiss before Dying*

1. Experiential function

Part One: *A Kiss before Dying*

Clause no.	Transitive	Ergative	Undercut agency	Background condition
1a. His plans had been running so beautifully, so goddamned beautifully, and now she was going to smash them all.		His plans (receptive/Medium) had been running so beautifully, so goddamned beautifully.(Process)	Progressive aspect	M/P/C Intransitive reading
1b. and now she was going to smash them all.		... and now (C/scope) she (Medium) was going to smash (Process) them all (C/scope)		Reverse C/M/P/C Intransitive reading
2. Hate erupted and flooded through him, gripping his face with jaw-aching pressure.		Hate (C/scope) erupted and flooded (Process) through him (Medium),	Depersonalization	Reverse C/P/M Unusual structure
		[hate] (Agent) gripping his face (Medium) with jaw-aching pressure (C/scope)	Depersonalization Progressive aspect	(undercut) Inanimate A/P/C Intransitive reading

3. *That was alright though, the lights were out.*		*That [the eruption of his hate] was alright though (C/scope entity) the lights were out. (C/scope)*	C (scope)
4. *He closed his eyes and spoke dreamily, intoning the words in a sedative chant.*		*He (Agent) closed (Process) his eyes (Medium) and [he] spoke dreamily, intoning the words in a sedative chant. (C/scope)*	Intentional A/P/M **Transitive reading** [Intentional Agent]/P/C **Intransitive reading**
5. *I had it planned so beautifully.*	DS		
6. *I would have come to New York this summer and you would have introduced me to him.*	DS		
7. *I could have got him to like me.*	DS		
8. *You would have introduced me to him.*	DS		

4 Disposition 279

(continued)

(continued)

Clause no.	Transitive	Ergative	Undercut agency	Background condition
9. I could have got him to like me.	DS			
10. You would have told me what he's interested in, what he likes, what he dislikes-' he stopped short, then continued.	DS he (Agent) stopped short, then continued. (Process)			Intentional A/P Transitive reading
11. 'And after graduation we would have been married.	DS			
12. Or even this summer.'	DS			
13. We could have come back here in September for our last two years.	DS			
14. A little apartment of our own, right near the campus –' (S)	DS			
15. He had discovered that she liked to be called 'baby'.		He (Medium) had discovered (Process) that she liked to be called 'baby'. (C/scope)	Perfective aspect	M/P/C Intransitive reading

4 Disposition 281

16. When he called her 'baby' and held her in arms he could get her to do practically anything.	When he called her 'baby' and held her in arms (C/scope) he (Agent) could get her to do (Process) practically anything. (C/scope)	Modality shift (Modality signal possibility *could*)	Reverse C/A/P/C Intransitive reading
17. He had thought about it, and decided it had something to do with the coldness she felt towards her father. (7)	He (Medium) had thought (Process) about it, (C/Range)	Perfective aspect	M/P/C Intransitive reading
	and [he] (Medium) decided (Process) it had something to do with the coldness she felt towards her father. (C/scope)	Perfective aspect	M/P/C Intransitive reading
18. What angered him most was that in a sense the responsibility for the entire situation rested with Dorothy.	What angered him most (C/scope) was (Process) that in a sense the responsibility for the entire situation (C/scope) rested (Process) with Dorothy. (Medium)		Reverse C/P/C/P/M Unusual structure
19. He wanted to take her to his room only once—a down-payment guaranteeing the fulfilment of a contract.	He (Medium) wanted (Process) to take her to his room only once—a down-payment guaranteeing the fulfilment of a contract. (C/scope)		M/P/C Intransitive reading

(continued)

(continued)

Clause no.	Transitive	Ergative	Undercut agency	Background condition
20. It was Dorothy, with her gently closed eyes and her passive, orphan hunger, who had wished for further visits.		It was Dorothy, with her gently closed eyes and her passive, orphan hunger, (C/scope) who (Medium) had wished (Process) for further visits. (C/scope)	Perfective tense	Reverse C/M/P/C Intransitive reading
21. He struck the table.	He (Agent) struck (Process) the table. (Medium)			Intentional A/P/M Transitive reading
22. It really was her fault! Damn her! (17)	FDT			
23. He sat at the back of the room, in the second seat from the window.	He (Agent) sat (Process) at the back of the room, in the second seat from the window. (C/ Location)			Intentional A/P/C Transitive reading
24. The seat on his left, the window seat, the empty seat, was hers.		The seat on his left, the window seat, the empty seat, (C/scope) was (Process) hers. (Medium)		C(scope)

4 Disposition

25. *It was the first class of the morning, a daily Social Science lecture, and their only class together this semester.*	*It was the first class of the morning, a daily Social Science lecture, and their only class together this semester.* (C/scope)	Existential *it*		C(scope)
26. *The speaker's voice droned in the sun-filled air.*	*The speaker's voice* (Medium) *droned* (Process) *in the sun-filled air.* (C/scope)	Depersonalization		M/P/C **Intransitive reading**
27. *Today of all days she could have made an effort to be on time.*	*Today of all days* (C/scope) *she* (Medium) *could have made an effort* (Process) *to be on time.* (C/scope)	Perfective aspect Modality shift (Modality signal possibility *could*)		C/M/P/C **Intransitive reading**
28. *Didn't she know he'd be frozen in an agony of suspense?* (21)	FDT			
29. *He put his books down on the grass.*	*He* (Agent) *put down* (Process) *his books* (Medium) *on the grass.* (C/Location)		Intentional	A/P/C **Transitive reading**
30. *The important thing was to get time, time to think.*	FDT			

(continued)

(continued)

Clause no.	Transitive	Ergative	Undercut agency	Background condition
31. *He was afraid his knees were going to start shaking.*		*He (Medium) was afraid (Process) his knees were going to start shaking.* (C/scope)		M/P/C Intransitive reading
32. *He took her by the shoulders, smiling.*	*He (Agent) took (Process) her by the shoulders, smiling.* (C/scope)			Intentional A/P/M/C Intransitive reading
33. *'That's the spirit.'*	DS			
34. *You just don't worry about anything.'*	DS			
35. *He took a breath.*	*He (Agent) took a breath.* (Process)			Intentional A/P Transitive reading
36. *'Friday afternoon we'll go down to the Municipal–'* (22)	DS			
37. *It still wasn't too late.*	*It still wasn't too late.* (C/scope)		Existential *It*	C(scope)

38. *People wrote suicide notes and then stalled around before actually doing it.*	FDT *People (Agent) wrote (Process) suicide notes (Medium) and then stalled around before actually doing it. (C/scope)*		Intentional A/P/M/C Transitive reading
39. *He looked at his watch: 9.20.*	*He (Agent) looked (Process) at his watch: (Medium) 9.20 (C/Location)*		Intentional A/P/C Transitive reading
40. *The earliest Ellen could get the note would be—three o' clock.*	FDT *The earliest (C/scope) Ellen (Agent) could get (Process) the note (Medium) would be—three o' clock. (C/ location)*	Modality shift (Modality signal possibility could)	Reverse C/A/P/M/C Transitive reading

4   Disposition   285

(continued)

(continued)

Clause no.	Transitive	Ergative	Undercut agency	Background condition
41. Five hours and forty minutes.	FDT			
42. No step by step planning now.	FDT			Temporal deictic *now*
43. It would have to be quick, positive.	FDT			
44. No trickery that counted on her doing a certain thing at a certain time.	FDT			
45. No poison.	FDT			
46. How else do people kill themselves?	FDT			
47. In five hours and forty minutes she must be dead. (55)		In five hours and forty minutes (C/scope) she (Medium) must be dead. (Process)	Modality shift (Modality signal obligation *must*)	Reverse C/M/P Intransitive reading

4 Disposition 287

Part Two: A Kiss before Dying

Clause no.	Transitive	Ergative	Undercut agency	Background condition
48. *He drove with his left hand, occasionally giving the steering wheel an inappreciable right or left movement to relieve the hypnotic monotony on the highway. …*	He (Agent) drove (Process) with his left hand, occasionally giving the steering wheel an inappreciable right or left movement to relieve the hypnotic monotony on the highway. … (C/scope)			Intentional A/P/C Transitive reading
49. *He told her everything…*	He (Agent) told (Process) her everything (Medium)			Intentional A/P/M Transitive reading
50. *So he told Ellen about the pills and the roof and why it had been necessary to kill Dorothy, and why it had been the most logical course to transfer to Caldwell and go after her, Ellen, knowing her likes and dislikes from conversation with Dorothy, knowing how to make himself the man she was waiting for—not only the most logical and inevitable course, going after the girl with whom he had such an advantage, but also the course most ironically satisfying, the course most compensatory for past bad luck …*	So he (Agent) told (Process) Ellen (Medium) about the pills and the roof …. C/scope		Progressive aspect	Intentional A/P/C Transitive reading

(continued)

(continued)

Clause no.	Transitive	Ergative	Undercut agency	Background condition
51. He told her these things with irritation and contempt; this girl with her hands over her mouth in horror had had everything given her on a silver platter; she didn't know what it was to live on a swaying catwalk over the chasm of failure, stealing perilously inch by inch towards the solid ground of success so many miles away. (175)	He (Agent) told (Process) her these things (Medium) ….	this girl (Medium) with her hands over her mouth in horror (C/scope) had had everything given (Process) to her on a silver platter; (C/Scope)	Proximal deictic these Proximal deictic this Perfective aspect Negation	Intentional A/P/M/C Transitive reading M/C/P/C Intransitive reading

Part Three: A Kiss before Dying

Clause no.	Transitive	Ergative	Undercut agency	Background condition
52. ... 'How did you get Dorothy to write that suicide note?' (264)	DS			
53. Everything fell away; the catwalk, the smelter, the whole world; everything melted away like sandcastles sucked into the sea, leaving him suspended in emptiness with two blue marbles staring at him and the sound of Leo's question swelling and reverberating like being inside an iron bell.		Everything (C/Scope) fell away (Process) the catwalk, the smelter, the whole world.... (C/scope)	swelling and reverberating Progressive aspect	C/P/C Unusual structure
54. Gant said, 'You killed Dorothy and Ellen and Dwight Powell!'	DS			
55. 'And almost killed Marion,' Leo said. 'When she saw that list- (266)	DS			
56. He swiped at his cheek. Control! Self-control!	He (Agent) swiped (Process) at his cheek. (C/scope) FDT Control! Self-control!			Intentional A/P/C Transitive reading
57. He dragged a deep breath into his chest ...		He (Medium) dragged a deep breath (Process) into his chest ... (C/scope)		Intentional A/P/C Intransitive reading

(continued)

(continued)

Clause no.	Transitive	Ergative	Undercut agency	Background condition
58. *Slow up, slow up ...*	FDT			
59. *They can't prove a thing, not a goddamn thing!*	FDT			
60. *They know about the list, about Marion, about the pamphlets—okay—but they can't prove a thing about ...*	FDT			
61. *He drew another breath ... (266–7)*		He (Medium) drew (Process) another breath		M/P Intransitive reading
62. *'Marion', he pleaded, 'stop them! They're crazy! They're trying to kill me! Stop them! They'll listen to you! I can explain about that list, I can explain everything! I swear I wasn't lying-'*	DS			
63. *'How do I know?' she asked.*	DS			
64. *'You swore so many things-' Her fingers appeared curving over the men's shoulders; long, white, pink-nailed fingers; they seemed to be pushing.*	DS	Her fingers (Medium) appeared curving (Process) over the men's shoulders; long, white, pink-nailed fingers; (C/scope) they (Medium) seemed to be pushing. (Process)	Modality shift *Appeared* *seemed*	M/P/C Intransitive reading M/P Intransitive reading

4 Disposition   291

65. 'Marion!' You wouldn't! Not when we—after we-'	DS			
66. Her fingers pressed forward into the cloth of the shoulders, pushing …		Her fingers (Agent) pressed forward … (Process) into the cloth of the shoulders, (C/scope) pushing (Process)	Depersonalization Progressive aspect	A/P/C/P **Transitive reading**
67. 'Marion,' he begged futilely. (271)	DS			
68. He looked down.		He (Agent) looked down (Process)	Intentional A/P	**Transitive reading**
69. The front of his pants was dark with a spreading stain that ran in a series of island blotches down his trouser leg.		The front of his pants (Medium) was dark (Process) with a spreading stain that ran in a series of island blotches down his trouser leg. (C/scope)		M/P/C **Intransitive reading**

(continued)

(continued)

Clause no.	Transitive	Ergative	Undercut agency	Background condition
70. *Oh God! The Jap—the Jap he had killed—that wretched, trembling, chattering pants-wetting caricature of a man—was that him? Was that himself?* (272)	FDT			
71. *—he had jumped*		he (Agent) had jumped (Process)	Perfective tense	A/P/C Transitive reading
and now he was letting go because he wanted to, that's all, and everything was alright and his knees weren't shaking any more, not that they had been shaking so much anyway, his knees weren't shaking anymore because he was in command again—he hadn't noticed his right hand open but it must have opened because he was dropping into the heat, cables were shooting up, someone was creaming like Dorrie going into the shaft and Ellen when the first bullet wasn't enough—this person was screaming this god awful scream and suddenly it was himself and he couldn't stop!		and now (C/scope) he (Medium) was letting go because ..... (C/scope)	Progressive aspect Negation Depersonalization Modality shift Proximal deictics *now*	Intentional C/M/P/C Intransitive reading
72. *Why was he screaming? Why? Why on earth should he be –*	FDT			

4 Disposition

73. The scream, which had knifed through the sudden stillness of the smelter, ended in a vicious splash.		Perfective aspect Depersonalization	C/P/C **Unusual structure**
	The scream, which (C/scope) had knifed (Process) through the sudden stillness of the smelter, ended in a vicious splash. (C/scope)		
74. From the other side of the vat a sheet of green leaped up.	Circumstance		C(Scope)
75. Arcing, it sheared down to the floor where it splattered into a million pools and droplets. (273–4)	Circumstance	Existential *it*	C(Scope)
76. They hissed softly on the cement and slowly dawned from green to copper.	They [Machines] (Agent) hissed softly (Process) on the cement and slowly dawned from green to copper. (C/scope)	Depersonalization	Inanimate A/P/C **Transitive reading**

Perpetrator Bud Corliss: *A Kiss before Dying*

2. **Interpersonal function**
3. **The truth-value**

Part One

Clause no.	Assertion	Narrative mode	Truth value NC (what is done)	EC (what is said)	Undercut agency
1. His plans had been running so beautifully, so goddamned beautifully, and now she was going to smash them all.		B(R)+ve Proximal deictic *now*	FC/comment		Perfective aspect Progressive aspect Proximal deictic *now*
2. Hate erupted and flooded through him, gripping his face with jaw-aching pressure.		B(N)+ve Evaluative adjective	FC/comment		Depersonalization Progressive aspect
3. That was alright though, the lights were out.	CA	B(N)+ve Evaluative adverbial *alright though*	FC/comment		
4. He closed his eyes and spoke dreamily, intoning the words in a sedative chant.	CA	B(N)+ve Evaluative adverbial *dreamily*)	Internal Correlative		Progressive aspect

4 Disposition   295

5. 'I had it planned so beautifully.	DS	Progressive aspect
6. I would have come to New York this summer and you would have introduced me to him.	DS	Modality shift
7. I could have got him to like me.	DS	Modality shift
8. You would have introduced me to him.	DS	Modality shift
9. I could have got him to like me.	DS	Modality shift
10. You would have told me what he's interested in, what he likes, what he dislikes-' he stopped short, then continued.	DS	Modality shift
11. 'And after graduation we would have been married.	DS	Modality shift
12. Or even this summer.	DS	
13. We could have come back here in September for our last two years.	DS	Modality shift
14. A little apartment of our own, right near the campus -' (5)	DS	

(continued)

(continued)

Clause no.	Assertion	Narrative mode	Truth value NC (what is done)	Truth value EC (what is said)	Undercut agency
15. He had discovered that she liked to be called 'baby'.	CA		Internal (intensifier that)		Perfective aspect
16. When he called her 'baby' and held her in arms he could get her to do practically anything.		B(N)+ve Action suspended for causality	FC/comment		Modality shift
17. He had thought about it, and decided it had something to do with the coldness she felt towards her father. (7)		B(N)+ve Action suspended for causality	FC/comment		Perfective aspect
18. What angered him most was that in a sense the responsibility for the entire situation rested with Dorothy.		B(N)+ve Action suspended for causality	Internal (intensifier that)		
19. He wanted to take her to his room only once—a down payment guaranteeing the fulfilment of a contract.		B(N)+ve	Internal (Correlative)		Progressive aspect

4 Disposition 297

20. It was Dorothy, with her gently closed eyes and her passive, orphan hunger, who had wished for further visits.		B(N)+ve		Perfective aspect
21. He struck the table.	CA	B neutral	NC(fixed)	
22. It really was her fault! Damn her! (17)	FIT			Existential *It*
23. He sat at the back of the room, in the second seat from the window.	CA	B neutral	FC/narrative	
24. The seat on his left, the window seat, the empty seat, was hers.	CA	B neutral	FC/narrative	
25. It was the first class of the morning, a daily Social Science lecture, and their only class together this semester.		B(R)+ve Proximal deictic *this*	FC/narrative	
26. The speaker's voice droned in the sun-filled air.		B(N)+ve Evaluative adverbial *droned*		Depersonalization
27. Today of all days she could have made an effort to be on time.		B(R)+ve Proximal adverbial *today*	FC/comment	Modality shift Proximal adverbial *today*
28. Didn't she know he'd be frozen in an agony of suspense? (21)	DT			Perfective aspect

(continued)

(continued)

Clause no.	Assertion	Narrative mode	Truth value NC (what is done)	EC (what is said)	Undercut agency
29. He put his books down on the grass.	CA	B neutral			
30. The important thing was to get time, time to think.	FIT		FC/comment		
31. He was afraid his knees were going to start shaking.		B(N)+ve	Internal (Correlative)		Depersonalization Progressive aspect
32. He took her by the shoulders, smiling.		B(N)+ve			Progressive aspect
33. 'That's the spirit.'	FIS				
34. 'You just don't worry about anything.'	FIS				Negation
35. He took a breath.	CA	B neutral	NC		
36. 'Friday afternoon we'll go down to the Municipal-' (22)	FIS				
37. It still wasn't too late.	FIT				
38. People wrote suicide notes and then stalled around before actually doing it.	FIT		FC/comment		

4 Disposition 299

#	Text	Cat	Features	Notes
39.	He looked at his watch: 9.20.	CA	B(N)+ve + B(R)+ve Proximal time **Double dipping** (dichotomy)	
40.	The earliest Ellen could get the note would be—three o' clock.	FDT	B(R)+ve Proximal time adverbial	FC/comment Modality shift
41.	Five hours and forty minutes.	FIT		
42.	No step by step planning now.	FIT		Proximal deictic *now*
43.	It would have to be quick, positive.	FIT		Modality shift
44.	No trickery that counted on her doing a certain thing at a certain time.	FIT		
45.	No poison.	FIT		
46.	How else do people kill themselves?	FIT		
47.	In five hours and forty minutes she must be dead. (55)		B(N)-ve Epistemic perception modality *must*	Embedded evaluation (comment by participant) Modality shift

Part Two: A Kiss before Dying

Clause no.	Assertion	Narrative modes	Truth value NC (what is done)	Truth value EC (what is said)	Devices undercut agency
48. He drove with his left hand, occasionally giving the steering wheel an inappreciable right or left movement to relieve the hypnotic monotony on the highway. …		B (N)+ve Evaluative adverbials	Internal (Correlatives)		Progressive aspect
49. He told her everything…	CA	B neutral	NC		
50. So he told Ellen about the pills and the roof and why it had been necessary to kill Dorothy, and why it had been the most logical course to transfer to Caldwell and go after her, Ellen, knowing her likes and dislikes from conversation with Dorothy, knowing how to make himself the man she was waiting for—not only the most logical and inevitable course, going after the girl with whom he had such an advantage, but also the course most ironically satisfying, the course most compensatory for past bad luck …	CA	B(N)+ve	Internal (Correlative)		Progressive aspect

Clause	Assertion	Narrative mode	Truth value NC	Truth value EC	Devices undercut agency
51. He told her these things with irritation and contempt;		B(N)+ve Evaluative adverbial irritation and contempt			Perfective aspect Progressive aspect Negation
this girl with her hands over her mouth in horror had had everything given her on a silver platter; she didn't know what it was to live on a swaying catwalk over the chasm of failure, stealing perilously inch by inch towards the solid ground of success so many miles away. (175)	+	B(R)+ve Proximal demonstrative *this, these*	FC/comment		

Part Three: *A Kiss before Dying*

			Truth value		
Clause no.	Assertion	Narrative mode	NC (what is done)	EC (what is said)	Devices undercut agency
52. ... 'How did you get Dorothy to write that suicide note?' (264)	FIS				
53. Everything fell away; the catwalk, the smelter, the whole world; everything melted away like sandcastles sucked into the sea, leaving him suspended in emptiness with two blue marbles staring at him and the sound of Leo's question swelling and reverberating like being inside an iron bell.		B(N)+ve Evaluative adjectives like *sandcastles sucked into the sea*, like *being inside an iron bell*	FC/comment		Progressive aspect

(continued)

(continued)

Clause no.	Assertion	Narrative modes	Truth value NC (what is done)	EC (what is said)	Devices undercut agency
54. Gant said, 'You killed Dorothy and Ellen and Dwight Powell!'	FIS				
55. 'And almost killed Marion,' Leo said. 'When she saw that list-' (266)	FIS				
56. He swiped at his cheek. Control! Self-control!	CA FIT	B(N)+ve + B(R)+ve (mediated through proximal perspective)			
57. He dragged a deep breath into his chest …	CA	B neutral	NC		
58. Slow up, slow up …	FIT		Internal (intensifier/ repetition)		
59. They can't prove a thing, not a goddamn thing!	FIT		Internal (Negation)		Negation
60. They know about the list, about Marion, about the pamphlets—okay—but they can't prove a thing about …	FIT		Internal (Negation)		Distal pronominal *they* Negation
61. He drew another breath … (266-7)	CA	B neutral			

4 Disposition   303

62. 'Marion', he pleaded, 'stop them! They're crazy! They're trying to kill me! Stop them! They'll listen to you! I can explain about that list, I can explain everything! I swear I wasn't lying-'	IS			
63. 'How do I know?' she asked.	IS			
64. 'You swore so many things-' Her fingers appeared curving over the men's shoulders; long, white, pink-nailed fingers; they seemed to be pushing.	FIS	B(R)-ve Words of estrangement seemed	Internal (Correlative)	Words of estrangement seemed
65. 'Marion!' You wouldn't! Not when we—after we-'	FIS			
66. Her fingers pressed forward into the cloth of the shoulders, pushing ...	CA	B(N)+ve	Internal (correlative)	Progressive aspect
67. 'Marion,' he begged futilely. (271)	DS			
68. He looked down.	CA		NC	
69. The front of his pants was dark with a spreading stain that ran in a series of island blotches down his trouser leg.	CA	B(N)+ve Evaluative adjective island blotches	Internal Intensifier that	Progressive aspect
70. Oh God! The Jap—the Jap he had killed—that wretched, trembling, chattering pants-wetting caricature of a man—was that him? Was that himself? (272)	FIT			

(continued)

(continued)

Clause no.	Assertion	Narrative modes	Truth value NC (what is done)	EC (what is said)	Devices
71. —he had jumped and now he was letting go because he wanted to, that's all, and everything was alright and his knees weren't shaking any more, not that they had been shaking so much anyway, his knees weren't shaking anymore because he was in command again—he hadn't noticed his right hand open but it must have opened because he was dropping into the heat, cables were shooting up, someone was creaming like Dorrie going into the shaft and Ellen when the first bullet wasn't enough—this person was screaming this god awful scream and suddenly it was himself and he couldn't stop!		B(N)+ve + B(R)+ve Proximal deictic *now*	Internal (Correlative)		Progressive aspect Negation Impersonal *this person for* Point of view shift *it* divided focus to undercut agency
72. Why was he screaming? Why? Why on earth should he be –	FDT				
73. The scream, which had knifed through the sudden stillness of the smelter, ended in a vicious splash.		B(N)+ve Evaluative adverbial *knifed*		Embedded evaluation (comment by teller)	Depersonalization Perfective aspect

Clause	Transitive	Ergative	Voice	Background condition
74. From the other side of the vat a sheet of green leaped up.	B(N)+ve			Spatial deictics other side
75. Arcing, it sheared down to the floor where it splattered into a million pools and droplets.	B(N)+ve			Internal (correlative) Progressive aspect Existential it
76. They hissed softly on the cement and slowly dawned from green to copper. (273–4)	B(N)+ve Evaluative adverbial hissed softly, slowly dawned			FC/comment Internal (correlative)

Appendix 4b

Perpetrator Raven: *A Gun for Sale*

1. Experiential function

Clause	Transitive	Ergative	Voice	Background condition
1. *Murder didn't mean much to Raven.*		Murder (C/scope) didn't mean much (Process) to Raven. C/scope	Negation	C/P/C Unusual structure

(continued)

(continued)

Clause	Transitive	Ergative	Voice	Background condition
2. You had to be careful.		You (Medium) had to be careful. (Process)	Perfective aspect	M/P Intransitive reading
3. You had to use your brains.		You (Medium) had to use (Process) your brains. (C/scope)	Perfective aspect	M/P/C Intransitive reading
4. It was not a question of hatred.		It [Murder] (C/Scope) was not (Process) a question of hatred. (C/scope)	Existential *It*	C/P/C Unusual structure
5. He had only seen the Minister once: he had been pointed out to Raven as he walked down the new housing estate between the small lit Christmas trees, an old grubby man without friends, who was said to love humanity. (1)	...	He (Experiencer/Medium) had only seen (Process) the Minister (Medium) once: (C/scope) ... he (Medium) had been pointed out (Process) to Raven (C/scope) as he walked down the new housing estate between the small lit Christmas trees, (C/location) an old grubby man without friends, who was said to love humanity.	Perfective aspect	M/P/M/C Intransitive reading M/P/C/C Intransitive reading Complex Cs

6. He snatched the automatic out of the case and shot the Minister twice in the back.	He (Agent) snatched (Process) the automatic (Medium) out of the case (C/location)	Intentional A/P/M/C **Transitive reading**
	and [Agent] shot (Process) the Minister (Medium) twice in the back. (C/location)	[Ellipted] Intentional A/P/M/C **Transitive reading**
7. The Minister fell across the oil stove; the saucepan upset and the two eggs broke.	The Minister (Medium) fell (Process) across the oil stove; (C/scope) the saucepan upset and the two eggs broke. (C/scope)	M/P/C/C **Intransitive reading**
8. Raven shot the Minister once more in the head, leaning across the desk to make quite certain, driving the bullet hard into the base of the skull, smashing it open like a china doll's.	Raven (Agent) shot (Process) the Minister (Medium) once more in the head, leaning across the desk to make quite certain, driving the bullet hard into the base of the skull, smashing it open like a china doll's. (C/scope)	Intentional A/P/M/C **Transitive reading**

(continued)

(continued)

Clause	Transitive	Ergative	Voice	Background condition
9. *Then he turned on the secretary; she moaned at him; she hadn't any words; the old mouth couldn't hold the saliva.*	*Then he (Agent) turned (Process) on the secretary;* (C/location) *she (Agent) hadn't any words;* (C/scope)	*she; (Agent) moaned (Process) at him* (C/ location)	Negation	Intentional A/P/C Transitive reading M/P/C Intransitive reading
		the old mouth (Medium) couldn't hold (Process) the saliva. (C/scope)	Depersonalization Modality shift Negation	Undercut A/P/C Intransitive reading M/P/C Intransitive reading
10. *He supposed she was begging him for mercy.*		*He (Medium/ Experiencer) supposed (Process) she was begging him for mercy.* (C/scope)	Progressive aspect	M/P/C Intransitive reading

11. He pressed the trigger again; she staggered under it as if she had been kicked by an animal in the side.	He (Agent) pressed (Process) the trigger again; (Medium)		Intentional A/P/M **Transitive reading**
	she (Medium) staggered (Process) under it (C/scope)		M/P/C **Intransitive reading**
	as if she (Medium) had been kicked (Process) by an animal (C/scope) in the side. (C/location)	Conditional *if* Perfective aspect	M/P/C/C **Intransitive reading**
12. But useless material in which she hid her body, had perhaps confused him.	But useless material in which (C/accompaniment) She (Agent) hid (Process) her body, (Medium) had perhaps confused him. (C/scope)	Perfective aspect	***Reverse C/** Intentional A/P/M/C **Transitive reading**
13. And she was tough, so tough he couldn't believe his eyes; she was through the door before he could fire again, slamming it behind her. (3)	a. *And she was tough, so tough* (C/point of view) *he couldn't believe his eyes;* (Process)	Negation	***Reverse C/M/P Intransitive reading**
	b. *she* (Agent) *was through the door* (Process) *before he could fire again, slamming it behind her.* (C/scope)		Intentional A/P/C **Transitive reading**

(continued)

(continued)

Clause	Transitive	Ergative	Voice	Background condition
14. *There was no time to waste.*			Existential *there*	C (scope)
15. *He stood away from the door and shot twice through the woodwork.*	*He (Agent) stood away (Process) from the door (C/location) and shot twice (Process) through the woodwork. (C/scope)*			Intentional A/P/C and [A]/P/C Transitive reading
16. *He could hear the pince-nez fall on the floor and break.*		*He (Medium) could hear (Process) the pince-nez (Medium) fall on the floor and break. (C/scope)*	Modality shift (modality signal possibility *could*)	M/P/M/C Intransitive reading Unusual structure
17. *The voice screamed again and stopped; there was a sound as if she were sobbing.*		*The voice (Medium) screamed again and stopped; (Process) there was a sound as if she were sobbing. (C/scope)*	Depersonalization Existential *there* Conditional *if* Progressive aspect	M/P Intransitive reading (C/scope)
18. *It was her breath going out through her wounds.*		*It was her breath (Medium) going out (Process) through her wounds. (C/scope)*	Existential *It*	M/P/C Intransitive reading

4 Disposition 311

19. Raven was satisfied.	Raven (Medium) was satisfied. (Process)		M/P **Intransitive reading**
20. He turned back to the Minister.	He (Agent) turned back (Process) to the Minister (C/scope)		Intentional A/P/C **Transitive reading**
21. A low voice whispered an appeal quite distinctly through the door.	A low voice (Agent) whispered (Process) an appeal (C/scope) quite distinctly through the door. (C/location)	Depersonalization	A/P/C/C **Transitive reading**
22. Raven picked up the automatic again; who would have imagined an old woman could be so tough?	Raven (Agent) picked up (Process) the automatic again; (Medium)		Intentional A/P/M **Transitive reading**
23. It touched his nerve a little just in the same way as the bell had done, as if a ghost were interfering with a man's job.	It (C) touched (Process) his nerve (Medium) a little (C/scope) just in the same way as the bell had done, as if a ghost were interfering with a man's job. (C/scope)	Existential *It*	*Reverse C/P/M/C **Intransitive reading**

(continued)

(continued)

Clause	Transitive	Ergative	Voice	Background condition
24. He opened the study door; he had to push it against the weight of her body.	He (Agent) opened (Process) the study door; (Medium) he (Agent) had to push (Process) it (Medium) against the weight of her body. (C/scope)		Perfective aspect Perfective aspect	Intentional A/P/M Transitive reading Intentional A/P/M/C Transitive reading
25. She looked dead enough, but he made quite sure with the automatic almost touching her eyes. (4)		She (Medium) looked dead enough, (Process) but he (Medium) made quite sure (Process) with the automatic (C/Scope) almost touching her eyes. (C/accompaniment)		M/P Intransitive reading Medium/P/C Intransitive reading

4 Disposition

... 26. These people [Dr. Yogel and his secretary] were of his own kind; they didn't belong inside the legal borders; for the second time in one day he had been betrayed by the lawless [the double-crossers].		These people (Medium) were (Process) of his own kind; (C/scope)	M/P/C Intransitive reading
	they (Agent) didn't belong (Process) inside the legal borders; (C/scope)	Negation	Negated intentional A/P/C Transitive reading
		for the second time in one day (C/extent/ duration) ... he (Medium) had been betrayed (Process) by the lawless. (C/scope)	Perfective aspect C/M/P/C Intransitive reading
27. He had always been alone, but never so alone as this.		He (Medium) had always been alone, (Process) but never so alone as this. (C/manner)	Perfective aspect M/P/C Intransitive reading
28. The telephone wire gave [in Yogel's surgery].	Circumstance		C/scope

(continued)

(continued)

Clause	Transitive	Ergative	Voice	Background condition
29. He wouldn't speak another word for fear his temper might master him and he might shoot.	He (Agent) wouldn't speak another word (Process)		Negation	Negated Intentional A/P Transitive reading
		for fear (C/scope) his temper (C/scope) might master (Process) him (Medium) double dipping and he (Medium) might shoot. (Process)	Modality shift (Modality signal possibility might)	*Reverse C/P/M Intransitive reading *Double dipping: Agent becomes Medium M/P Intransitive reading
30. This wasn't the time for shooting. (25)			Negation	C (Scope)

... 31. Raven could never realize other people; they didn't seem to him to live in the same way as he lived [to play fair (16), Raven did not go back on a fellow who treated him right (24), he kept a promise (41)]; and though he bore a grudge against Mr Cholmondeley, hated him enough to kill him, he couldn't imagine Mr Cholmondeley's own fears and motives.	Raven (Medium) could never realize (Process) other people; (C/Scope)	Negation	M/P/C (Scope) Unusual structure
	they (Medium) didn't seem (Process) to him (C/Scope) to live in the same way as he lived; (C/manner)	Stative verb seem	M/P/C/C Intransitive reading
	c. and though (C/concession) he (Agent) bore a grudge (Process) against Mr Cholmondeley, (C/scope)		*Reverse C/M/P/C (scope) Intransitive reading
	[he] hated (Process) him enough (Medium) to kill him, (C/scope)	Negation	[M]/P/M/C Unusual structure
	he (Medium) couldn't imagine (Process) Mr Cholmondeley's own fears and motives. (C/scope)		M/P/C Intransitive reading

(continued)

(continued)

Clause	Transitive	Ergative	Voice	Background condition
32. He was the greyhound and Mr Cholmondeley the mechanical hare; but in this case the greyhound was chased in its turn by another mechanical hare. (p. 29)		a. He (Medium) was (Process) the greyhound and Mr Cholmondeley the mechanical hare; (C/adjective)		M/P/C (Scope)
		b. but in this case (C (Scope) the greyhound (Medium) was chased in its turn (Process) by another mechanical hare. (C/scope)		*Reverse C/M/P/C Intransitive reading
... 33. He was used to fear. It had lived inside him for twenty years.		He (Medium) was used (Process) to fear. (C/scope)		M/P/C Unusual structure
		It [fear] (C/scope) had lived (Process) inside him (C/scope) for twenty years. (C/duration)	Existential It	C/P/C/C Unusual structure
34. It was normality [human feelings] he couldn't cope with. (39)		It was normality (C/scope) he (Medium) couldn't cope with. (Process)	Negation	*Reverse C/M/P Intransitive reading

#	Text	Clause analysis	Notes	Reading
35.	'People don't trouble to keep their word to me,' Raven said (41) …	IS		
36.	He made no sound, the tears seemed to run like flies of their own will from the corners of his eyes. (42) …	He (Agent) made no sound, (Process)		Intentional A/P **Intransitive reading**
		… the tears (Medium) seemed to run (Process) like flies (C/ manner) of their own will (C/scope) from the corners of his eyes. (C/location) **double dipping**	Stative verb: seemed to run Depersonalization	M/P/C+C+C **Intransitive reading** **Complex Cs** C (manner + scope+ location) *Double dipping: Agent also as Medium
37.	He remembered the kitten he had left behind in the Soho café.	He (Medium) remembered (Process) the kitten (Medium)		M/P/M **Unusual structure**
		he had left behind in the Soho café. (C/scope)	Perfective aspect	Intentional A/P/C **Transitive reading**
38.	He had loved that kitten.	He (Agent) had loved (Process) that kitten. (Medium)	Perfective aspect	Intentional A/P/M **Transitive reading**

(continued)

(continued)

Clause	Transitive	Ergative	Voice	Background condition
39. She never knew, he thought, that he had meant to kill her; she had been innocent of his intention as a cat he had once been forced to drown; and he remembered with astonishment that she had not betrayed him, although he had told her that the police were after him.	She (Agent) never knew, (Process)		Negation	Negated Engaged A/P Intransitive reading
	he (Agent) thought, (Process) that he had meant to kill her; ... (C/scope)		Perfective aspect	Engaged A/P/C Intransitive reading
		...she (Medium) had been innocent (Process) of his intention as a cat (C/scope) he had once been forced to drown; (C/manner)	Perfective aspect	M/P/C Intransitive reading
		...and he (Medium) remembered with astonishment (Process) that she had not betrayed him, (C/scope)	Perfective aspect	M/P/C Intransitive reading
	although (C/concession) he (Agent) had told (Process) her (Medium) that the police were after him. (C/matter)		Perfective aspect	*Reverse C/ intentional A/P/M/C Transitive reading

... 40. It was even possible that she had believed him. (61)	It was even possible that (C/scope) she (Medium) had believed (Process) him. (Medium)	Perfective aspect	*Reverse C/M/P/M **Unusual structure**
41. These thoughts were colder and more uncomfortable than the hail.	These thoughts were colder and more uncomfortable than the hail. (C/scope)	Proximal deictic *these*	C (Scope)
42. He wasn't used to any taste that wasn't bitter on the tongue.	He (Medium) wasn't used (Process) to any taste that wasn't bitter on the tongue. (C/scope)	Negation	M/P/C **Intransitive reading**
43. He had been made by hatred; it had constructed him into this smokey murderous figure in the rain, hunted and ugly.	He (Medium) had been made (Process) by hatred; (C/scope) it [hatred] (C/Scope) had constructed (Process) him (Medium) into this smokey murderous figure in the rain, hunted and ugly. (C/scope) **Double dipping**	Perfective aspect	M/P/C **Intransitive reading** C/P/M/C **Unusual structure** **Double dipping** Medium as circumstance

(continued)

(continued)

Clause	Transitive	Ergative	Voice	Background condition
44. His mother had borne him when his father was in gaol, and six years later when his father was hanged for another crime, she had cut her throat with a kitchen knife; afterwards there had been home.	His mother (Agent) had borne him (Medium) when his father was in gaol. (C/time)		Perfective aspect	Intentional A/P/M/C Transitive reading
	...	... and six years later when (C/time) his father (Medium) was hanged (Process) for another crime, (C/scope)		C/M/P/C Intransitive reading
	she (Agent) had cut (Process) her throat (Medium) with a kitchen knife; (C/accompaniment) afterwards there had been home. (C/scope)			Intentional A/M/C/C Transitive reading
45. He had never felt the least tenderness for anyone; ... he didn't want to be unmade.		He (Medium) had never felt (Process) the least tenderness for anyone; ... (C/scope)	Perfective aspect Negation	M/P/C Intransitive reading
	he (Agent) didn't want (Process) to be unmade. (C/scope)c			Intentional A/P/C Transitive reading

4 Disposition 321

46. He had a sudden terrified conviction that he must be himself now as never before if he was to escape.	He (Medium) had a sudden terrified conviction (Process) ... that he (Medium) must be (Process) himself now (Medium) as never before (C/scope) if he was to escape. (C/cause)	Perfective aspect Modality shift Conditional *if* Modality shift (modality signal obligation *must*)	M/P **Intransitive reading** M/P/M/C/C **Unusual structure**
47. It was not tenderness that made you quick on the draw. (62) ...	It was not tenderness that made you quick on the draw. (C/scope)	Negation	C(scope)
48. He thought: give her time and she too will go to the police.	IT		
49. That's what always happens in the end with a skirt, (63)	That [betrayal by skirt] 's what always happen in the end with a skirt, (C/scope)		C (scope)
50. A police man came up the street, as Raven stared into the window, and passed without a glance.	A police man (Agent) came (Process) up the street, (C/location) as Raven stared into the window, (C/scope) and passed without a glance. (C/scope)		Intentional A/P/C/C **Transitive reading**

(continued)

(continued)

Clause	Transitive	Ergative	Voice	Background condition
51. *Had the girl told them her story?*	FDT			FIT
52. *He supposed .... it would be in the paper, and he looked.*		He (Medium) supposed (Process) .... [that] it would be in the paper, and he looked. (C/scope)	Stative verb *supposed*	M/P/C Intransitive reading
53. *There was not a word about her there.*		The was not a word about her there. (C/scope)	Presentational Negation	C (scope)
54. *It shook him.*		It [not a word about her/Anne] (C/matter) shook him. (Medium)	Existential *It*	*Reverse C/P/M Unusual structure
55. *He's nearly killed her and she hadn't gone to them: that meant she had believed what he'd told her [that he never stole the notes, and he did not know why he was double-crossed (43)].*	He (Agent)'s [is] nearly killed her (Medium) and she (Agent) hadn't gone (Process) to them: (C/scope)	that meant (C/scope) she (Medium) had believed (Process) what he'd told her (C/scope)	Perfective aspect	Intentional A/P/M Transitive reading Negated Intentional A/P/C Transitive reading C/M/P/C Intransitive reading

4 Disposition   323

... 56. 'give her time ... it always happens with a skirt'.	FDT	
57. He said bitterly, ... 'If you were a God, you'd know I wouldn't harm her: you'd give me a break, you'd let me turn and see her on the pavement,' and he turned with half hope, but of course there was nothing there. (86)	DS	
58. 'It was you,' Raven said, 'who tried to kill...' my friend [Anne].' ...	DS	
59. Mr Davis shook all over. ...		*Mr Davis* (Medium) *shook* (Process) *all over* (C/scope) M/P/C Intransitive reading
60. He said, 'She wasn't a friend of yours.	DS	

(continued)

(continued)

Clause	Transitive	Ergative	Voice	Background condition
61. *Why are the police here if she didn't ... who else could have known ...?* [that Raven was after Davis, who paid Raven with stolen notes, who was Mr Cholmondeley as revealed by Anne (58) and they will be in the Tannery]' ...	FDT			
62. *How could he have expected to have escaped the commonest betrayal of all: to go soft on skirt?*	FDT			
63. *Raven shot him [Davis].*	*Raven* (Agent) *shot* (Process) *him* (Medium)			Intentional A/P/M Transitive reading

4 Disposition 325

64. With despair and deliberation he shot his last chance of escape, as if he were shooting the whole world in the person of stout moaning bleeding Mr Davis.	With despair and deliberation (C/scope) he (Agent) shot (Process) his last chance of escape, (C/scope)	Conditional *if*	***Reverse** C/intentional A/P/C **Transitive reading**
	as if (C/scope) he (Medium) were shooting (Process) the whole world in the person of stout moaning bleeding Mr Davis (C/scope) double dipping	Progressive aspect	C/M/P/C **Intransitive reading Double dipping** Agent also as Medium
65. There was no other way of confession, and it had failed him for the usual reason.	There was no other way of confession, and it (C/scope) had failed (Process) him (Medium) for the usual reason. (C/ scope)	Perfective aspect	***Reverse** C/P/M/C **Unusual structure**
66. There was no one outside your own brain whom you could trust: not a doctor, not a priest, not a woman. (164)	There was no one outside your own brain (C/scope) whom you (Medium) could trust: (Process) not a doctor, not a priest, not a woman. (C/scope)	Modality shift	***Reverse** C/M/P/C **Unusual structure**

(continued)

(continued)

Clause	Transitive	Ergative	Voice	Background condition
67. He was only aware of a pain and despair which was more like a complete weariness than anything else.		He (Medium) was only aware of a pain and despair (Process) which was more like a complete weariness than anything else. (C/scope)		M/P/C Intransitive reading
... 68. He couldn't work up any soreness, any bitterness, at his betrayal.		He (Medium) couldn't work up any soreness, any bitterness, (Process) at his betrayal. C/scope)	Modality shift Negation	M/P/C Intransitive reading
... 69. For the first time the idea of his mother's suicide came to him without bitterness, as he reluctantly fixed his aim and Saunders shot him in the back through the opening door.	as he reluctantly fixed his aim (C/scope) and Saunders (Agent) shot him (Process) in the back through the opening door. (C/location)	For the first time (C/scope) the idea of his mother's suicide (C/scope) came (Process) to him without bitterness, (C/scope)		*Reverse C/P/C Unusual structure A/P/C Intransitive reading Intentional A/P/M/C Transitive reading
70. Death came to him in the form of unbearable pain.		Death (C/scope) came to (Process) him (Medium) in the form of unbearable pain. (C/scope)		*Reverse C/P/M/C Unusual structure

4 Disposition

71. It was as if he had to deliver this pain as a woman delivers a child, and he sobbed and moaned in the effort. (166)	It was as if (C/scope) he (Agent) had to deliver (Process) this pain (C/scope) as a woman delivers a child, (C/scope)		Perfective aspect	*Reverse C/conditional Intentional A/P/C Transitive reading
		and he (Medium) sobbed and moaned in the effort. (Process)		M/P/C Intransitive reading
72. At last it came out of him and he followed his only child into a vast desolation. (166)		At last (C/duration) it [death] (C/scope) came out (Process) of him (C/scope)	Existential *It*	C/C/P/C Unusual structure
	... and he (Agent) followed (Process) his only child (C/Scope) into a vast desolation. (C/location)			Intentional A/ Process/C/C Transitive reading A poetic ending. Raven is now a wilful being who wilfully followed his death, which metaphorically is his child representing something he nurtured to be safe

Perpetrator Raven

2. Interpersonal function
3. The truth-value

Clauses	Assertions	Narrative modes	Truth value			
			NC (what is done)	EC (what is said)		Devices undercut agency
1. *Murder didn't mean much to Raven.*		B(N)+ve Negation	FC/comment			Negation
2. *It was just a new job.*		B(N)+ve Evaluative adjective *just a new job*	FC/comment			Existential *it*
3. *You had to be careful.*		B(N)+ve Evaluative adverbial *careful*	FC/comment			Perfective aspect
4. *You had to use your brains.*		B(N)+ve	FC/comment			Perfective aspect
5. *It was not a question of hatred.*		B(N)+ve		FC/comment		Negation

4 Disposition 329

6. He had only seen the Minister once: he had been pointed out to Raven as he walked down the new housing estate between the small lit Christmas trees, an old grubby man without friends, who was said to love humanity. (1)		B(N)+ve Evaluative adverbial only seen once	FC/narrative > NC (fixed)	Perfective aspect
... 7. He snatched the automatic out of the case and shot the Minister twice in the back.	CA	B neutral	NC (fixed)	
8. The Minister fell across the oil stove; the saucepan upset and the two eggs broke.	CA	B neutral	NC (fixed)	
9. Raven shot the Minister once more in the head, leaning across the desk to make quite certain, driving the bullet hard into the base of the skull, smashing it open like a china doll's.	CA	B(N)+ve Evaluative adverbial once more, quite certain	NC (fixed)	EC Internal (Correlative) Progressive aspect
10. Then he turned on the secretary; she moaned at him; she hadn't any words; the old mouth couldn't hold the saliva.		B(N)+ve Modalized discourse	NC (fixed)	Modality shift Negation

(continued)

(continued)

Clauses	Assertions	Narrative modes	NC (what is done)	EC (what is said)	Devices undercut agency
11. *He supposed she was begging him for mercy.*		B(R)-ve Words of estrangement *supposed*	FC/narrative		
12. *He pressed the trigger again; she staggered under it as if she had been kicked by an animal in the side.*	CA	B neutral Action suspended for causality **Double dipping**	NC (fixed)		Perfective aspect
13. *But useless material in which she hid her body, had perhaps confused him.*		B(R)-ve Words of estrangement *perhaps*	FC/comment	Embedded evaluation (comment by teller)	Perfective aspect
14. *And she was tough, so tough he couldn't believe his eyes; she was through the door before he could fire again, slamming it behind her. (3)*	CA	B(N)+ve Modalized discourse	FC/comment NC (fixed) Internal (Correlative)		Negation Modality shift Progressive aspect
15. *There was no time to waste.*		B(N)+ve Action suspended for causality	FC/narrative		Existential *there* Negation

4 Disposition 331

16. He stood away from the door and shot twice through the woodwork.	CA	B neutral	NC (fixed)	
17. He could hear the pince-nez fall on the floor and break.		B(N)+ve Modalized discourse	NC (fixed)	Modal shift
18. The voice screamed again and stopped; there was a sound as if she were sobbing.	CA	B(R)-ve Perception *if*	NC (fixed)	Depersonalization Existential *it* Conditional *if*
19. It was her breath going out through her wounds.	CA	B neutral	NC (fixed)	Progressive aspect
20. Raven was satisfied.	CA	B neutral	FC/narrative	
21. A low voice whispered an appeal quite distinctly through the door.	CA	B(N)+ve Evaluative adverb *quite distinctly*	NC (fixed)	Depersonalization Embedded evaluation (comment by teller)
22. Raven picked up the automatic again; who would have imagined an old woman could be so tough?	CA	B neutral B(N)+ve Modalized discourse	NC (fixed)	Modality shift Embedded evaluation (comment by teller)

(continued)

(continued)

Clauses	Assertions	Narrative modes	Truth value			Devices undercut agency
			NC (what is done)	EC (what is said)		
23. It touched his nerve a little just in the same way as the bell had done, as if a ghost were interfering with a man's job.		B(N)+ve Evaluative adverb *a little, just in the same way* B(N)-ve Perception *if*	FC/narrative			Existential *it*, Perfective aspect, Conditional *if* Progressive aspect
24. He opened the study door; he had to push it against the weight of her body.	CA	B neutral	NC (fixed) >FC/Narrative			Perfective aspect
25. She looked dead enough, but he made quite sure with the automatic almost touching her eyes. (4)		B(N)+ve Evaluative adverb *dead enough, quite sure*	FC/comment FC/narrative	Embedded evaluation (comment by teller)		Progressive aspect

4 Disposition

... 26. These people [Dr. Yogel and his secretary] were of his own kind; they didn't belong inside the legal borders; for the second time in one day he had been betrayed by the lawless [the double-crossers]. ...	B(R)+ve Proximal deictics *these* vs. distal *they*		FC/narrative	Embedded evaluation (comment by participant comment)	Negation Perfective aspect
27. He had always been alone, but never so alone as this.	B(R)+ve Proximal deictic *this*			Embedded evaluation (comment by participant)	
28. The telephone wire gave [in Yogel's surgery].		CA	NC (fixed)		
29. He wouldn't speak another word for fear his temper might master him and he might shoot.	B(N)+ve Modalized discourse			Embedded evaluation (comment by teller)	Negation
30. *This* wasn't the time for shooting. ... (25)	B(R)+ve Proximal deictic *this*		FC/comment	Embedded evaluation (comment by participant)	

(continued)

(continued)

Clauses	Assertions	Narrative modes	Truth value			Devices undercut agency
			NC (what is done)	EC (what is said)		
...31. Raven could never realize other people; they didn't seem to him to live in the same way as he lived [to play fair (16). Raven did not go back on a fellow who treated him right (24), he kept a promise (41)]; and though he bore a grudge against Mr Cholmondeley, hated him enough to kill him, he couldn't imagine Mr Cholmondeley's own fears and motives.		B(N)+ve Modalized discourse B(R)+ve Perception modality seem **Double dipping**		Embedded evaluation (comment by teller)		Modality shift Negation
32. He was the greyhound and Mr Cholmondeley the mechanical hare; but in this case the greyhound was chased in its turn by another mechanical hare. (29)		B(R)+ve Proximal deictic this		Embedded evaluation (comment by the participant)		

4 Disposition 335

33. He gazed at her with faint astonishment: her [Anne Crowder] smile, ... he was more used to the absent-minded routine endearments of prostitutes than to this natural friendliness, this sense of rather lost and desperate amusement. (37)		B(R)+ve Proximal deictic *this*		Embedded evaluation (comment by the participant) Perfective aspect
34. he was used to fear. It had lived inside him for twenty years. (30) It was normality [human feelings] he couldn't cope with. (39) ...		B(N)+ve Modalized discourse		Embedded evaluation (comment by teller)
35. 'People don't trouble to keep their word to me,' Raven said (41)	IS			Embedded evaluation (comment reported)
... 36. He made no sound, the tears seemed to run like flies of their own will from the corners of his eyes. (42) ...	CA	B(R)+ve Perception modality *seemed*	NC (fixed)	Embedded evaluation (comment by participant)
37. He remembered the kitten he had left behind in the Soho café.		B neutral	FC/narrative	Perfective aspect

(continued)

(continued)

Clauses	Assertions	Narrative modes	Truth value		Devices undercut agency
			NC (what is done)	EC (what is said)	
38. *He had loved that kitten.*		B neutral	FC/comment		Perfective aspect
... 39. *She never knew, he thought, that he had meant to kill her; she had been innocent of his intention as a cat he had once been forced to drown; and he remembered with astonishment that she had not betrayed him, although he had told her that the police were after him.*		B(N)+ve Evaluative adverbials with *astonishment*	FC/comment Internal (intensifier *that*)	wholly external (subordination)	Perfective aspect
40. *It was even possible that she had believed him.* (61)		B(R)-ve Limited knowledge *even possible*		Internal (intensifier *that*)	
41. *These thoughts were colder and more uncomfortable than the hail. ...*		B(R)+ve Proximal deictics *these*		Embedded evaluation (comment by participant)	

4 Disposition   337

42. He wasn't used to any taste that wasn't bitter on the tongue.	B(N)+ve Action suspended for causality	Internal (intensifier *that*)		Negation
43. He had been made by hatred; it had constructed him into this smokey murderous figure in the rain, hunted and ugly.	B(N)+ve Evaluative adjective *smokey murderous figure* Action suspended for causality	FC/comment	Embedded evaluation (comment by teller)	Perfective aspect
44. His mother had borne him when his father was in gaol, and six years later when his father was hanged for another crime, she had cut her throat with a kitchen knife; afterwards there had been home.	B(N)+ve Action suspended for causality		Wholly external (in subordination)	Perfective aspect
45. He had never felt the least tenderness for anyone; ... he didn't want to be unmade.	B(N)+ve Action suspended for causality	FC/comment	Embedded evaluation (comment by teller)	Perfective aspect Negation

(continued)

(continued)

Clauses	Assertions	Narrative modes	Truth value: NC (what is done)	Truth value: EC (what is said)	Devices undercut agency
46. *He had a sudden terrified conviction that he must be himself now as never before if he was to escape.*		B(N)+ve Modalized discourse Evaluative adverbials *sudden* *terrified* + B(R)+ve Perception *as if* **Double dipping**	Internal (Intensifier)	Embedded evaluation (comment by teller)	
47. *It was not tenderness that made you quick on the draw. (62) ...*		B(N)+ve Action suspended for causality	FC/comment	Embedded evaluation (comment by teller)	
48. *He thought: give her time and she too will go to the police.*	IT			Embedded evaluation (comment reported)	
49. *That's what always happens in the end with a skirt,... (63)*		B(N)+ve moralizing		Embedded evaluation (comment by teller)	

4 Disposition   339

50. A police man came up the street, as Raven stared into the window, and passed without a glance.	CA	B neutral	NC (fixed)	
51. Had the girl told them her story?	FIT		NC (fixed)	
52. He supposed .... it would be in the paper, and he looked.		B(R)+ve Perception modality *supposed*	FC/narrative	
53. There was not a word about her there.	CA		NC (fixed)	Existential *there*
54. It shook him.	CA			Existential *it*
55. He's nearly killed her and she hadn't gone to them: that meant she had believed what he'd told her [that he never stole the notes, and he did not know why he was double-crossed (p. 43)].		B(N)+ve Evaluative adverbial *nearly killed* + B(R)+ve Tense alternation *he's > he had told* **Double dipping**	Internal (intensifier *that*)	Perfective aspect Embedded evaluation (comment by participant)

(continued)

(continued)

Clauses	Assertions	Narrative modes	NC (what is done)	EC (what is said)	Devices undercut agency
... 56. *'give her time ... it always happens with a skirt'.*	FIT			Embedded evaluation (comment reported)	
57. *He said bitterly, ... 'If you were a God, you'd know I wouldn't harm her: you'd give me a break, you'd let me turn and see her on the pavement,' and he turned with half hope, but of course there was nothing there.* (86)		B(N)+ve Evaluative adverbials *bitterly, of course*		Embedded evaluation (comment reported)	
58. *'It was you,' Raven said, 'who tried to kill...' my friend [Anne].' ...*	IS			Embedded evaluation (comment reported)	
59. *Mr Davis shook all over.*	CA	B neutral	NC (fixed)		
60. *He said, 'She wasn't a friend of yours'.*	IS			Embedded evaluation (comment reported)	

4 Disposition 341

61. Why are the police here if she didn't ... who else could have known ...? [that Raven was after Davis, who paid Raven with stolen notes, who was Mr Cholmondeley as revealed by Anne (58) and they will be in the Tannery]	FIT	Proximal locative *here* Present tense	Embedded evaluation (comment reported)	Modality shift Present tense
... 62. How could he have expected to have escaped the commonest betrayal of all: to go soft on skirt?	FIT	Present tense	Embedded evaluation (comment reported)	Modality shift Present tense
63. Raven shot him [Davis].	CA	B neutral	FC/narrative	
64. With despair and deliberation he shot his last chance of escape, as if he were shooting the whole world in the person of stout moaning bleeding Mr Davis.		B(N)+ve Evaluative adverbial despair and deliberation Present tense	FC/narrative	Wholly external (subordination)	Progressive aspect Present tense
65. There was no other way of confession, and it had failed him for the usual reason.		B(N)+ve Action suspended for causality		Embedded evaluation (comment by teller)	Perfective aspect

(continued)

(continued)

Clauses	Assertions	Narrative modes	Truth value		Devices undercut agency
			NC (what is done)	EC (what is said)	
66. *There was no one outside your own brain whom you could trust: not a doctor, not a priest, not a woman.* (164)	FDT	B(N)+ve Action suspended for causality		Embedded evaluation (comment by teller)	
... 67. *He was only aware of a pain and despair which was more like a complete weariness than anything else.*		B(N)+ve Action suspended for causality	FC/comment	Embedded evaluation (comment by teller)	
68. *He couldn't work up any soreness, any bitterness, at his betrayal. ...*		B(N)+ve Action suspended for causality		Embedded evaluation (comment by teller)	Modality shift
69. *For the first time the idea of his mother's suicide came to him without bitterness, as he reluctantly fixed his aim and Saunders shot him in the back through the opening door.*	CA	B(N)+ve Evaluative adverbial *For the first time, reluctantly*	NC (fixed)	Wholly external (subordination)	

70. Death came to him in the form of unbearable pain.	B(N)+ve Evaluative adverbial *unbearable pain*	NC (fixed)	Embedded evaluation (comment by teller)
71. It was as if he had to deliver this pain as a woman delivers a child, and he sobbed and moaned in the effort.	B(R)+ve Modal perception *if*	FC/comment NC (fixed)	Embedded evaluation (comment by participant)
72. At last it came out of him and he followed his only child into a vast desolation. (166)	B(N)+ve Evaluative adverbial *at last*	NC (fixed)	Embedded evaluation (comment by teller)

Appendix 4d

Offender Mrs. Eleanor Maxie: *Cover Her Face*

1. Experiential function

Clause	Transitive	Ergative	Undercut agency	Background condition
Frame 1: [Mrs. M remembered the ritual gathering of her guests for the summer church fete that took place three months before the killing of Sally Jupp]				
1. *Exactly three months before the killing at Martingale Mrs Maxie gave a dinner party.*	*Exactly three months before the killing at Martingale* (C/scope) *Mrs Maxie (Agent) gave (Process) a dinner party.* (C/scope)			Reverse C/intentional A/P/C Transitive reading
2. *Years later, when the trial was a half-forgotten scandal and the headlines were yellowing on the newspaper lining of cupboard drawers, Eleanor Maxie looked back on that spring evening as the opening scene of tragedy.*	*Years later, when the trial was a half-forgotten scandal and the headlines were yellowing on the newspaper lining of cupboard drawers,* (C/scope) *Eleanor Maxie (Agent) looked back (Process) on that spring evening as the opening scene of tragedy.* (C/scope)			Reverse C/Engaged A/P/C Transitive reading

			A/P/M/C/C Intransitive reading
3. Memory, selective and perverse, invested what had been a perfectly ordinary dinner party with an aura of foreboding and unease.	Memory, selective and perverse, (Agent) invested (Process) what had been a perfectly ordinary dinner party (C/scope) with an aura of foreboding and unease. (C/role)	Depersonalized Agent Perfective aspect	
4. It became, in retrospect, a ritual gathering under one roof of victim and suspects, a staged preliminary to murder.	It became, in retrospect, a ritual gathering under one roof of victim and suspects, a staged preliminary to murder.	Existential *it*	**Complex Cs** (scope, + location, matter + role)
5. In fact not all the suspects had been present.	In fact not all the suspects (Medium) had been present. (Process)	Negation Perfective aspect	C/M/P Intransitive reading
6. Felix Hearne, for one, was not at Martingale that week-end.	Felix Hearne, for one, was not at Martingale that week-end.(C/scope)	Negation	C/scope

(continued)

(continued)

Clause	Transitive	Ergative	Undercut agency	Background condition
7. Yet, in her memory, he too sat at Mrs Maxie's table, watching with amused, sardonic eyes the opening antics of the players.	Yet, in her memory, (C/location) he too (Agent) sat (Process) at Mrs Maxie's table, (C/location) watching with amused, sardonic eyes (C/scope) the opening antics of the players. (C/matter)			Reverse C/intentional A/P/C/C Transitive reading Complex Cs (location + location + matter)
8. At the time, of course, the party was both ordinary and rather dull. ...	At the time, of course, the party was both ordinary and rather dull. ... (C/scope)			C(scope)
9. Mrs Maxie had just employed one of Miss Liddell's unmarried mothers as house-parlourmaid and the girl was waiting at the table for the first time.	Mrs Maxie (Agent) had just employed (Process) one of Miss Liddell's unmarried mothers (Medium) as house-parlourmaid (C/role)	and the girl (Medium) was waiting (Process) at the table for the first time. (C/location)	Perfective aspect Progressive aspect	Intentional A/P/M/C Transitive reading M/P/C intransitive reading

4 Disposition   347

10. But the air of constraint which burdened the meal could hardly have been caused by the occasional presence of Sally Jupp who placed the dishes in front of Mrs Maxie and removed the plates with a dextrous efficiency which Miss Liddell noted with complacent approval. (5)	But the air of constraint which burdened the meal (C/scope) could hardly have been caused (Process) by the occasional presence of Sally Jupp(Medium, C/scope)	Perfective aspect	**Reverse C/P/M + C Unusual structure Blending** of Medium Sally as C
	Blending Sally as the C		**A/P/M/C Transitive reading**
	who [Sally] (Agent) placed (Process) the dishes (Medium) in front of Mrs Maxie (C/location) and [Sally] (Agent) removed (Process) the plates (M) with a dextrous efficiency (C/manner)		Intentional Agent/P/M/C **Transitive reading**
	which Miss Liddell (experiencer/ Medium) noted (Process) with complacent approval. (C/manner)		**M/P/C Intransitive reading**

Frame 4: [SJ's sudden and brief change of attitude from *Sally the submissive* to *Sally the enigma*, as Miss Liddell noticed.]

(continued)

(continued)

Clause	Transitive	Ergative	Undercut agency	Background condition
11. Miss Liddell watched Sally Jupp as she moved about the table. …		Miss Liddell (experiencer/Medium) watched (Process) Sally Jupp (Medium) as she moved about the table. … (C/scope)		M/P/M/C intransitive reading
12. Suddenly Miss Liddell was visited by an irrational spasm of affection.		Suddenly (C/scope) Miss Liddell (Medium) was visited (Process) by an irrational spasm of affection. (C/scope)		Reverse C/M/P/C Intransitive reading
13. Sally was really doing nicely … Suddenly their eyes met.	Sally was really doing nicely (C/scope)	… Suddenly (C/scope) their eyes (Medium) met. (Process)	Depersonalization	C/scope Reverse C/M/P Intransitive reading
14. For a full two seconds they looked at each other. Then Miss Liddell flushed and dropped her eyes.	For a full two seconds (C/scope) they (Agent) looked (Process) at each other. (C/scope) Then Miss Liddell (Agent) flushed and dropped her eyes. (Process)			Reverse C/Engaged A/P/C Transitive reading Engaged A/P Transitive reading

4 Disposition   349

... 15. Confused and horrified she tried to analyze the extraordinary effect of that brief contact. ... she had read in the girl's eyes, not the submissive gratitude which had characterizes Sally Jupp. ... but amused contempt, a hint of conspiracy and a dislike which was almost frightening in its intensity.	Confused and horrified (C/scope) she (Medium) tried to analyze (Process) the extraordinary effect of that brief contact. (C/scope) ... she (Medium) had read (Process) in the girl's eyes, (C/location) not the submissive gratitude which had characterizes Sally Jupp. (C/scope) ... but amused contempt, a hint of conspiracy and a dislike which was almost frightening in its intensity. (C/scope)	Progressive aspect	**Reverse** C/M/P/C Intransitive reading M/P/C/C Intransitive reading

(continued)

Clause	Transitive	Ergative	Undercut agency	Background condition
16. Then the green eyes had dropped again and Sally the enigma became once more Sally the submissive, the subdued, ... She had recommended Sally without reserve.		Then the green eyes (Medium) had dropped again (Process)	Perfective aspect	M/P Intransitive reading
		and Sally the enigma (C/Scope) became (Process) once more Sally the submissive, the subdued, (C/scope) **blending** Sally as C		(Sally) C/P/C (Sally) Unusual structure
	... She (Agent) had recommended (Process) Sally (Medium) without reserve.		Perfective aspect	Intentional A/P/M (Sally) Transitive reading
... 17. The girl was a most superior type.	The girl was a most superior type (C/scope)			C(scope)
... 18. The decision had been taken.		The decision (C/scope) had been taken. (Process)	Progressive aspect	C(scope)/ Process Unusual structure Sally as C
19. It was too late to doubt its wisdom now. (10)	It was too late to doubt its wisdom now (C/scope)		Existential *it*	C(scope)

4 Disposition 351

The omniscient narrator

20. *Miss Liddell was aware for the first time that the introduction of her favourite to Martingale might produce complications.*	*Miss Liddell (Medium) was aware (Process) for the first time that the introduction of her favourite to Martingale (C/scope) might produce complications (C/manner)*	Modality shift	**M/P/C Sally/C Intransitive reading Blending** Sally as C, as the scope of the process
21. *She could not be expected to foresee the magnitude of those complications nor that they would end in violent death.'* (10)	*She (Medium) could not be expected (Process) to foresee the magnitude of those complications nor that they would end in violent death.'* (C/scope) **Double dipping**	Negation Modality shift (Modality signal obligation *could*)	**Sally M/P/C (Sally) Sally presented as the scope of the process Double dipping**

(continued)

(continued)

Clause	Transitive	Ergative	Undercut agency	Background condition
Frame 11: [Sally overslept on the morning of the summer fete, as CB observes.]				
22. '... *Catherine remembered that there had been some trouble that morning [the day of the annual church summer fete at Martingale House] with Martha because the girl [Sally] had overslept.... she had to rush to make up the lost time for she looked flushed and was, Catherine thought, concealing some excitement behind an outward air of docile efficiency.'* (36) **Sally's secret**	... *she* (Agent) *had to rush* (Process) *to make up the lost time for she looked flushed* (C/scope)	*Catherine* (Medium) *remembered* (Process) *that there had been some trouble that morning [the day of the annual church summer fete at Martingale House] with Martha because the girl [Sally] had overslept.* (C/scope) *and* [Sally] (Medium) *was, concealing* (Process) *Catherine thought, some excitement behind an outward air of docile efficiency.* (C/scope)	Perfective aspect Perfective aspect Progressive aspect	M/P/C **(Sally)** Intransitive reading Blending Sally as C Intentional A/P/C **(Sally)** Transitive reading M/P/C **(Sally)** Blending Sally presented as the scope of the process

Perpetrator Mrs. Eleanor Maxie: *Cover Her Face*

2. Interpersonal function
3. The truth-value

Clauses (Frames)	Assertions	Narrative modes	Truth value NC (what is done)	Truth value EC (what is said)	Devices undercut agency
Frame 1: Mrs. M remembered the ritual gathering of her guests for the summer church fete that took place three months before the killing of Sally Jupp					
1. *Exactly three months before the killing at Martingale Mrs Maxie gave a dinner party.*	B(N)+ve	Evaluative adverb *Exactly*	FC/narrative		
2. *Years later, when the trial was a half-forgotten scandal and the headlines were yellowing on the newspaper lining of cupboard drawers, Eleanor Maxie looked back on that spring evening as the opening scene of tragedy.*	B(N)+ve	Birds eye panoramic view	Internal evaluation (Correlative)		Progressive aspect

(continued)

(continued)

Clauses (Frames)	Assertions	Narrative modes	Truth value		Devices undercut agency
			NC (what is done)	EC (what is said)	
3. *Memory, selective and perverse, invested what had been a perfectly ordinary dinner party with an aura of foreboding and unease.*	B(N)+ve	Evaluative adverb *perfectly* Evaluative adjective *selective and perverse foreboding and unease*		Embedded evaluation (comment by teller)	Perfective aspect
4. *It became, in retrospect, a ritual gathering under one roof of victim and suspects, a staged preliminary to murder.*	B(N)+ve	Evaluative adjective *staged preliminary to murder*		Embedded evaluation (comment by teller)	
5. *In fact not all the suspects had been present.*	B(N)+ve	Evaluative adverb *In fact*			Perfective aspect
6. *Felix Hearne, for one, was not at Martingale that week-end.*	B(N)+ve	Evaluative adverb *for one*	Internal evaluation Intensifier Deictic *that*		

4 Disposition   355

7. Yet, in her memory, he too sat at Mrs Maxie's table, watching with amused, sardonic eyes the opening antics of the players.	B(N)+ve Evaluative Adverb and adjective *amused, sardonic eyes, opening antics*	Internal evaluation (Explicatives)	Progressive aspect
8. At the time, of course, the party was both ordinary and rather dull.	B(N)+ve Evaluative Adverb *At the time, of course*	FC/comment	
... 9. Mrs Maxie had just employed one of Miss Liddell's unmarried mothers as house-parlourmaid and the girl was waiting at the table for the first time.	B(N)+ve Evaluative aspects		Perfective aspect Progressive aspect
10. But the air of constraint which burdened the meal could hardly have been caused by the occasional presence of Sally Jupp who placed the dishes in front of Mrs Maxie and removed the plates with a dextrous efficiency which Miss Liddell noted with complacent approval. (5)	B(N)+ve Evaluative adjective *dextrous efficiency, complacent approval*		Embedded evaluation (comment by teller) + Wholly external (subordination) Modality shift

(continued)

(continued)

Clauses (Frames)	Assertions	Narrative modes	NC (what is done)	EC (what is said)	Devices undercut agency

Frame 4: SJ's sudden and brief change of attitude from *Sally the submissive* to *Sally the enigma*, as Miss L noticed,

Clauses (Frames)	Assertions	Narrative modes	NC (what is done)	EC (what is said)	Devices undercut agency
11. 'Miss Liddell watched Sally Jupp as she moved about the table.	CA			Wholly external (subordination)	
... 12. Suddenly Miss Liddell was visited by an irrational spasm of affection.		B(N)+ve Evaluative Adverb *Suddenly* and adjective *irrational spasm*		Embedded evaluation (comment by teller)	
13. Sally was really doing nicely ... Suddenly their eyes met.		B(N)+ve Evaluative Adverb *really doing nicely*, *Suddenly*	FC/comment		
14. For a full two seconds they looked at each other. Then Miss Liddell flushed and dropped her eyes.		B(N)+ve Evaluative Adverb *For a full two seconds*	FC/narrative		

... 15. Confused and horrified she tried to analyze the extraordinary effect of that brief contact. ... she had read in the girl's eyes, not the submissive gratitude which had characterizes Sally Jupp. ... but amused contempt, a hint of conspiracy and a dislike which was almost frightening in its intensity.	B(N)+ve Evaluative Adverb Confused and horrified, almost frightening	Embedded evaluation (comment by teller)	Perfective aspect
16. Then the green eyes had dropped again and Sally the enigma became once more Sally the submissive, the subdued, ... She had recommended Sally without reserve.	B(N)+ve Evaluative adjective Sally the enigma, Sally the submissive, the subdued	Embedded evaluation (comment by teller)	Perfective aspect
... 17. The girl was a most superior type.	B(N)+ve Evaluative adjective most superior type	Embedded evaluation (comment by teller)	

(continued)

(continued)

Clauses (Frames)	Assertions	Narrative modes	Truth value		Devices undercut agency
			NC (what is done)	EC (what is said)	
... 18. *The decision had been taken.*	CA		FC/narrative		CA with Perfective aspect
19. *It was too late to doubt its wisdom now.'* (10)		B(R)+ve Proximal deictic *now* Reflector Miss Liddell		Embedded evaluation (from another participant)	
20. *'Miss Liddell was aware for the first time that the introduction of her favourite to Martingale might produce complications.*		B(N)+ve Evaluative adverb *for the first time*	Internal evaluation (Intensifier *that*)		Modality shift
21. *She could not be expected to foresee the magnitude of those complications nor that they would end in violent death.'* (10)		B(N)+ve Panoramic view of the *magnitude of those complications* B(R)+ve Distal deictic *those*	Internal evaluation		Modality shift Negation

Frame 11: Sally overslept on the morning of the summer fete, as Catherine Bower observes,

	B(N)+ve	Internal evaluation (intensifier + explicative)	Embedded evaluation (from another participant)	Perfective aspect	Progressive aspect
22. '... Catherine remembered that there had been some trouble that morning [the day of the annual church summer fete at Martingale House] with Martha because the girl [Sally] had overslept. ... she had to rush to make up the lost time for she looked flushed and was, Catherine thought, concealing some excitement behind an outward air of docile efficiency.' (36) Sally's secret (the conspiracy)					

Appendix 4e

Perpetrator Dr. Sheppard: *The Murder of Roger Ackroyd*

1. Experiential function

Clause	Transitive	Ergative	Undercut agency	Background condition
Frame 2: [Dr. Sheppard met Mrs. Ferrars a week before she died,] *'Her manner had been normal enough considering—well considering everything.'* (p. 15)	FDT		Perfective aspect	FIT
Frame 14: *'Could I do anything with the boy [Ralph Paton]? I thought I could.'* (p. 27)	FDT		Modality shift	FIT

4 Disposition 361

				Reverse C/P/C **Unusual structure**
Frame 21: [Dr. S recalls,] 'Suddenly before my [Dr. Sheppard] eyes there rose the picture of Ralph Paton and Mrs Ferrars side by side.	FDT	*Suddenly before my [Dr. Sheppard] eyes there (C/scope) rose (Process) the picture of Ralph Paton and Mrs Ferrars side by side. (C/matter)*		
.... I felt a momentary throb of anxiety. Supposing—oh! but surely that was impossible.' (p. 37)		*.... I (Medium) felt a momentary throb of anxiety. (Process)*		M/P **Intransitive reading**
		IT Supposing—oh! but surely that was impossible.	Distal deictic *that* ... *surely that was impossible*	(C/scope) What was impossible? **(Ellipted)** Dr. Sheppard contemplating Ralph Paton blackmailed Mrs. Ferrars (Frame 14)
Frame 29: [Parker leaves Ackroyd's study to ring the police. Dr. Sheppard alone in the study narrates,] 'I did what little had to be done' (p. 45)	FDT	*I (Agent) did (Process) what little had to be done (C/scope)*	Perfective aspect	Intentional A/P/C **Intransitive reading** What little was done by Dr. Sheppard? **(Ellipted)** Dr. Sheppard removed the Dictaphone that framed Ralph Paton as the blackmailer, and put back the armchair that concealed it.

(continued)

(continued)

Clause	Transitive	Ergative	Undercut agency	Background condition
Frame 33:				
a. 'If Parker heard anything about blackmail,' [Sheppard] said slowly, 'he must have been listening outside this door with his ear glued against the keyhole.' ... Davis nodded. ...	DS			DS
b. I took an instant decision. ...	NRT *I (Agent) took (Process) an instant decision (C/scope)*			Intentional A/P/C **Transitive reading** *instant decision about what?* (**Ellipted**) to frame Ralph Paton as the blackmailer.
c. And then and there [I] narrated the whole events of the evening as I have set them down here.	NRA *And then and there (C/scope) [I] (Agent) narrated (Process) the whole events of the evening as I have set them down here. (C/scope)*	Proximal deictic *here*		**Reverse Cs** C/[intentional A]/P/C **Transitive reading** Inspector **Engaged** A/P/C **Transitive reading**

4 Disposition 363

d. The inspector listened intently, occasionally interjecting a question.

The inspector (Agent) listened intently, (Process) occasionally interjecting a question. (C/scope)

DS

... 'And you say that letter has completely disappeared? It looks bad—it looks very bad indeed. It gives us what we've been looking for—a motive. For the murder.' (p. 57)

DS

Perpetrator Dr. Sheppard: *The Murder of Roger Ackroyd*

2. Interpersonal function
3. The truth-value

Frame no.	Assertions	Narrative modes	Truth value NC (what is done)	EC (what is said)	Devices undercut agency
Frame 2: [Dr. Sheppard met Mrs. Ferrars a week before she died.] 'Her manner had been normal enough considering—well— considering everything.' (15)	A(N)+ve	Action suspended for causality Evaluative adverbial considering—well— considering everything	Internal evaluation (repetition)	Embedded evaluation (comment by teller)	Perfective aspect
Frame 14: 'Could I do anything with the boy [Ralph Paton]? I thought I could.' (27)	A(N)+ve	Modalized discourse		Embedded evaluation (comment by teller)	Modality shift

4 Disposition   365

Frame 21: [Dr. Sheppard recalls,] '*Suddenly before my* [Dr. S] *eyes there rose the picture of Ralph Paton and Mrs Ferrars side by side. ... I felt a momentary throb of anxiety. Supposing—oh! but surely that was impossible.*' (37)	A(N)+ve Evaluative adverbial *Suddenly, momentary throb, Supposing, surely*	Embedded evaluation (comment by teller)
Frame 29: [Parker leaves Ackroyd's study to ring the police. Dr. Sheppard alone in the study narrates.] '*I did what little had to be done*' (45) [remove the evidence: the letter and Dictaphone]	A(R)+ve Perfective aspect undercutting Narrator intervention.	Perfective aspect **Double dipping** Juxtaposing the Reflector I with the Narrator-Reflector I
Frame 33: a. '*If Parker heard anything about blackmail,*' *I said slowly,* '*he must have been listening outside this door with his ear glued against the keyhole.*' ... *Davis nodded.* ...	A(N)+ve Evaluative adverbial *slowly*	
b. *I took an instant decision.* ...	A(N)+ve Evaluative adverbial *instant decision*	

(continued)

(continued)

Frame no.	Assertions	Narrative modes	Truth value NC (what is done)	EC (what is said) NC (fixed type)	Devices undercut agency
c. *And then and thee narrated the whole events of the evening as I have set them down here.*		A(R)+ve Proximal deictics here + A(N)+ve			Double dipping Juxtaposing the Reflector in proximal deictics with the Narrator-Reflector
d. *The inspector listened intently, occasionally interjecting a question.*		Evaluative adverbials *listened intently, occasionally interjecting* Double dipping			
... *'And you say that letter has completely disappeared? It looks bad—it looks very bad indeed. It gives us what we've been looking for—a motive. For the murder.'* (57)					

Appendix 4f

Abettor John Dowell: *The Good Soldier*

1. Experiential function

Note: The story in TGS develop through indirect thought (IT) of the principal character Dowell, who is also the narrator in the story. In the discourse below, the direct and indirect thought and speech of the principal character Dowell being the diegetic world in the narrative is analyzed over direct or indirect discourse of other characters.

Clause	Transitive	Ergative	Undercut agency	Background condition
The Protest scene				
Frame 11: [Dowell senses Florence was up to something,]		IT		Reverse C/Dowell Engaged A/P/C
'But on this occasion I knew that something was up. (49) ... I must say that, until the astonishment came [the Protest scene]	... I (Agent) must say that, (Process) until the astonishment came [the Protest scene] (C/scope)	But on this occasion (C/scope) I (Agent) knew (Process) that something was up. (49) (C/scope)	Proximal deictic *this* Modality shift (Modality signal obligation *must*)	Transitive reading
I got nothing but pleasure out of the little expedition. (50)		I (Medium) got nothing (Process) but pleasure out of the little expedition. (50) (C/scope)	Negation	Intentional A/P/C Transitive reading
I was aware of something treacherous, something frightful, something the evil in the day (53)		I (Medium) was aware (Process) of something treacherous, something frightful, something the evil in the day (53) (C/scope: indefinite)		M/P/C Intransitive reading M/P/C Intransitive reading

(continued)

(continued)

Clause	Transitive	Ergative	Undercut agency	Background condition
Frame 12: [At the museum in the city of M- Florence explains the letter about the Protest and compliments Edward.]	DS			
'It's because of that piece of paper [draft of the Protest drawn up by Luther and others] that you're honest, sober, industrious, provident and clean-lived. If it weren't for that piece of paper you'd be like the Irish or the Italians or the Poles, but particularly the Irish...' (53)				
Frame 13: [Leonara reveals to Dowell the affair between E and F,]	DS			
"I can't stand this," she said [to Dowell] with a most extraordinary passion;	DS			
"I must get out of this." "... Don't you [Dowell] see?" she said, "don't you see what's going on)]?' [Florence was Edward's mistress ... committing adultery in hired rooms. (83–84)	NRT DS			
The panic again stopped my heart.		The panic again (C/scope) stopped (Process) my heart. (C/scope)		C/P/M Unusual structure
...				
'Don't you see,'' ... of the eternal damnation of you and me and them [alluding to Florence and Edward who lack constancy] (55)				

Frame 36: [Dowell narrating Leonora's reaction to Florence's comment in Frame 12.] "It would be better if Florence said nothing at all against my co-religionists, because it is a point that I am touchy about."	DS		
That was the hint that, accordingly I conveyed (Process) to Florence when, shortly afterwards, she and Edward came down from the tower.		Distal deictic *that* (C/scope) I (Agent) conveyed (Process) to Florence when, shortly afterwards, she and Edward came down from the tower. (C/scope)	**Reverse C/** intentional A/P/M/C **Transitive reading**
That was the hint that, accordingly I conveyed to Florence when, shortly afterwards, she and Edward came down from the tower. And I want you [the reader] to understand that, from that moment until Edward and the girl and Florence were all dead together		And I (Medium) want (Process) you [the reader] (Medium) to understand that, ... from that moment until Edward and the girl and Florence were all dead together (C/scope)	Distal demonstrative *that*	M/P/M/C **Intransitive reading**
glimpse, not the shadow of a suspicion, that there was anything wrong [the affair between E and F], as the saying is. ... How in the world should I get it? ... I was just a male sick nurse. ... I was a deceived husband. And that Leonora was pimping [alluding to Maisie and Nancy affair] for Edward.' (81)	DT as the saying is. (C/scope): ... How in the world should I get it? ...	I was just a male sick nurse. ... (c/role) I (Medium) was (Process) a deceived husband. (c/role) And that Leonora was pimping for Edward.' (c/ scope) I (Medium) had never the remotest glimpse, not the shadow of a suspicion, (Process) that there was anything wrong, (C/scope):	Negation	M/P/C **Intransitive reading** **Complex C** C(role + scope) M/P/C

(continued)

(continued)

Clause	Transitive	Ergative	Undercut agency	Background condition
Frame 135: [following the Protest scene, L warned D about F making eyes at her husband.] "Your wife is a harlot who is going to be my husband's mistress ..." ... A week after Maisie Maiden's death she was aware that Florence had become Edward's mistress.' (221)	DS	... A week after Maisie Maiden's death (C/scope) she (Medium) was aware (Process) that Florence had become Edward's mistress."(C/matter)	Perfective aspect	C/M/P/C
The conspiracy **Frame 51:** [just as they were to go away for their voyage, D got to know of F's heart condition for the first time.]	DS			
"I wanted to know, so as to pack my trunks." ... I may be ill, you know. I guess my heart is a little like Uncle Hurlbird's. It runs in families. ... Now I wonder what had passed through Florence's mind during the two hours that she kept me waiting at the foot of the ladder. ... Till then, I fancy she had no settled plan in her mind. She certainly never mentioned her heart till that time." (99, 101)		Now (C/scope) I (Medium) wonder (Process) what had passed through Florence's mind during the two hours that she kept me waiting at the foot of the ladder. ... (C/scope)	Proximal temporal deictic now Perfective aspect Presentational what	Reverse C/M/P/C Intransitive reading
		She (Agent) certainly never mentioned (Process) her heart (C/matter) till that I (Medium) fancy (Process) she had no settled plan in her mind. (C/matter)	Negation Distal demonstrative that	C/M/P/C Intransitive reading
		Till then, (C/scope)	Negation	Florence **(negated)** intentional A/P/C Transitive reading Complex Cs (matter + scope)

Frame 53: [Ship doctor warned Dowell of Florence's heart.]

Florence went down into her cabin and her heart took her. An agitated stewardess came running up to me, and I running down. I got my directions how to behave to my wife. Most of them came from her, though it was the ship doctor who discreetly suggested to me that I had better refrain from manifestations of affection. ... I wonder, though, how Florence got the doctor to enter the conspiracy—the several doctors ... Anyhow, she and they tied me pretty well down—and Jimmy, of course, that dreary boy—...' (101)

Florence (Agent) went down (Process) into her cabin (C/location) and her heart took her. (C/scope)	Intentional A/P/C/C **Transitive reading** **Complex C** (location + scope) Intentional A/P/M **Transitive reading**
An agitated stewardess (Agent) came running up (Process) to me, (Medium) and I (Agent) running down. (Process)	Dowell A/P **Intransitive reading** M/P/C **Intransitive reading**
I (Medium) got (Process) my directions how to behave to my wife. (C/scope)	Reverse C/P/M **Unusual structure** Reverse C/ Intentional A/P/M/C **Transitive reading**
Most of them (C/scope) came (Process) from her, (Medium)	
though it was the ship doctor who (Agent) discreetly suggested (Process) to me (Medium) that I had better refrain from manifestations of affection. (C/scope)	M/P/C **Intransitive reading** C/Intentional A/P/M/C **Transitive reading**
I (Medium) wonder, (Process) though, how Florence got the doctor to enter the conspiracy—the several doctors ... (C/scope)	
Anyhow, (C/scope) she and they (Agent) tied (Process) me (Medium) pretty well down—and Jimmy, of course, that dreary boy—(C/scope)	

(continued)

(continued)

Clause	Transitive	Ergative	Undercut agency	Background condition
Florence and Jimmy affair				
Bagshawe incident: revelation of Florence's conspiracy				
Frame 71: [Dowell with Bagshawe at the hotel lounge at 4th August 1913 the last day of my absolute happiness (117)	4th August 1913 the last day of my absolute happiness (C/scope)			(C/scope)
Frame 73: [Leonora wanted Nancy Rufford to be chaperoned with Edward and wanted Florence to join them]	n/a			
Frame 74: [Dowell and Leonora sat in the lounge waiting until 10pm]	n/a			
Frame 75: [Bagshawe from Ludlow Manor near Ludbury joined D at the hotel lounge]	n/a			
Frame 76: [Dowell then saw Florence running back into the hotel lounge. Florence rushed in at the swing doors, looked round to see Bagshawe speaking to Dowell,]	She (Agent) stuck (Process) her hands (Medium) over her face (C/location)			Intentional A/P/M/C **Transitive reading**
She saw the man who was talking to me. She stuck her hands over her face as if she wished to push her eyes out. (118)		She (Medium) saw (Process) the man who was talking to me. (C/scope)	Progressive aspect	M/P/C **Intransitive reading**
		as if (C/scope) she (Medium) wished (Process) to push her eyes out (C/scope)	Conditional *if*	C/M/P/C **Intransitive reading**

	DS		
Florence and Jimmy affair			
Frame 77: [Bagshawe surprised to find Florence and remarks,] "By Jove: Florry Hurlbird." …. Do you know who that is?" he asked. "The last time I saw that girl she was coming out of the bedroom of a young man called Jimmy at five o' clock in the morning. In my house at Ledbury.' (118)			
Frame 78: [Dowell pulls himself up after this to go up to F's room]			
Frame 79: [4th August 1913, lying dead, the first night Florence does not lock her room]	*She* (Agent) *had* (Process) *a little phial* (Medium)	Perfective aspect	Intentional A/P/M **Transitive reading** Reverse C/P/M/C **Intransitive reading**
She had a little phial that rightly should have contained nitrate of amyl, in her right hand. (119)	… *that rightly* (C/scope) *should have contained* (Process) *nitrate of amyl,* (Medium) *in her right hand.'* (C/location)	Modality shift (Modality signal obligation *should*)	

(continued)

(continued)

Clause	Transitive	Ergative	Undercut agency	Background condition
F's intention according to character Dowell in narrative				
Frame 37: [Dowell accusing Florence of trying to reunite Edward and Leonora when she was Edward's mistress.]				
'She should not have done it. She should not have done it.' (83)		She (Medium) should not have done (Process) it. (C/scope) She should not have done it.'	Modality shift (Modality signal obligation *should*) Negation Repetition	M/P/C Intransitive reading M/P/C Intransitive reading
[Florence tried to convince L about her affair with E was of spiritual kind, and tried to reunite Edward to his wife, when L accused her,] "You come to me straight out of his bed to tell me that is my proper place." (84)		DS		
Frame 38: Leonora in her bedroom doing her hair when reminded Florence of how Leonora and Florence murdered her. 'You and I murdered her [Maisie Maiden] between us.' (84)	DS			
Frame 140: [Dowell's frame of mind] Florence's contaminating influence, was vulgar, unstoppable talker (214)	FDT Florence's contaminating influence, was vulgar, unstoppable talker (C/scope)			C(scope)

			C/intentional A/P/M
		Proximal deictic	Transitive reading
Frame 80: [Leonora reminded Dowell of his remark.]			
'Now I can marry the girl [Nancy].' To which Leonora replied, "of course you might marry her," and, when I asked whom, she answered: "The girl." (123)	IS 'Now (C/scope) I (Agent) can marry (Process) the girl' (Medium) IS	now	
Frame 85: Dowell's remark, 'Now I can marry the girl'. (129)	To which Leonora replied, "of course you might marry her," and, when I asked whom, she answered: "The girl."		

(continued)

(continued)

Clause	Transitive	Ergative	Undercut agency	Background condition
The motive: Dowell				
Frame 87: [Dowell's retrospective narration on Edward's actions in the Casino Park with Nancy Rufford,]	NRT			
'And it appears that Edward Ashburnham led the girl not up the dark trees of the park. Edward Ashburnham told me all this in his final outburst. I have told you that, upon that occasion, he became deucedly vocal. I didn't pump him, I hadn't any motive. 'At the time I didn't in the least connect him with my wife.' (130)	And it appears that (C/scope) Edward Ashburnham (Agent) led (Process) the girl (Medium) not up the dark trees of the park. (C/location)		Negation Existential *it*	C/intentional A/P/M/C Transitive reading
	Edward Ashburnham (Agent) told (Process) me (Medium) all this in his final outburst. (C/scope)			Intentional A/P/M/C Transitive reading
	I (Agent) have told (Process) you that, (Medium) upon that occasion, he became deucedly vocal. (C/scope)			Intentional A/P/M/C Transitive reading
	I (Agent) didn't pump (Process) him, (Medium)		Negation	Intentional A/P/M Transitive reading
		I (Medium) hadn't (Process) any motive. (c/scope)	Negation	M/P/C Intransitive reading
		At the time (C/scope) I (Medium) didn't in the least connect (Process) him (Medium) with my wife. (C/scope)	Negation	Reverse C/M/P/M/C Unusual structure
Frame 92: Florence heard Edward from behind the tress as Nancy being the person he cared most (137)	n/a			

Frame 110: [Edward realizes what he was doing and Dowell narrates,] '… wicked thing Edward ever did in his life. … to corrupt a young girl from convent (134)	'… wicked thing (C/scope) Edward (Agent) ever did in his life. (Process) … to corrupt a young girl (C/scope)/ from convent (C/location)		C/intentional A/P/C **Transitive reading** **Complex Cs** (scope + location)
The motive: Dowell **Frame 116:** [Dowell narrating.]			
'Why she was like the sail of a ship, … And to think she will never … Why, she will never do anything again. I can't believe it…' (150)	Why she was like the sail of a ship, … (C/manner)		C(manner)
	And to think she will never … Why, (C/scope) she (Medium) will never do anything again.(Process)	Negation	**Reverse C/M/P** **Transitive reading**
	I (Agent) can't believe (Process) it…'(C/scope)	Existential *it* Negation	A/P/C **Transitive reading**
Frame 120: [Leonora could trust Edward with Nancy and she knew that Nancy could be trusted, Leonora slackened her vigilance of Edward and Nancy being together, which was a mistake, 'This is perhaps the most miserable part of the story.' (158)	'This (C/scope) [she (Nancy Rufford) will never do anything again] is perhaps (Process) the most miserable part of the story (C/angle)	Proximal deictic *this*	C/P/C **Unusual structure**

(continued)

(continued)

Clause	Transitive	Ergative	Undercut agency	Background condition
Frame 158: [The quote below sums up the end to come in this final part of the story.] 'The end was plain … Edward must die, the girl must lose her reason because Edward died—… that end, on that night, whilst Leonora sat in the girl's bedroom and Edward telephoned down below—that end was plainly manifest.' (268)	whilst Leonora (Agent) sat (Process) in the girl's bedroom (C/scope) and Edward (Agent) telephoned (Process) down below—that end was plainly manifest. C (location + scope)	The end was plain … (C/scope) Edward (Medium) must die, (Process) the girl (Medium) must lose her reason (Process) because (C/cause) Edward (Agent) died—… (Process) that end, on that night, (C/time)	Modality shift (Modality signal obligation must) Modality shift (Modality signal obligation must) Distal demonstrative that	**Reverse C/M/P** Intransitive reading (Girl)M/P/C Intransitive reading **Reverse C/** Intentional A/P/C Intransitive reading **Complex C** (location + scope)
Frame 170: [Edward in the stables one afternoon talking to Dowell. A stable-boy bought the telegram, which read,] "Safe Brindisi. Having rattling good time. Nancy." (293)	DS			
Frame 171: [Edward got out a penknife from his waistcoat pocket, asked Dowell to take the telegram to Leonora, Dowell realized Edward's intention but did not interfere with Edward's intention to **commit suicide**.] 'And he looked at me with a direct, challenging, brow-beating glare. I guess I could see in my eyes that I didn't intend to hinder him. Why should I hinder him?' (294)	And he (Medium) looked (Process) at me with a direct, challenging, brow-beating glare. (C/scope) I guess (Process)	I (Medium) could see (Process) in my eyes (C/location) that I didn't intend to hinder him. Why should I hinder him? C(scope)	Progressive aspect Modality shift (Modality signal possibility *could*)	M/P/C Intransitive reading Dowell **Engaged** A/P Intransitive reading M/P/C Intransitive reading **Complex C** (Location + scope)

Abettor John Dowell: *The Good Soldier*

2. Interpersonal function
3. The truth-value

Frame no.	Assertions	Narrative modes	Truth value		Devices undercut agency
			NC (what is done)	EC (what is said)	
The Protest scene					
Frame 11: [Dowell senses Florence was up to something.] 'But on this occasion I knew that something was up. (49) ... I must say that, until the astonishment came [the Protest scene] I got nothing but pleasure out of the little expedition. (50) I was aware of something treacherous, something frightful, something the evil in the day (53)		A-ve (R) (suppressed, limited knowledge)	Internal evaluation (intensifier *that*)		Modality shift Negation Proximal deictic *this*

(continued)

(continued)

Frame no.	Assertions	Narrative modes	Truth value		Devices undercut agency
			NC (what is done)	EC (what is said)	
Frame 12: [At the museum in the city of M- Florence explains the letter about the Protest and compliments Edward.] 'It's because of that piece of paper [draft of the Protest drawn up by Luther and others] that you're honest, sober, industrious, provident and clean-lived. If it weren't for that piece of paper you'd be like the Irish or the Italians or the Poles, but particularly the Irish.... (53)	DS				
Frame 13: [Leonara reveals to Dowell the affair between E and F.] "I can't stand this," she said [to Dowell] with a most extraordinary passion; "I must get out of this." ... Don't you [Dowell] see?" she said, "don't you see what's going on [Florence was Edward's mistress ... committing adultery in hired rooms. (83–84)]?" The panic again stopped my heart. ... 'Don't you see," ... of the eternal damnation of you and me and them [alluding to Florence and Edward who lack constancy] (55)	DS				

4 Disposition 381

Frame 36: [Dowell narrating Leonora's reaction to Florence's comment in Frame 12.] "It would be better if Florence said nothing at all against my co-religionists, because it is a point that I am touchy about." That was the hint that, accordingly I conveyed to Florence when, shortly afterwards, she and Edward came down from the tower. And I want you [the reader] to understand that, from that moment until Edward and the girl and Florence were all dead together I had never the remotest glimpse, not the shadow of a suspicion, that there was anything wrong [the affair between E and F], as the saying is. …. How in the world should I get it? …. I was just a male sick nurse. …. I was a deceived husband. And that Leonora was pimping [alluding to Maisie and Nancy affair] for Edward.' (81)	DS	A+ve (N) Evaluative adverbials *shortly afterwards, that moment* adjectives *just a male sick nurse*	Internal evaluation (intensifier *that*)	Distal demonstrative *that* Negation Progressive aspect

(continued)

(continued)

Frame no.	Assertions	Narrative modes	Truth value NC (what is done)	EC (what is said)	Devices undercut agency
Frame 135: [following the Protest scene, L warned D about F making eyes at her husband.]	DS				
"Your wife is a harlot who is going to be my husband's mistress ..." ... A week after Maisie Maiden's death she was aware that Florence had become Edward's mistress.' (221)	CA				Perfective aspect
The conspiracy					
Frame 51: [just as they were to go away for their voyage, D got to know of F's heart condition for the first time.]	DS				
"I wanted to know, so as to pack my trunks." ... I may be ill, you know. I guess my heart is a little like Uncle Hurlbird's. It runs in families. ...		A-ve (R) (limited knowledge) +	Internal evaluation (Correlative)		Proximal temporal deictic *now* Perfective aspect
Now I wonder what had passed through Florence's mind during the two hours that she kept me waiting at the foot of the ladder. ... Till then, I fancy she had no settled plan in her mind. She certainly never mentioned her heart till that time." (99, 101)		A+ve (N) Evaluative adverbials *fancy, certainly* Double dipping			Presentational *what* Negation Distal demonstrative *that*

4 Disposition   383

	CA		
Frame 53: [Ship doctor warned Dowell of Florence's heart.]			
'Florence went down into her cabin and her heart took her. An agitated stewardess came running up to me, and I running down. I got my directions how to behave to my wife. Most of them came from her, though it was the ship doctor who discreetly suggested to me that I had better refrain from manifestations of affection.	+	A+ve (N) Evaluative adverbials *discreetly, Anyhow, pretty well down*	Embedded evaluation (comments by teller)
… I wonder, though, how Florence got the doctor to enter the conspiracy—the several doctors … Anyhow, she and they tied me pretty well down—and Jimmy, of course, that dreary boy—…' (101)		+ A-ve (R) Suppressed limited knowledge *wonder, though* **Double dipping**	
Florence and Jimmy affair **Bagshawe incident: revelation of Florence's conspiracy**			
Frame 71: [Dowell with Bagshawe at the hotel lounge at 4th August 1913 *the last day of my absolute happiness* (117)		A+ve (N) Evaluative adverbial *the last day, absolute happiness*	Embedded evaluation (comment by teller)

(continued)

(continued)

Frame no.	Assertions	Narrative modes	Truth value		Devices undercut agency
			NC (what is done)	EC (what is said)	
Frame 73: [Leonora wanted Nancy Rufford to be chaperoned with Edward and wanted Florence to join them]	n/a				Conditional *if*
Frame 74: [Dowell and Leonora sat in the lounge waiting until 10pm]	n/a				
Frame 75: [Bagshawe from Ludlow Manor near Ludbury joined D at the hotel lounge]	n/a CA				
Frame 76: [Dowell then saw Florence running back into the hotel lounge. Florence rushed in at the swing doors, looked round to see Bagshawe speaking to Dowell.] 'She saw the man who was talking to me. She stuck her hands over her face as if she wished to push her eyes out.' (118)		+ A(R)-ve Conditional *if* Perception *wished*			

Florence and Jimmy affair

Frame 77: [Bagshawe surprised to find Florence and remarks,]

"*By Jove: Florry Hurlbird." …. Do you know who that is?" he asked. "The last time I saw that girl she was coming out of the bedroom of a young man called Jimmy at five'oclock in the morning. In my house at Ledbury.'* (118) — DS

Frame 78: [Dowell pulls himself up after this to go up to F's room]

Frame 79: [4th August 1913, lying dead, the first night Florence does not lock her room]

'*She had a little phial that rightly should have contained nitrate of amyl, in her right hand.*' (119)

— A+ve (N) Evaluative adverbial *rightly should have*

— Internal evaluation (intensifier *that*)

— Perfective aspect
Modality shift

(continued)

(continued)

Frame no. F's intention according to character Dowell in narrative	Assertions	Narrative modes	Truth value NC (what is done)	EC (what is said)	Devices undercut agency
Frame 37: [Dowell accusing Florence of trying to reunite Edward and Leonora when she was Edward's mistress.] *'She should not have done it. She should not have done it.'* (83) [Florence tried to convince L about her affair with E was of spiritual kind, and tried to reunite Edward to his wife, when L accused her.] *"You come to me straight out of his bed to tell me that is my proper place."* (84)	DS	A+ve (N) Obligation modality	Internal evaluation (Intensifier repetition)		Modality shift Negation Repetition
Frame 38: Leonora in her bedroom doing her hair when reminded Florence of how Leonora and Florence murdered her. *'You and I murdered her* [Maisie Maiden] *between us.'* (84)	DS				

Frame 140: [Dowell's frame of mind] *Florence's contaminating influence, was vulgar, unstoppable talker* (214)		A+ve (N) Evaluative adverbial *contaminating vulgar, unstoppable talker*	Embedded evaluation (comment by teller)
The cardinal point	DS		
Frame 80: [Leonora reminded Dowell of his remark.]			
'Now I can marry the girl [Nancy].'	IS		
To which Leonora replied, "of course you might marry her," and, when I asked whom, she answered: "The girl." (123)	DS		
Frame 85: Dowell's remark, *'Now I can marry the girl'.* (129) **cardinal point: Dowell**			Embedded evaluation (comment by teller) Proximal deictic *now*

(continued)

(continued)

Frame no.	Assertions	Narrative modes	Truth value NC (what is done)	Truth value EC (what is said)	Devices undercut agency
The motive: Dowell					
Frame 87: [Dowell's retrospective narration on Edward's actions in the Casino Park with Nancy Rufford.] 'And it appears that Edward Ashburnham led the girl not up the dark trees of the park. Edward Ashburnham told me all this in his final outburst. I have told you that, upon that occasion, he became deucedly vocal. I didn't pump him, I hadn't any motive. 'At the time I didn't in the least connect him with my wife.' (130)	n/a	A-ve (R) Perception modality *appears* + A+ve (N) Evaluative adverbials *outburst, in the least* Double dipping	Internal evaluation (intensifier *that*)		Negation Existential *it* Distal demonstrative *that*
Frame 92: Florence heard Edward from behind the tress as Nancy being the person he cared most (137) **cardinal point: Florence**					
Frame 110: [Edward realizes what he was doing and Dowell narrates,] '... *wicked thing Edward ever did in his life.* (133) ... *to corrupt a young girl from convent* (134)		A+ve Evaluative adjective *wicked thing*		Embedded evaluation (comment by teller)	

The motive: Dowell

Frame 116: [Dowell narrating.]
'Why she was like the sail of a ship, … And to think she will never … Why, she will never do anything again. I can't believe it…' (150)

| A-ve (R) Perception modality *think* + A+ve (N) (futurity) **Double dipping** | Embedded evaluation (comment by teller) | Negation Existential *it* |

Frame 120: [Leonora could trust Edward with Nancy and she knew that Nancy could be trusted, Leonora slackened her vigilance of Edward and Nancy being together, which was a mistake, 'This is perhaps the most miserable part of the story.' (158)

| A-ve (R) Perception modality *perhaps* | Embedded evaluation (comment by teller) | Proximal deictic *this* |

Frame 158: [The quote below sums up the end to come in this final part of the story.]
'The end was plain … Edward must die, the girl must lose her reason because Edward died—… that end, on that night, whilst Leonora sat in the girl's bedroom and Edward telephoned down below—that end was plainly manifest.' (268)

| A+ve (N) Obligation modality *must die* | Embedded evaluation (comment by teller) | Modality shift |

(continued)

(continued)

Frame no.	Assertions	Narrative modes	Truth value NC (what is done)	Truth value EC (what is said)	Devices undercut agency
Frame 170: [Edward in the stables one afternoon talking to Dowell. A stable-boy bought the telegram, which read.] "*Safe Brindisi. Having rattling good time. Nancy.*" (293)	DS				
Frame 171: [Edward got out a penknife from his waistcoat pocket, asked Dowell to take the telegram to Leonora, Dowell realized Edward's intention but did not interfere with Edward's intention to **commit suicide**.] '*And he looked at me with a direct, challenging, brow-beating glare. I guess I could see in my eyes that I didn't intend to hinder him. Why should I hinder him?*' (294)		A+ve (N) Evaluative adverbials *direct, challenging, brow-beating glare* + A-ve (R) Perception, probability modality *guess, could see* **Double dipping**	Internal evaluation (intensifier *that*)		Modality shift Negation

Appendix 4g

Offender, Perpetrator Engagement Discourses

Bud Corliss: *A Kiss before Dying*

Part One

1. *His plans had been running so beautifully, so goddamned beautifully, and now she was going to smash them all.* 2. *Hate erupted and flooded through him, gripping his face with jaw-aching pressure.* 3. *That was alright though, the lights were out.* (4)

...

4. *He closed his eyes and spoke dreamily, intoning the words in a sedative chant.* 5. *'I had it planned so beautifully.* 6. *I would have come to New York this summer and you would have introduced me to him.* 7. *I could have got him to like me.* 8. *You would have introduced me to him.* 9. *I could have got him to like me.* 10. *You would have told me what he's interested in, what he likes, what he dislikes-' he stopped short, then continued.* 11. *'And after graduation we would have been married.* 12. *Or even this summer.* 13. *We could have come back here in September for our last two years.* 14. *A little apartment of our own, right near the campus -'* (5)

...

15. *He had discovered that she liked to be called 'baby'.* 16. *When he called her 'baby' and held her in arms he could get her to do practically anything.* 17. *He had thought about it, and decided it had something to do with the coldness she felt towards her father.* (7)

...

18. *What angered him most was that in a sense the responsibility for the entire situation rested with Dorothy.* 19. *He wanted to take her to his room only once—a down-payment guaranteeing the fulfilment of a contract.* 20. *It was Dorothy, with her gently closed eyes and her passive, orphan hunger, who had wished for further visits.* 21. *He struck the table.* 22. *It really was her fault! Damn her!* (17)

...

23. *He sat at the back of the room, in the second seat from the window.* 24. *The seat on his left, the window seat, the empty seat, was hers.* 25. *It was the first*

class of the morning, a daily Social Science lecture, and their only class together this semester. 26. *The speaker's voice droned in the sun-filled air.* 27. *Today of all days she could have made an effort to be on time.* 28. *Didn't she know he'd be frozen in an agony of suspense?* (21)

...

29. *He put his books down on the grass.* 30. *The important thing was to get time, time to think.* 31. *He was afraid his knees were going to start shaking.* 32. *He took her by the shoulders, smiling.* 33. *'That's the spirit.* 34. *You just don't worry about anything.'* 35. *He took a breath.* 36. *'Friday afternoon we'll go down to the Municipal-'* (22)

...

37. *It still wasn't too late.* 38. *People wrote suicide notes and then stalled around before actually doing it.* 39. *He looked at his watch: 9.20.* 40. *The earliest Ellen could get the note would be—three o' clock.* 41. *Five hours and forty minutes.* 42. *No step by step planning now.* 43. *It would have to be quick, positive.* 44. *No trickery that counted on her doing a certain thing at a certain time.* 45. *No poison.* 46. *How else do people kill themselves?* 47. *In five hours and forty minutes she must be dead.* (55)

....

Part Two

48. *He drove with his left hand, occasionally giving the steering wheel an inappreciable right or left movement to relieve the hypnotic monotony on the highway. ...*
49. *He told her everything...* 50. *So he told Ellen about the pills and the roof and why it had been necessary to kill Dorothy, and why it had been the most logical course to transfer to Caldwell and go after her, Ellen, knowing her likes and dislikes from conversation with Dorothy, knowing how to make himself the man she was waiting for—not only the most logical and inevitable course, going after the girl with whom he had such an advantage, but also the course most ironically satisfying, the course most compensatory for past bad luck ...*
51. *He told her these things with irritation and contempt; this girl with her hands over her mouth in horror had had everything given her on a silver platter; she didn't know what it was to live on a swaying catwalk over the chasm of failure, stealing perilously inch by inch towards the solid ground of success so many miles away.* (175)

Part Three

52. ... 'How did you get Dorothy to write that suicide note?' (264)
53. *Everything fell away; the catwalk, the smelter, the whole world; everything melted away like sandcastles sucked into the sea, leaving him suspended in emptiness with two blue marbles staring at him and the sound of Leo's question swelling and reverberating like being inside an iron bell.*
...
54. Gant said, 'You killed Dorothy and Ellen and Dwight Powell!'
55. 'And almost killed Marion,' Leo said. 'When she saw that list- (266)
...
56. *He swiped at his cheek. Control! Self-control!* 57. *He dragged a deep breath into his chest* ... 58. *Slow up, slow up* ... 59. *They can't prove a thing, not a goddamn thing!* 60. *They know about the list, about Marion, about the pamphlets—okay—but they can't prove a thing about* ... 61. *He drew another breath* ... (266–267)
...
62. 'Marion', he pleaded, 'stop them! They're crazy! They're trying to kill me! Stop them! They'll listen to you! I can explain about that list, I can explain everything! I swear I wasn't lying-'
...
63. 'How do I know?' she asked.
...
64. 'You swore so many things-' *Her fingers appeared curving over the men's shoulders; long, white, pink-nailed fingers; they seemed to be pushing.*
65. 'Marion!' You wouldn't! Not when we—after we-'
66. *Her fingers pressed forward into the cloth of the shoulders, pushing* ...
67. 'Marion,' he begged futilely. (271)
...
68. *He looked down.* 69. *The front of his pants was dark with a spreading stain that ran in a series of island blotches down his trouser leg.* 70. *Oh God! The Jap—the Jap he had killed—that wretched, trembling, chattering pants-wetting caricature of a man—was that him? Was that himself?* (272)
...
... 71.—*he had jumped and now he was letting go because he wanted to, that's all, and everything was alright and his knees weren't shaking any more, not that they had been shaking so much anyway, his knees weren't shaking any more*

because he was in command again—he hadn't noticed his right hand open but it must have opened because he was dropping into the heat, cabels were shooting up, someone was creaming like Dorrie going into the shaft and Ellen when the first bullet wasn't enough—this person was screaming this godawful scream and suddenly it was himself and he couldn't stop! 72. *Why was he screaming? Why? Why on earth should he be—*
73. *The scream, which had knifed through the sudden stillness of the smelter, ended in a vicious splash.* 74. *From the other side of the vat a sheet of green leaped up.* 75. *Arcing, it sheared down to the floor where it splattered into a million pools and droplets.* 76. *They hissed softly on the cement and slowly dawned from green to copper.* (273–274)

Raven: *A Gun for Sale*
Before the murder of the War (Czech) Minister

1. *Murder didn't mean much to Raven.* 2. *It was just a new job.* 3. *You had to be careful.* 4. *You had to use your brains.* 5. *It was not a question of hatred.* 6. *He had only seen the Minister once: he had been pointed out to Raven as he walked down the new housing estate between the small lit Christmas trees, an old grubby man without friends, who was said to love humanity.* (1)
...

Contracted to murder the War (Czech) Minister

... 7. *He snatched the automatic out of the case and shot the Minister twice in the back.*
8. *The Minister fell across the oil stove; the saucepan upset and the two eggs broke.* 9. *Raven shot the Minister once more in the head, leaning across the desk to make quite certain, driving the bullet hard into the base of the skull, smashing it open like a china doll's.* 10. *Then he turned on the secretary; she moaned at him; she hadn't any words; the old mouth couldn't hold the saliva.* 11. *He supposed she was begging him for mercy.* 12. *He pressed the trigger again; she staggered under it as if she had been kicked by an animal in the side.* 13. *But useless material in which she hid her body, had perhaps confused him.* 14. *And she was tough, so tough he couldn't believe his eyes; she was through the door before he could fire again, slamming it behind her.* (3)
...
15. *There was no time to waste.* 16. *He stood away from the door and shot twice through the woodwork.* 17. *He could hear the pince-nez fall on the floor*

and break. 18. *The voice screamed again and stopped; there was a sound as if she were sobbing.* 19. *It was her breath going out through her wounds.* 20. *Raven was satisfied.* 21. *He turned back to the Minister.*
...
22. *A low voice whispered an appeal quite distinctly through the door.* 23. *Raven picked up the automatic again; who would have imagined an old woman could be so tough?* 24. *It touched his nerve a little just in the same way as the bell had done, as if a ghost were interfering with a man's job.* 25. *He opened the study door; he had to push it against the weight of her body.* 26. *She looked dead enough, but he made quite sure with the automatic almost touching her eyes. (4)*
...

At Dr. Yogel's surgery when Raven went to sort out his harelip to conceal his identity from police

... 27. *These people [Dr Yogel and his secretary] were of his own kind; they didn't belong inside the legal borders; for the second time in one day he had been betrayed by the lawless [the double-crossers].* 28. *He had always been alone, but never so alone as this.* 29. *The telephone wire gave [in Yogel's surgery].* 30. *He wouldn't speak another word for fear his temper might master him and he might shoot.* 31. *This wasn't the time for shooting. (25)*
...
... 32. *Raven could never realize other people; they didn't seem to him to live in the same way as he lived* [to play fair (16), Raven did not go back on a fellow who treated him right (24), he kept a promise (41)]; *and though he bore a grudge against Mr Cholmondeley, hated him enough to kill him, he couldn't imagine Mr Cholmondeley's own fears and motives.* 33. *He was the greyhound and Mr Cholmondeley the mechanical hare; but in this case the greyhound was chased in its turn by another mechanical hare. (29)*
...

Raven kidnaps Anne Crowder the fiancée of Detective Sergeant Mather

34. *He gazed at her with faint astonishment: her [Anne Crowder] smile, ... he was more used to the absent-minded routine endearments of prostitutes than to this natural friendliness, this sense of rather lost and desperate amusement. (37)*
...

... 35. *he was used to fear. It had lived inside him for twenty years. 30. It was normality [human feelings] he couldn't cope with. (39)*
...
36. *'People don't trouble to keep their word to me,' Raven said (41)* ... 37. *He made no sound, the tears seemed to run like flies of their own will from the corners of his eyes. (42)* ... 38. *He remembered the kitten he had left behind in the Soho café. 39. He had loved that kitten.* ... 40. *She never knew, he thought, that he had meant to kill her; she had been innocent of his intention as a cat he had once been forced to drown; and he remembered with astonishment that she had not betrayed him, although he had told her that the police were after him. 41. It was even possible that she had believed him. (61) 42. These thoughts were colder and more uncomfortable than the hail. 43. He wasn't used to any taste that wasn't bitter on the tongue. 44. He had been made by hatred; it had constructed him into this smokey murderous figure in the rain, hunted and ugly. 45. His mother had borne him when his father was in gaol, and six years later when his father was hanged for another crime, she had cut her throat with a kitchen knife; afterwards there had been home. 46. He had never felt the least tenderness for anyone;* ... *he didn't want to be unmade. 47. He had a sudden terrified conviction that he must be himself now as never before if he was to escape. 48. It was not tenderness that made you quick on the draw. (62)* ... 49. *He thought: give her time and she too will go to the police. 50. That's what always happens in the end with a skirt, (63)*
...

Raven let Anne free

51. *A police man came up the street, as Raven stared into the window, and passed without a glance. 52. Had the girl told them her story? 53. He supposed* ... . *it would be in the paper, and he looked. 54. There was not a word about her there. 55. It shook him. 56. He's nearly killed her and she hadn't gone to them: that meant she had believed what he'd told her* [that he never stole the notes, and he did not know why he was double-crossed (43)]. ... 57. *'give her time* ... *it always happens with a skirt'. 58. He said bitterly,* ... *'If you were a God, you'd know I wouldn't harm her: you'd give me a break, you'd let me turn and see her on the pavement,' and he turned with half hope, but of course there was nothing there. (86)*
...

Raven caught up with Mr Cholmondeley known as Mr Davis and realized of Anne's betrayal

59. 'It was you,' Raven said, 'who tried to kill...' my friend [Anne].'...
60. Mr Davis shook all over. ... 61. He said, 'She wasn't a friend of yours.
62. Why are the police here if she didn't ... who else could have known ...? [that Raven was after Davis, who paid Raven with stolen notes, who was Mr Cholmondeley as revealed by Anne (58)] and they will be in the Tannery]'... 63. *How could he have expected to have escaped the commonest betrayal of all: to go soft on skirt?*
...
64. Raven shot him [Davis]. 65. *With despair and deliberation he shot his last chance of escape, as if he were shooting the whole world in the person of stout moaning bleeding Mr Davis*. 66. *There was no other way of confession, and it had failed him for the usual reason*. 67. *There was no one outside your own brain whom you could trust: not a doctor, not a priest, not a woman*. (164)
...

Raven comes to term with Anne's betrayal

... 68. *He was only aware of a pain and despair which was more like a complete weariness than anything else*. 69. *He couldn't work up any soreness, any bitterness, at his betrayal*. ... 70. *For the first time the idea of his mother's suicide came to him without bitterness*, as he reluctantly fixed his aim and Saunders shot him in the back through the opening door. 71. *Death came to him in the form of unbearable pain*. 72. *It was as if he had to deliver this pain as a woman delivers a child, and he sobbed and moaned in the effort*. 73. *At last it came out of him and he followed his only child into a vast desolation*. (166)

Tom Ripley: *The Talented Mr. Ripley*

Tom Ripley (Ripley) realized he was being followed by a man coming out of Green Cage. The man later turned out to be Dickey's father Mr. Greenleaf.

1. *My God, what does he want?* 2. *He certainly wasn't a pervert, Tom thought for the second time, though now his tortured brain groped and produced the actual word, as if the word could protect him, because he would rather the man be pervert than a policeman.* 3. *To a pervert, he could simply say, 'No thank you,' and smile and walk away.* 4. *Tom slid back on the stool, bracing himself.*
5. *Tom saw the man make a gesture of postponement to the barman, and come around the bar towards him.* 6. *Here it was! Tom stared at him paralyzed.* 7. *They couldn't give him more than ten years, Tom thought.* 7. *Maybe fifteen, but with good conduct—In the instant the man's lips parted to speak, Tom had a pang of desperate, agonized regret. (6)*

Note: A false trail in lexical choice '*pervert*' when Ripley's sexual jealousy is apparent later in his imaginative hypothetical world of punishing (being violent) Marge.

Intransitive clause, e.g. *regret* for what? A curiosity suspense conflict in inexplicit information related to Tom's *regret* as an intransitive clause. Tom's regret was about not being able to cash the cheques posted by clients he threated of tax error (9, 14). The regret was therefore he worked out the tax error but could not gain from this and the whole affair was no more than a practical joke (14).

Ripley's imagined (hypothetical) world
A clean slate

8. *When Mr. Greenleaf's money was used up, he might not come back to America.* 9. *He might get an interesting job in a hotel, for instance, where they needed somebody bright and personable who spoke English.* 10. *Or he might become a representative for some European firm and travel everywhere in the world.* 11. *Or somebody might come along who needed a young man exactly like himself, who could drive a car, who was quick at figures who could entertain an old grandmother or squire somebody's daughter to a dance.* 12. *He was versatile, and the world was wide!* 13. *He swore to himself he would stick to a job once he got it. Patience and perseverance! Upward and onward! (32)*

About aunt Dottie (an unfinished event in his imagined (hypothetical) world)

14. *Aunt Dottie had hated him when he had a cold; she used to take her handkerchief and nearly wrench his nose off, wiping it. …*

15. *He remembered the vows he had made, even at the age of eight, to run away from Aunt Dottie, the violent scenes he had imagined—Aunt Dottie trying to hold him in the house, and he hitting her with his fists, flinging her to the ground and throttling her, and finally tearing the big brooch off her dress and stabbing her a million times in the throat with it.* 16. *He had run away at seventeen and had been brought back, and he had done it again at twenty and succeeded.* 17. *And it was astounding and pitiful how naïve he had been, how little he had known about the way the world worked, as if he had spent so much of his time hating Aunt Dottie and scheming how to escape her, that he had not had enough time to learn and grow.* (35–36)

Tom joined join Dickie and Marge for lunch at Dickie's house in Mongibello

18. *Dickie and Marge began to talk about … minute changes in the neighbourhood.* 19. *There was nothing Tom could contribute.* 20. *He spent the time examining Dickie's rings.* 21. *He liked them both: … Dickie had long bony hands, a little like his own hands, Tom thought.* (44)
… 22. *Tom wondered if Dickie and Marge were having an affair, one of those old, faute de mieux affairs that wouldn't necessarily be obvious from the outside, because neither was very enthusiastic.* 23. *Marge was in love with Dickie, Tom thought, but Dickie couldn't have been more indifferent to her if she had been the fifty-year-old Italian maid sitting there.* (45)
…

Tom's feelings for Dickie

… 24. *The first step, anyway, was to make Dickie like him.* 25. *That he wanted more than anything else.* (47)
…
26. *'I think I'll go up to see Marge,' Dickie said. 'I won't be long, but there's no use in your waiting.'*
… 27. *About half-way up the hill he stopped …with another impulse to go down to Giorgio's for a drink … and with another impulse to go up to Marge's house, … .* 28. *He suddenly felt that Dickie was embracing her, or at least touching her, at this minute, and partly he wanted to see it, and partly he loathed the idea of seeing it. …* 29. *He slowed as he climbed the last flight of steps.* 30. *He would say, 'Look here, Marge, I'm sorry if I've been causing the strain around here.* 31. *We asked you to go today, and we mean it. I mean it.'* (67)

Note: the Discourse World above is an imagined Storyworld

...

32. *Tom stopped as Marge's window came into view: Dickie's arm was around her waist. Dickie was kissing her, little pecks on her cheek, smiling at her. ... now Marge's face was tipped straight up to Dickie's, as if she were fairly lost in ecstasy, and what disgusted Tom was that he knew Dickie didn't mean it, that Dickie was only using this cheap obvious, easy way to hold on to her friendship.*
33. *What disgusted him was the big bulge of her behind in the peasant skirt below Dickie's arm that circled her waist. And Dickie -! Tom really wouldn't have believed it possible of Dickie!* (67)
34. *Tom turned away and ran down the steps, wanting to scream.*
35. *He went up to Dickie's room and paced around for a few moments, his hands in his pockets.* 30. *He wondered when Dickie was coming back?* 37. *Or was he going to stay and make an afternoon of it, really take her to bed with him?* 38. *He jerked Dickie's closet door open and looked in. ...* 39. *he took off his knee-length shorts and put on the grey flannel trousers. ...* 40. *He reparted his hair and put the part a little more to oneside, the way Dickie wore his.*
41. *'Marge you must understand that I don't love you,' Tom said into the mirror in Dickie's voice, with Dickie's higher pitch on the emphasized words.* 42. *With little growl in his throat at the end of the phrase that could be pleasant or unpleasant, intimate or cool, according to Dickie's mood.* 43. *'Marge, stop it!'* 44. *Tom turned suddenly and made a grab in the air as if he were seizing Marge's throat.* 45. *He shook her, twisted her, while she sank lower and lower, until at last he left her, limp, on the floor. He was panting.* 46. *He wiped his forehead the way Dickie did, reached her handkerchief and, not finding any, got one from Dickie's top drawer, then resumed in front of the mirror.* 47. *Even his parted lips looked like Dickie's lips when he was out of breath from swimming, drawn down a little from his lower teeth.* 48. *'You know why I had to do that,' he said, still breathlessly, addressing Marge, though he watched himself in the mirror.* 49. *'You were interfering between Tom and me—No, not that! But there is bond between us!'*

...

50. *He turned, stepped over the imaginary body, and went stealthily to the window. He turned, stepped over the imaginary body, and went stealthily to the window.* 51. *Dickie was not on the steps or on the parts of the road that he could see.* 52. *Maybe they were sleeping together, Tom thought with a tighter twist in his throat.* 53. *He imagined <u>it</u>, awkward, clumsy, unsatisfactory for*

Dickie, and Marge loving it. 54. *She'd love it even if he tortured her!* 55. *Tom darted back to the closet again and took a hat from the top shelf.* ... 56. *He put it on rakishly.* 57. *It surprised him how much he looked like Dickie with the top part of his head covered.* (69)

Note: the use of inanimate pronoun *it*. Inanimate *it* reduces the feeling between Dickie and Marge. The effect is of someone not willing to acknowledge an emotional experience by reducing an entity to an inanimate it.

...
58. *'What're you doing?'*
59. *Tom whirled around. Dickie was in the doorway.* ... *Dickie advanced to the room.* ... *Dickie stood petrified with fear.* (69)
60. *'I wish you'd get out of my clothes,' Dickie said.* ...
61. *Dickie looked at Tom's feet. 'Shoes, too? Are you crazy?'*
62. *'No.' Tom tried to pull himself together* ... *then he asked, 'Did you make it up with Marge?*
... 63. *Dickie snapped in a way that shut Tom out from them.* ... *'Another thing I want to say,* ... *looking at Tom, 'I'm not queer. 58. I don't know if you have the idea that I am not.'*
64. *'Queer?' Tom smiled faintly. 'I never thought you were queer.'*
... 65. *'Well Marge thinks you are.'*
... 66. *'Why should she? What've I ever done?' He felt faint. Nobody had ever said it outright to him, not in this way.*
...
... 67. *'Dickie, I want to get this straight,' Tom began. 63. 'I'm not queer either, and I don't want anybody thinking I am.'*
...
... 68. *Tom asked quietly, 'Are you in love with Marge, Dickie?'*
... 69. *One thing Tom was sure of: Dickie was glad to have him here.* 70. *Dickie was bored with living by himself, and bored with Marge, too.* (69–73)

Tom and Dickie in San Remo without Marge

...
71. *They took only one suitcase of Dickie's between them,* ... . 72. *Dickie was in a slightly more cheerful mood, but the awful finality was still there, the*

feeling that this was the last trip they would make together anywhere. ... 73. It occurred to Tom that Dickie was trying to sell him on the town and might try to persuade him to stay there alone instead of coming back to Mongibello. 74. Tom began to feel an aversion to the place before they got there. (84)

...

They arrived at Cannes around eleven o'clock that night and left for San Remo that afternoon.
75. Dickie said absolutely nothing on the train. 76. Tom sat opposite him, staring at his bony, arrogant, handsome face, at his hands with the ring and the gold signet ring. 77. It crossed Tom's mind to steal the green ring when he left. 78. It would be easy: Dickie took it off when he swam. ... 79. He would do it the very last day, Tom thought. 80. A crazy emotion of hate, of affection, of impatience and frustration was swelling in him, hampering his breathing. 81. He wanted to kill Dickie. 82. It was not the first time he had thought of it. ... 83. what was there to be ashamed of anymore? 84. He had failed with Dickie, in every way. 85. He hated Dickie, because, however he looked at what happened, his failing had not been his own fault, not due to anything he had done, but due to Dickie's inhuman stubbornness. 86. And his blatant rudeness! 87. He had offered Dickie friendship, companionship, and respect, everything he had to offer, and Dickie had replied with ingratitude and now hostility. 88. Dickie was just shoving him out in the cold. If he killed him on this trip, Tom thought, he could simply say that some accident had happened. 89. He could— He had just thought of something brilliant: he could become Dickie Greenleaf himself. 90. He could do everything that Dickie did. ... receive Dickie's cheques every month and forge Dickie's signature on it. 91. He could step right into Dickie's shoes. ... 92. The danger of it, ... only made him more enthusiastic. He began to think how. (84–88)

...

... 93. Tom lifted the oar and came down with it on the top of Dickie's head.

...

94. Tom swung a left-handed blow with the oar against the side of Dickie's head. ...

...

95. He stooped and yanked at Dickie's green ring. He pocketed it. (91)

...

96. Tom had an ecstatic moment when he thought of all the pleasures that lay before him now with Dickie's money, other beds, tables, seas, ships, suitcases, shirts, years of freedom, years of pleasure. 97. Then he turned the light out and put his head down and almost at once fell asleep, happy, content, and utterly confident, as he had never been before in his life. (97)

The imagined circumstance

35. *He went up to Dickie's room and paced around for a few moments, his hands in his pockets. 30. He wondered when Dickie was coming back? 37. Or was he going to stay and make an afternoon of it, really take her to bed with him? 38. He jerked Dickie's closet door open and looked in. ... 39. he took off his knee-length shorts and put on the grey flannel trousers. ... 40. He reparted his hair and put the part a little more to oneside, the way Dickie wore his.*
41. *'Marge you must understand that I don't love you,' Tom said into the mirror in Dickie's voice, with Dickie's higher pitch on the emphasized words. 42. With little growl in his throat at the end of the phrase that could be pleasant or unpleasant, intimate or cool, according to Dickie's mood. 43. 'Marge, stop it!' 44. Tom turned suddenly and made a grab in the air as if he were seizing Marge's throat. 45. He shook her, twisted her, while she sank lower and lower, until at last he left her, limp, on the floor. He was panting. 46. He wiped his forehead the way Dickie did, reached her handkerchief and, not finding any, got one from Dickie's top drawer, then resumed in front of the mirror. 47. Even his parted lips looked like Dickie's lips when he was out of breath from swimming, drawn down a little from his lower teeth. 48. 'You know why I had to do that,' he said, still breathlessly, addressing Marge, though he watched himself in the mirror. 49. 'You were interfering between Tom and me—No, not that! But there is bond between us!'*
...
50. *He turned, stepped over the imaginary body, and went stealthily to the window.*
55. *Tom darted back to the closet again and took a hat from the top shelf. ... 56. He put it on rakishly. 57. It surprised him how much he looked like Dickie with the top part of his head covered.* (69)

The epistemic sub-world

72. *Dickie was in a slightly more cheerful mood, but the awful finality was still there, the feeling that this was the last trip they would make together anywhere. ... 73. It occurred to Tom that Dickie was trying to sell him on the*

town and might try to persuade him to stay there alone instead of coming back to Mongibello. 74. Tom began to feel an aversion to the place before they got there. (84)
77. It crossed Tom's mind to steal the green ring when he left. 78. It would be easy: Dickie took it off when he swam. ... 79. He would do it the very last day, Tom thought. 80. A crazy emotion of hate, of affection, of impatience and frustration was swelling in him, hampering his breathing. 81. He wanted to kill Dickie. 82. It was not the first time he had thought of it. ... 83. what was there to be ashamed of anymore? 84. He had failed with Dickie, in every way. 85. He hated Dickie, because, however he looked at what happened, his failing had not been his own fault, not due to anything he had done, but due to Dickie's inhuman stubbornness. 86. And his blatant rudeness! 87. He had offered Dickie friendship, companionship, and respect, everything he had to offer, and Dickie had replied with ingratitude and now hostility. 88. Dickie was just shoving him out in the cold. If he killed him on this trip, Tom thought, he could simply say that some accident had happened. 89. He could—He had just thought of something brilliant: he could become Dickie Greenleaf himself. 90. He could do everything that Dickie did. ... receive Dickie's cheques every month and forge Dickie's signature on it. 91. He could step right into Dickie's shoes. ... 92. The danger of it, ... only made him more enthusiastic. He began to think how. (84–88)

The actual world

71. They took only one suitcase of Dickie's between them, ...
75. Dickie said absolutely nothing on the train.
93. Tom lifted the oar and came down with it on the top of Dickie's head.
...
94. Tom swung a left-handed blow with the oar against the side of Dickie's head. ...
...
95. He stooped and yanked at Dickie's green ring. He pocketed it. (91)
...
96. Tom had an ecstatic moment when he thought of all the pleasures that lay before him now with Dickie's money, other beds, tables, seas, ships, suitcases, shirts, years of freedom, years of pleasure. 97. Then he turned the light out and

put his head down and almost at once fell asleep, happy, content, and utterly confident, as he had never been before in his life. (97)

Bibliography

Sources cited: Chapter 4

Abbott, H. Porter. 2007. Story, Plot and Narration. In *The Cambridge Companion to Narrative*, ed. David Herman, 39–51. Cambridge: Cambridge University Press.
Biber, D., and E. Finegan. 1989. Styles of Stance in English: Lexical and Grammatical Marking of Evidentiality and Affect. *Text* 9 (1): 93–124.
Boltanski, L. 2014. *Mysteries and Conspiracies*. Translated by Catherine Porter, 3, 49, 77, 102, 123, 132–133, 144–145. Cambridge: Polity Press.
Chatman, Seymour. 1978 (1st published) (1980, 1st printing). *Story Discourse: Narrative Structure in Fiction and Film*. Ithaca and London: Cornell University Press.
Christies. 1993. *The Murder of Roger Ackroyd* (henceforth Ackroyd).
Davidse, Kirstin. 1992. Transitivity/Ergativity: The Janus-headed Grammar of Actions and Events. In *Advances in Systemic Linguistics: Recent Theory and Practice*, ed. Martin Davidse and Louise Ravelli, 116–129. London: Pinter Publishers.
Davidse, Martin, and Louise Ravelli, eds. 1992. Advances in Systemic Linguistics: Recent Theory and Practice, 116–129. London and New York: Pinter Publishers.
Davies, Martin, and Louise Ravelli. 1992. *Advances in Systemic Linguistics: Recent Theory and Practice*, 229–244. London and New York: Pinter Publishers.
Flanders, Reshmi D. 2014. Concealment and Revelation: An Interdisciplinary Approach to Reader Suspense. *Style* 48 (2) (Summer): 219–242.
Flanders, R. Dutta. 2012. Functional Nativeness in Outer and Expanding Circle. In *Linguistic and Extra-linguistic Problems of Communication*. Collection of Academic and Research Papers, Issue 9. N P Ogarev Mordovia State National Research University, Faculty of Foreign Languages, 285–321.
Fowler, Roger. 1977. *New Accents: Linguistics and the Novel*. London and New York: Methuen.

Genette, Gerard. 1988. *Narrative Discourse Revisited*. Ithaca, NY: Cornell University Press.
Halliday, M.A.K. 1974. The Place of Functional Sentence Perspective in the System of Linguistic Description. In *Papers on Functional Sentence Perspective*, ed. F. Danes. The Hague: Mouton; Prague: Academia.
———. 1994. *An Introduction to Functional Grammar*. 2nd ed. London: Edward Arnold.
———. 2004. *An Introduction to Functional Grammar*. 3rd ed. (revised by C.M.I.M. Matthiessen). New York: Hodder Arnold.
———. 2004. *The Language of Science*, Collected Works of Michael Halliday. Vol. 5. London and New York: Continuum.
Harding, Jennifer Riddle. 2007. Evaluative Stance and Counterfactuals in Language and Literature. *Language and Literature* 16 (3): 263–280.
Herman, David. 2007. Cognition, Emotion, and Consciousness. In *The Cambridge Companion to Narrative*, ed. David Herman, 245–259. Cambridge: Cambridge University Press.
Herman, David. 2014. Cognition, Emotion, and Consciousness. In *The Cambridge Companion to Narrative*, ed. David Herman. doi:10.1017/ CCOL0521856965.017. Accessed August 5, 2014.
Jermyn, Deborah. 2015. He's a Young Man...He's Strong...He Knows Criminology... and He's Intelligent': Desire, Doubling, and the Search for the Killer in *The Fall* 'The Most Feminist Show on Television'?: *The Fall*, The Female Detective and the Future of TV Crime Drama. Unpublished conference paper for workshop: *CSI series Finale Screening & Workshops*, Oxford Brookes University.
Labov, W. 1972. *Language in the Inner City*. Phiildelphia: University of Pennsylvania Press.
Lyons, J. 1977. *Semantics*. Cambridge: Cambridge University Press.
Kies, Daniel. 1992. The Uses of Passivity: Suppressing Agency in *Nineteen eighty-four*. In *Advances in Systemic Linguistics: Recent Theory and Practice*, ed. Martin Davis and Louise Ravelli, 229–244. London: Pinter Publishers.
Nash, Walter. 1990. *The Writing Scholar: Studies in Academic Discourse*. Newbury Park, London, and New Delhi: Sage Publications.
Opas-Hanninen, L.L., and Tapi Seppanen. 2010. 2D and 3D Visualization of Stance in Popular Fiction. In *Language and Style: In Honour of Mick Hort*, ed. Dan McIntyre and Beatrix Busse, 272–286. Basingstoke: Palgrave Macmillan.
Opas, L.L., and F.J. Tweedie. 2000. Come into My World: Styles of Stance in Detective and Romantic Fiction. *Poster. ALLC-ACH2000*, Glasgow, UK.

Pavel, Thomas G. 2014. Gerald Prince and Narrative Studies. *Narrative* 22 (3): 298–303.
Quirk, R., S. Greenbaum, G. Leech, and J. Svartvik. 1972. *A Grammar of Contemporary English*. London: Longman.
Rimmon-Kenan, S. 2002. *Narrative Fiction: Contemporary Poetics*, 7–28. London: Routledge.
Shibatani, Masayoshi. 1976. The Grammar of Causative Constructions: A Conspectus. In *Syntax and Semantics: The Grammar of Causative Constructions*, ed. M. Shibatani, vol. 6, 1040. New York: Academic Press.
Simpson, Paul. 1993. *Language, Ideology and Point of View*, Chs. 1, 2. London: Routledge.
———. 2014. Just What is Narrative Urgency? *Language and Literature* 23 (1): 3–22.
Thompson, Geoff. 1996. *Introducing Functional Grammar*. London: Arnold.
Todorov, T. 1966. Les categories du recit litterature. In *The Poetics of Prose*, ed. T. Todorov. Translated by Richard Howard and Jonathan Culler, 43–52. Ithaca, NY: Cornell University Press. Reprint 1977.
Toolan, Michael. 1988 (first published) (2001, 2nd ed.). *Narrative: A Critical Linguistiic Introduction*. Oxon, New York, and Canada: Routledge.
Youngs, Donna, and David Canter. 2012. Offenders' Crime Narratives as Revealed by the Narrative Roles Questionnaire. *International Journal of Offender Therapy and Comparative Criminology* 57 (3): 289–311.
Ziegeler, Debra. 2000. *Hypothetical Modality: Grammaticalisation in an L2 Dialect*. Amsterdam and Philadelhia: John Benjamins.

5

Orientation

5.1 Introduction

Designing the narrative of the past into what is currently relevant to the present and to a potential imagined future, brings out not only what happened, but also presents an authentic sense of the person who is doing the telling. In offender engagement discourse, this authentic sense of the person is privileging and confessional, as if there is a positional layer beyond or behind the self in which the narrating 'I' or the narrating 'he/she' is agentively or inagentively (suffering or victimization) engaged in the narrative discourse. In the sorting out of past events as a sequence of 'I' positions in the 'there-and-then' (relative to the 'here-and-now') in the narrative, leads up to a 'me' who the 'I' (or the 'he') wants to be understood as an **anticipated** other in a retrospective narrative. In so doing, a speaker's *self* is thematized, revealing its past in relation to the personal and the private issues. For example, the implied self of a *retrospective post-murder participant* is conceptualized in a way that the **speaker self** is subjected to the way a homodiegetic or heterodiegetic narrator position themselves with their story; either as,

- **Agent-oriented** (desire, obligation, ability, root possibility, permission) e.g., '*Todd has to go home at five on Thursdays.*' Speaker is reporting on a situation, and the modality predicates certain conditions on the agent on completion of an action or event.
- **A-state-oriented** (Epistemic-oriented) modality in epistemic (possibility, probability) reading of a situation related to the degree of truth-value. (For example, '*Todd has probably reached home by now.*')
- **Speaker-oriented** (imperative, hortative (moralizing), optative (mood). For example, '[May] *we go home now?*' (The speaker is doing something with the utterance, for example, seeking permission or simply speaking aloud.)

(Bybee et al. 1994)

Each orientation is discussed further in the framework (Sect. 5.4.2), where the overall distinction is evident between the types of orientations constructed in discourse. Such orientation is linked with an **overt** and **covert** analysis of the narrator for dual effect.

Orientation of a participant as an **anticipated other** in the offender narrative makes sense only in relation to what the teller/perpetrator is **countering** in the dominant narrative in a murder mystery or thriller narrative. This is influenced by the positioning of the speaker self in relation to the sequence of **'I' positions** in the narrative, and is synonymous to the relationship between *counternarratives* to *master* (dominant) *narratives*; that is, what is *resistant* and what is *dominant*. In Bamberg and Andrews (2004), the fluidity of these relational categories is based on the complexity of **inside/outside dynamics** of **the self**, which form the context of counternarratives and is understood in the way that the speaker positions themselves in respect to what they are countering in the story. From a behavioral (orientation) perspective, the act of killing is **circular**. It is an instrument to achieve the prime goal of homicide, and serves as a **motivation** for the self-gratification through crime.

'*A common theme in the classical perception of homicide pictured the murderer as being instrumentally oriented with material gain as the prime goal of the killing.*'

(Holmes and Burger 1988: p. 50)

Hence, positioning of **self-gratification** of the self as the **goal** of the offender is from a **reflective vantage point** of the perpetrator, as crime stories are retrospective narratives. Events are therefore picked out by the speaker to make way for the self that is relevant as an emerged character (the quest for **identity**), which is also connected to the self as the speaker (**author/animator**) in the here-and-now of the **story world**.

As mentioned above, an **anticipated other** is about the relationship formed between **resistant narratives** with the **dominant master narrative**. Master narratives are **culturally** accepted frames from which an accepted course of events is easily plotted. They naturalize and normalize the sequence of actions, which **constrain** and delineate the agency of subjects (Bamberg and Andrews 2004: p. 360). By countering the invoked master narrative, readers re orientate to the **alternative** (authentic) **self**, an anticipated other in the embedded sub-world (the second story) in murder mystery or thriller narrative. In the reorientation of narrative events, as seen in **Reverse Cs** in clauses for marked focus where the offender setting modifies the Process in clauses for an **undergoer** disposition (as Medium or C/scope), which came into being in a Process-participant active voice constellation relative to the I-perspective in offender discourse. The **anticipated alternative** undergoes a self-transformation, in marked focus, from a stereotypical agentive subject to a **Narrative Object** (**NO**). As a speaker, this narrative object then juggles claims as to who they are and justifies their working from within the **existent dominant narrative frame**, when oscillating between being **complicit** and the **countering** aspects of master narratives.

In Chap. 4, the **analytical focus** in relation to the **intermediary disposition** revealed the presentation of the protagonist as '**becoming**', or as **undergoing** a process of transformation in the syntactic devices for undercutting narrator Agency for an **intermediary participant**, especially in functional contrast. The intermediary disposition in functional contrast was observed with the crossing over into new modal territories in static syntax to undercut agency for a **restricted omniscience**, and in epistemic modal assertions to minimize narrator intervention within dominant diegetic A(N)+ve and B(N)+ve narrative mode. This minimized mode was distinct from a neutral narrative mode in **categorical assertions** for a factual disposition, with a **controlling Agent C**, as we shall see in this chapter (Sect. 5.5).

The **analytical focus** of Chap. 4 is mainly on **analytical causation** where Reverse C causes an intransitive reading of perpetrator circumstance as the grammatical subject. This functions as a counterstrategy in linguistic dysfunction which instantiates a marked focus on the offender setting for criminal justification. In this way, in the **narrativizing** of past events in offender discourse, past-lived moments in the dysfunctions are sensed and experienced as deep layers of the **experiencing 'I'**, which shape the dominant narrative of the perpetrator. A narrative format is provided thus in the **linguistic dysfunction** that privileges the character/perpetrator to foreground its backgrounded circumstance that is currently relevant to the perpetrator's present self.

The dominant narrative of homicide is thus a counternarrative of resistance for the perpetrator in crime narratives (for example, the embedded narrative with the sub-theme of desire and greed for Dr. Sheppard and Ripley, the story of betrayal for Raven, and Ripley's sexual jealousy). **Thematization** of these sub-themes for the perpetrator self, creates a **criminally oriented** specific **entity** which becomes the primary backdrop for the story of crime and violence, and is also the central strand for this **anticipated self** in criminal discourse. The sub-theme arguably becomes the **second story** in the dual structure of the crime story as suggested in Howard and Culler (1977: p. 44), where the **first** is the story of crime and **second** is a *story* of investigation. The sub-theme creates a tripartite structure of crime story (first story of crime, second embedded/**backgrounded story** of the perpetrator and third story of investigation).

In the second story, the state of a affairs display the coming into existence of the **criminally oriented behavior** that is backgrounded in the first and revealed in the third story of crime, where the **stimulus** for the act of killing may not be for a material gain, but a psychological gain for fulfilling ones **fantasy**, for instance, the **self-gratification** or the ultimate possession. From a psychological perspective, Canter (1994: p. 69) proposes, with reference to behavioral characteristics, two opposing themes about the nature of people,

> The first is the quest for **identity**, related to the social context and consequently the actions that make each person distinct
> The second is the development and the **change of the self**.

In the criminal context, the identity first leads to an individual that makes the self **unique** (the distinctiveness of people). Leary (1957) in Youngs and Canter (2012: p. 293) conceptualized this behavioral orientation toward the **unique self** as two dimensions of an **interpersonal disposition**; by that Leary captures an individual's approach to dealing with others: the **dominance/submission** and the **love/hate polarities**. For instance, in search of the **offender identity** (or the **personality** as psychologists call it), the obsession of the perpetrator in the (fictional) Ripper diaries concern his wife's unfaithfulness, his voyeurism and overall resentment towards his wife for her betrayal, presents an image of the self in which he is an emotionally injured man. This provides the justification for his desire to recover his power and control over women which he achieves through murder. For instance,

> '*The thought of him* [wife, Florie's lover] *taking her* [Florie] *is beginning to thrill me, perhaps I will allow her to continue, some of my thoughts are indeed beginning to give me pleasure. Yes I will visit Michael for a few weeks, and allow her to take all she can from the whoring master. Tonight I shall see mine* [the mistress]. *I may return to Battlecrease and take the unfaithful bitch* [Florie]. *Two in a night, indeed pleasure.*'
> Diary transcript 208, (voyeurism theme)

> '... *I* [Maybrick?] *struck deep into her* [victim]. ... *The bitch opened like a ripe peach. I have decided next time I will rip all out. My medicine will give me strength and the thought of the whore* [wife Florie] *and her whoring master will spur me on the road.*'
> Diary transcript 217 (decapitation theme)

Maybrick, presented with a question mark in the quote, is a disputed identification of Jack the Ripper, who was responsible for five murders in Whitechapel in London in 1888.

Alongside his secret act of voyeurism (watching his wife with her unnamed lover in Harrison (2010: pp. 70, 74), the Ripper perpetrator recorded his killings and mutilation. In Harrison, the killings and mutilations that are described appear as a way of dealing with his sexual jealousy towards his wife Florie on the one hand, '*banishment from Florie's bed, Maybrick was insanely jealous*' (2010: p. 78), and on the other, his deep resentment manifesting as uncontrollable rage, when carrying out mutilations of the body following the murder. David Forshaw in Harrison (2010: p. 152) mentions, the deep resentment **countering** the killer's inadequacy surfacing in the boastful style of writing in the diary, '*I have left the stupid fools a clue which I am sure they* [Inspector Abberline] *will not solve. Once again, I have been clever, very clever.*' (Diary transcript 221)

The interpersonal disposition of the Ripper contains a **polarity** of love and hate in his approach to his secret voyeurism, and in dealing with his personal inadequacy and resentment. Later in the diary transcripts, Ripper admitted that it was *love that spurred him on* [his *campaign*] and *it was love that shall put an end to it.* (Harrison 2010: p. 178)

> '*I could not find it in my heart* [hate/resentment] *to strike* [to murder], [as] *visions of my dear Bunny* [Florie] *overwhelm me. I still love her. But how I hate her. She has destroyed all and yet my heart aches for her, oh how it aches. I do not know which pain is the worse my body or my mind.*'
>
> Diary transcript 266

Recall that a speaker's self may be thematized, revealing the personal and private issues of the speaker. For example, it may be said contextually that the **implied self** of the Ripper is portrayed as a *retrospective post-murder participant* in transcript 266, which is conceptualized against the backdrop of an **authentic sense** of the **offender self** in transcript 217, which is confessional and is engaged in the agentive discourse *opened*, or in the deontic sense, *will*.

In a social context, the 'me' of the Ripper's self is opposed to the Ripper 'I', '*I am convinced God placed me here to kill all whores … Nothing will stop me now.*' (Transcript 241). In Holmes and Burger (1988: p. 11), here is a **mission-oriented** social type (Sect. 5.4.1). Again, with reference to the opposing theme in Canter (1994), the quest for the **identity** of the self is in opposition to the actions that inform of the characteristics of the person that makes that person distinct. In the idea of the **speaker self** in relation to the **sequencing of 'I' positions** in the narrative form (Bamberg and Andrews 2004: p. 355), the opposition of the self align to the ways the 'I' in the *there-and-then lead up to a 'me' as* [the] '*I' want to be understood.* In Chap. 4, this opposition exists between the worlds of modal assertions, identifying the disposition of this **anticipated other** of the **narrating I**.

5 Orientation   415

One is then contextually inclined to predict the perspective, for instance, in the Ripper transcripts 208 and 217, are a counternarrative to the utterance in diary transcript 266. If the **counternarrative** is one of disruption and fragmentation, then which offender orientation, following **topicality strength** in Sect. 5.4.2, is being fragmented or **undercut** to license the manner in which the violence is narrated in the diary transcripts 217 and 208? This question is taken up, first with reference to the idea that,

> '… *there is some central theme as the core or objective to a series of crimes that in some way represents the criminal's way of dealing with other people* [the interpersonal actions].'
>
> (Canter 1994: p. 61)

In Canter, **interpersonal actions** and the **violence** of the criminal as a *way of dealing with other people* **remained constant** even when the degree of violence in crime developed or underwent change. For instance, perpetrator, John Duffy, in Canter (1994: p. 61) dropped his guard when involved in violence that he did not think of as criminal (forcing his ex-wife to have sex at knifepoint). This contrasts with the offender being skilled and cautious at avoiding arrest when he was consciously going out to rape and then violently murder. There is opposition between the **controlled covert** criminal behavior and an **overt central nature** of the **self**, where Duffy's central violent nature represents the underlying self for the criminal actions. Duffy, as the self, showed his appetite for treating women as a vehicle for his control and sexuality when he raped many women and then started to deliberately kill his victims.

In **real world**, Duffy was infertile, and some of his violent assaults, as Canter (p. 67) states, took place after he discovered that his ex-wife had become pregnant by another man. Duffy's ensuing anger and frustration, stemming from his personal inadequacy (like the Ripper's sexual jealousy towards his wife) became the **trigger** for his identity to be in control in criminal actions in the **dominant (master) narrative**. Anger and frustration, as a means of disruption and fragmentation of an **intermediate experiencing self**, finds its way into the dominant narrative, which turns into a **narrative of resistance** found in murder, **countering** the inadequacy of the **experiencing self**. Consequently, an **embedded secondary** narrative, a **second story of self-conflict** is perpetuated in the counter-positioning of the **agentive I**, who is now committing violence and murder, which is in opposition with the **experiencing self** (following Leary's love/hate instead of submissive/control polarity, as in Ripper diary, '*I still love her. But how I hate her*').

5.2 Hypothesis: Narrating-I, Narrating-He and Experiencing Self

The chapter aim is to analyze with linguistics the orientation of the **anticipated (experiencing) self (me)**, set in opposition to a dominant **narrating (agentive) -I**.

Orientation of the **identity** of self is in opposition to the increased violence with an **evolved/evolving I**, progressing to murder as the process of development and change. In the midst of this, contextually there is an '**aggressor trigger**' fuelled by anger and frustration which is **triggered in a past situation** that urged transgression from an **undergoer** (inagentive) entity to an Actor orientation. The **transgression trigger** is at the point when the transition is for committing a number of crimes and not just one sudden outburst. In **behavioral science**, this then becomes a lifestyle of breaking the law, or living beyond the law. This **evolving 'I'** or the *core you* (Sect. 6.4 in Chap. 6) is dynamic and it is the participant of a dominant narrative where action fulfils a goal to achieve self-gratification. This orientation is set in opposition to an entity, which is stative and relational to a state of lifestyle beyond the law, countering the underlying quest to be presented as an '**intermediary**' participating character.

It should then be assumed that the orientation of the **evolving I** is dynamic and Agent-oriented, while the **experiencing self** or an *autobiographical you* (Sect. 6.2 in Chap. 6) is a state-oriented disposition. Assume also that the state-oriented self is the **countering** (in the **inter diegesis space** in the offender story world) by an intermediary participating character for an identity, which makes the perpetrator distinct as a person (the personality) in relation to his criminal behavior.

Ziegeler (2000: p. 18) raises the question,

'What is not so obvious is the nature of the linguistic devices that contribute to the creation of a hypothetical or counterfactual implicature, and [the question is] *whether or not they can be isolated.'*

Ziegeler goes on to state that such interpretation appears to be based solely on the matters of contextual interpretation. However, when readers do not have the (**realis**) contextual information about the offender-self and the offender-I, they do not have a real set of circumstances to judge the truth or falsity (the **counterfactual implicature**) for instance as in the Ripper diaries if this was an account of a real offender.

In another case of a real serial killer, Ted Bundy did not confess to being the killer of 30 victims (disputed as more) in his interviews, but he presented a predicative statement of an offender who **distanced** himself from all the murders in his **third-person account**. In third-person narration, Bundy had the chance to talk without **overtly** implicating himself in the murders. Until the final weekend of his life, he did not confess to the murders he was convicted of. A third-person interview technique gave Bundy the chance to talk directly about himself without the stigma of confession.

'[Bundy provided] *a matter-of-fact account in third person* [about] *how a person performing the act of killing might act under any specific circumstance.* [The account was more about his experiencing self], *who he was* and *why he had become a killer* [than about the facts related to the killings he carried out].'
(Michaud and Aynesworth 2005: p. 15)

In contrast to the Bundy case, the level of **hypotheticality** implied in the Ripper diary transcripts reveals the offender's ballooning compulsion which drives him to violence. While *counterfactuality* (not fact, but a predicative statement) was a **cognitive state** in Bundy's account, in the Ripper's diaries the accounts foregrounded a **counternarrative** in temporality and **hypotheticality**. In other words, the diary is not counterfactual but rather hypothetical with counterfactual inferences. This difference in narration techniques then positioned the **experiencing self** of the two serial killers Ted Bundy and Jack the Ripper differently.

The offender orientation is the **analytical focus** in this chapter with reference to counterfactuality and hypotheticality (or a hypothetical context with counterfactual inferences) in which the orientation is a-state-oriented disposition in an Agent-oriented discourse.

5.3 Offender Texts: The Characteristics

To analyze **identity** and distinguish an *evolving I* from the *experiencing self*, the texts selected are true narratives in contrast to the fictional offender narratives selected in the last 3 chapters. This is because the extracts for analysis so far were akin to offender engagement discourse. It is therefore logical to analyze actual criminal discourse alongside fictional offender discourses from crime fiction. This intuition is supported by Jones in the Introduction for *True Crime* who states,

> '*Detective fiction of classic variety* [like Christie's murder-mystery] *bears little relation to real crime … real murders are in many ways much more interesting than the fictional ones … as they are much more extraordinary. Things which a novelist would not dare to put in the story would crop up in reality.*'
> (Glyn Jones 1992)

Secondly, the **killer-victim relationship** takes place inside the killer's mind, which is not **overt**, but discussed at length when analysing the story telling in classic detective stories unlike the true crime discourses of Bundy and Ripper. Thirdly, in detective fiction of the classic variety the killer knows the victim. When victims are unknown to the killer, there is a need for psychological accuracy to get into the murderer's **mind** in order to realize the **process of distortion**, which is the focus in Chap. 6. This is a *process-focused* murder which is distinct from an *act-focused* way of ending a victim's life (Holmes and Burger 1988: p. 52). In the event of **redundant overkill** and violence, the murderer is *process-focused*; the brutality of the process is of more importance than simply ending a victim's life, as in classic detective fictions. The multiple murders committed by fictional offenders like Ripley, Bud Corliss, Eleanor Maxie and Dr. Shepphard are *act-focused* and directed towards accomplishing their goal, unlike *process-focused* which serves as a psychological gain in the form of expressive killing for **self-gratification** by serial killers. *Cover*

Her Face by James is regarded as a psychological crime story like Ruth Rendell's crime novel, *A demon in my view*, where the focus is on an **inward-looking** rather than an **outward-looking** killer; who may not necessarily be a psychopath. With reference to mindstyle, the last crime novel is analyzed in Chap. 6. In this chapter, criminal discourses are analyzed to understand the criminal orientation by use of linguistic devices. These are extracts from the Ted Bundy interviews and from the Ripper Diary transcripts, where the serial killer Bundy's discourse is compared with the fictional offender in the Ripper diaries for counterfactual and hypothetical implicature with counterfactual inferences.

5.4 The Framework: Orientation Techniques

The framework is used to consider the linguistic devices that the countering self invoked in the master narrative of the killer. In Chap. 4, the narrative of murder and violence was the consequence of the criminal disposition of the protagonist. It is contextually the **resistant narrative**, countering personal experiences that underlie the **autobiographical offender experience**, such as in the Ripley discourse with reference to his homosexual disposition, his hidden identity and consequently his revenge due to sexual jealousy which lead him to commit to murder. These experiences are beyond the control of the participating character, constituting the **disposition** of the **perpetrator self** as inagentive (an **undergoer**), while the **criminal behavior** appears **volitional** and in control. This disposition is an **Agent-affected participant** in a **circumstantial setting**, established in an Actor-Affected schema (Sect. 4.4.1.1 in Chap. 4). It is a **secondary agent, Ag$_2$**; different from a disposition in **Actor-Goal schema**, with a primary Agent, Ag$_1$, in clauses.

Contextually, the **Causer role** of this anticipatory participant is **superventive**, as in clause 6a and clause 7a, in Fig. 4.2. This is because; the participant (**a deontic-Agent**) is orientating its world of desire and obligation that compelled a criminal disposition. Alternatively, the participant is imposing a specific mood (**Speaker-oriented**) on the addressee, or causing **a-state-oriented** assertion. **A-state-oriented** assertion is an epistemic reading, which calls for a stative interpretation of the main verb. This understanding was not evident in the analysis of linguistic dysfunctions in Chap. 4.

5.4.1 Orientation in Behavioral Science

In behavioral science, orientation is described as,

- **Behavioral** (behavioral background in response to what is gained from homicidal violence),
- **Visionary** (voices or visions that demand that a person or category of persons be destroyed)
- **Mission-oriented** (mission to rid the world of a category of people who are undesirable or unworthy of living with other human beings),
- **Hedonistic** (no qualms about murdering others as means of his own enjoyment of life)
- **Power-oriented** (profound satisfaction from the process of having complete life-or-death control over the victim)

(Holmes and Burger 1988: pp. 56–59)

5.4.2 Orientation in Modal Senses

In the **grammaticalization** of a speaker's subjective attitudes and opinions, orientations in Bybee et al. (1994: pp. 177–180) are modal senses corresponding to the **mood** (traditionally associated with imperative, optative, conditional and subordinate verb forms) and **modality** (indicating obligation, probability and possibility) notions. The behavior of modals differs in accordance with the type of main verb in the utterances. Verbs of action and telic verb (action with a clear endpoint) are **agent-oriented** whilst stative verbs have **epistemic focal sense**. However, this classification is not straightforward. For instance, *have known* gravitates towards Agent-oriented uses, while 'know' as in 'be acquainted with' has an epistemic use. This issue is tackled in **topicality strength** with reference to epistemic/root contrast and in relation to the expression of possibility in English. The main modal senses classified in Bybee and Fleischman (1995: p. 25) are,

5 Orientation

Agent-oriented—modality reports the existence of **internal and external** conditions on an Agent with respect to completion of an action expressed in the main predicate. **Semantically** specific notions are,

- **Obligation**—reports existence of **external social conditions** compelling an Agent to complete the predicate action (e.g., All students **must** obtain [obligation sense] the consent of the Dean; I called her Miss Tillman, but one **should** [advice sense) call her President)
- **Necessity**—reports the existence of **physical conditions** to complete the predicate action (e.g., I **need** to hear a loud alarm to wake me up)
- **Ability**—reports existence of **internal enabling conditions** in the Agent with respect to predicate action (e.g., I **can** only type, as I am a beginner)
- **Desire**—reports existence of **internal volitional conditions** in the Agent with respect to predicate action (e.g., 'Juan called them loudly in Indian tongue, if they would (= wanted to) save their lives')

(Coates 1983: p. 212 in Bybee et al. 1994: p. 178)

Speaker-oriented modalities are directives, and do not report the existence of conditions on the Agent, but allow the Speaker to **impose** such **conditions** on the addressee. Speaker-oriented modalities are,

- **Imperative**—performs commands as prohibitive/negative (e.g., don't run too fast)
- **Optative**—is about wish/hope in a main clause, (e.g., may we go!)
- **Hortative**—is encouraging/inciting some action, (e.g., keep up the good work!)
- **Admonitive**—is warning, (e.g., be careful, it is hot!)
- **Permissive**—is granting permission (e.g., you may go now)

Epistemic-oriented modalities are assertions that indicate the extent to which the speaker is committed to the truth proposition. The unmarked case is in total commitment to the truth of the proposition. Markers of epistemic modality indicate,

- **Possibility**—proposition may be true (e.g. I **may have** put them down on the table)

- **Probability**—greater likelihood that the proposition is true (e.g., The storm **should** be clear by tomorrow, **inferred certainty**: There **must** be some way to get to New York)
- **Counterfactual propositions**—which are contrary to the fact (e.g. I **should** have mailed this yesterday, **but** I forgot)

Subordinating moods—express both epistemic and Speaker-oriented modalities, and are often marked in certain subordinating clauses which are,

- **Complement** (I suggested **that he should call you immediately**)
- **Concessive** (**Although** he may be a wise man, he made mistakes)
- **Purpose clauses** (We are working now **so that I can take summer off**)

Epistemic reading of situations also calls for a **stative interpretation** of the main verb. For example,

1. *'He must understand what we want (or we'll never get it).'*

An **epistemic reading** here calls for a stative interpretation of main verb *must*. However, an **obligation reading** requires a dynamic interpretation such as, 'he must be made to understand'.

2. *'He must play tennis a lot (or he won't win the tournament).'*

(Bybee et al. 1994: p. 201)

There are thus **two readings**.
An **epistemic reading** which has a present **habitual aspect**, and an **Obligation reading** which is **future projecting**.
A **stative predicate** (for example, *know, want*) describes an unchanging situation which will continue unless something happens to change it. A **dynamic predicate** in Bybee et al. (1994: p. 55) typically describes a situation, which involves some sort of change (for example, *write, walk, drop*). In example 1, a stative interpretation of *He must understand* is a **statement** in the sense that 'He certainly knows what we wants'.

5 Orientation   423

However a **dynamic interpretation** of a (possible) change of state makes a **hypothetical utterance** have **counterfactual inference**, for instance, 'If he does **not understand**, then they (we) **may** lose the deal'. Similarly, the second reading of example 2 is, *He **must** practice hard or else he **will** lose the tournament*. With **extra-world knowledge** like the encyclopedic knowledge, the **hypothetical meaning** in the **utterance** can overshadow the temporal meanings in future.

In these variations there is dichotomy. Following Ricoeur (1985: p. 88) the variation is because,

*'When the discourse spoken by one of the characters concerning their experience is incorporated in the **diegesis**, the **pair utterance/statement** ... can be reformulated in a vocabulary that personalizes the two terms. The **utterance** becomes the discourse of the narrator, while the **statement** becomes the discourse of a character.* [Ricoeur then goes on to pose the question in italics], *The question will then be to determine by which special narrative means the narrative is constituted as the discourse of a narrator* [such as the retrospective post murder participant as Narrator in criminal context] *recounting the discourse of the character* [as the criminal].' (My emphasis)

The narrative as MC in Chap. 2, constituted the narrator discourse in the first story of crime. The re-sequence of events in this '**inter diegesis**', was formulated by the re-positioning of events in the metanarrative at the horizontal and vertical axis of the victim and murderer's diegesis space (alternative storyworld), based on their respective PoR in Chap. 2 (Figs. 2.2, 2.3, 2.5, and 2.6). In Chap. 4, the offender engagement discourse in this **offender-substituted** narrative came with its own language of suspense in **functional contrast** and in the **deviation from the norm**. An 'intermediary' participant disposition as a **narrative object** was identified in the manner of **thematization** of Speaker circumstance, in which the self was the central focus setting of circumstance which overshadows the perpetrator focus.

With reference to the **focal sense** of Agent or Epistemic-oriented modality, the **intermediary participant** may be **Speaker oriented (S)**, the **controlling Agent (Agent C)** or can differ in modality with the **modal force (F)**. The controlling Agent C is typically **coded** as the sentence subject. The topicality strength with reference to epistemic/root contrast and in relation to the expression of possibility in English is,

Topicality strength

- There is some **force F** that has an interest in an event either occurring or not occurring, (for example, *he has to sleep*); This surfaces the question of who is responsible for the fact that he has to sleep—a focal sense of Agent-oriented modality
- That event is to be **performed by** some Agent **A** (For example, *he has to sleep*)
- The event **is dynamic** (**D**) (For example, *I want to come* (D) versus *I would like to come* (F)).
- The event has not taken place at **reference time**, it will be taking place at a later time than the reference time (**L**) (For example, *he has to sleep*)
- The event is **non-factual**, but there is certain degree of **probability** (**P**) that it will occur. For example, when a modal expresses a high degree of probability = strong obligation)

(Heine in Bybee and Fleischman 1995: p. 56)

These **conceptual** properties **F, A, D, L** and **P** are prototypical instances of **Agent-oriented modality**. Prototypical instances of **epistemic modality** lack all these properties except **P**, creating a **counterfactual context** in probability, as in modal 'will'.

By employing the **modal senses** as above, along with **high/low topicality** related to **functional factors** in the discourse roles below, the type of **context** initiated in a discourse is valuable in relation to a participant orientation in offender engagement discourse. These contexts inform varying levels of counterfactuality and hypotheticality.

5.4.3 Counterfactual Implicature

A **Counterfactual utterance** (contrary to the known fact) is an *irrealis* statement and therefore not a true assertion. Assertions only involve *realis* statements. Whilst a speaker is only aware of the counterfactuality of statements, the reader (hearer) has to deduce counterfactuality from linguistic indicators and contextual **cues**.

The nature and the form of the indicators associated with **counterfactuality** in Ziegeler (2000) are,

- In past temporal reference, the likelihood of a counterfactual interpretation increases; that is, **inferences** of counterfactuality are in the present and co-exist with past temporality.
- The counterfactuality of a statement is unrelated to the temporality, for instance, a statement in the future suggesting that the past tense morphology has strengthened to the point at which the past reference is no longer required to convey the meaning. For example, if the speaker was in full knowledge that Grannie had died,

3. '*If Grannie had missed the bus on Friday, she would have walked home.*'

the **implied falsity** in the conditional 'if' clause provide extra-linguistic contextual information necessary to decode meaning at the time of **utterance**, that is, if Grannie was alive, it was habitual of her to take the same bus home. The hypothetical meaning in example 3 then overshadows the temporal meaning in the statement. Quirk et al. (1987: p. 782) in Ziegeler (2000: p. 17), do not use the term counterfactual. They apply the term *hypothetical* to indicate an **implied rejection** of the conditional premise, for example,

4. '*If you had listened to me, you wouldn't have made mistakes (but you didn't listen to me)*'   **counterfactual premise**

A hypothetical meaning is distinguished between the past, present or in future, where the meaning may be one of negative expectation, for example,

5. '*If you listen to me, you wouldn't make mistakes (but I don't suppose you will listen to me)*'   **hypothetical premise**

Examples 4 and 5 could be interchangeable as hypothetical conditional and as counterfactual. That is, if the **conditional premise** be suffixed in 5 with, *but you don't listen to me* (habitually), then it suggests implied rejection of the conditional premise and **time reference** is neither in the future nor in the past, but in **habitual present**. Similarly, if 4 could be suffixed with, *but I don't suppose you did listen to me*, indicating the past hypothesis is just a surmise and not backed by a known fact, it is then a counterfactual utterance. Ziegeler proposes that all counterfactual meaning is pragmatically implied. In 5, the speaker's intent was to express an **assertion,** but the speech act was only a **predicative statement**. **Counterfactuality** is not equivalent to lying, but **an intention** of concealing the contravened known facts from the hearer.

> '*Counterfactuality* [thus] *permits the hearer* [reader] *to infer the negation of reality from the expression of only partial reality* [Bundy implied as innocent of a first degree murder], *the means by which this is inferred is from the structure of* **utterance** [such as in topicality strength above], *from the world knowledge about a situation, or from various* **discourse clues.**' (My emphasis)   (Ziegeler 2000: p. 16)

In Dannenberg (2008: p. 59),

> '*The counterfactual is ... an alternate world that is viewed, with hindsight, an* **ontologically subordinate event**—*something that might have been but was not.*' (My emphasis)

Counterfactuality is further informed in functional factors related to discourse roles. This approach has been useful, as Myhill states (in Schiffrin et al. 2001: p. 166), in providing a typological perspective on **functional alternations**, clarifying discourse motivations underlying these alternations. Functional factors in discourse roles may be,

Functional factors in discourse roles

- Functionally **direct** (for example, a construction where the **Agent** is more **topical**[1] (what the sentence is about, or about something), I (**Agent**) broke a vase)

---

[1] Topic—discourse-based definition of a topic is, what a sentence is about, or something, which sets a spatial, temporal, or individual frame work within which prediction holds. (Chafe 1976: p. 50) in Schiffrin et al. (2001: p. 164).

- Functionally **inverse** (for example, a construction where **Patient** is high in topicality (for example, The vase (**Patient**) broke)
- Functionally defocusing (**passivization**) (for example, a construction where **Agent** 'I' is **low** in topicality,[2] e.g. in Reverse Circumstantiation (Reverse C), (Ripper diary 209: *And oh what deeds* (**Reverse C**) I (Agent) *shall commit* (Process))
- Functionally **antipassive** (e.g. construction where **Patient** is very **low in topicality**, e.g. (TB extract 4: ... *having exposed **himself** to that kind of situation* (**Patient of passive**))

5.4.4 Hypothetical Implicature

In contrast, a **hypothetical implicature** (predictive meanings) is intensified over a counterfactual utterance (non-factual/irrealis statement) in undercutting the lexical sense of volition and intention in hypothetical modals such as, *could*, and *shall*, alongside counterfactual inferences in **negation** and modal *would* (as underlined below). This linguistically formulating distinction by Myhill (in Schiffrin 2001: p. 63), between counterfactuals and alternate hypothetical world creates a **binary pair of events**, a *factual* one and its hypothetical other (the *counterfactual*). Contextually, following the diary transcript below,
Ripper diary transcript (DT) 209

*'I am beginning to believe it is unwise to continue writing. ... **If** Smith should find this **then** I am done before my campaign begins. And oh what deeds I **shall** commit. For how **could** one suspect that I **could** be capable of such things, for **am I not**, as all believe, a mild man, who it has been said **would** never hurt a fly. Indeed only the other day **did not** Edwin [Ripper/(Maybrick's? brother with whom Florie was implied to have an affair)] **say** me I was the most gentlest of men he **had encountered?'***

While, the '**if then**' construction is **counterfactual** with reference to the context in transcript 209, denoting falsity of an utterance (similar to example 3 above). A sense of obligation is provided in the probability

---

[2] Topicality—discourse function of a particular form or construction is not necessarily high in topicality, though the term topic in English might be used for a clause-initial constituent. This phenomenon is noticed cross-linguistically.

modals *will, shall* and *could* in the sense of future prediction. In the diary transcript 211 below, for instance, a future '*if*' has reached the stage of prediction, and is used to make predictions about the present, *thrills me*, but at the same time interpreted as probability *will throw* in transcript 209 constituting a **hypothetical world** as a **binary pair of event**.

Ripper DT 211

'*... do not know if I have the courage to go back to my original idea. Manchester was cold and damp very much like this hell hole. Next time I **will throw** acid over them* [*the prostitutes*]. *The thought of them ridling and screaming while the acid burns deep **thrills** me, ha, what a joke it would be if I could gorge an eye out and [then] leave it by the whores body for all to see, to see, ha, ha.*'

5.4.5 Binary Pair of Events: Hypotheticality in Counterfactual Inferences

Finally, the level of hypotheticality is also implied with counterfactual inferences in **temporal features** when present in a hypothetical context and formed in,

- Past and perfect morphology that marks events and situations generally accepted as completed.
- Negation that presupposes a corresponding positive proposition.
- First person subjects that have first-hand information about the factual premise for the speaker's utterance.
- Extra-world knowledge where temporal meanings in future are overshadowed by the hypothetical meanings.

(Ziegeler 2000: p. 40)

5.5 Findings: Counterfactual Recount and Hypothetical Utterance

The dichotomy of the grammatical person of a narrator is distinct from the character, that is, distinction between the **narrating discourse** (**utterance**) and the **narrated discourse** (**statement**) is maintained in the grammatical distinctions between person and verb tenses (Ricoeur 1985: p. 91). This distinction gets tricky when the difference between the narrator and the character is not marked by the distinction of personal pronouns. The analysis of this dichotomy in orientations is carried out first in Ted Bundy (TB) extracts followed by the extracts from Ripper diaries (Appendix 5). For space constraint, only selected texts from Ripper transcripts, as '**killer in anticipation**' is compared with the discourse of '**post killing reminiscences**' by the offender.

5.5.1 A Counterfactual Context

The four extracts adopted from Ted Bundy's (TB) interviews (Appendix 5) with journalists Stephen Michaud (SM) and Hugh Aynesworth (HA) were to reinvestigate the murder allegations against him. The interviews were to disengage TB as a suspect in any of the two dozen killings he was then accused of, or suspected of having committed. The chance that Bundy would tell the truth to prove his innocence encouraged the journalists to take up the project, only to discover that all Bundy intended was to provide a picture of who he was and why he had become a killer and his innate need to **manipulate**. His sole intention, as the journalists later discovered, was to emphasize the mystery surrounding him, and to use the publicity to bolster his defense (p. 278) and have strong supporters for his book to sell, and for this, he needed the journalists as tools to carry out his intention.

The extracts quoted in Appendix 5 are in italics, emphasis in italics in the original text is underlined. Linguistic elements are in bold to draw attention for the analysis.

Ted Bundy (TB) confesses to '*possession*' as being the motive for his crime. The extracts below adopted for analysis, center on this **sub-theme of possession**, which reappears when police question Bundy about the *overkilling* committed following a murder. In the interviews, Bundy presented a **predicative statement** of an offender distanced in his third person account (extracts 3 and 4).

Bundy's narrative about being a thief (extract 1) is relational in the first person, *I was*, and is Agent-oriented in, *I really enjoyed, I had wanted*. Bundy started as a thief prior to his activities as a serial killer (extract 3

and 4). He also played the role of a Defendant in extract 2, and the narrative technique in extract 2 is factual similar to that of extract 1.
TB: thief discourse (extract 1)

6. '*TB: The big payoff for me **was** actually possessing whatever it **was** I had stolen. It wasn't the act, necessarily. ... **I really enjoyed** having something on my wall or sitting in my apartment that **I had wanted** and gone out and taken.*'
(Michaud and Aynesworth 2005: p. 41)

In the discourse below, he records his feelings in the first person, soon after he failed to convince the jury in the Leach murder case of being innocent of first-degree murder.
TB: Defendant discourse (extract 2)

7. '*TB: ... while for at least six months **I had prepared** myself in every way possible for a conviction, this defense mechanism began to slowly disintegrate once I became involved in the active conduct of the trial. **I guess** there were several factors which **forced me**, which **influenced me** to play the role. To play the role of the defendant, who had every hope and expectation of being acquitted of a crime of which **he knew himself** to be innocent*' [PP could be suffixed with modal, 'supposed to be', or relational Process 'was' for a factual value]. (My emphasis)
(Michaud and Aynesworth 2005: pp. 41 and 45)

To provide context, Bundy was sentenced to death for Kim Leach's murder (p. 55). The twelve-year-old had disappeared from her school and prosecution witness Andy Wilson testified he had seen Bundy driving with Miss Leach in a white van (p. 50). Bundy denied (concealed) this (p. 57). This murder was in Bundy's final disorganized phase, a **development scenario** in Canter, which began with the slaughter at Chi Omega, a women's hostel, where he killed two victims while they slept, with another two escaping death. One of the victims, Levy, sustained an injury that journalists described as overkilling—to *stick an instrument up a person's vagina or you cut a person or bite a person that seems to indicate a certain amount of rage* (p. 247). Journalist (HA) questioned that such violence was an act of sexual (self) gratification. TB denied his rage, it was more to do with the intensification of stressful factors (unmentioned in original text), which drove him to seek more stimulation that resulted in him causing pain and mutilation. (pp. 244–248)

Bundy defended his innocence by **countering** his identity of a perpetrator accused of being a serial killer. The distance between the narrating discourse and the narrated discourse in the Defendant narrative (by the same grammatical person 'I') varied depending on the degree to which the Narrator/Defendant discourse dominated in relation to that of the character TB's discourse.

Linguistically, the **distancing act** in the Agentive Subject, *I* was, is performed in the switch in participant roles from **Actor** (*I had prepared, I became, I guess*), to **object**, *forced me, influenced me*, to third person **Senser** *he knew* to a functionally **passive** entity disposition, *himself to be innocent*. Pronouns I (the Actor/performer) *he* (the Senser) and *himself* (the entity to be) refer to the same participant Ted Bundy. The participant Bundy is an Agentive 'I', *play* [ing] *the role of the defendant* in the extract 2, but shifts in the final clause to an Agentive Senser role *he* (the one who experiences the process *knew*), with corresponding **entity**/phenomenon, *himself to be innocent*. Furthermore, clause-initial circumstantial, *To play the role of the defendant, who had every hope and expectation of being acquitted of a crime*, in the final clause is a **linguistic dysfunction** in Reverse circumstantiation. Reverse Circumstantiation as **scope** (where **process and participant are blended together**) functions as the overall **topic** of the sentence, as well as in the extract, and is similar to the function of circumstantial/scope, *That book*, in *That book I don't like*.

There is a predominance of **intransitive activity** in the prepositional form of the final clause, maintaining Agent-orientation of the Defendant *I* in the PP, but Senser *he* in comparison is less strongly agentive. This is also because of functional factors, such as **low topicality** in the discourse role, explained below. Alternatively, a **transitive proposition** would be **high** in **topicality**, where the clause becomes a construction with an **endpoint** (state and activity that have terminated and have an endpoint (Ziegeler 2006: p. 14)). However, this is not the case with the Senser/Phenomenon role, an entity/phenomenon *himself to be innocent*, is an **(hypothetical) entity to be** which in the Defendant discourse does not have an endpoint, because in reality Bundy failed to prove he was innocent of first-degree murder in the Leach murder case.

Distancing the act of the **narrating** Agentive *I* from Senser *he* as the **narrated discourse** is further evident in **discourse roles**. Senser *he* in the Defendant narrative is the convicted murderer, who is playing the Defendant role as a **direct** Actor, while remaining a focused constituent in clause-initial PP, despite the **shift** from a Narrating/Actor *I* to a narrated *he* as a Senser and then passive Agent. The discourse role of Agentive *I* (*I had prepared, I became, I guess*) is high in topicality compared to the low topicality in the discourse function of Senser *he*, in passive object *me* (in *forced me, influenced me*) and in the entity/phenomenon *to be* considered by the jury as *innocent* in the Defendant discourse. Further, the pronoun *himself* in the subordinate clause, *of which he knew himself to be innocent*, is a **counterfactual entity** of *he* as a Senser.

In positioning the Senser *he* as an **experiencing self** of offender Bundy in the 'here-and-now' relative to the 'there-and-then' of Defendant Bundy's utterance leads up to the **entity** 'me' (*himself to be innocent*), who the Defendant *I* wanted to be understood as the **anticipated other** in a retrospective recording. Between this experiencing self and the Agentive I, the established relationship is between a resistant and dominant narrative. The Defendant *I* was **countering** the identity of a serial killer when presented as the Senser *he* (the convicted serial killer implied) and as an entity *himself to be innocent* with a low topicality discourse role in PP.

For a linguistically aware reader, the shift in participant disposition is from Actor/Agent to Senser/Phenomenon, and following Myhill's discourse function (S), is deduced as counterfactual in the structurally constructed PP. In the PP, the proposition made, of *which he knew himself to be innocent*, contextually is a **hypothetical utterance**; however, the recounted recording of Bundy in a defendant role is **counterfactual**. The countering role as direct Actor/Defendant 'I' is structurally distinct from Senser *he* as a counterpart of 'I', and distinct from the pronoun *himself* with a passive discourse function characterized with the auxiliary verb *to be*. A **Senser disposition** formulates a low topicality for the participant *he*, who is the serial killer in the master narrative; a **binary opposite** to the high topicality **direct** Defendant role in the Defendant discourse.

Counterfactual statements defined in Ziegeler (2000: p. 41) are mere **abstraction** (withdrawal) from the real world. They are not backed by any known fact and are not the polar opposite to factuality. Therefore the defendant role of Bundy is a mere withdrawal, as Bundy himself states that the trial was a *defense mechanism*, [where] *we were actually in the process of seeking the truth* (my emphasis) (Michaud and Aynesworth 2005: p. 47)—a **process focused** performance over an **act-focused** action.

Further, in Harding (2007: p. 263), *counterfactuals* as **scenarios** which are described or imagined by the character or narrator are not realized in the story, and are regarded as unrealized by the speaker who introduce them. Then, Bundy's emotional gamut in the Defendant role is a **scenario** regarded as a missed opportunity for him to ultimately establish his innocence. Bundy was aware of the truth concealed in the quoted recount in extract 2 where, he used an FSU van to abduct Kim Leach, who was later murdered (p. 57).

To conclude, if Bundy's Defendant discourse is a speaker **intention** to conceal the contravened known facts from the hearer, then the **hypotheticality** was in the stative entity, presented as functionally passive with the auxiliary verb *to be* for low topicality. This is reinforced in the prepositional form for an **intransitive activity** that maintained the Agent-oriented disposition in an intransitive perspective, which is not goal-oriented and less strongly agentive in topicality; a **functional contrast** in the narrated discourse.

This theme of 'playing a role', was his ***organized*** **phase** (the development phase in Canter) and (the role) is repeated when he persuaded his victims to help him with his faked disability before abducting them. After having picked up Kathy Parks hitchhiking (extract 3), he persuaded her to join him to a party at his place. They continued drinking. Roberta (Kathy) Parks was 22, when she was abducted (May 6, 1974) from the campus of Oregon State University. Her skull was later discovered on Tylor Mountain where other bodies were also found (p. 110), and described as his [TBs] *garbage disposal*. (Michaud and Aynesworth 2005: (hardback): p. 104).

TB initially explained that his act of killing was necessary to avoid being caught, an organized phase.

8. ... *And the killing of the victim, we* **would** *expect,* ***would have seemed*** *a rather extreme act—but one that the individual* ***considered necessary*** *to eliminate the possibility of his getting caught.*

The assertions in modal *would* indicate the extent to which speaker Bundy is committed to the truth proposition.

9. *'The initial sexual encounter* **would be** *more or less a voluntary one. .... Well, it* **would be**—*in dealing with the kind of profile <u>we've created</u> (coughs) as I've stated before, nothing is clearcut and nothing is simple.'*

Modal *would* intensifies the hypothetical implicature of the proposition. Although the victim was under the control of the offender, it was still necessary to kill for fear of being caught. However, when compared to the proposition as complements in the subordinating clauses, they form **epistemic-oriented** possibility such as, *that perhaps it came to be seen* **that the ultimate possession** *was, in fact, the taking of the life.* **And then** *the purely, the physical possession of the remains (my emphasis)*. In these clauses TB is a post-murder participant speaking from jail, and the proposition is considered as a (**factual**) possibility. This is also because, at the level of **causal reasoning, aspectual conflict** in the progressive aspect, '**killing** *of the victim. Uh, then* **using**—**examining** *that kind of attitude* [*for purposes of gratification*]', form **causation** as a necessary condition, termed as **causal-sufficient** which is an effect necessary to justify/instigate/trigger the *over killing*. This **causation** is separate from causation as action (***causal-manipulative***), which involves someone directly manipulating some pre-existing objects, or causation as progeneration (***causal-progenerative***) as something causal and linear (for example, the conception of time and plot) (Dannenberg 2008: p. 26).

There is **conflict** between counterfactuality and hypotheticality when modal *would* is indexical to the actualization of an event. That is, lexical senses of volition and intention are retained in the meaning of the modal *would*. However, modal *would* is made **non-stative** with reference to the perception modality *would have seemed,*

10. *And the killing of the victim, we* **would** *expect,* **would have seemed** *a rather extreme act—but one that the individual considered necessary to eliminate the possibility of his getting caught.*

As with extract 3, there is a dichotomy of disposition. Like the animate first person subject 'we' with the perception verb *seemed* in *we would expect, would have seemed*, the modal *would* is Agent-oriented. This disposition is reduced to an inanimate pronoun *it* (4th section in extract 4) to thematize the scope of the abnormal self, which is the compulsion *for purposes of gratification—the killing of the victim … it came to be seen … the ultimate possession* (extract 3). With the inanimate subject *it* and a stative verb *came*, the proposition that the killing was for the purpose of ultimate possession has a **focal epistemic sense**.

11. *Uh, then using—examining that kind of attitude—that perhaps **it came** to be seen that the ultimate possession was, in fact, the taking of the life. And then the purely, the physical possession of the remains.* (Michaud and Aynesworth 2005: p. 125)

Further, Agent-oriented *we* (*we would expect*) contrasts with the Senser *I think* (extract 4), *I guess* (extract 2) and also as scope created in the **blending of process and participant** in clause-initial position for **the entity**—*… the control, the possession aspect, came to include*; *… that kind of attitude—that perhaps it came to be seen* (extract 4).

12. ***I think** we see a point reached—slowly, perhaps—where the control, the possession aspect, came to include, uh, uh, within its demands, the necessity … for purposes of gratification—the killing of the victim.*

In Agent-oriented modality, (*the killing of the victim, **we would expect, would have seemed**… one that the individual considered necessary to eliminate the possibility of his getting caught* (extract 3)) there is existence of external physical conditions on Agent TB that are necessary to complete the **predicate action** of explaining the aspect of *overkilling*. In contrast, Senser I in subordinating clauses in the here-and-now of the narration **blends** the telling of the crime as a scope/circumstance, which is a-**state-oriented** stative assertion in past tense form.

What is made of this analysis is that in the transition from third person *he* to a first person *I, we*, and then to an inanimate entity *it* referring to the phenomenon of ultimate possession as gratification for the purpose of killing, the participant *he* is a **controlling Agent C** (he *strangled her to death*). While the same participant as *I* and *we*, is both a **controlling Agent C** and refers to the Speaker with modal Force (*would*) for **epistemic focal sense**, therefore giving a **double reading**. **Clues** to the referential identity of this inanimate subject *it*, are implied to the entity with the other behavior, **the need** to *totally possess her, after she's passed out, as she lay there in a state somewhere between coma and sleep*.

The individual in the extract was under the grip of a different behavior for the transition from an entity, *the need to possess*, to a controlling Agent, *he strangled to kill*, with the completed action in aspectual content, *had intended*. To conceptualize the **'self'** from the **narrating 'I'**, the different behavior relates to the individual who *considered* [it] *necessary* to kill for fear of being caught. This then relates to being **compelled** to strangle *his victim to death for that ultimate possession*. The controlling Agent, *he* (the serial killer) thus becomes a **Patient** with low topicality because of his implied behavior to possess, although structurally *he* is a controlling participant type, hence **a functional contrast**. The meaning of an Agent-oriented proposition of the evolving—I, who *considered* [it] *necessary to eliminate the possibility of his getting caught* then becomes **hypothetical** and is in opposition to the **Speaker-oriented experiencing-self** in subordination, expressed as *the control, the possession aspect … the necessity … for the killing of the victim—for purposes of gratification* [the motivation].

According to Michaud and Aynesworth, Bundy revealed two different selves that co-existed which were **cyclical**. According to TB, it was collaboration between the **malignant condition** with the **rational self** (extract 4 in hardback, p. 110). The malignant condition was the concealed other self, the abnormal **entity**, which was concerned with engineering abduction for gratification, for control and ultimate possession, factors that nurtured his psychopathological condition, in Bundy's words, *an antisocial pathological mental condition that was just a different part*. (pp. 117–118)

There is **negation** when reinforcing different behavioral patterns with different minds in relation to the *public self* and the other in extract 4,

13. *We are **not talking about** two different minds, normal self,*
    *... the public self—normal self, which is **not necessarily latent** but which **would certainly have** its latent phases* [when the other condition/behavior of ultimate possession is on demand]. *... Yet that was **not the kind of worry** or concern that was pervasive* [fear of being captured or the remorse of killing for gratification].

With reference to the (public) normal self, the adverbial '*very much*' is used with psychological processes, *in favor of, shocked, moved, suppose*. While at the same time constructing a counterfactual inference in the hypothetical context (a **binary event**) such as with the conditional, *as if,* modal *would*, adverbial *almost*, and subordination *that*,

14. *It was **almost as if** he said it was wrong for all these things to happen. ...*
    *The inhibitions **that would** normally prevent **a person** from acting that way were specifically excised, removed, diminished, repressed ... in such a way (as to) **not affect** all other inhibitions—or to result in the deterioration of entire personality.*

In Ziegeler (2006: p. 140),

*Counterfactual implicature is a conversational implicature derived from the contextual assessment of the speaker's knowledge of the facts to the contrary of a hypothetical utterance. **Counterfactual conditionals** are found where **underlying utterance** of the counterfactual is generally **believed to be factual**.* (My emphasis)

The example cited in Ziegler is,

If it had rained, the picnic would have been cancelled.

The **factual premise** is that it did not rain and therefore picnic was not cancelled. The hearer's assessment of the **utterance** in the counterfactual conditional is conditional and not an assertion of truth.

Similarly, in the TB quotes above, the factual premise is that Bundy was aware of contrary facts that corresponded to the past situation of killing for self-gratification, but this is not asserted. Connecting this analysis further with **counterfactual markers** (the **negation** and **adverbial** *almost*) implicates the negation of a stronger proposition of the malignant condition as the **other self** of Speaker TB, who had full knowledge of the facts relating to his *overkilling*. However, the meaning in the utterance in extract 4 is merely hypothesized. The hearer needs to work out in the discourse, the speaker's knowledge of contrary information, which is not expressed as part of the counterfactual utterance. In reality TB was using these linguistic measures (**cues**) in order to avoid his commitment to the killings in the interviews.

As the **narrating self**, Agentive 'I' or 'he' is replaced by a circumstantiation of a **state of coexistence** (public self with the malignant condition), *The uniqueness of the whole situation, the inhibitions that would normally prevent a person from acting that way* (extract 4). This allows the Speaker to impose coexistences as a future condition with modal *would* for the killer,

15. *On the other hand, he* ***would have*** *a combination of fear or capture or remorse for having exposed* ***himself*** *to that kind of situation. Yet that was* ***not the kind of worry*** *or concern that was pervasive. There was no thought given to the long-range consequences of this kind of behavior [an antisocial pathological mental condition that was just a different part]*.

The Speaker *me* (below), as in extract 1, is a **Patient** in an **inverse construction**.

16. *"It is wrong for* ***me*** *to jaywalk. It is* [for me] *wrong to rob a bank. It is wrong* [for me] *to break into other people's houses. It is wrong for* ***me*** *to drive without a driver's license. It is wrong* [for me] *to pay your parking tickets. It is wrong* [for me] *not to vote in elections. It is wrong* [for me] *to intentionally embarrass people."*

Speaker *me* in the inverse construction has a high topicality like Speaker *I* (in all extracts), *this person, this individual* (extract 4) with a malignant condition to kill for gratification and which has high topicality in the extracts. However, there is low topicality of the same individual as a **Passive** Agent *himself* in *having exposed **himself** to that kind of situation* (extract 4), and *himself to be innocent* in extract 2. The **shift** from direct **controlling Agent C** to **Passive Agent** with low topicality contributes to levels of counterfactuality in the discourse. The use of **conditionals** and **negation** as **counterfactual markers** further in the discourse also contributes to an underlying counterfactual premise in the **utterance** that is believed to be factual alongside the modal *would* with **modal force** in an epistemic sense counters this factuality. The embedded **experiencing self**, '*me*', '*himself*' in the extracts is distinct from the dominant narrative with Agent-oriented **narrating 'I'** (the serial killer).

5.5.2 A Hypothetical Context

In contrast to TB extracts, in the Ripper Diary (Appendix 5) the hypothetical implicature in the predictive meanings is intensified.

The Ripper's idea of violence for self-gratification is determined first in his imagination, and then carried out in reality. Contextually the characteristics that are in motion in the Ripper diaries for the hypothetical implicature (in the hypothetical relation between the uttered and the inferred statement) is in the sense of imaginary self-gratification for the offender (to be) who seeks revenge on his wife, '*I long for peace of mind …. That **will** not come until I have sought my revenge on the whore and the whore master*' (diary transcript (DT) 207). This motivation gradually places him in an **imaginary space** of control and power, while building on his confidence (diary transcripts 207–213, 217). Having dwelt on this imaginary self-fulfillment, the diary author was restless and dissatisfied and switches from fictional imaginary victims, '*I **will** take the first whore I encounter and show her what he is really like*' (DT 215), to carrying out his fantasies on real, living people,

> '*Within the quarter of the hour I found another dirty bitch willing to sell her wares. … The thrill she gave me was unlike the others, I cut deep deep deep.*'
> (Diary transcript 232)

The tone changes to someone fantasizing due to his,

- deep-rooted jealousy and inferiority towards his wife and his brothers (DTs 210, 219, 223, 225, 226, 240, 241, 249, 253, 258, 261);
- delusionary and self-serving justifications (DTs 230, 241, 247);
- thrills and self-gratification achieved from butchery and mutilation of his murdered victims; and
- taunting games and sarcasm towards the Mets (officer Abberline in particular) (DTs 222, 226, 231, 233, 236, 237, 239, 245).

In contrast to his concern,

- over his children (transcripts 208, 221, 230, 246);
- his obsession over his deteriorating health and addiction (208, 212, 213, 239, 240, 246, 246); and
- his desire to take revenge on his wife and her whoring master (voyeurism, which is a parallel theme that runs through nearly all pre- and post-murder transcripts).

The diary ends with the writer wishing to be dead, but does not have the courage to take his own life (transcript 268). He wanted to be poisoned by his wife as he lacked the strength to end his life by himself (transcript 269). This transition starts in DT 266, when the Ripper admits how *tired* he feels, '*I shall return to Battlecrease with the knowledge I can no longer continue my campaign.*'

The Ripper DTs are to date considered as being a forgery. It is seen as an imaginary Victorian hoaxer deluding himself that he committed the murders. However, this has been contested, especially due to the discovery of a gold pocket watch with the signature, J. Maybrick, and the initials of five prostitutes murdered in Whitechapel and the confession, '*I am Jack*'. (Harrison 1993: p. xi)

By considering the diary transcripts as fictional, and keeping to the discourse of offender engagement in this book, the orientations of the **experiencing self** is linguistically set in opposition to a dominant **agentive-I** with a-state-oriented or speaker-oriented disposition.

Contextually, the underlying motive, which influenced the Ripper in his criminal activities, from an offender perspective, was the discovery that his wife Florie was being unfaithful. He admits in DT 264, that it was,

'an eye for an eye [when he discovered his wife's affairs]. *The bitch, the whore is not satisfied with one whore master, she now has eyes on another* (DT 253).

His imagination of taking revenge for his wife's betrayal ended, when he realized he was unable to continue with his revenge killings. He was unable to strike when visions of his wife overwhelmed him because he still loved her (DT 266). The transition from **behavior to character-based focus**, from the act of revenge to personal regret (DT 257) is evident in the extracts from the diaries in Appendix 5. It is difficult to subdivide the diary transcripts into specific **themes**; but roughly, they may be as a **killer in anticipation** and in **post killing reminiscences.**

In the transcripts, there is predominant use of the progressive, some perfective aspects, modal *must* and future *will* that contribute to a **Speaker based focus** in Agent-oriented properties (**a double function**). In future *will* and modal *must*, the utterance imposes or proposes a course of action or pattern of behavior, and indicates that it will be carried out, constituting a **Speaker-oriented discourse.** The Speaker-oriented **sense**, while allowing the **speaker** to impose conditions on himself as the addressee, the Agent-oriented **writer** also reports the existence of conditions on him when he commits to *make them* [the prostitutes he planned to murder] *suffer as she* [the wife, by betraying him] *has made me suffer*—a **juxtaposing** of the Speaker with Agent-orientation.

Following Bybee and Fleischman (1995: p. 26), [a] *focal epistemic sense is likely if the main verb is in progressive, perfective or stative.* The main verbs in the **progressives** below, mainly from 'Killer in anticipation' transcripts, indicate the necessity for a course of actions due to **external conditions** on the writer as an Agent. The external condition here was Florie's unfaithfulness that led to the campaign of revenge on prostitutes in Whitechapel (the post murder reminiscences). In the **progressive aspect**, the subject is located in the midst of an activity at reference time (in the here-and-now of the narrative), and displays a **developing** state. It is more an active involvement in an activity over a **characterizing state** providing a dynamic state over a stative predicate, making the discourse oriented towards a **controlling Agent (C)**. Additionally, modal *will* (12 in total) add the highest Agent values, where there is some Force (**Agent F/Engaged Agent**) for an event occurring or not occurring, constituting a participant type, which is a **controlling Agent (C)** with epistemic **modal Force (F)**. While the modal *must* in, '*All whores must suffer first and my God I will make them suffer as she has made me*,' triggers an **Agent (C) orientation**, orientating in the progressive aspect his **alternative world** of fantasy and feelings for his wife. For example,

> '*The thought* [of controlling his wife through possessing her] *is beginning to thrill me, I will allow her to continue* (DT 208), *the thought of them* [the prostitutes] *ridling and screaming while the acid burns deep thrills me*' (DT 211),
> '*I keep assuring myself if I have done no wrong. It is the whore who has done so, not I*' (DT 247), when justifying his criminal behavior,
> '*I keep seeing blood pouring from the bitches.*' (DT 250), when expressing gratification in his overkilling,
> '*I am fighting a battle within me*' (DT 231), when struggling with his conscience, over his decision to seek out revenge (on defenseless prostitutes because of his wife's betrayal),
> '*The bitch is vexing me more so as each day passes*' (DT 231), [finally, when the writer is increasingly more annoyed by his wife's affairs].

Further, in the transcript, the use of main verbs like, *I have taken, I have walked, I have become I said, I travel* (DT 217), *I have no doubt*, and similar VPs have the modal sense of obligation associated with an Agent C. As a **dynamic** predicate, the VPs describe a situation which involved a change where the writer familiarized the locality of where he was to start his campaign of revenge killing.

Other features also found in the text are,

Repetition ('*It's love that spurned me so, 'tis love that shall put an end*' (DT 266)),

Transitive clauses ('*The next time I travel to London I shall begin* '[the personal campaign of killing all prostitutes (DT217)),

Conditional 'if then' clauses (with or without an overt 'then') (*'If I was to do so* [kill Florie's lover, who was implied as the writer's brother] *I would surely be caught'* (DT231)).
Repetitions are not goal-oriented; stylistically, they create emphasis.
Intransitives are agent-oriented, and not goal-oriented.

With reference to **hypotheticality** (Sect. 5.4.4), the future marker, *will* and the first person subject contribute to a high level of hypotheticality. Features in the transcript that also imply hypotheticality are in,

- **Perfect morphology** (*I have had*) (DT 230),
- The **causal link between two clauses** of a conditional, e.g. *'as if it* [my heart] *had left my body'* (DT 232), If *'Smith should find this* **then** *I am done before my campaign begins'* (DT 209),
- The **negation** (*'For how could one suspect that I could be capable of such things* [the mutilation] *for I am not, as all believe, a mild man, who it has been said* [by his brother Edwin] *would never hurt a fly.'*)

Presence of the above features enforces hypotheticality with counterfactual inference. Ziegeler (2000: p. 38) points out that a grammatical device that indicates an **utterance** as being counterfactual may not be reliable to realize levels of hypotheticality.

'Grammatical devices are available to indicate that the utterance [in the diary] *is irrealis, but are not reliable indicators for disambiguating levels of hypotheticality. ... hypotheticality is based on the presence and absence of a number of features,* [which] *together may contribute to an overall optimum situation for the expression of hypothetical notions.'*

A **realis** situation as **extra-knowledge** is that the Ripper diaries are considered as forgery. An investigative journalist from Sweden (John Christopher Holmgren) concluded the identity of the Whitechapel murderer was a delivery man named Charles Allen Lechmer (Cross) who was working in the area, making him well placed to commit the crimes in 1888. Based on this extra-world knowledge, and along with grammatical indicators of hypotheticality above, one may treat the diary transcripts as an **alternate world** constructed by the diary writer. As seen in DT 266, the account is confessional and the individual steps out of his **fantastical world** (DT 267) set in a **hypothetical context** of committing murder to avenge his wife for being unfaithful. He eventually realizes the value of his wife and children and overcomes his vices like jealousy and personal inadequacy (DT 268). Contextually the diary reads more like a **confessional fantasy**, a catharsis to overcome a personal crisis and able to be forgiven.

For space constraint, I will not carry out an exhaustive comparative analysis of offender discourses in Appendix 4. However, a brief understanding of the linguistic devices that point out the **Speaker-orientation** in the **Agent-oriented** discourse is realized in the Ripley discourse when applying the functional factors in discourse roles as orientation techniques.

Extract 5 (Ripley)

> 7. 'Aunt Dottie **had hated him** when **he had a cold**; *she used to take her handkerchief and nearly wrench his nose off, wiping it. ...*'
> 8. 'He remembered the vows he had made, even at the age of eight, to run away from Aunt Dottie, the violent scenes he had imagined—Aunt Dottie **trying to hold him** *in the house, and* **he hitting her with his fists, flinging her to the ground and throttling her,** *and* **finally tearing the big brooch off her dress and stabbing her** *a million times in the throat with it.*' 9. 'He **had run away** at seventeen and **had been brought back,** and **he had done it again** at twenty and succeeded.' 10. 'And it was astounding and pitiful how naïve **he had been,** how little **he had known** about the way the world worked, as if he had spent so much of his time **hating Aunt Dottie and scheming how to escape her,** that **he had not had enough time to learn and grow.**' (35–36)

In extract 5, the '**narrating**' Ripley uses perfective aspects alternating occasionally with the **imagined hypothetical world** in progressive aspect, *'as if he had spent so much of his time hating Aunt Dottie and scheming how to escape her, that he had not had enough time to learn and grow.'*

There is no contextual evidence that Aunt Dottie was physically abusive to Ripley, on the contrary, in the short extract above, Ripley stabbed his aunt, *'stabbing her a million times in the throat with it'* [aunt's brooch], when aunt Dottie tried to restrain him from fleeing away from home. As explained in Canter with reference to the Duffy case quoted above, in an offender profile the stabbing is a **behavioral trace** considered as a **trigger factor** for the murder. In the story, readers are told that Ripley received regular checks from his aunt even when he left home. However, he did not give her his forwarding address when he informed her of him being away to meet his school friend Dickie in Spain; as he states he wanted to cut himself off from all the '*second-rate people*' (p. 31), and aunt Dottie was one of them.

In the extract for the **oriented discourse**, there is evidence of **external conditions** on the **narrating Agent** to complete the **predicated action**; that is, to run away from an aunt '*who never* [gave] *him credit for anything he had stuck to*' (p. 35), making the discourse Agent-oriented.

However, in Ziegeler with reference to the distinction between counterfactuality and hypotheticality, **past and perfect morphology** mark events and situations that indicate **speaker-hearer interaction**. With no extra-world knowledge about Ripley being mistreated by his aunt, and with no other **hypothetical devices** (negation, first person subject and temporal meanings in future) counterfactuality inferences in extract 5 are dominant over hypotheticality.

Speaker Ripley uses the **dual premise** of an Agent-oriented third-person narrator narrating about himself, the narrated character, when he was growing up at his aunt's place. Like Bundy in extracts 3 and 4, the third-person narrating, 'he' is the **anticipated self**, who would like to be understood in the retrospective third-person narrative as a victim of abuse and poverty that he wanted to flee. Following this rationale, the discourse in extract 5 is **state-oriented** in the perfective and progressive aspect. This overrules an Agent-oriented subject position, from where the **narrating 'he'** narrates the perspective of character Ripley to differentiate the **retrospective 'me'** in his own offender discourse.

In extracts 1–5, the discourse of an **experiencing self** (me) is also a functional premise for Bundy and Ripley's desire to avoid a murder conviction or to become rich respectively. This **overlapping** of the Agent-oriented narrator desire from the character language surfaces as a **dual effect** distinguishing the same individual (the narrating from the narrated). This dual effect is studied further in mind style in Chap. 6 in offender discourse.

5.6 Conclusion

Without the grammatical devices in the discourse, the Speaker or the implied self is anticipated and not visible. The Ripper diary and Defendant TB's discourses are in the first person and are **overtly** Agent-oriented offender utterances with a controlling Agent, Agent type C. However, Bundy's third-person interview technique (extracts 3–4) avoids the stigma of a confession in the first person, while the discourse in extract 5 is like a first-person offender utterance, Agent-oriented with a controlling Agent, Agent type C. From a functional perspective, this finding contradicts the observation in Bybee and Fleischman,

> 'An utterance is most likely to have an agent-oriented interpretation when subject referent is first-person and least likely when it is third-person; conversely, epistemic modality correlates most strongly with third-person and least strongly with first-person subjects.'

(1995: p. 25)

The hypothesis was that that orientation of the **evolving (narrating) 'I'** is dynamic and Agent-oriented, while the **experiencing self** is a-state-oriented in relation to the 'here-and-now' of the countering story world of narrating 'I' for an identity, which makes the self of perpetrator 'I' distinct as a person (the personality). The transition in orientation is discovered in discourse roles with high or low topicality of the Agent-oriented narrating participant 'I' and then as the narrated, 'he' or 'himself' as in TB's Defendant discourse.

Similarly the transition from the first-person Agent-oriented narrator in the Ripper diaries with epistemic modal force (*will, shall, could would*), formulates a state-oriented focus in Agent-oriented modal properties; a **double function** characteristic in the criminal discourses analyzed thus far. For instance, the low topicality of agentive 'I' as a passive Agent in Defendant TB's narrative discourse **counters** the violent orientation of the offender TB, while in the Ripper discourse, the modal force of modal *will, shall, could, would* formulates **levels of hypotheticality**. These linguistic devices manifest the way psychological accuracy is achieved in an offender's mind for counterfactuality or for an alternative hypothetical world. Otherwise, for a linguistically untrained reader the discourses in the Ripper diary transcripts are received as mere expression of extreme violence, when epistemic **sense** in modal force is for the self-conflict of the perpetrator Ripper with reference to his voyeurism, constituting **covertly** a control/submission polarity, besides the **overt** love/hate polarity scale in the Ripper diaries.

Similarly, in the Bundy extracts, as state-oriented discourse in linguistics devices (a Patient as passive Agent, a Senser as Engaged Agent), there is a **reflective act** of a convicted serial killer. The linguistic devices provide an understanding of the *overkilling* as a self-gratification with reference to the underlying premise of TB's normal public self, and connecting this with the overall Agent-oriented third person; countering the realis narrative of a serial killer. Similarly, in the Ripley extract, inadequacy of the self of the perpetrator Ripley is highlighted in aspects **transiting** from past tense narrative form. This transition to an abnormal self is otherwise unnoticed as a mere childhood situation in the life of the perpetrator without the causal link to the desired world of Ripley in order to counter his inadequacy to persevere and become rich at the expense of Dicky's murder, and in the sequence of other murders that help to maintain his rich social status.

With levels of counterfactuality and hypotheticality, the distinction is found in the **modal behavior**, which foregrounds the transition from an Agent-oriented to epistemic meanings in modal Force (participant type F) more representative of a stative-oriented discourse for the criminal's way of dealing with his criminal behavior from a reflective vantage point.

In the search for compelling clues of a referential identity in the epistemic modal force and aspect, there is an opposition between the quests for identity of the self and the Agent-oriented actions that inform of the characteristics of a serial murderer. When the linguistic features are linked with the orientation (the behavior) the perpetrator fulfils the intention of an experiencing self, rather than simply ending a victim's life (**act focused**), as found in mystery stories that conceal an identity. Such affects the degree of factuality in the discourse formulating in offender discourse a **hypothetical alternative world** or a **counterfactual alternative**, or even a **binary event** with both counterfactual and hypothetical inferences.

While Agent-oriented criminal behavior is volitional, orientating the world of desire and obligation that compelled the criminal disposition is in opposition with the epistemic focal sense in Agent-oriented modality. In the use of aspect and functional factors with low topicality set against direct Agent discourse roles in offender discourse formulates an **anticipated other** in an epistemic state-oriented assertion.

Appendix 5

Ted Bundy: Conversations with a Killer: The Death Row Interviews (2005)

The extracts are from Ted Bundy's (TB) account of his school days, his criminal activities (the killings) to journalists Stephen Michaud (SM) and Hugh Aynesworth. The journalists' task was to reinvestigate the murder allegations against Ted, interview him TB was a suspect in two dozen killings he was accused of or suspected of having committed. The chance that Bundy would tell the truth to prove him innocent encouraged the journalists to take up the project. They did this only to discover that all Bundy intended was to provide a picture of who he was and why he had become a killer, and to highlight his innate need to manipulate. TB's sole intention, as the journalists later found out, was to gather publicity to bolster his defense (p. 278), and to gather strong supporters for his book to sell, for which he needed the journalists as tools to carry out his intention.

Note: as the extracts are in italics, emphasis in italics in the original text is underlined here.

Extract 1

> *'The big payoff for **me** was actually possessing whatever it was I had stolen. It wasn't the act, necessarily. … **I really enjoyed** having something on my wall or sitting in my apartment <u>that</u> I had wanted and gone out and taken.'*
> (Michaud and Aynesworth 2005: p. 41)

5 Orientation 449

Speaker-oriented in subordinating moods
Extract 2

'TB: ... while for at least six months **I had prepared myself** in every way possible for a conviction, this defense mechanism began to slowly disintegrate once **I became** involved in the active conduct of the trial. **I guess** there were several factors which <u>**forced**</u> me, which **influenced me** to play the role. ***To play the role of the defendant, who had every hope and expectation of being acquitted of a crime*** of which he knew himself to be innocent.'
(Michaud and Aynesworth 2005: p. 45)

Speaker-oriented in subordinating moods
Extract 3
Playing a role (The organized phase)

'The initial sexual encounter **would be** more or less a voluntary one. .... Well, it **would** be—in dealing with the kind of profile <u>we've created</u> (coughs) as **I've stated** before, nothing is clearcut and nothing is simple.' (p. 114)

'And the killing of the victim, **we would** expect, **would have seemed** a rather extreme act—but one that the individual **considered necessary** to eliminate the possibility of his getting caught.' (p. 125)
...
'Uh, then **using—examining** that kind of attitude—**that perhaps it came** to be seen **that the** <u>**ultimate**</u> **possession** was, in fact, the taking of the life. **And then** the purely, the physical possession of the remains.'

Extract 4
Different minds
TB explains the parameters of the notion of possession, and how this connects with the killing, and not stops at satisfying the urge for power and controls from sexual encounter with his kidnapped victim.

'**I think** we see a point reached—slowly, perhaps—**where the control, the possession aspect, came** to include, uh, uh, within its demands, the necessity ... **for purposes of gratification—the killing of the victim.**'
(Michaud and Aynesworth 2005: p. 125)

'We are **not talking about** two different minds, normal *self,*

... *the public self—normal self, which is **not necessarily latent** but which **would certainly have** its latent phases* [when the other condition/behavior of ultimate possession is on demand]. ... *Yet that was **not the kind of worry** or concern that was pervasive* [fear of being captured or the remorse of killing for gratification].'
   *'It was **almost as if** he said it was wrong for all these things to happen.* ...
   *The inhibitions **that would** normally prevent **a person** from acting that way were specifically excised, removed, diminished, repressed ... in such a way (as to) **not affect** all other inhibitions—or to result in the deterioration of entire personality.'*
   'On the other hand, he would have a combination of fear or capture or remorse for having exposed **himself** to that kind of situation. Yet that was not the kind of worry or concern that was pervasive. There was no thought given to the long-range consequences of this kind of behavior [an antisocial pathological mental condition that was just a different part].'
   *'It is wrong for **me** to jaywalk. It is* [for me] *wrong to rob a bank. It is wrong* [for me] *to break into other people's houses. It is wrong for **me** to drive without a driver's license. It is wrong* [for me] *to pay your parking tickets. It is wrong* [for me] *not to vote in elections. It is wrong* [for me] *to intentionally embarrass people.'*
   (Michaud and Aynesworth 2005: pp. 18–120)

The Diary of Jack the Ripper: The chilling confessions of James Maybrick (2010)

Ripper's idea of violence for self-gratification is determined first in his mind through his imagination, and then carried out in reality. Contextually the characteristics that are in motion in Ripper diaries for hypothetical implicature (hypothetical relation between the uttered and the inferred statement) is first in the sense of imaginary self-gratification for the offender (to be) who seeks revenge on his wife, '*I long for peace of mind …. That will not come until I have sought my revenge on the whore and the whore master*' (diary transcript 207). This motivation gradually places him in an imaginary space of control and power, while building on his confidence (diary transcripts 207–213, 217). Having dwelt on this imaginary self-fulfilment, the individual was restless and dissatisfied and switches from fictional imaginary victims, '*I will take the first whore*

I encounter and show her what hell is really like' (diary transcript 215) to carrying out his fantasies on real, living people. It is difficult to subdivide the diary transcripts into specific themes, roughly they may be as, **killer in anticipation** (diary transcripts 213, 214, 215, 216, 217, 220, 225, 230, 255) and **post killing reminiscence** (diary transcripts 217 (final paragraph) 221, 222, 224, 230, 232, 241, 250, 253, 254, 257).

The diary ends with the writer wishing to be dead, but does not have the courage (268) to carry out his wish. He desired to be poisoned by his wife as he lacked the strength to end on his own (269). This transition starts in transcript 266, when Ripper admits how *tired* he feels, '*I shall return to Battlecrease with the knowledge I can no longer continue my campaign.*'

The underlying narrative which influenced Ripper to his criminal activities, from offender perspective, appear to be the discovery that his wife Florie was being unfaithful. Ripper admits in diary transcript 264, that it was '*an eye for an eye,*' when he discovered his wife's affairs, '*The bitch, the whore is not satisfied with one whore master, she now has eyes on another*' (diary transcript 253). His imagination of taking revenge of his wife's betrayal ends, when he realized he was unable to continue with his revenge killings. He realized he was unable to find in his heart to strike when visions of his wife overwhelmed him and he still loved her (266). The transition from behavior to character-based focus, from the act of revenge to personal regret is evident in the extracts from the diaries below.

Diary transcript 207

'*I long for peace of mind but I sincerely believe that that will not come until I have sought my revenge on the whore and the whore master*'.

Diary transcript 208 (paragraph 2)

'*Foolish bitch, I know for certain she has arranged a rondaveau with him in Whitechapel. So be it. My mind is firmly made.* [To start the campaign of killing whores at Whitechapel]'

Diary transcript 208 (paragraph 4)

The thought of him taking her is beginning to thrill me, perhaps I will aloe her to continue, some of my thoughts are indeed beginning to give me pleasure. Yes

I will visit Michael for a few weeks, and allow her to take all she can from the whoring master. Tonight I shall see mine. I may return to Battlecrease and take the unfaithful bitch. Two in a night, indeed pleasure.'

Diary transcript 211

'*I long for peace but my work is only beginning. I will have a long wait for peace. All whores must suffer first and my God how I will make them suffer as she* [wife Florie] *has made me. ... I will take the bitch* [wife Florie] *tonight.'*

Diary transcript 220

'*The whore seen her master today it did not bother me. I imagined I was with them. The very thought thrills me. I wonder if the whore has ever had such thoughts? I believe she has, has she not cried out when I demand she takes another. The bitch! She will suffer but not yet.'*

Diary transcript 221 (following first killing)

'*I ripped open my God I will have to stop thinking of the children they distract me so I ripped open. It has taken me three days to recover, I will not feel guilty it is the whoring bitch to blame not I. I ate all of it* [body part from murdered victim]'

Diary transcript 230 (second paragraph)

'*I am fighting a battle within me. My desire for revenge is overwhelming. The whore has destroyed my life. I try whenever possible to keep all sense of respectability.'*

Diary transcript 231 (final paragraph)

'"*The bitch is vexing me more so as each day passes. If I could I would have it over and done with. ... The whore still believes I have no knowledge of her whoring master. I have considered killing him, but if I was to do so I would surely be caught. I have no desire for that, curse him and the whore their time will come.'*

Diary transcript 247

'I have lost my battle and shall go on until I am caught. Perhaps I should top myself and save the hangman a job. ... I keep assuring myself if I have done no wrong. It is the whore who has done so, not I. Will peace of mind ever come?'

Diary transcript 253

'The bitch, the whore is not satisfied with one whore master, she now has eyes on another. I could not cut like my last, visions of her flooded back as I struck. I tried to quosh all thoughts of love. I left her dead, that I know. It did not amuse me. There was thrill. I have showered my fury on the bitch. I struck and struck [Florie]. The whore will unlike she has ever suffered. May God have mercy on her for I shall not, so help me.'

Diary transcript 261

'... the bitch gave me the greatest pleasure of all. Did not the whore see her whore master in front of all, true the race was the fastest I have seen, but the thrill of seeing the whore with the bastard thrilled me more so ... if the greedy bastard would have known he was less than few feet away from the name all England was talking about he would have died there and then. Regret I could not tell the foolish fool. To hell with sovereignty, to hell with all whores, to hell with the bitch who rules.'

...

'I struck her several times an eye for an eye ... once more the bitch is in my debt, my God I will cut her. Oh how I will cut her. I will visit the city of whores I will pay her dues and shall take mine, by God I will. I will rip rip May seek the bastard out who stopped my funny little games and rip him to. I said he would pay. I will make sure he damn will.'

Diary transcript 266

'My God I am tired, I do not know if I can go on. Bunny [wife Florie] and the children are all that matter. No regrets, no regrets. I shall not allow such thoughts to enter my head. Tonight I will take the shinning knife and be rid of it. ... It's love that spurned me so, 'tis love that shall put an end.'

Diary transcript 267

'I am afraid to look back on all I have written. Perhaps it would be wiser to destroy this, [the diary] but in my heart I cannot bring myself to do so. I have tried once before, but the coward I am, I could not. Perhaps in my tormented mind I wish someone to read this and understand that the man I have become was not the man I was born.'

The participant in this offender engagement discourse is orientating his world of desire and obligation to avenge himself on his wife, Florie, for her betrayal and hence should be Agent-oriented.

Diary transcript 209

*'I am beginning to believe it is unwise to continue writing. … **If** Smith should find this **then** I am done before my campaign begins. And oh what deeds I shall commit. For how could one suspect that I could be capable of such things, for am I not, as all believe, a mild man, who it has been said would never hurt a fly. Indeed only the other day did not Edwin* [Ripper/ (Maybrick's? brother with whom Florie was implied to have an affair)] *say me I was the most gentlest of men he had encountered.'*

Diary transcript 211

*'… do not know **if** I have the courage to go back to my original idea. Manchester was cold and damp very much like this hell hole. Next time I will throw acid over them* [the prostitutes]. *The thought of them ridling and screaming while the acid burns deep thrills me, ha, what a joke it would be **if** I could gorge an eye out and leave it by the whores body for all to see, to see, ha, ha.'*

Bibliography

Texts

Harrison, Shirley. 2010. *The Diary of Jack the Ripper: The Chilling Confessions of James Maybrick*. Irving, TX: John Blake Publishing Ltd.

Michaud, Stephen G., and Hugh AynesWorth. 2005. *Ted Bundy: Conversations with a Killer: The Death Row Interviews*. New York: Barnes and Noble Books.

Sources cited: Chapter 5

Bamberg, Michael, and Molly Andrews. 2004. *Considering Counter-Narratives: Narrating, Resisting, Making Sense*. Amsterdam and Philedelphia: John Benjamins.
Bybee, Joan. 1995. The Semantic Development of Past Tense Modals in English. In *Modality in Grammar and Discourse*, ed. John Bybee and Suzanne Fleischman, 503–517. Amsterdam: John Benjamins.
Bybee, John, Revere Perkins, and William Pagliuca, eds. 1994. *The Evolution of Grammar: Tense, Aspect, and Modality in the Languages of the World*. Chicago: University of Chicago Press.
Canter, David. 1994. *Criminal Shadows: Inside the Mind of the Serial Killer*. Hammersmith, London: Harper Colins Publisher.
Chafe, W. 1976. Givenness, Contrastiveness, Definiteness, Subjects, Topics, and Point of View. In *Subject and Topic*, ed. C.N. Li, 25–55. New York: Academic Press.
Coates, Jennifer. 1983. *The Semantics of Modal Auxiliaries*. London: Croom Helm.
Dannenberg, Hilary P. 2008. *Coincidence and Counterfactuality: Plotting Time and Space in Narrative Fiction*. Lincoln and London: University of Nebraska Press.
Harding, Jennifer Riddle. 2007. Evaluative Stance and Counterfactuals in Language and Literature. *Language and Literature* 16 (3): 263–280.
Holmes, Ronald M., and James De Burger. 1988. *Serial Murder: Studies in Crime, Law and Justice Volume 2*. Newbury Park, CA: Sage Publications.
Howard, Richard, and Jonathan Culler. 1977. *Tzvetan Todorov: The Poetics of Prose*. Ithaca, NY: Cornell University Press.
Jones, Richard Glyn. 1992. *The Giant Book of True Crime*. London: Magpie Books.
Leary, T. 1957. *Interpersonal Diagnosis of Personality*. New York, NY: Ronald Press.
Quirk, Randolph, Sidney Greenbaum, Geoffrey Leech, and Jan Svartvik. 1985. *A Comprehensive Grammar of the English Language*. London: Longman.
Quirk, Randolph, Geoffrey Leech, and Jan Svartvik. 1987. *A Grammar of Contemporary English*. Harlow: Longman.

Ricoeur, Paul. 1985. *Time and Narrative Volume 1*. Trans. Kathleen McLaughlin and David Pellauer. Chicago and London: University of Chicago Press.
Schiffrin, Deborah, Deborah Tannen, and Heidi E. Hamilton. 2001. *The Handbook of Discourse Analysis*. Oxford: Blackwell.
Youngs, Donna, and David Canter. 2012. Offenders' Crime Narratives as Revealed by the Narrative Roles Questionnaire. *International Journal of Offender Therapy and Comparative Criminology* 57 (3): 289–311.
Ziegeler, Debra. 2000. *Hypothetical Modality: Grammaticalization in an L2 Dialect*. Amsterdam and Philadelphia: John Benjamins.
Ziegeler, Debra. 2006. *Interfaces with English Aspect: Diachronic and Empirical Studies*. Amsterdam: John Benjamins.

nd-styles

and in the modal senses for Actor–Patient topicality in Chap. 5. In this chapter, in imagery metaphor the offender fantasy is revisited to reflect the mind-style of an offending character. For instance in the saying '*an English man's home is his castle*' a number of **alternative interpretations** can be intended by the word *castle*. **Intended meaning** associated with castle could be about opulence, or about defense and protection, or it could be perceived as a restricted or confined space in which one is metaphorically imprisoned. Thus, the evocation of *castle* **triggers** an association that comes into play which **indexes** the **referent** in a way to which the intended use of *castle* relates to. This could be a **world-view** that contrasts with the **real (actual) world**. **Alternative inferences** drawn from an **image-schematic structure** (Sect. 6.2) can be set in opposition to the potential **conventional** meaning of an image-structure and therefore cannot be taken as a one-to-one mapping of the word with its most common meaning; we have to look deeper for the intended meaning. This enables one to further reflect on the patterns of **dual function** strategies.

In Fowler, **mind-style** is a phenomenon in literary fictions where it is about the world-view of an author, or a narrator or a character constituted by the ideational structure of the text (1986: p. 150). Semino (2008: p. 269) develops Fowler's (1996) notion of mind-style to focus on the individual rather than social consciousness. **World view** for Semino is the overall view of reality of the text actual world. For the author, the ideological point of view, and mind-style are terms to capture different aspects of world views projected by texts, such as the offender view of reality. In Leech and Short (2007: p. 150), mind-style is defined **how** a *fictional world* of **what** is comprehended is conceptualized and varies on a scale from *normality* to *deviance* (pp. 154–166), and is foregrounded in linguistic patterns that index salient cognitive habits or deficits. For example, from Faulkner's *The Sound and the Fury* (1929), deviance is captured by the transitive verb *hit* in the character Benji's sentence, '*they* [the golfers] were *hitting little, across the pasture*', where Benji uses the adjective *little* as if it were an adverb. This created effect is either to foreground ignorance or to perceive a sense of no purpose in the golfer's actions. The intransitive sentence overall foregrounds Benji's cognitively abnormal disposition, and this fictional world is indexed through Benji's imperfect understanding of cause and effect created in the VP *hitting little* [golf balls].

6 Contrasting Mind-styles 459

Mind-style and the **fictional world** are two sides of the same coin. The notion of mind-style when applied to an individual or a group who may have similar cognitive characteristics, e.g. a shared stage of cognitive development, as in young children from families with offending background, may foreground salient features that are associated with **criminality** and may shape their cognitive characteristics. For instance, from the crime fiction stories, offenders Tom Ripley, Raven, and Bud Corliss all had a difficult upbringing. Ripley fled home to get away from his aunt who brought him up. She was very strict and Ripley always failed to live up to her expectations. The same theme of 'not living up to expectation' is found with Corliss who grew up listening to his mother complaining of his dad's incompetence to provide a respectable living. By trying to marry into a rich family he was trying to please his mother, his urgency to marry someone rich, however, when unsuccessful, ultimately led to his killings; the mythic ***Oedipus complex***[1] in a criminal **profiling context** associated with ritual killings (Danesi 2014: p. 117). Raven felt betrayed by his mother when she committed suicide. She was his only guardian as his father was in jail and she died when he was very young. Similarly, in the true crime narratives of the Bundy interviews, it was <u>implied</u> that his mother was actually his sister and he was brought up by his abusive grandfather. These offenders all **share deviant family background** and this have **affected** their propensity to behave in certain ways.

The concern in this chapter is with, **how** the fictional world of a disaffected participant in their narrative is apprehended or conceptualized. In Leech and Short (2007: p. 150) ***apprehension*** and ***conceptualization*** are opposite sides of two coins. Conceptualization of a world presupposes a world referred to, and a **mind** is through which that world is reflected. Devices commonly used to reveal ones **point of view** (see note 2) are in the choices of manner of expressions rather than content, such as metaphorical expressions in **personifying metaphor**, *the <u>cruel sea</u>*, also in **mixing metaphors** with similes, for example, ... *its <u>Titanic form</u> seemed to await something; but <u>it</u> had waited thus* ... (My emphasis)) (Leech

---

[1] Oedipus complex—is based on Oedipus myth, which Freud believed explained the process of development. Love of the mother and jealousy of the father is a general phenomenon of early childhood. Freud goes on to say, *Every member of the audience was once a budding Oedipus in fantasy and this dream fulfilment played out in reality causes ... horror, with the full measure of repression which separates his infantile from his present state.* (cited in Danesi 2014: p. 117)

and Short 2007: p. 160). In the realignment of conceptual bounda
such as, animacy extended to inanimate objects can account for di
ent interpretations creating changing contexts for reading purposes,
function is *metaphorical mapping* (Simpson 2004: p. 215), where
key idea is about *salience*—a judgement of **match** between the inc
ing text from the **source domain** (cruel, a human trait) and betw
's expectations to the in (the sea). By gi

the source domain, with respect to different concepts wi
context, are mapped on to the target, such as in the exa
surrealist writer Andre Breton (in Germain 1978: p. 69 ci
2004: p. 214),

'My wife ... whose waist is an hourglass.'

of the expression and make possible to comprehend the idea implicitly asserted for reference. **Mapping** thus is an action which involves moving beyond the simple mapped restructuring of **image-schemas** (Simpson 2004: p. 214).

For instance, in Rendell's psychological thriller, *A Demon in my View*, the metaphorical reading of *dark/darkness* and the *white lady* (Sect. 6.4) is in reference to the killer Arthur, and is constituted in the **repeated** use of these expressions in the narrative. Conventionally as the first-order reading, the linguistic element, *white*, may first invoke a **binary sense** of white versus black, or white as innocent versus black as evil. To identify which significant use of *darkness* and *white lady* is associated to the offender Arthur, the analyst has to look beyond the conventional concept associated with *darkness* and a *white* woman, and then formulate the relevance of these adjectival repetitions in the offender discourse with reference to the offender's **backgrounded** desire, fantasy or motivation as projected in the story.

6.3 Text and Hypothesis: Fictional World

The text, for the analysis of the offender fictional world is a psychological thriller by Ruth Rendell, *A Demon in My View*.
Jones (1992) observes,

> 'Murder is a mirror. A dark, distorting mirror in which we see unfamiliar faces. It shows us uncomfortable things, aspects of the human mind that we might not wish to see or acknowledge, but which we are nonetheless, and if we wish fully to understand ourselves we should look into it.'

To understand **oneself**, one should look into ones **inner self**, where fantasies and desires are imagined and even acted out, such as in Ripley's functionally oriented transitive world without purpose, and in Ripper's hypothetical modal world. The **self** is the difference between the immediate single mental event and a state, a condition with respect to circumstance that continues over time in terms of two selves: the seemingly

'*Arthur collected the drill. **The darkness ... The pitch darkness** of wartime. **In the dark** ... he had touched her,* [Arthur was 22] *to run one finger down the side of her warm neck. **Her scream as she fled was more beautiful in his ears than the squeaking of the mouse.** ... He knew what he wanted to do* [to strangle], *but thought intervened to stay with him.'* (p. 57) (My emphasis)

In the extracts above, the offender desire was for power over his victim by strangulation in the dark. This power he did not have over his aunt, and is understood when his aunt ridiculed him for his inadequacies and his birth,

'... *who needed to cleanse himself of the taint of his birth and background.*' (p. 24)

Arthur's inadequacy was to do with a stigma about *an unnamed boy* [himself] ... *he could never shake off* (p. 55). He overheard Auntie Gracie and her two friends' discussion about this stigma, which was to do with his mother. Possibly, but not explicit in the narrative, Arthur was an illegitimate child and Auntie Gracie was conventionally rigid. She had bought Arthur from his mother for a hundred pounds. Arthur had never seen his mother since then, *She was off like greased lightning* (p. 28).

Arthur is implied as a psychopath in the story, a medical condition that was the underlying cause for his deviant behavior. By looking at the imagery of *darkness*, the *white lady*, and the personifying metaphors (in extracts below) associated with them, one can understand the conflict between his desire to kill, this desire related to his cognitive development, and his deviant view of women forming a deviant *fictional world*[3] with gaps based on presupposition. For example, this is revealed in his desire to strangle the mannequin dressed as his aunt,

'*There was only one thing he had ever been able to do to women and, advancing now, smiling, he did it* [strangled the mannequin his white lady].' (p. 10)

---

[3] Fictional world—in fiction there are gaps, which are temporary and filled later in the discourse, for example, the identity of the murderer in a whodunit, while some gaps are implicit and permanent. This implicitness in Palmer (2004: p. 34) is based on presupposition, which is the source for fictional world construction.

6 Contrasting Mind-styles

True to the characteristics of a psychopath, Arthur was asocial, and was unable to form an emotional relationship. Arthur was forced to go out with Beryl to the cinemas, who was someone his aunt was keen he got close to, and this he was extremely unhappy about,

> '... *he liked things better before they* [Arthur and Aunt Gracie] *knew Beryl* ... .' (p. 107) (My emphasis)

Using a pretext, Arthur escapes from the cinema leaving Beryl behind and strangles a prostitute on his way back home after *dark*.

In line with the **profile** of a **serial killer**, there is a recurring pattern surrounding the mode of Arthur's killing by strangulation. There was then his self-gratification from the act of strangulation as he gained power over his victim. *Darkness* was the **trigger factor** that engulfed Arthur with its compelling urge to strangle victims, an act consistent with the characteristics of a serial killer. Amongst this deviant orientation however, there is a mind-style which follows an imagery pattern of Arthur as a typical individual, who happened to have a small peculiarity like all normal men, but he was able to keep under control (p. 25).

When the imagery-structure in the story narrative is contextualized, a **killer signature** appears in the narrative linked with the Oedipus complex (see note 1). The imagery-structure foregrounds his battle with his asocial and deviant self. This is set in opposition to Anthony Johnson who was a tenant in the same house and ironically, conducting research about psychopaths after his separation from his Helen.

Treated as a point of view, the above extracts index a particular mind set which is of a deviant kind. It is necessary in the Arthur and Anthony extracts analyzed below, to separate the **fictional world** from the **mind-style** in order to find out the extent to which the way the represented world deviates from the **common-sense version** of reality in the two extracts. By following mind-styles, the constructed **worldview** in each extract easily strikes a reader as natural and uncontrived. However in the Anthony extract as opposition to Arthur's worldview, there is a clear implication of an unorthodox conception of the fictional world in the ideological worldview of love.

'*He had never known how to talk to women. There was only one thing he had ever been able to do to women* [strangle them].'

The conceptual structure of a **child schemata** is instantiated in the centrally prototypical features of a *plastic shop model*, and in the way, like a child impersonating the shop model as a *white lady* who was his *protectress* like Auntie Gracie whom Arthur was infatuated with (p. 107).

In addition, in line with child-schemata, the prototypical feature of *darkness* is always associated with unpleasant things that may happen to children, as '*Auntie Gracie had always been most eloquent on the subject of night air and its evil effects*' (p. 37).

The **first-order metaphorical** reading of *darkness* then activates the domain of a child, where the fear of darkness is childlike and is animated, where **the mouth of the dark** *opened and called him* [Arthur]. *The* **jaws of darkness** *received him*, **the streets** *received him*, **taking him** *into their arteries like a grain of poison*. In addition, the Oedipus complex unfolds in Arthur's **adult fantasy** carried out on the mannequin in the cellar on the one hand, and on the other impersonating in childlike manner by dressing the mannequin with his aunt's '*handbag ... hooked over one of her arms and scuffed* [aunt's] *black shoes.*'

Arthur also fulfilled his **adult desire** for power in meeting his infatuation through strangulation, a psychotic behavior. This **second-order of metaphorical reading** of the salient features of *darkness* and *the plastic shop window model* in the child-schema as the source domain, beyond their conventional concept when **mapped** onto the *core you* **(self)** of offender disposition, generates the adult concept of desire and power. Contextually this is understood in Arthur's sense of knowing in that he *knew* he was a perfectly normal man with a small peculiarity like all normal men he was able to keep under control (p. 25). The *small peculiarity* was only associated (Oedipus complex) with his feelings for Auntie Gracie was,

Arthur extract:

'*Arthur always remembered those kisses when, ... he reminded himself how happy their relationship had been. And he felt a savage anger against Beryl's mother for a comment she had once made.*'

*For the first time the idea of his mother's suicide came to him without bitterness, as **he reluctantly fixed his aim and Saunders shot him** in the back through the opening door. Death came to him in the form of unbearable pain. **It was as if he had deliver this pain as a woman delivers a child, and he sobbed and moaned in the effort. At last it came out of him and he followed his only child into a vast desolation.**'* (166)

The episodic link between Raven's recollections of his mother's suicide when he is shot foregrounds the self- relocation of Raven as an Agent in the discourse. Raven emotionally sets himself free from his recurring cycle of betrayal, though he was shot dead by Officer Saunders in **story logic**. By drawing such inference from the above extracts, a **circular link** is drawn between his mother's suicide and his underlying circumstance of betrayal at the time of being shot dead; such inference makes Raven again in control of his actions.

The figurative use of *pain* and *child* is also poignant at this point in Raven's discourse. Like Arthur, he also lost his mother when he was very young. Image-structure mapping enables one to understand Raven's **self-locations** relative to the violence and thus relate them to the **discursive contexts** in the text. For example, the second-order metaphorical reading of the salient features associated with *pain* and *child* map (beyond their conventional concept) the **image schema** of 'birth' and 'death' on to the target domain as Raven, who, in his death experiences pain synonymous to a mother giving birth to a child. The child is a **symbol** of new beginning following the *pain* of birth; this rebirth '*At last it came out of him,*' setting him [Raven] free of earthly pain and could follow his new self into eternity,' *followed his only child into a vast desolation*' (p. 166). The **semantic field** of endlessness as a *vast desolation* links with the image of eternity. Eternity thus influences the domain of freedom that emerges following the death. In Raven's case, this is a freedom from betrayal that bonded him to violence.

Raven's sense of knowing his ***core self***, that is his bondage to violence, was also realized when he was unable to make sense of Annie Crowder's actions, who was a friend of the police officer he had kidnapped in order to protect himself from being caught. The extract below from *A Gun for*

6 Contrasting Mind-styles 471

Sale, particularly in the clauses in bold, contextualizes Raven's sense of captivity.

'People don't trouble to keep their word to me,' Raven said (41) ... He remembered the kitten he had left behind in the Soho café. He had loved that kitten. ... She [Anne Crowder] never knew, he thought, that he had meant to kill her; **she had been innocent of his intention as a cat he had once been forced to drown;** *and he remembered with astonishment that* **she had not betrayed him,** *although he had told her that the police were after him.* **It was even possible that she had believed him.***' (61)*
'These thoughts were colder and more uncomfortable than the hail. He wasn't used to any taste that wasn't bitter on the tongue. **He had been made by hatred; it had constructed him into this smokey murderous figure in the rain, hunted and ugly.** *His mother had borne him when his father was in gaol, and six years later when his father was hanged for another crime, she had cut her throat with a kitchen knife; afterwards there had been home.* **He had never felt the least tenderness for anyone;** ... **he didn't want to be unmade.** *He had a sudden terrified conviction that* **he must be himself now as never before if he was to escape. It was not tenderness that made you quick on the draw.** *(62) ... He thought: give her time and she too will go to the police. That's what always happens in the end with a skirt,'* (p. 63) (My emphasis)

The fictional world construction is incomplete and is full of blanks and gaps. As stated in Palmer (2004: p. 34) some gaps are temporary and filled in later in the discourse. However, the permanent gaps like the process of cognitive development of the **core self** as a **code** for Arthur's neurotic behavior, or as a **code** for Raven's sense of captivity, is **covert**. In reconstructing this **covert** *storyworld*[5] (Ryan's **possible world**) in image-schematic structure-mapping, the mapping closes the **ontological** (study of existence) **gaps** inferred from the text and when associated with the real

---

[5] Covert storyworld—In Palmer (2004: p. 34) the storyworld has three elements. It has the source domain, which is a real world in which the reader is processing the text; the target domain that constitutes the output of the reader's processing; and the system of textual features that triggers various kinds of reader-held real-world knowledge in a way that projects the reader from source domain to target domain.

offender characteristics and scenarios that contribute as the 'going on' that resulted in a criminal process for self-fulfillment.

Using an applied approach to crime and criminality in fiction and in true crime narratives, crime analysis shows a way of understanding the criminal process. This approach uses a case-by-case study of crime fiction, which is not restricted to the mystery or the suspense surrounding the crime. The mystery surrounding the perpetrator is relevant to the act of crime, and is an end or a start of a criminal process. Such a study was not possible without the interdisciplinary approach given here. Frameworks and analytical models from different fields were necessary to tackle different aspects of crime and criminality in each chapter.

Suspense in crime fiction is primarily about the conflict of interests between narrative universals, *curiosity*, *surprise* or *suspense* in the content plane (story), which results in narrative gaps like *curiosity gaps* in retrospect and *suspense gaps* in prospective narration, moving the narrative both backwards and forwards. A third-level narration in anticipation, in the *discourse-now* of the narrating-I provides an insight into the offending process. In the storytelling in anticipation, the offender simultaneously correlates its retrospective past with the prospective future to its underlying self-gratification, which tends to be backgrounded in the story. This embedding is achieved by the thematization of offender experience, the revelation of situations that affected the participant to a life of crime but that remain secret in the prospective and retrospective storytelling by the diegetic Narrator. By foregrounding the backgrounded situations of the affected participant an embedded storyworld unravels, unpacking situations that juxtapose the circumstantial relation to the personal motive in the offender engagement discourse; this motive scenario becoming the second story in anticipation. Conventionally, there is a *first story of crime* in prospection and a *second story of investigation* in retrospection. The embedded sub-world of an offender in anticipation initiates a tripartite narration alongside the acts of prospection and retrospection in a criminal context.

This led me to focus on issues like the manipulation technique in the complex plotting system found in crime fiction. This issue, tackled by an event-by-event frame analysis of the content plane, revealed microcontexts centering on the motive frame, which, as the hinge point in the story,

Conclusion 477

formulated alternative event relations when mapped against the relevance to the victim and the perpetrator in the narrative. As a result, alternative narrative relations index to a sequence of events that are altered for narrative outcomes in offender context, other than for solving the crime. Subsequently, when plotted against the offender motive narratives substituted to conceal the criminal became evident. Different narrative relations thus define a manipulated context in the murder mystery. This context is a discourse in which the perpetrator is engaged in the offending process, and the 'offender-substituted' narrative relations become distinct from the victim scenario in crime stories.

The double function as a method of analysis dominates the offending process. At clause level, the analysis of linguistic devices in their reciprocal stylistic functions reveals a dual narrative act in criminal discourse. Based on the principle of alternation as a technique, in this dual narrative act the offender-Narrator alternates between the telling and the showing, as well as the state of affairs that surfaces the embedded offender disposition in anticipation. In offender in anticipation discourse, the stimuli that trigger the criminal act reveal the criminality in process; sidestepped in the story because of the popular preoccupation with the revelation of the murderer and with the resolution of the mystery centering on the anti-hero. The alternation technique also benefited the analysis of narrative gaps in episodic links, inserted for a situated focus in the offender storytelling process, when shifting between the dynamic and a static storyworld and alternating between its Narrator and Reflector roles. Also inserted between two roles within the default diegetic mode of the offender discourse is an indirect intermediary participant disposition of the narrating perpetrator. Hence, this narrative act in alternation also drew up an 'inter diegesis' story space for the offending participant, from where the offender setting for an agentive 'evolving-I' comes together with the 'experiencing self', to portray itself as an undergoer over an agentive-Actor in the offending process.

By thematizing the offender's past, juxtaposed with its personal controversies, justifies the offending act and reveals behavioral issues that were not linked to the criminal act in the storytelling. In so doing, the thematized circumstantial elements for the situated focus on the offender setting, reveals facts that are central to the offending situation; the 'going

———. 2006. The Disnarrated. In *The Routledge Encyclopaedia of Narrative Theory*, ed. D. Herman, M. Jahn, and M.-L. Ryan, 442–443. London: Routledge.

Sources cited: Chapter 1

Pavel, Thomas G. 2014. Gerald Prince and Narrative Studies. *Narrative* 22 (3): 298–303.
Prince, Gerald. 1988. The Disnarrated. *Style* 22: 1–8.
———. c2003. *A Dictionary of Narratology*. Rev. ed. London: University of Nebraska Press.
———. 2003[1987]. *A Dictionary of Narratology*. Lincoln: University of Nebraska Press.
Todorov, T. 1987. *The Poetics of Prose*. Trans. Richard Howard and Jonathan Culler, 43–52. Ithaca, NY: Cornell University Press. Reprint, 1977.

Sources cited: Chapter 2

Ariel, Mira. 1988. Retrieving Propositions from Context: Why and How. *Journal of Pragmatics* 12: 567–600.
Barthes, R. 1977. *Image Music Text*. Translated by Stephen Heath, 81–124. London: Fontana Press.
Bloor, T., and Bloor, M. 2013. *The Functional Analysis of English*. 3rd ed., 95–96. Oxon: Routledge.
Bock, J. Kathryn, and Richard K. Warren. 1985. Conceptual Accessibility and Syntactic Structure in Sentence Formulation. *Cognition* 21: 47–67.
Boltanski, L. 2014. *Mysteries and Conspiracies*. Translated by Catherine Porter, 3, 49, 77, 102, 123, 132–133, 144–145. Cambridge: Polity Press.
Brown, G., and George Yule. 1983. *Discourse Analysis*. Cambridge, New York, Melbourne: Cambridge University Press.
Canter, D.V. 1994. *Criminal Shadows: Inside the Mind of the Seriel Killer*. London, UK: Harper Collins.
Chatman, Seymour. 1978. *Story Discourse: Narrative Structure in Fiction and Film*. Ithaca, NY: Cornell University Press.
Chatman, S. 1980. *Story and Discourse: Narrative Structure in Fiction and Film*, 15–107. New York: Cornell University.

Glenn, A.L., and A. Raine. 2014. Neurocriminology: Implications for the Punishment, Prediction and Prevention of Criminal Behaviour. *Nature Reviews Neuroscience* 15 (1): 54–63. doi:10.1038/Nrn3640.

Goffman, E. 1975. *Frame Analysis. An Essay on the Organization of Experience*. Harmondsworth: Penguin Books.

Grice, H.P. 1975. Logic and Conversation. In *Syntax and Semantics III: Speech Acts*, ed. P. Cole and J. Morgan. New York: Academic Press. Reprint, A. Jaworski and N. Coupland, eds. *The Discourse Reader*, 2nd ed., 66–77. London: Routledge.

Hayes, P.J. 1980. The Logic of Frames. In *Frame Analysis: Text Understanding*, ed. D. Metzing. Berlin and New York: Walter de Gruyter.

Herman, D. 2007. Cognition, Emotion, and Consciousness. In *The Cambridge Companion to Narrative*, ed. David Herman, 245–259. Cambridge: Cambridge University Press.

Holmes, Ronald M., and Stephen T. Holmes, eds. 1998. *Contemporary Perspectives on Serial Murder*. London and New Delhi: Sage Publications International Educational and Professional Publisher.

Howard, Richard, and Jonathan Culler. 1977. *Tzvetan Todorov: The Poetics of Prose*. Ithaca, NY: Cornell University Press.

James, P.D. 1974. *Cover Her Face*. 3rd ed. London: Penguin Books.

Kayama, Misa, Wendy Haight, Priscilla A. Gibson, and Robert Wilson. 2015. Use of Criminal Justice Language in Personal Narratives of Out-of-School Suspensions: Black Students, Caregivers, and Educators. *Children and Youth Services Review* 51: 26–35. doi:10.1016/j.childyouth.2015.01.020.

Malmkjaer, K. 2013. *The Routledge Linguistics Encyclopedia*. 3rd ed. London and New York: Routledge.

Moser, Thomas C. 2008. Introduction. In *The Good Soldier*, ed. Ford Madox Ford, 3rd ed. Oxford: OUP.

Lemert, Charles, and Ann Branaman. 1997. *The Goffman Reader*. USA, UK, Australia: Blackwell Publishing.

Metzing, Dieter, ed. 1980. *Frame Conceptions and Text Understanding*. Berlin and New York: Walter de Gruyter.

Minsky, M. 1980. A Framework for Representing Knowledge. In *Frame Analysis: Text Understanding*, ed. D. Metzing. Berlin and New York: Walter de Gruyter.

Opas-Hanninen, Lisa Lena, and Tapi Seppanen. 2010. 2D and 3D Visualization of Stance in Popular Fiction. In *Language and Style*, ed. Dan McIntyre and Beatrix Busse, 272–286. Basingstoke and New York: Palgrave Macmillan.

Palmer, Alan. 2004. *Fictional Minds*. Lincoln and London: University of Nebraska Press.

Prince, Gerald. 1982. *Narratology: The Form and Functioning of Narrative*. Berlin, New York, and Amsterdam: Mouton Publishers.
Quirk, R., et al. 1985. *A Comprehensive Grammar of the English Language*. London: Longman.
Rimmon-Kenan, S. 2002. *Narrative Fiction: Contemporary Poetics*. London and New York: Routledge.
Rosenberg, St.T. 1980. Frame-based Text Processing. In *Frame Analysis: Text Understanding*, ed. D. Metzing. Berlin and New York: Walter de Gruyter.
Schank, R.C., and R. Abelson. 1977. *Scripts, Plans, Goals and Understanding*. Hillsdale, NJ: Lawrence Erlbaum.
Scott, Jeremy. 2009. *The Demotic Voice in Contemporary British Fiction*. New York: Palgrave Macmillan.
Scott, J. 2014. Creative Writing and Stylistics. In *The Routledge Handbook of Stylstics*, ed. M. Burke, 423–438. London and New York: Routledge.
Short, Mick. 1996. *Exploring the Language of Poems, Plays and Prose: Learning About Language*, 306–325. London and New York: Routledge.
Sperber, Dan, and Deirdre Wilson. 1986. *Relevance: Communications and Cognition*. Oxford: Basil Blackwell.
Sternberg, M. 2003. Universals of Narrative and Their Cognitivist Fortunes (I). *Poetics Today* 24 (2): 395.
Sussex, L. 2010. *Women Writers and Detectives in Nineteenth-Century Crime Fiction: The Mothers of the Mystery Genre*. Basingstoke: Palgrave Macmillan.
Todorov, T. 1987. *The Poetics of Prose*. Translated by Richard Howard and Jonathan Culler, 43–52. Ithaca, NY: Cornell University Press. Reprint, 1977.
Toolan, M. 1995. Discourse Style Makes Viewpoint: The Example of Carver's Narrator in 'Cathedral'. In *Twentieth-Century Fiction: From Text to Context*, ed. Jean Jacques Weber, 126–137. London and New York: Routledge.
———. 2004. *Language in Literature. An Introduction to Stylistics*. London: Arnold.
———. 2014. Stylistics and Film. In *The Routledge Handbook of Stylistics*, ed. M. Burke, 455–469. London and New York: Routledge.
Van Dijk, T.A. 1977. *Text and Context. Explorations in the Semantics and Pragmatics of Discourse*. London and New York: Longman.
Van Gelder, Jean-Louis, and S. Van Daele. 2014. Innovative Data Collection Methods in Criminological Research: Editorial Introduction. *Crime Science* 3 (6). http://www.crimesciencejournal.com/content/3/1/6. Accessed 24 September 2014.
Wales, Katie. 2001. *A Dictionary of Stylistics*. 2nd ed. Harlow, Essex, UK: Pearson Education Limited.
Weizman, E., and M. Dascal. 1991. On Clues and Cues: Strategies of Text-understanding. *Journal of Literary Semantics* 20 (1): 19–29.

Butler, Christopher S. 1985. *Systemic Linguistics Theory and Applications*, 47, 77–79, 170–176. London: Batsford Academic and Educational.

Chatman, Seymour. 1978 (1st published) (1980, 1st printing). *Story Discourse: Narrative Structure in Fiction and Film*. Ithaca and London: Cornell University Press.

Christies. 1993. *The Murder of Roger Ackroyd* (henceforth Ackroyd).

Davidse, Martin, and Louise Ravelli, eds. 1992. *Advances in Systemic Linguistics: Recent Theory and Practice*, 116–129. London and New York: Pinter Publishers.

Davies, Martin, and Louise Ravelli. 1992. *Advances in Systemic Linguistics: Recent Theory and Practice*, 229–244. London and New York: Pinter Publishers.

Davidse, Kirstin. 1992. Transitivity/Ergativity: The Janus-headed Grammar of Actions and Events. In *Advances in Systemic Linguistics: Recent Theory and Practice*, ed. Martin Davidse and Louise Ravelli, 116–129. London and New York: Pinter Publishers.

Fowler, Roger. 1977. *New Accents: Linguistics and the Novel*. London and New York: Methuen.

Flanders, R. Dutta. 2012. Functional Nativeness in Outer and Expanding Circle. In *Linguistic and Extra-linguistic Problems of Communication*. Collection of Academic and Research Papers, Issue 9. N P Ogarev Mordovia State National Research University, Faculty of Foreign Languages, 285–321.

Flanders, Reshmi D. 2014. Concealment and Revelation: An Interdisciplinary Approach to Reader Suspense. *Style* 48 (2): 219–242.

Genette, Gerard. 1988. *Narrative Discourse Revisited*. Ithaca, NY: Cornell University Press.

Greenbaum, Sidney, and Randolpg Quirk. 2010. *A Student's Grammar of the English Language*. 23rd ed. China: Longman.

Halliday, M.A.K. 1974. The Place of Functional Sentence Perspective in the System of Linguistic Description. In *Papers on Functional Sentence Perspective*, ed. F. Danes. The Hague: Mouton; Prague: Academia.

———. 1994. *An Introduction to Functional Grammar*. 2nd ed. London: Edward Arnold.

———. 2004a. *The Language of Science*, Collected Works of Michael Halliday. Vol. 5. London and New York: Continuum.

———. 2004b. *An Introduction to Functional Grammar*. 3rd ed. (revised by C.M.I.M. Matthiessen). London: Hodder Arnold.

———. 2014. *Halliday's Introduction to Functional Grammar*. 4th ed. (revised by C. M. I. M. Matthiessen). London: Routledge.

Rapp, David N., and Richard J. Gerrig. 2006. Predilections for Narrative Outcomes: The Impact of Story Contexts and Reader Preferences. *Journal of Memory and Language* 54: 54–67.
Rimmon-Kenan, S. 2002. *Narrative Fiction: Contemporary Poetics*, 7–28. London and New York: Routledge.
Shibatani, Masayoshi. 1976. The Grammar of Causative Constructions: A Conspectus. In *Syntax and Semantics: The Grammar of Causative Constructions*, ed. M. Shibatani, vol. 6, 1040. New York: Academic Press.
Simpson, Paul. 1993. *Language, Ideology and Point of View*, Chapters 1 and 2. London and New York: Routledge.
———. 2014. Just What is Narrative Urgency? *Language and Literature* 23 (1): 3–22.
Thompson, Geoff. 1996. *Introducing Functional Grammar*. London and New York: Arnold.
Todorov, T. 1966. Les categories du recit litterature. In *The Poetics of Prose*, ed. T. Todorov. Translated by Richard Howard and Jonathan Culler, 43–52. Ithaca, NY: Cornell University Press. Reprint 1977.
Toolan, Michael. 1988 (first published) (2001, 2nd ed.). *Narrative: A Critical Linguistiic Introduction*. Oxon, New York, and Canada: Routledge.
Uprichard, Emma. 2011. Narratives of the Future: Complexity, Time and Temporality. In *Innovation in Social Research Methods*, ed. Malcolm Williams and W. Paul Vogt, Chapter 5, 103–421. Los Angeles, London, New Delhi, Singapore, and Washington: Sage.
Youngs, Donna, and David Canter. 2012. Offenders' Crime Narratives as Revealed by the Narrative Roles Questionnaire. *International Journal of Offender Therapy and Comparative Criminology* 57 (3): 289–311.
Youngs, Donna E., David V. Canter, and Nikki Carthy. 2016. The Offender's Narrative: Unresolved Dissonance in Life as a Film (LAAF) Responses. *Legal and Criminological Psychology* 21 (2): 251–265.
Ziegeler, Debra. 2000. *Hypothetical Modality: Grammaticalisation in an L2 Dialect*. Amsterdam and Philadelphia: John Benjamins.
———. 2012. The Grammaticalization of Modality. In *The Oxford Handbook of Grammaticalization*, ed. Bernd Heine and Heiko Narrog. www.oxfordhandbooks.com. Accessed 26 February 2015.

Sources cited: Chapter 5

Bamberg, Michael, and Molly Andrews. 2004. *Considering Counter-Narratives: Narrating, Resisting, Making Sense.* Amsterdam and Philedelphia: John Benjamins.
Butler, Christopher S. 1985. *Systemic Linguistics: Theory and Applications.* London: Batsford Academic and Educational.
———. 1990. Qualifications in Science: Modal Meanings in Scientific Texts. In *The Writing Scholar*, ed. Walter Nash. Newbury Park, CA: Sage Publications.
———. 2003a. *Structure and Function: A Guide to Three Major Structural-Functional Theories Part 1.* Amsterdam: John Benjamins.
———. 2003b. *Structure and Function: A Guide to Three Major Structural-Functional Theories Part 2.* Amsterdam: John Benjamins.
Bybee, Joan, Revere Perkins, and William Pagliuca, eds. 1994. *The Evolution of Grammar: Tense, Aspect, and Modality in the Languages of the World.* Chicago: University of Chicago Press.
Bybee, Joan. 1995. The Semantic Development of Past Tense Modals in English. In *Modality in Grammar and Discourse*, ed. John Bybee and Suzanne Fleischman, 503–517. Amsterdam: John Benjamins.
Canter, David. 1994. *Criminal Shadows: Inside the Mind of the Serial Killer.* Hammersmith, London: Harper Colins Publisher.
Chafe, W. 1976. Givenness, Contrastiveness, Definiteness, Subjects, Topics, and Point of View. In *Subject and Topic*, ed. C.N. Li, 25–55. New York: Academic Press.
Coates, Jennifer. 1983. *The Semantics of Modal Auxiliaries.* London: Croom Helm.
Dannenberg, Hilary P. 2008. *Coincidence and Counterfactuality: Plotting Time and Space in Narrative Fiction.* Lincoln and London: University of Nebraska Press.
Davidse, Kirstin. 1992. Transitivity/Ergativity: The Janus-headed Grammar of Actions and Events. In *Advances in Systemic Linguistics: Recent Theory and Practice*, ed. Martin Davidse and Louise Ravelli, 116–129. London and New York: Pinter Publishers.
Davis, Martin, and Louise Ravelli. 1992. *Advances in Systemic Linguistics: Recent Theory and Practice.* London: Pinter Publishers.
Fowler, Roger. 1977. *New Accents: Linguistics and the Novel.* London and New York: Methuen.

Lakoff, George, and Mark Turner. 1989. *More than Cool Reason: A Field Guide to Poetic Metaphor*. Chicago and London: The University of Chicago Press.
Leech, G., and M. Short. 2007. *Style in Fiction: A Linguistic Introduction to English Fictional Prose*. 2nd ed. Harlow: Pearson Education Limited.
Mithen, S. 1996. *The Prehistory of the Mind: The Cognitive Origins of Art and Science*. London: Thames and Hudson.
Oatley, Keith. 2015. World of the Possible: Abstraction, Imagination, Consciousness. *Pragmatics and Cognition* 21 (3): 448–468.
Palmer, Alan. 2004. *Fictional Minds*. Lincoln and London: University of Nebraska Press.
Quirk, Randolph, Sidney Greenbaum, Geoffrey Leech, and Jan Svartvik. 1985. *A Grammar of Contemporary English*. Harlow: Longman.
Semino, Elena. 1997. *Language and World Creation in Poems and Other Texts*. London and New York: Longman.
———. 2008. A Cognitive Stylistic Approach to Mind-style in Narrative Fiction. In *The Language and Literature Reader*, ed. Ronald Carter and Peter Stockwell, 268–277. London and New York: Routledge.
Simpson, Paul. 2004. *Stylistics: A Resource Book for Students* (Unit 11). London and New York: Routledge.
———. 2010. Point of View. In *Language and Style: In Honour of Mick Short*, ed. Dan McIntyre and Beatrix Busse, 293–310. London: Palgrave Macmillan.
Wber, Jean Jacques. 1992. A Three-Level Approach to Stylistic Analysis. In *Critical Analysis of Fiction: Essays in Discourse Stylistics*, ed. Jean Jacques Weber, 13–40. Amsterdam and Atlanta, GA: Rodopi.

B

bidirectional, 6, 7, 14, 22–4, 28, 29, 46, 57, 64–6, 70, 138, 139, 201, 201n3
binary, 232, 275, 427, 428, 432, 437, 447, 462

C

cardinal function, 23, 27, 29, 54n18, 70, 138
cardinal point, 5, 10, 13, 15n10, 16, 19, 20, 22–5, 27, 32, 33, 36, 46, 52, 55–8, 62, 71, 73, 91, 132, 133, 141, 157, 158, 171, 179–80, 198
causal, 18, 29, 42, 43, 57, 58, 62, 64, 66, 71, 188, 247, 434, 443, 447
causality, 24, 138, 180, 191, 214, 245, 247, 255
causation, 201n3, 202–6, 225, 231, 264, 276, 412, 434
character(s), 2, 141n5, 142, 189, 411, 457
circularity, circular narrative(s), 12, 22, 51, 57, 70, 191
circumstantial, 3, 48, 188, 200, 201, 206, 208, 219, 225, 227, 244, 275, 419, 431, 476, 477
circumstantiation, 193, 201, 206–9, 225, 232, 248, 261, 264, 265, 275, 276, 427, 431, 438
common sense assumption, 25, 26, 34, 35
concealer(s), 5, 10, 17, 20, 23, 25, 28, 29, 37, 40–3, 70, 71, 138, 169, 174, 188

consecution of events, 12, 139
consequence of events, 6, 25
content factor(s), 11–13, 33, 44
the content plane, 2, 16, 476
context of situation, 13
contextual assumptions, 13, 44
contextual effect(s), 9, 12, 13, 91, 139, 148
contextual frames, 6, 16, 26n16, 78
contrasting mind styles, 457–73
countering, 410, 411, 414–16, 419, 431, 432, 446, 447
counter narrative, 73
covert, 27, 34, 410, 415, 471, 471n5, 478
cues, clues, 9, 9n4, 10, 12, 13, 34, 148, 156, 158, 169, 174, 181, 183, 244, 245, 247, 255, 264, 265, 277, 414, 424, 426, 436, 438, 447, 472n7
curiosity gaps, 7, 10, 10n6, 22, 36, 42, 188, 265, 476

D

desire(s), 2, 6, 7, 13, 15, 16, 18, 19, 21, 22, 24, 27–9, 32, 35, 36, 41, 44, 50–8, 65, 67, 133, 148, 152, 188, 214, 235, 260, 261, 264, 265, 269, 275, 277, 279, 410, 412, 413, 419, 421, 440, 445, 448, 452, 454, 457, 462–4, 468, 469
deviation from norm, 143, 157, 188, 225, 232, 423
DF. *See* double function (DF)
diegesis, 147–9, 153, 181, 183, 416, 423

diegetic, 10, 27, 143, 235, 277, 367, 411, 476, 477
discourse, 2, 6, 138, 150–6, 188, 391–405, 409, 460, 475
discourse cue(s), 9, 9n4, 14, 34, 51
discourse markers, 146, 149
discourse referent (DR), 6, 7, 13, 14, 16, 20, 22–9, 32–5, 37, 42, 46, 53–8, 66, 70, 71, 93–7, 138, 139, 275
disposition(s), 3, 9, 137, 187–405, 411, 457, 477
distortion(s), 11, 20–8, 36, 62, 143, 145, 147, 148, 190, 193, 418
domain(s), 148, 173, 206n5, 235, 460, 461, 468, 470, 471n5, 472, 472n6
double dipping, 187, 218, 223, 225, 245, 265, 269
double function (DF), 3, 6, 23, 25, 27, 137–84, 188, 202, 202n4, 441, 446, 477
DR. *See* discourse referent (DR)
dual function, 24, 29, 45, 62, 143, 144, 206, 209, 458
dual processing, 461

E

EC. *See* evaluative clause (EC)
effector, 189, 192, 199, 200, 208, 225, 226, 244, 255
embedding, 49, 141, 149, 149n7, 151, 152, 184, 476
enactor(s), 148, 149, 213, 226
entity(ies), 12n9, 14, 19, 25–7, 34, 35, 56, 57, 70, 81, 141n4, 146, 184, 187–9, 193, 199, 201–4, 206–8, 213, 214, 219, 220, 226, 231, 232, 235–7, 244, 252, 255, 260, 264, 265, 275, 276, 401, 412, 416, 431–33, 435, 436
episode(s), 8, 10, 11, 15, 21, 30, 34–6, 44, 51, 53, 55–9, 73, 78, 84, 91, 97, 99, 169, 174, 181, 191
episodic links, 6, 9, 11, 12, 16, 19, 20, 24, 29, 30, 32, 34–6, 41, 53, 56, 57, 73, 78, 138, 140, 151, 174, 190, 275, 470, 475, 477
ergative, 203–6, 220–2, 225, 237
evaluative clause (EC), 217, 220, 221, 224
events, 1, 5–8, 10n5, 12, 14–27, 29, 33–7, 42–6, 48, 50, 54–8, 63, 65, 66, 70, 71, 73, 81, 99, 127, 133, 137n1, 138–41, 143, 146–8, 149n7, 151, 154, 156, 158, 170, 174, 180, 181, 187, 188, 190, 191, 193, 194, 196, 199, 200, 208, 213, 214, 216, 218–20, 232, 268, 269, 275–7, 409, 411, 412, 423, 427, 428, 445, 463, 463n2, 472, 477
evidentiality, 216, 223
existents, 19, 190, 199, 411
experiencing I, 26, 148, 213, 412
experientialist novels, 7, 7n3
experiential role, 207, 220
the expression plane, 2

F

fantasy, 197, 201, 412, 442, 444, 457, 458, 459n1, 462, 466–8

498 Index

NC. *See* narrative clause (NC)
negation, negated, 64–6, 68, 175, 181, 182, 220, 252, 263, 269, 275–7, 426–8, 436, 438, 439, 443, 445
NO. *See* narrative object (NO)

O

offender, 1, 157–75, 261–70, 391–405, 409, 418–19, 457, 475
offender self, 414, 417
omnipresent, 141, 173, 174, 188
omniscience, 48, 140, 152, 174, 175, 184, 190, 214, 226, 234, 237, 245, 264, 275, 277, 411
orientation, 2, 3, 11n8, 12, 14, 23, 35, 46, 56, 58, 59, 66, 67, 69, 158, 190, 216, 225, 252, 253, 277, 409–54, 465, 478
overt, 221, 410, 415, 418, 443, 447

P

paralepsis, 140, 142, 190
paralipsis, 140, 142, 190
paraphrases, 10, 10n7
participant(s), 3, 137, 187, 410, 457, 476
patient, 16, 47, 50, 82, 103, 141, 142, 187, 189, 196, 244, 427, 436, 438, 447, 457, 458, 467, 478
performed, 137, 143–5, 189, 218, 219, 424, 431
perspective(s), 7, 17, 19, 20, 28, 36, 41, 63–6, 71, 133, 140, 169, 170, 173, 180, 190, 197, 214, 216, 218, 221–3, 225, 237, 275, 410–12, 415, 426, 433, 441, 445, 446, 451, 463, 463n2, 475
phase, 125, 430, 433, 437, 449, 450
polarity, 183, 413, 414, 416, 447
PoR. *See* Principle of Relevance (PoR)
post hoc, 9, 11, 29, 34, 41, 472
predicate(s), 208, 227, 236, 410, 421, 422, 435, 442, 457
prefocalization, 190, 192, 218, 232, 244, 265
priming, 6, 25, 27, 56, 70, 139
Principle of Relevance (PoR), 6, 7, 23, 25, 29, 36–43, 49, 58–68, 71, 138, 188, 423
process-focused, 418, 433
profile, 181, 213, 260, 434, 445, 449, 465
profiling, 2, 66, 69, 459, 472n7, 475
prospection, 1, 2, 6n2, 7, 14, 21, 22, 24–6, 29, 33, 36, 41, 42, 45–8, 51, 57, 79, 95, 100, 138–41, 143, 147, 148, 150, 153, 158, 169, 171, 174, 183, 184, 188, 234, 263–5, 475, 476
prospective reading, 6

R

realis, 417, 424, 443, 447
recalled context, 9
reference(s), 3, 8, 9, 10n7, 12–14, 17, 20, 21, 25–9, 33, 41, 44, 46, 49, 53, 56, 57, 65, 70, 96,

T

telling, 7, 21, 24, 99, 139, 140, 148–53, 171, 181, 197, 211–14, 409, 418, 435, 477
text-world, 213, 232, 277
thematization, 412, 423, 476
topicality, 227, 415, 420, 423, 424, 426, 427, 427n2, 431–3, 436, 438, 439, 446, 448, 458, 478
transformation, 140, 200–9, 219, 220, 411, 457, 472
transitive, 201, 412, 458
trigger(s), 2, 26, 35, 56, 64, 66, 69, 193, 197, 260, 276, 394, 415, 416, 434, 442, 445, 458, 463, 465, 471n5, 477

U

undercut, 169, 212, 217, 219, 223, 225, 234, 244, 245, 260, 261, 263, 268, 275, 277, 411, 415, 427
unreliable narrator, 76
utterance, 3, 6, 8, 9, 9n4, 11, 13, 14, 19, 20, 22, 23, 25, 26, 28, 32–4, 39, 41, 44–6, 48, 67, 73, 139, 143, 145, 146, 152, 153, 155, 157, 158, 169, 182–4, 187–90, 209, 231, 244, 252, 410, 415, 420, 423–46
utterance-act, 8, 9

V

vantage point(s), 7, 16, 137, 139, 148, 150–2, 154, 158, 175, 184, 411, 447
vertical axis, 37
victim(s), 7, 12, 15, 16, 19, 20, 36, 44, 50, 53, 62–8, 70, 71, 92, 96, 127, 139, 171, 173, 174, 196, 226, 226n10, 232, 244, 247, 252, 261, 263–5, 269, 275, 276, 413, 415, 417, 418, 420, 423, 430, 433–6, 439, 440, 445, 447, 449, 450, 452, 460, 463–5, 467, 469, 477
villains, 67, 69, 125, 189, 193–200, 473
voice, 27n17, 140, 142, 143, 150, 189, 190, 198, 199, 206, 209, 216, 217, 223, 225, 231, 260, 392, 395, 400, 403, 411, 420

W

withheld frame, 9, 36, 44, 55, 65
worldview(s), 457, 458

Printed by Printforce, the Netherlands